BY JOHN CLARKSON

John Clarkson

NEW LOTS

A novel of redemption

Second Edition published 2020 by John Clarkson Inc.
11 Schermerhorn Street, Suite 6WB, Brooklyn, NY 11201

ISBN 978-0-9992155-6-2 (softcover)
ISBN 978-0-9992155-7-9 (e-book)

Subjects of this book.
Fiction – Crime
Fiction – Drug trafficking
Fiction – Gangs
Fiction – Brooklyn, NY.
Fiction – NYPD police procedural

Cover and interior design: Design for Writers
Printing history: A Forge Book; Tom Dougherty Associates, hardcover edition, September 1998
Paperback edition, October 2000

PRAISE FOR NEW LOTS

"*New Lots* is prime-time crime fiction. The action starts fast, roving past drug-ravaged streets, deadly dealers, killers hunting their next target. Clarkson writes with fierce reality, pages filled with characters tabloid-fresh, street-corner dialogue vibrating with the fear which populates the hard zone of the city. *New Lots* is a roller coaster thrill ride from the opening riff down to a pulse-shredder of a climax. As with many of the characters he has created, Clarkson has bagged himself a hit. *New Lots* is the proof."

– Lorenzo Carcaterra, NY Times best selling author

"*New Lots* will satisfy readers looking for a fast-paced cop thriller with sympathetic leads."

– Publishers Weekly

"Thrillingly complex drug-war novel set in Brooklyn's Browns-ville section…steel-edged dialogue…intensively researched…hard-driving realism.

– Kirkus Reviews

"Clarkson has created an assortment of vibrant, realistic players – not exactly likeable but certainly watchable…recommended for fans of gritty crime drama."

– Booklist

"Vibrant, realistic players…Clarkson keeps us caring until the end…Recommended for fans of gritty crime drama."

– American Library Association

*To Ellen, who reminded me
at a crucial moment
that she married a writer.*

AUTHOR'S NOTE:

THIS BOOK WAS FIRST PUBLISHED BY TOR/FORGE TWENTY-FIVE years ago. The story takes place in Brownsville, Brooklyn during the last days of the crack epidemic that ravaged poor neighborhoods throughout New York. There was a housing project on New Lots Avenue that I used as the main locale in the book. That setting became a composite of the systemic problems that plagued neighborhoods like Brownsville and its largely African American residents.

When I decided to publish *New Lots*, I realized that a novel written so long ago wasn't exactly timely. But as I finish this effort, America is living through the Black Lives Matter movement, George Floyd protests, and a re-evaluation of race relations and police department policies. During the editing of *New Lots,* I researched what has happened over the years to the original housing project. Sadly, not much has changed. As of 2015, the courtyard was an open-air drug market. Buildings were taken over by squatters and drug dealers. Over twenty apartments were commandeered for selling drugs. Real estate investors were still trying to profit from the situation.

As of 2018, Brownsville has the highest infant mortality rate in NYC. The most drug related deaths. This is true for premature deaths, psychiatric hospitalizations, rates of diabetes, poor access to healthcare, childhood obesity, poor housing quality, air pollution, and so on. It's been twenty-five years and not much has changed. So, perhaps this story is more relevant than ever.

ACKNOWLEDGEMENTS:

THANKS to NYPD First Grade Detective Michael Greene, without whose help I could not have written this book. Also, many thanks to Kathy and all the other NYPD police officers who shared their time and information with me. Thanks to Abdul Karim. Thanks to Norm Siegel for his invaluable technical advice.

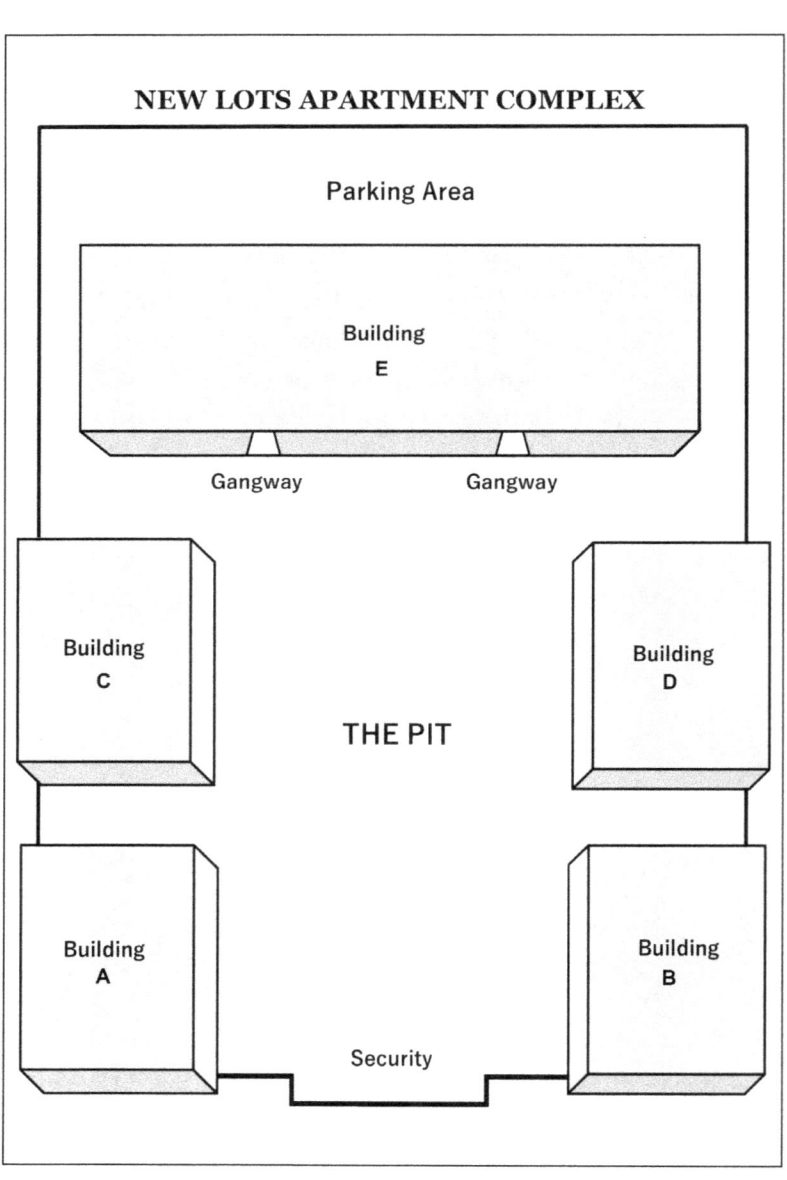

CHAPTER 1

Christmas lights in April.

A little out of season, thought Loyd Shaw.

Multicolored, twinkling rope-lights framed the front window of an old neighborhood bar. Behind the window, a sign displayed the words EARL'S PLACE in a glowing red neon script. Behind the neon, black velvet drapes blocked the view into the bar.

Shaw tried to push open the heavy front door. Locked. Yep, he thought, this must be the place.

Shaw rapped on the door. It opened just wide enough to reveal a scowl on the dark, broad face of a white-haired black man.

"Loyd Shaw, friend of Jake's."

The frown disappeared, and the door opened.

Shaw stepped into a bar like none he had ever seen. His head bumped into a Christmas ornament hanging from the ceiling. He noted a spray of cardboard shamrocks plastered on a wall, a HAPPY NEW YEAR sign drooped over the back bar, birthday streamers, Valentine's hearts, tinsel, and more multicolored lights hung on walls and fixtures.

A bar for all seasons.

Shaw breathed in the smell of beer, whiskey, and cigarette smoke. He listened to the Motown music that filled the air.

While Shaw looked around trying to spot Jake Bennett, he thought about all the holidays and occasions represented by the jumble of decorations. Everything but weddings. Shaw smiled. This is a place where wedding vows are broken.

He spotted Big Jake Bennett sitting at the far end of a long wooden bar where it curved around to meet the wall. Shaw politely made his way through the crowd, noticing that, as the only white person in the place, he made a few heads turn his way.

Jake spotted him and yelled out, "Shaw! Get your ass over here, boy."

Shaw walked into a bear hug. Not surprising, since Jake Bennett was about the size of a black bear.

"I didn't think you'd come, man."

"Why the hell not?"

"How's it going, Loyd?"

Shaw made a face. "The usual shit. Counting the days, brother, counting the days."

"Until when?"

"Until I put in my damn twenty and get the hell out."

"Out of what?"

"You know what. The damn job, the bullshit with my wife, all of it."

"No wonder you're up in the middle of the night comin' to see old Jake."

"These days, there are a lot of nights I can't sleep, Jake. So why not haul my ass out to Brooklyn and drink down some birthday booze with Big Jake Bennett?"

"And here you are, goddamn it."

"Here I am. Where am I, exactly, Jake?"

"Bushwick."

"Sounds right. Whose place is this? This ain't a regular bar, Jake."

"No, this is Earl's place. He only opens it up when he feels like it. Mostly for private parties. Goddamn, I'm glad you came out, Shaw."

"Me, too. How old are you, man? You been around for so damn long it seems like everything else came after you."

"Old enough. How'd you get out here?"

"Drove."

"Shit, now you be careful drivin' back. Don't get so drunk you can't drive."

Shaw knew that as big and gruff as Jake Bennett was, Jake would, in fact, worry about him driving back.

"I don't have the energy to get really drunk."

"Yeah, we'll see about that. What the fuck you lookin' around at?"

"All these women you've got here. Christ, how's an old man like you get so many good-looking women out here in the middle of the night for your birthday?"

Jake looked sideways at Shaw. "Old? Who the hell you talkin' to, son?"

"Big Jake Bennett. Three hundred pounds of fun for everyone."

"Goddamn right. What're you drinkin'?" Jake shouted at the bartender, "Eddie, get my friend a drink."

The bartender leaned close to Shaw to hear his order above the party noise.

"Jack rocks, soda back."

The bartender nodded, grabbed glasses and ice, and started pouring. Shaw looked at his friend Jake sitting on his barstool as if it were attached to his broad rear end, settled in, smiling, sipping double shots of Johnny Walker Black out of a heavy-bottomed old-fashioned glass. Shaw noticed that, as busy as the bartender was, he never allowed Jake's glass to get empty.

Shaw's drink and chaser landed in front of him. He took the first cold swig of icy whiskey, leaned back against the bar, and watched a steady stream of friends and relatives come by to wish Jake a happy birthday.

Jake would smile and nod and shake a hand or accept a kiss, then his guest would move on.

Shaw remained standing next to Jake, mostly because he didn't know anybody else in the bar. The partygoers were polite to him, mostly because he stood with Jake.

Shaw kept to himself but couldn't help noticing that one of Jake's female friends seemed to be taking an interest in him. He had no problem returning her gaze, and it didn't seem to make her the least bit uncomfortable.

She was nearly tall enough to look the six-foot-two Shaw eye-to-eye and confident enough to do it without a hint of shyness. She wore a black spaghetti-strap dress that revealed plenty *café au lait* cleavage and long, sleek legs below.

Shaw particularly enjoyed the view when she bent over to kiss Jake's cheek.

She reached out to shake Shaw's hand.

"I'm Denise."

"Loyd. Loyd Shaw."

"Pleased to meet you."

Denise smiled, revealing a right front tooth rimmed in gold. Her smile made Shaw wish she would kiss his cheek, too. The warmth of Denise's smile lingered over him as she turned and melted back into the party. For a moment, Shaw felt less like an outsider.

Jake looked at his friend watching Denise saunter off and said, "It's all that sperm backed up into your brain."

"Maybe I need a black woman, Jakey."

"Why?"

"I have the feeling they are more understanding of a man's needs. A man such as me."

"Dude, you're crazy."

Shaw took a long sip from his tumbler of iced bourbon. "I suppose."

The cold whiskey warmed Shaw's belly. He swung an arm across Jake's broad shoulders. "You are one big happy fucking birthday boy, aren't you?"

Jake laughed a booming birthday laugh that made Shaw laugh, too. He looked around the bar, enjoying the sight of Jake's guests. Although most of the people were Jake's family and close friends, they weren't typical family and friends. Jake Bennett didn't attract typical people. Everybody had dressed with style. Jake wore the only pair of jeans in the bar. These were people who partied in after-hours clubs until dawn. The kind of people who knew about a bar like Earl's Place and were quickly admitted once they tapped on the locked front door.

Suddenly, Shaw felt like an outsider. Like he didn't belong.

"Keep lookin'; you might find something, Loyd. You're welcome to anything I don't want."

"Oh, Jakey, how marvelous it would be. A young, toned, smooth-skinned, voluptuous black girl snuggled up next to me, naked, in postcoital bliss, in some quiet little Bushwick bungalow."

"What kind of bliss?"

"After-fucking-me bliss."

"After laughin' at your…"

"Hey, no racial stereotyping, please."

"And they ain't no innocent women in this bar, Shaw. At least none that I know of."

"Forget innocent. Young is good enough. Young and wicked. Twenties. Late twenties, I don't care. Maybe thirties. Like Denise."

"Oh, boy, here we go."

"What do you think?"

"Hey. It could happen. I saw the way she smiled at you, all nice and friendly. Ask her husband over there; maybe he'll say okay."

Jake's big laugh boomed again. Shaw smiled but didn't laugh back. "Story of my life, Jake. I find no humor in tormenting a man already in torment."

"You wanna get laid, Shaw, just stand where you are and keep drinking with old Jake. I'll get you laid. Maybe not some young, smooth whatever, but I'll get the job done."

"God knows how."

"So?"

This time they both laughed. But Shaw's laughter faded quickly. He reached over and picked up his drink from the bar and drained it. The ice had watered it down to the point where it had no bite, but he finished it off anyway.

"Fuck it," Shaw said. He reached over and squeezed Jake's meaty shoulder and told him, "So long, big guy. You have a happy birthday. And many more to come."

"What's the matter, man? We just gettin' started."

"I don't know. Don't have the energy to drink until dawn and hope for a miracle. Don't mind me. Your fat ass is gonna be sittin' in that spot for a long time, and I want you to enjoy every minute of it."

Jake answered, "Till the dawn's early light, brother."

"Yes, sir, you must meet the first day of your new birth year drunked up, smellin' of perfumed women and smoke and booze."

"Sounds good to me."

"We don't do that often enough anymore, do we?"

"Wouldn't still be here if we did."

"Well, there you go. Blow out the candle, brother, and make a wish. See ya."

"You okay?"

"Yeah, of course I'm okay."

"Cheer up, Shaw, you're gonna make it. How long you got left till you're out?"

"With sick time, vacation days, all that bullshit…thirteen, fourteen months."

"Shit, you're good."

"I am."

"You know where you are?"

"Yeah, and I know the way home. Have fun."

"Hey, man, sorry about the situation with Jane. It happens."

Damn, thought Shaw. Old Jake had to slip that in just as I'm about to leave.

Shaw answered, "I'd say it's pretty much over. It shits, but what else is new?"

"Hang in."

"Oh yeah. Not to worry, brother. Take care, Jake. I love you. Happy birthday, man."

"Thanks for comin' out to see me." Jake began to rise from his stool. "Come on, I'll walk you to your car."

Shaw pushed him back down. He knew the offer was genuine on Jake's part, but he said, "No way. I'm not taking you from your party."

Jake eased back down and gripped his scotch. They shook hands so that no more could be said about the sadness that suddenly surrounded them. Shaw held on to Jake's solid hand for a couple more beats than he normally would have, then released his grip and headed for the front door. He eased his way through the partygoers. Nobody urged him to stay.

He unlocked the front door himself and stepped out onto the darkened street.

He stood for a moment, letting the cool, early morning April air clear his head a bit, listening to the faint bass beat emanating from the bar. A muffled laugh penetrated the closed door. Denise? Laughing at something her husband said? Shaw heard the lock snap shut behind him.

Now what? he asked himself.

He checked his watch – almost three in the morning. To hell with it, he thought, I'm going home.

He pictured crawling into bed with Jane. He didn't relish waking her and facing that steely silence that continued to separate them.

Should have built that second bedroom in the back of the loft, he told himself. Nah, no way. That would've just caused open warfare. She'd have started the divorce rolling just to save face. No, he told himself, just go home and keep your distance, pal.

He had parked four or five blocks from the bar. After two blocks, he started looking for his seven-year-old, dark green Mercury Marquis, trying to remember exactly where he'd parked. He passed two black men standing under the streetlight. Seeing them brought to mind that he was a white man walking in a disadvantaged black neighborhood at three in the morning. The two men checked out Shaw. Shaw looked at them for no more than five seconds and judged them to be working men. Maybe four-to-midnight guys getting home after eating a late dinner or an early breakfast. Not a problem.

He started thinking about Jane again and the loneliness her presence caused and the unfulfilled needs. He frowned, wondering just how much longer he could keep the peace. And then the frown deepened into a scowl as he heard the unmistakable low-pitched thud that seemed specifically created to annoy.

Shaw turned and saw the car coming his way. Even at a distance of a city block, he could hear the music. Gangsta rap. Loud. With that booming, thudding bass and the angry, insistent lyrics.

Shaw shook his head. What the hell is that incomprehensible shit? Yelling like that, over and over and over again.

As the car approached, the music blasted out so loudly and the bass boomed so deeply that Shaw could feel the sound waves thudding against his chest. He thought, this is fucking ridiculous.

The car passed by, and three dark faces glared at him, daring Shaw to say something.

He wanted to yell back, turn that shit off. He didn't, but he did say the words in his head. And when they glared at him,

Shaw didn't look the other way. He didn't look down. He lifted his chin and defiantly stared right back at the dark threatening faces. And in his mind, he said, *fuck you, assholes.* In the middle of the night, alone, on the streets of Bushwick.

CHAPTER 2

Less than a mile from where Shaw stood glaring at the rolling boom box, six bearded black men wearing knit skullcaps stood in a dark stairwell inside Building A of a five-building housing complex called New Lots Apartments located on Rockaway Avenue in Brownsville, Brooklyn.

Each of the six men occupied a step. At the highest step stood an ex-convict named Walter Harris, who had changed his name to Rachman Abdul X during his last stay at the Eastern Correctional Facility in upstate New York as part of his conversion to Islam.

The five men standing behind Rachman Abdul X were also Muslims. Rachman knew their Muslim names but referred to them as Gunmen. When Rachman pictured each of the men, he thought about how they fired their weapons more than he thought about their names. Efram fired steadily but always squinted at the discharge. Ahmad, a small man, employed a two-handed grip to compensate for his slight size. Abdul, Mahmoud, Suli, each of them had their own quirks.

Rachman had matched each gunman with a specific weapon. The three standing directly behind him gripped Tec-9 guns loaded with thirty-two bullet magazines. The next two held Glock 17 9mm semiautomatics. Rachman gripped a powerful 50 Magnum Desert Eagle. He was the only one strong enough to fire it single-handed. All the weapons had full clips. And each man had a second clip.

Rachman turned to check his gunmen one last time, but the narrow, unlit stairwell was too dark to see anything other than indistinguishable, shadowy forms. He decided they were ready when he heard the last man chamber a round.

Once the weapons were cocked, Rachman slowly led the way up the stairs. He headed for the fourth floor, but by the time Rachman reached the second floor, the blood thudding in his ears made it difficult for him to hear the shuffling footsteps of those behind him. It wasn't just the walk up the stairs that made Rachman's blood pound. The last prison doctor had called it hypertension.

"What's hypertension?" Rachman had asked.

"High blood pressure," the doctor had told him.

More poisonous words from the white devil trying to weaken him. Rachman had ignored the doctor, just as he had ignored all the other prison doctors who had examined him throughout his years in the New York prison system – at Sing-Sing, Dannemora, Attica, Eastern, Rikers, all the way back to the Spofford Juvenile Detention Center which he had entered at the age of sixteen.

Rachman remembered that word now: hypertension. High blood pressure. He didn't need a doctor to tell him living in the New York State prison system would cause pressure and tension. What he felt standing in the darkness with his five gunmen coming up behind him, semiautomatic weapons pressed against their legs, hands on the stair railing, slowly climbing the dark stairs, ready to do what they were about to do – that went way past tension.

Rachman pushed all such thoughts out of his mind and concentrated on climbing up onto each invisible step, slowly, carefully up, up, every so often catching a bit of light seeping out from doors that opened onto the hallways of each floor.

A few more steps up and Rachman stopped outside the door to the fourth-floor hallway.

The sudden stop caused the gunman directly behind Rachman to bump into him. For a moment, the gunman thought he had bumped into the door. Rachman's two hundred-thirty-pound frame hadn't moved an inch.

Rachman hissed, "Careful."

The column stopped without further mishap and stood in the order: Rachman with the .50 Magnum. Then the three Tec-9s. And finally, the two Glocks.

Out in the hallway, about twenty feet from the stairwell, a man named Ellis slouched next to one of the few functioning elevators in the entire five-building complex. Ellis belonged to the crack gang that had taken over New Lots Apartments three months previously. The gang called themselves the Blue-Tops after the color of the caps on their crack vials. They were the ones who had smashed all the lights inside the hallways and stairwells of New Lots Apartments. Less light meant more terror for those who walked the halls of New Lots. The more terrified people were, the easier it was for the Blue-Tops to control New Lots. The darkness also made it easier to keep the cops out of their business inside the dark halls of New Lots Apartments.

Ellis was chosen for his job because of his bulk. Even if someone shot him, he was so big he would block the doorway to the crack apartment.

Rachman stood in the dark stairwell, waiting patiently. He knew Ellis stood outside two apartments commandeered by the Blue-Tops. One apartment for selling crack, the other for smoking it.

He also knew how the Blue-Tops ran their operation. Police pressure and rivalries had driven much of the drug business indoors. It was safer and easier to sell inside rather than out on the street. Steerers surrounded the five-building complex directing customers into the central courtyard, known as The Pit, where gang members would direct them into one of the five downstairs lobbies. From there, the buyer would take the elevator up to a designated floor, money in hand. Once they entered New Lots, no one was allowed to reach into their pockets. The customer handed the cash to Ellis, who slipped it into a slot in one of the apartment doors. The proper amount of crack would come out the same slot.

Rachman knew everything there was to know about how the Blue-Tops ran their operation. He knew exactly where to send six more of his gunmen so they could cover each of the Blue-Tops working in The Pit and the lobby.

Soon now, Rachman told himself. Soon. He breathed slowly, willing the blood to stop pounding in his ears. For the hundredth time, he pictured the layout of the two apartments. In the first apartment were two rooms. Behind the front door sat one man taking in money and handing out crack – a pair of armed men behind him. In the second room, four people sat around a table measuring and packing the vials of cocaine. Rachman assumed there would also be a runner in that room to fetch more supplies as needed.

Then there was the smoking apartment, next door to the selling apartment: dark, littered with filth, stifling. The only piece of furniture in it was a battered old couch that had been hauled in off the street, something dogs and derelicts had slept on. The windows in the apartment hadn't been opened in four months. Rachman knew that an acrid stench permeated the place, a gagging combination of burning crack, rank body odor, and the human waste deposited in a bathroom that no one ever bothered to clean. He didn't bother estimating how many crackheads might be in there. They did not concern him.

One of the occupants, a glassy-eyed, wasted woman named Marlene who had been smoking for almost two days, worked the crack den. At one time in her life, before she'd lost twenty pounds and her teeth loosened and her skin began to look like dirty clay and her hair like filthy, rusted steel wool, Marlene had been an attractive girl with a lovely shape. Even now, at three in the morning, she somehow managed to conjure up a smile that helped but wasn't the main attraction. The main attraction was her unbuttoned blouse and lack of a bra.

Marlene had run out of money one hour into her binge and continued to finance her habit by offering oral sex for five dollars. She'd shuffle on her knees between the legs of whatever male crackhead would allow it, kneeling there, stroking his thigh, smiling at him, exposing her breasts while she gently cupped his genitals, softly whispering the required graphic sexual pleas as she asked for five dollars, describing what she would do and how good it would feel and how much she wanted him in her mouth. She'd let them grab her breasts and pinch her nipples, no matter how much it hurt. Anything to make them feel like they owed her something. She asked for five, and some of the men would simply push her away after abusing her for as long as she, or they, could stand it. But some gave her money. Maybe five dollars, maybe only one dollar. And as soon as Marlene had done enough to get ten dollars, she turned those dollars into rock and smoked the crack with frightening need.

Rachman didn't know about the woman working the den, but he knew the misery crack had caused people like her. And when he heard the elevator open out in the hallway, he knew it was almost time to end that misery. For her and for everyone else in New Lots. At least for tonight.

John X stepped out of the elevator and smiled at Ellis. Ellis did not smile back. Nobody smiled when they saw John X. Like the others, John X was bearded, but he wore his beard to hide his pockmarked skin and diminish a pronounced underbite that exposed a badly misshapen row of teeth. John X was bigger than Ellis, which made him very big. Ellis would normally have pulled his gun the second he saw someone John X's size and demeanor, but John X had been in and out of New Lots buying crack enough times so that Ellis recognized him. As usual, Ellis put out his hand for the money without saying anything.

Unfortunately for Ellis, this time was different.

When John X stepped out of the elevator, he grabbed Ellis's throat with his extra-large left hand and shoved a long-barrel .38 revolver far enough into Ellis's gaping mouth to make him gag.

With the long barrel pressing into the back of Ellis's throat, John X swung the guard around and backed him up against the wall next to the elevator. Ellis instinctively grabbed John X's wrist, but when John X pulled back the hammer of the .38, Ellis froze. John X brought his big, ugly, pockmarked face closer to Ellis and repeatedly nodded at him as if to say, that's right, that's right, don't move. Don't move, and I won't squeeze this trigger and blow off the back of your head.

Rachman heard the sounds of the elevator and Ellis choking on the gun barrel. He shoved open the hall door and walked quickly into the dim corridor, moving fast along the outside wall of the two adjoining apartments. The others followed as he raised the Desert Eagle and fired three booming shots. The high-caliber explosions deafened everybody in the corridor.

Ellis flinched at the booming blasts, likely wondering what the hell Rachman was shooting at, since only he and John X were in the hallway.

But Rachman wasn't shooting people. He was shooting walls. Three shots opened up three holes: one in the cinder-block wall, one in the front door of the selling apartment, and a third in the wall of the smoking room.

The exploding walls and door had the desired effect on the people inside. They dropped as if they had been shot. If they could have burrowed under the hard floors, they would have. One of the Blue-Tops sitting at the table doling out crack rocks and counting money dove under the table so quickly that his forehead hit the corner, splitting open a gash that ran from just above his eyebrow to his scalp.

The only person who didn't immediately drop down was the strung-out woman in the smoke room. She froze in her kneeling position, hands covering her ears, and began screaming nonstop.

Her screams were not audible for long.

CHAPTER 3

LOYD SHAW MIGHT HAVE PREFERRED THE CRACK ADDICT'S SCREAMS to the booming rap that blasted him as the car rolled past. His angry scowl had not pleased the car's occupants. Shaw saw the passenger in the backseat lean forward and say something to the driver. The car slowed, turned right at the corner, ten feet in front of Shaw, and stopped.

Shaw muttered, "Shit." And then, "Shit, fuck," as he felt fear hit his chest as if someone had thrown a bucket of ice water on him, penetrating down, creating that sickening loose bowel feeling. His heart began pounding. He ruthlessly suppressed the fear, shutting off any image of vulnerability. He forced himself to walk toward the car. He stopped and looked behind him. He was too far away from the bar to run back, and the car was too close to let him. He looked around. Nobody on the street.

Shaw found himself short of breath. The adrenaline had kicked in. He knew he would be strong and fast for a short time, and then a shaky weakness would set in. One way or another, whatever was about to happen, it couldn't last long.

He continued forward, approaching the car, the passenger side of the vehicle blocking his way.

He looked into the car; a Chevy Nova tricked out with chrome and trim and wheel covers and ridiculously large speakers in the back window well. He could make out a driver, a passenger in the back, and one in the front. All black. All young.

Now that the car had stopped in front of him, the music sounded even louder. Shouting at him, beating him with that pounding bass like a weapon they were using on him. Shaw felt as if someone were smacking him in the head with the Brooklyn phone book.

Now it started. The two passengers in front and back opened their doors and stepped out. The driver stayed behind the wheel but leaned forward to watch with a malicious grin.

That's right, Shaw said to himself. Smile, you cocksucker. Whitey about to be maimed for your amusement.

With the car doors open, the music boomed out even louder. The two young blacks blocked Shaw's passage. They seemed to Shaw like a George and Lennie act – one big, one small. The big one responsible for the heavy work, the small one giving directions.

Shaw did not miss noticing how the Nova had visibly lifted when the big one stepped out of the front seat. He wore his homeboy uniform: a black hooded sweatshirt, baggy denim pants, untied Timberland boots. His face reminded Shaw of a dimwitted heavyweight fighter, nose flat and eyes blank. The sides of his head shaved. A short pile of dreads sprouted like a nest of fat black worms coming out of the top of his skull.

He tilted his head back, looked down at Shaw, and said, "What's your fuckin' problem, bitch?"

Shaw knew which of the two he would go for. He saw everything he needed to and more. The smaller one stood a step back from his big homey. He was lean and nasty, nothing extra on him, with a face that reminded Shaw of a Doberman. Every angle of his bony skull stood out underneath his skin. Shaw checked the smaller one's hands, saw that they were empty, but the heavyweight had his right hand stuck in the front pouch pocket of his hooded sweatshirt. He was the one with the gun. Shaw could already see the big, stupid kid dressed in those ridiculous baggy clothes, surrounded by that awful booming din, pulling out the gun and squeezing the trigger, shooting him, alone, on this strange street in Bushwick. Squeezing the trigger, no questions, no statements, without thought or concern, mindlessly inflicting terrible pain and damage to him. Or killing him. And with that horrible music so loud, no one would hear the shots.

Just the idea of it made Shaw so furious that the anger inside him blossomed like something alive. Like a dark hand reaching up his spine into his head, pushing aside everything – good sense, fear, caution, all of it. He went for the heavyweight powered by a ferocious red wave of anger.

The heavyweight didn't see the anger take over. He was too accustomed to terrifying people.

He said, "I axed you a question, motherfucker."

But Shaw was already moving for him, fast. It confused him. A white guy, alone, middle of the night, coming at him. No way. The confusion made the heavyweight hesitate.

The smaller one yelled, "Yo, Dred, cap this crazy motherfucker."

But by the time Dred tried to pull his gun, Shaw was already too close.

The gun came halfway out of the sweatshirt pouch.

Shaw's left hand was already coming up toward Dred, Shaw twisting at the hip for added leverage, thumb and forefinger spread wide, turning his upper body, driving the crook of his left hand into the heavyweight's throat.

The contact jarred Shaw's wrist and arm all the way to his shoulder. It felt as if he'd hit a small tree. The big kid barely moved back, but the blow paralyzed him where he stood as he reached for his throat, struggling to breathe.

Without any hesitation between blows, Shaw made his next and last move.

He bunched his right hand into a fist, circling up and around, driving the side of his right fist in a hammer strike right into the center the heavyweight's collarbone. He put everything he had into the blow. All his strength, all his weight, up from the balls of his feet, concentrating everything into one fast, brutal overhand smash. Shaw knew he couldn't let this turn into a fight. He had one chance, just one blow, full strength.

He heard the crack and felt the heavyweight's thick bone break under his fist. It was at once both sweetly satisfying and sickening.

Shaw heard a short, choking scream and watched the big kid deflate. The pain hit so intensely, so suddenly, that the scream didn't last long. The heavyweight dropped to his knees. Moving either arm now would grind the broken ends of his left collarbone, so he didn't move.

But Shaw moved fast, ripping the gun out of his attacker's limp hand just as the smaller one swung at him. Shaw thought it was a punch, but the hand coming at his face held a hooked, carpet cutter knife. Shaw just managed to duck before the blade tore open the left side of his face.

Shaw came up out of his crouch fast, the gun in his right hand. With no time to aim, he backhanded the gun barrel across the smaller one's face, breaking his nose. The attacker's head snapped around, blood flew out of his nostrils, and he went down hard on his left hip.

Now the driver came out of the car, pointing a revolver. Shaw pulled back the slide on the gun he'd taken from the heavyweight, a 9mm semiautomatic.

The driver fired wildly, too pumped up and rushed to aim. The bullet went wide. Shaw returned fire, but he did not shoot at the driver. He shot at the back speaker in the Chevy Nova. That idiotic noise had been booming at him the entire time he had been fighting for his life. His first shot blew out the back window. The driver ducked and ran, and the two others some-how made it to their feet and disappeared. But not the music. It still pounded out at Shaw, driving him even further over the edge. He pumped another shot at the speakers, yelling at the car in between shots. Shouting, "Goddamn – fucking – music!"

He emptied the gun into the speakers and the dashboard, and the music finally died.

Shaw stood staring at the car, breathing hard. It took a few seconds, maybe longer, for him to come back to the present time and space. He was just about to toss Dred's gun, a beat-up old Browning, into the wrecked Nova and stumble off, find his car, and drive out of the neighborhood when the first police car screeched to a halt behind him. The second blue-and-white appeared two seconds after the first, stopping in front of him.

Shaw stood motionless, frozen in the glare of four headlights, and forgot about tossing the gun. He dropped it where he stood.

For some reason, as he dropped the gun, he noted that, despite its poor condition, the gun was an expensive weapon, probably stolen. Strange thoughts to be having standing there with his hands raised while at least four cops, four nervous cops, all had their guns drawn and pointed at him.

He wondered who'd called the cops. Maybe those two black guys under the streetlamp. He supposed it was good of them to do that. Too bad the uniforms hadn't arrived sooner. Now, even though he'd survived the other three guys, if he made any sudden move, one of these four nervous, shouting patrol cops would shoot him.

CHAPTER 4

AFTER FIRING THE DEAFENING BLASTS FROM THE DESERT EAGLE, Rachman Abdul X could barely hear the hysterical screams of the crack whore or the pounding footsteps of the three rushing gunmen behind him. Each of them shoved the muzzle of his Tec-9 into the holes Rachman had blasted open and fired short ripping bursts into the two apartments. Bullets banged and ripped and ricocheted in the confined interiors. Fire from the muzzles burned the walls. Acrid gun smoke filled the rooms. The exploding nine-millimeter ammunition deafened. Everyone in the apartment expected to die.

But they didn't. Rachman had made sure the holes were about six feet high. And the gunmen made sure to aim level or slightly upward, so the nightmare erupted over the heads of the dealers and buyers.

The Blue-Tops, the crazed crack addicts, all of them squirmed and writhed on the floor under the withering gunfire that seemed to go on forever.

Finally, the machine pistols ran out of ammunition. But it wasn't over.

The two trailing gunmen with the Glocks stepped up to the two holes in the selling apartment and began methodically pulling their triggers. There were fewer bullets, but each of the nine-millimeter shots delivered a withering blast into the rooms.

Finally, out of a desperate survival instinct, the two Blue-Tops guards inside started shooting back. They lay on their backs, cowering under the gunfire, and blindly shot at the exploding hole in the front door.

Rachman saw his gunman duck and step away from the shooting holes. He rushed to the door, shoved the barrel of the Desert Eagle into the hole, and fired. The big gun bucked and banged. Rachman growled and kept on firing, aiming downward because someone inside had dared to shoot back. He tried to envision the position of the shooters on the other side of the door, willing his bullets to hit them, tear into them, and kill them.

Rachman yelled with each pull of the trigger. Inside, both guards scrambled out of the line of fire as the big .50 Magnum bullets slammed into the floor around them and the wall behind them, tearing out chunks of wood and sheetrock. One of Rachman's shots caught the side of a guard's leg and tore away a wad of flesh the size of a fist. Both Blue-Tops stopped shooting.

And then, just as suddenly as the hellish assault had started, it ended. Everything stopped except the screaming of the crack whore and the hollow click of Rachman's empty Desert Eagle. The gunmen with the Glocks had already turned and walked back to the stairwell. The gunmen with the machine pistols had reloaded. They stood pointing their weapons at the apartment door in case anyone dared to come out shooting.

Rachman stepped back from his firing hole, slid a fresh clip into the Desert Eagle, chambered a round, and motioned for John X to leave. John eased his long-barreled revolver out of Ellis's mouth while Rachman pressed the hot muzzle of the Desert Eagle into Ellis's chest and brought his face up close to the Blue-Tops guard. While Ellis stared at him, Rachman told the guard, "Lie down. Put your face on the floor. Ask Allah to forgive you. Stay here, or I will kill you."

Inside the smoking room, someone finally punched the screaming crack whore, ending her hysterical shrieks.

After a few moments, the others slowly rose from the floor, touching themselves, squinting in the smoke-filled rooms, deafened from the gunfire, unable to comprehend what had just happened except that somehow they were still alive.

As Rachman and his men rumbled down the inside stairwell, the gunmen outside emerged almost invisibly from the night air, appearing next to each one of the Blue-Tops working around the complex. Every member of the gang felt a gun pressed firmly into the side of his head. If they had weapons, practiced hands found them and stripped them away. Then each Blue-Top heard a message hissed into his ear: "Tonight, we shoot above your heads. Next time, we shoot *in* your heads. Get out. New Lots belongs to MS-Two."

By the time Rachman and the others burst out the door at the bottom of the stairwell, the muzzles of their guns still hot, their clothes stinking of gun smoke, the outside gunmen had gathered near the rear door of Building A. The gunmen gathered around a small man holding open a canvas bag. Each of them carefully placed their weapons and the guns confiscated from the Blue-Tops in the bag. The gunmen quietly scattered and walked away from the scene. Rachman watched the bag man place the satchel filled with weapons into the trunk of a beat-up '86 Ford LTD that looked like one of the gypsy cabs that plied the Brownsville neighborhood.

Rachman looked around. No one had called the police. For the moment, all was quiet in the complex. Rachman got into the Ford and drove off, knowing the calm would not last for long.

CHAPTER 5

Loyd Shaw stood on Tilden Avenue, hands lifted in the air. The beams of three police squad cars illuminating him. Six cops yelled, "Get down, get down. Down. Down."

Shaw slowly sank to his knees, keeping his hands raised. The cops kept shouting, "Get down! Get down!"

Shaw carefully placed his hands on the pavement and lowered himself to the street and spread his arms and legs wide.

The gritty asphalt felt cold against his cheek. Better than a hot bullet slamming into my head, thought Shaw. He knew that cops called out in the middle of the night to a black neighborhood where shots had been fired were going to make damn sure they didn't get shot. Shaw had been standing next to a shot-up car with a gun in his hand. He knew if he'd been a black man, he would probably be dead.

He lay on the cold, dirty street motionless. He wasn't about to give anybody a reason to launch a kick or pull a trigger now.

At least a couple of the cops held their guns pointed at Shaw while two others knelt next to him and cuffed his hands behind his back. They roughly lifted him to his feet, pulled him over to a squad car, and shoved him into the backseat.

They left him in the squad car as they checked the scene.

Shaw leaned over and rested against the side door of the car. He couldn't sit back comfortably with his hands cuffed behind him. He carefully rolled his shoulders, testing to see if any damage had been done when they lifted him off the street.

Outside, the cops prowled around the wrecked Chevy Nova and confirmed the area was free of witnesses, dead, or wounded.

After about ten minutes, one of the older cops came over and squatted down next to the back window of the squad. He held up the empty Browning by the trigger guard so Shaw could see it.

"This your gun?"

Shaw answered, "No, it's not my gun."

"Whose is it?"

"Two guys came out of that car, approached me, and one of them pulled out that gun. I took it away from him."

The cop raised an eyebrow. "You took it away from him?"

"Yeah."

"Uh-huh. How'd you manage to do that?"

"Very quickly."

"Oh, really."

Shaw clamped his mouth shut instead of saying, yeah, really, so the cop asked him another question.

"That's their car?"

"Yeah. There were three guys in it. The two, plus the driver."

"And they came after you."

"'Right. When I got the gun, the driver came out and pegged a shot at me."

"Why?"

"Cuz I took his pal's gun, I guess."

"No, why were these guys after you?"

Shaw thought about the answer for a moment. Because I dissed them? Because I was white, alone, in the wrong neighborhood? Because they weren't nice guys?

"I didn't like their music."

"You didn't like their music."

"I'm using the term music very loosely. I don't consider rap exactly music. Maybe musical, but not music."

"What are you, a fucking critic?"

Shaw didn't answer.

"I see. So you shot up their car?"

"Not the whole car. Just the speakers and the dashboard."

"Because you didn't like the music?"

"It was self-defense."

"Uh-huh. The guys with the guns you didn't give a shit about. It was the music that was killing you?"

Shaw smiled at that one.

The cop said, "Yeah, well, maybe, but shooting up cars ain't allowed. I'm going to have to take you in."

When they brought Shaw into the 77th Precinct, the desk sergeant didn't do much more than glance at Shaw. He saw a well-built white guy, brown hair long enough to go over the collar of his blue shirt, a dark brown leather jacket, black jeans. He noticed that Shaw was bigger than the cops on either side of him, but he didn't bother to look beyond that. The desk sergeant looked down at his logbook and made an entry.

Shaw, on the other hand, recognized the desk sergeant from a long time ago but didn't feel like reminding the old cop. The arresting officer waited for the sergeant to make his notes and hand him a report form. Then he walked Shaw over to the property clerk's cage, handed over Shaw's wallet, keys, pocket change. Next, he walked Shaw through double doors into a large open room, sat at an empty desk, and pulled out an arrest form from the bottom desk drawer.

Shaw sat and took it all in. The cop pulled an old IBM Selectric typewriter into position, shoved the arrest form in the roller, and kicked shut the desk drawer.

Midnight to eight shift, thought Shaw. Guy's pissed off now that he can't get out of here on time. Not this shift, pal. Not for a couple of hours at least.

Shaw said to the cop, "Well, at least you'll be getting some overtime."

"What?"

"Nothing," said Shaw.

The cop ratcheted a form into position and began poking at the keys with two fingers.

Shaw thought about how much the precinct looked like most others he'd been inside. Concrete-block walls. Green paint. Harsh fluorescent lighting. Gray metal desks and a motley assortment of desk chairs. Always a bunch of mismatched chairs.

Shaw noticed that this precinct seemed particularly messy. Piles of papers lay everywhere – in folders, on desks, in piles next to desks, on bulletin boards. Lots of paper, lots of forms, one of which his arresting cop labored over. Shaw watched him peck away and wondered if the NYPD would ever fully computerize their precincts. So many useless words pecked into mountains of forms that sat in mute phalanxes of old file cabinets.

Shaw turned sideways in his chair and leaned his shoulder against the back. His hands were still cuffed. He couldn't comfortably sit back. Shaw decided he'd about had enough of the damn handcuffs. He was about to tell the arresting cop to uncuff him when the property clerk appeared and said, "We got a problem here, Joe."

Joe kept hunting for typewriter keys as he said, "What?"

The property clerk said, "You arrested a cop."

"Huh?"

"His ID is in his wallet. This is Detective First Grade Loyd Shaw." The cop stopped poking at the typewriter keys. He looked up and stared at Shaw for about three seconds, then asked, "You're a detective?"

"Yeah."

"First grade?"

"Yeah."

"Where's your fucking shield and gun?"

"I don't have them."

"Who does?"

"My CO."

"You're on the rubber-gun squad?"

Shaw nodded.

"And you're out on Tilden Avenue shooting up cars?"

"Not cars. One car. One piece of shit Chevy Nova."

The cop grimaced, "Whoa. Fuck me, man." He stood up and said, "This one's outta my hands." He told the property clerk, "Watch him." The clerk looked at Shaw. For a moment, he didn't say anything. Then he asked, "Why didn't you tell 'em you're a cop?"

"I don't know. There was a moment when it seemed appropriate to mention it, and then it somehow slipped away."

The clerk looked at Shaw again and said, "Are you really Loyd Shaw?"

"Yeah."

The property clerk blinked twice, mumbled something about deep shit, and sat down.

Within five minutes, the cuffs were off, and Shaw was locked away in a small office on the second floor of the precinct.

Shaw sat in the cramped office trying to figure out who worked in the small space. Probably the detective who recorded assignment calls for the precinct's detective squad. There was the old green ledger used for such purposes sitting on the desk. On the far wall, someone had taped a map of Brooklyn showing the various boundaries of each Brooklyn precinct. Phones would be ringing all over Brooklyn about now, thought Shaw. In other boroughs, too.

Shaw began to make a mental list of the law enforcement personnel who would be called in the next hour or so. He knew the precinct commander wouldn't be on duty at nearly three a.m., so they'd call in the zone commander to handle the situation. The zone commander would call Shaw's CO, Captain Richard Parnell, commander of the Special Investigation Division that had jurisdiction over Shaw's unit – the Major Case Squad.

Shaw pictured Parnell awakened by an early morning phone call. Parnell reminded Shaw of a bulldog, both in appearance and demeanor – squat, dour, tough Irish cop who had been around, knew the ropes and didn't suffer fools easily. Nope, Shaw told himself, Richard won't be happy about this.

Parnell would call the Detectives' Endowment Association and talk to the head delegate who would probably call the local delegate who would call the lawyer assigned to Shaw's restricted duty case, Morton Siegel. The zone commander would call the Internal Affairs Bureau and the Brooklyn District Attorney's Office. Both entities would send personnel.

Shaw figured there would be anywhere from six to ten people assembled to figure out what to do with him. The possibilities ranged from letting him go home to locking him up and indicting him for attempted murder.

"Shit," he muttered to himself. That was going to be one room full of disgruntled people forced to deal with this mess at five in the morning.

Shaw leaned back in his chair and propped his feet on the desk, shifting until he achieved a somewhat comfortable position. It would be some time before the Assistant District Attorney and Internal Affairs investigator interviewed him. Nothing he could do until then except try to catch some sleep. Hell of a way to end a goddamn birthday party.

CHAPTER 6

THREE HOURS LATER, WHILE SHAW SLEPT IN THE SMALL OFFICE on the second floor, Captain James Raiford, Brooklyn borough zone commander, sat at the precinct commander's desk on the second floor writing notes on a legal pad. The commander's office wasn't much bigger than the office where Shaw sat dozing in a desk chair.

If Raiford had been wearing a judge's robe instead of his police captain's executive white shirt and black tie, he would have fit the image of a stern, no-nonsense criminal court judge. Everything about him communicated rectitude – his hawk-like features, his ramrod-straight posture, his thinning hair combed straight back. Even the meticulous way he scrutinized his notes reminded the men who sat before him of a judge.

Shaw's estimate of six to ten participants proved accurate. Eight men were crowded into the small office, sitting or standing, looking at the zone commander. But Raiford's interest focused on three men only: Shaw's CO, Richard Parnell; Shaw's lawyer, a disheveled, bald, gnome-like man named Morton Siegel; and the assistant district attorney, an intense young black man named Philip Johnson whose white shirt and blue suit seemed remarkably crisp and wrinkle-free as if kept that way by the force of Johnson's will.

Raiford finally looked up from his notes.

"All right, you know the drill, gentlemen. It's my job to decide what happens to Detective Shaw tonight. After tonight, Internal

Affairs and the DA's office will do whatever they decide, but the next move is my call. I want your input, but I'm not looking for arguments or extended debates. You've all read the report. I think Captain Parnell has made Detective Shaw's personnel file available. Internal Affairs and Mr. Johnson have completed their interviews of the arresting officers. Mr. Siegel, you've finished?"

"Yes, sir."

"All right. The union delegates have already given their opinion that Detective Shaw should be awarded a commendation and sent home. Mr. Johnson, you represent the District Attorney here, what's your recommendation?"

"I'm looking at indicting him for attempted murder."

A voice from the back of the room commented, "You gotta be kidding."

Johnson's head snapped in the direction of the voice and said, "You think I'm kidding, just watch me. First of all, this line about a twenty-year veteran who never had a problem is bullshit. The man's already on restricted duty for what, assaulting a superior officer?"

Siegel gently interrupted, "Excuse me, Mr. Johnson, I happen to be handling that case. It's not assault. In fact, it's not at all clear who struck the first blow in the altercation."

Johnson shuffled his papers and referred to a report on the incident. "Well, it's damn clear who ended up with a broken jaw and chipped teeth." Johnson held up a hand to preclude Siegel's response. "Hold on. I haven't even started. This other report notes that Shaw was involved in a shooting incident with multiple wounded and two deaths. This man is a killer. This is a serious incident. I'll want the more details, but it says here he saw Psych Services for weeks afterward. Now three years later, he's back in Psych Services, been going twice a week for two months. Sounds like Detective Shaw has problems. Significant problems."

Siegel tried to get a word in, but Johnson continued over him.

"Now the guy shows up on Tilden Avenue at three in the morning, drunk, shooting a gun while he's on restricted duty. The man shouldn't even be touching a gun, and he's shooting up a car, which for all I know was filled with civilians. Hell, at the very least, I've got weapon's possession and property damage. If there were people in that car, I've got attempted murder. You folks have a cop out of control, Captain Raiford. He should be held for arraignment. Let a judge set bail and give the Department of Corrections custody of this man and let my office go in front of the Grand Jury and figure out just what we want to indict him for."

Raiford turned to the lawyer. "Mr. Siegel?"

Siegel grimaced as if in pain. He spoke at half the volume of Johnson but with just as much intensity.

"This *man*? Turn this *man* over to the Department of Corrections? This *man* is not a common criminal. Loyd Shaw is a nineteen-year, not twenty-year yet, Mr. Johnson, a nineteen-year veteran of the NYPD. A first grade detective. Gentlemen, some perspective, please."

Siegel looked around the room as if to assess for himself if everyone was keeping the proper perspective before he continued.

"Where is the criminal case against this officer? Mr. Johnson referred to a shooting incident three years ago. *Three* years ago? In the line of duty. What does that have to do with anything? Psych Services counseling is *mandatory* after shooting incidents. A full and proper investigation was conducted. There were no charges. No improprieties. Officer Shaw was awarded a commendation, for God's sake. And this is now being turned against him? That's outrageous. Not to mention irrelevant. As is his recent use of Psych Services. The department encourages its officers to use those services. You don't know why Detective

Shaw is seeking counseling. Perhaps Detective Shaw is dealing with a marital problem, a death in the family, the loss of a fellow officer, there could be any number of reasons. It's this kind of prejudicial attitude displayed by the assistant district attorney that discourages cops who need help from getting it. Detective Shaw should be commended, not condemned.

"And this characterization that Detective Shaw was drunk? Based on what? There's no evidence of intoxication. The arresting officer made no mention of it. There's nothing about alcohol in his arrest report. I just interviewed Detective Shaw, and I can assure you the man is sober. Detective Shaw attended a birthday gathering for a fellow police officer. He was present for a total of no more than thirty minutes. And suddenly he's running the streets of Brooklyn in a wild drunken spree? Hardly. He was walking back to his car, and he was assaulted.

"If there's a crime here, Detective Shaw is not the one who committed it. There's no evidence of a crime. The gun was not Detective Shaw's. There was no sign of injury on the street. No blood. No witnesses. There is no case. By all means, Mr. Johnson, I encourage you to go back to your office and figure out what charges to bring. A closer, more dispassionate appraisal will reveal there are none." Siegel turned to Raiford. "Captain, Detective Shaw should be sent home. He shouldn't have even been arrested in the first place, but in deference to the uniformed officers on the scene, Detective Shaw didn't try to badge his way out of this. He went along with the proper procedure. And look what it got him?"

Johnson responded, "Mr. Siegel, you are being disingenuous at best. You know the relevance of his Psych Services record. Whether it's fair or not, you know as well as I do that once a cop does that, he's basically kissing off his career. A cop who doesn't give a damn about his career anymore is a dangerous cop."

Siegal interrupted. "Absolutely ridiculous."

Johnson continued. "Now, there might not have been any victims on the scene, but the man fired off eight rounds. *Eight.* If he intended to drive off these so-called assailants, one or two warning shots in the air would suffice, don't you think? The man unloaded a nine-millimeter weapon at a car. You consider that rational behavior? He claims he was assaulted by three black men, but there's not a mark on him. No sign of a struggle. How do I know that gun wasn't his? How do I know he didn't just decide these kids were making too much noise and felt a little street justice was in order?"

Siegel interrupted. "Kid? Who said they were kids? Where are you getting that?"

Johnson ignored Siegel. "Again, I think you've got a cop out of control here. He should be locked up."

Raiford raised a hand. He knew that, exaggerations aside, Johnson had finally stated the critical issue.

"All right, gentlemen, thank you."

Raiford's demeanor made it clear he didn't want to hear any more from Siegel and Johnson.

"Mr. Siegel, I tend to agree with you that without witnesses or victims, there isn't much of a chance that any criminal proceedings will go forward. Of course, if Internal Affairs comes up with the owner of that car and a victim, Mr. Johnson might be able to make a case.

"However, Mr. Johnson does have a point. Detective Shaw, by any standards, went over the line tonight. Most of us in this room are familiar with the shooting incident Detective Shaw engaged in a few years back."

Johnson interrupted. "Enlighten me."

Raiford held up a hand. "I don't have time for that. I've got to decide if this cop is stable enough to be allowed out of here. He is seeing Psych Services. He seemed to be acting a bit crazy this morning, even given the circumstances. Captain Parnell, you're the person in this room who knows him best. I don't want to hold a good cop for arraignment before the department completes a thorough investigation, but I can't let him back out there if he's lost it. Is Detective Shaw a danger?"

Parnell rubbed his jowly face as if he were trying to rouse a response from somewhere deep inside. Raiford carefully observed him, calculating how much of Parnell's answer would be contrived to distance himself from Shaw, and how much would be the simple truth as he knew it.

Parnell started with an equivocation.

"I don't deal with Shaw closely on a day-to-day basis. But I've known him for a lot of years. I put him on the Major Case Squad."

Parnell shifted in his chair. He knew whatever he said would be the deciding factor for Raiford.

Parnell continued, "Fact is, Shaw's a damned good detective. Not exactly a team player, but he gets the job done. Maybe a little too smart for his own good. Does things his way. Always has. But, like I said, he gets the job done. I don't know if he's about to go off his nut. How the hell do you know that? Who knows how all this shit we deal with affects a guy? Maybe you should have dragged his shrink in here and asked her. But I do know one thing."

"Yes?" asked Raiford.

"I know the guy wants to finish his twenty and get the hell out. He's made no bones about that. Told me so himself. He's got a place up in Massachusetts. A weekend place. I don't think he deserves to sit in some goddamn cell until he gets arraigned. I'd tell him to get the hell out of town. Go up to his place out of state and stay there until his departmental hearing. Suspend him. Tell him if he shows up inside the city before his investigation is complete, he goes into the can. If he's gonna go off his nut and shoot something or somebody, let him do it up in the woods."

Parnell crossed his arms and sat back in his chair.

Raiford looked around the room one time to see if anyone had anything else to say.

Johnson saw the decision coming and simply announced, "Do what you want. I'm pursuing an investigation."

Raiford responded, "That's your prerogative, Mr. Johnson. In the meantime, Detective Shaw is suspended pending a departmental hearing and investigation of tonight's events. I suggest IAB get on this as soon as possible.

"Captain Parnell, I'll give Shaw the news, but I want you to accompany him out of this precinct, take him home, and tell him if he doesn't leave town, I'll have him locked up. And I want you to keep a tight rein on him until he does. Don't let him near your squad. They work out of One Police?"

"Yes."

"He shouldn't even go in there to clean his desk. Tell him to get out of town and stay out until his hearing. He can talk to his lawyer from Massachusetts. That's it, gentlemen. Thank you. Go home and get whatever sleep you can."

CHAPTER 7

As Parnell and Raiford slowly walked up to the second floor of the 75th Precinct to deliver the news to Loyd Shaw, a phone rang in Saddle Brook, New Jersey, bringing news to Archie Reynolds.

Archie lay sleeping in a queen-size bed, dressed only in purple silk boxer shorts. His slim, muscular, mocha-colored body contrasted against the white sheets. Before the first ring finished, Archie snatched the receiver from the cradle.

"What?"

"Ar-Man, we, we got hit."

Archie knew the stuttering voice belonged to one of his three managers, Reggie Whack.

"Slow down, motherfucker. Where?"

"New, New Lots?"

"New Lots?"

"Yeah."

"Who? Cops?"

"Nuh, nuh, no. Wasn' no cops."

"Who? What they get?"

"Nu, nuthin'. The crew got the rocks and money out."

"So, what's the fuckin' problem? Anybody dead?"

Reggie answered, "No. Mayon ga, ga, got, hit in the leg. Got a, a big chunk blowed out, but he ain't dead."

"So what you so fucked up about, man?"

"'Dis wasn't no regular thing, Arch. This was different. They didn't *try* to shoot nobody, except for Mayon cuz I guess he wa, wa, was shootin' back. They unloaded all kinds a shit into the place, coulda kilt everybody, taken everything, but they didn't. This was a warning kind of thing."

"A warning? What the fuck you mean, a warning?"

"They had guys inside, outside. Got the drop on everybody. They said New Lots belong to, to, to them now, and we got to get the fuck out or the next time they shoo, shoo, shoot us in the head."

"Wait a minute, wait a minute. Who's they?"

"Don't know, man. Some initial shit."

"Some what?"

"Initials. Like em, em, MSG or M-Two, I don't know. Some shit like that."

"And they tellin' *us* to get the fuck out?"

"Yeah."

"What they hit us with?"

"Ellis said it was Tec-nines and Glocks. A shi, a shitload of firepower, man."

"That's drug gang guns."

"Yeah, but it wasn't no drug gang, Archie. They didn't kill no one. And they had everybody c, c, covered, man. The guys in The Pit. The steerers. The lookouts on the street. They could have kilt all of 'em, but they didn't. Just said to get out."

Archie said, "Yeah, okay, I got it."

"Got what? Who the fuck are these guys?"

"You suppose to know that, motherfucker. Somebody shoots shit up and tells me and mines to get out, you suppose to know."

"Yeah, man. I, I know."

"No, you don't fuckin' know. That's the trouble. You call everybody walking. You get everybody over to the shop. You make sure Little Marvin is there. He's lieutenant of the operation, ain't he?"

"Yeah."

"You suppose to be the manager, right?"

"Yeah."

"Get your people, your wagons, your shit over there now. I be leaving here after I shower and dress an' shit."

Archie dropped the receiver back into the cradle and lay back in bed. A frown marred his otherwise handsome, dark face. Archie stroked the slight goatee that decorated his upper lip and chin.

"What the fuck is goin' on now?" he asked himself.

He thought about it for a few seconds, then jackknifed himself out of his bed in one quick move and headed slowly for his bathroom. Archie did not rush through the hour he spent showering, shaving, slipping on his matching gold chains on wrist and neck, and dressing. Archie moved casually, stepping into light wool pleated pants, buttoning his stylish silk and rayon shirt. But his mind ticked off several scenarios trying to explain what had happened at New Lots that night.

By the time he slid behind the wheel of his Saab 900 SE convertible, Archie had stopped trying to figure all the angles and concentrated on two facts – his men had not seen the attack coming. Whoever had attacked them was telling him to get out of New Lots. The first fact made him angry. The second drove him into a slow, simmering rage.

The rage simmered and burned as Archie drove along Route 80 toward New York.

When Archie had first checked a road map to figure out the way from Saddle Brook to Brownsville, he thought Route 80 looked like a long, fat blue vein. A thick, blue vein that ran right next to his condo in Saddle Brook headed straight to the George Washington Bridge, crossed the bridge, and merged with another highway vein that pulsed through the Bronx, curved over to the Whitestone Bridge, continued into Queens along the Van Wyck, looping slowly around in a lazy J along the Interboro Parkway right into the heart of Brooklyn, right into the misery of Brownsville.

Archie rode the vein to Brownsville, checking the Saab's speedometer to make sure he stayed between fifty-five and sixty mph. It didn't matter that the traffic was light. Archie Reynolds knew better than to give some eager state trooper a reason to pull him over.

Archie knew that Jersey troopers or Port Authority police didn't need genuine probable cause to stop him. To them, a young black man in a new car was cause enough.

Archie reminded himself – fuckin' crackers be smacking and crackin' my nappy head and putting me in cuffs before I know it.

Nope, just be cool, Archie told himself. Don't want nuthin' to stop me from getting into Brownsville tonight.

CHAPTER 8

ZONE COMMANDER JAMES RAIFORD WALKED INTO THE SMALL, second-floor precinct office. He didn't sit down while he told Loyd Shaw he'd been exiled. Raiford recited the verdict while Parnell stood behind him. Shaw glanced at Richard Parnell while Raiford spoke in a bureaucrat's monotone. Parnell's fleshy face displayed no emotion.

Shaw expected Raiford's dispassion and found himself surprised that he expected something more from Richard Parnell. A look of regret. A scowl of anger. Anything. Something to convey that his commanding officer gave a shit.

Raiford's speech to Shaw ended. He turned to Parnell and said, "Please see that Detective Shaw leaves the precinct immediately."

The zone commander left without another word. Shaw hadn't bothered to rise from his chair. Parnell simply said, "Let's go."

As they walked down to the ground floor, Parnell said, "I don't have to bother telling you they mean business, do I?"

"No."

"Don't even think about hanging around, Shaw. When can you leave?"

Shaw said to himself, is that the best you can come up with, Dick? When can you leave? Shaw opened his mouth to answer, but anger and bitterness choked off his words. He wouldn't give Parnell the satisfaction of hearing what he felt. He said, "Now."

"What?" said Parnell.

"I'm leaving now. Give me a ride back to my car in Bushwick."

Parnell heard a tone in Shaw's voice that told him, don't push it. He shot a quick sidelong glance at Shaw and decided to keep his mouth shut.

Parnell's deference mollified Shaw just enough so that he endured being led out of the police precinct like a criminal. He caught the looks of the uniformed cops as he walked through the lobby of the precinct. For a moment, he considered turning to Parnell and telling him, no thanks. I don't need a fucking ride. I'll find my car myself and leave when I damn well feel like it. But when they reached the ground floor, Shaw spotted big Jake Bennett standing in the lobby. Jake's smiling birthday face had turned glum and worried.

When Shaw saw that look on Jake's face, he forgot about Parnell. Shaw thought, goddamn it, they went and pulled him out of Earl's. Shit.

Jake stood there, brow furrowed, head down, looking as if he had done something terrible. Shaw turned to Parnell and said, "Wait a minute."

Parnell didn't try to follow him.

"Don't even say it, Jake."

"Damn, Shaw. I'm sorry."

"I told you don't say it. This has nothing to do with you."

"I should have walked you to your car."

"Oh, bullshit. It just happened, that's all."

"Yeah, but you can't be…"

"Forget it. I told you in the bar it's over."

Jake shook his head, forcing himself not to comment or belabor the fact that Shaw's career was over.

"Jake, listen, damn it, don't stand there feeling sorry for me. You want to do something; I'll tell you what to do."

"What? Name it."

"You heard about what happened?"

"Yeah."

"Three knuckleheads. In a Chevy Nova. Get the plate from the arresting officer. Find those fucks."

Shaw described the three assailants, making sure to tell Jake one of them would be walking around with a broken collarbone and one with a busted nose.

"Find them if you can, brother. Find them before the ADA's investigators or IAB guys. Make sure those pricks don't show up at my hearing with some bullshit story."

Jake stood close to Shaw, listening carefully, nodding.

"You got it, brother. It's done. Guaranteed."

Shaw knew if his attackers were still in Brooklyn, Jake Bennett would find them. Jake had been on the Brooklyn Warrants Squad for a long time. He knew how to find people, particularly in Bushwick. They shook hands, and then Jake pulled Shaw into his meaty shoulder and wrapped his arm around him. The embrace was quick, but it made Shaw feel as grateful as he'd felt in a long time.

Jake let him go. Shaw headed out of the precinct, Parnell following silently two steps behind him.

After speaking with Jake, Parnell's presence didn't bother Shaw nearly as much as it had. It suddenly didn't matter so much what the brass wanted to do. Shaw never paid much attention to the brass anyhow. The guys you work with in the trenches, those were the ones who determine whether or not you made it. Always had been. Always will be. Fuck Parnell and Raiford and all the rest.

At that moment, all Loyd Shaw wanted to do was get into his car and get the hell out of New York.

Parnell drove Shaw back to Bushwick. They quickly located Shaw's car.

Neither of the men spoke during the ride. When Shaw stepped out of Parnell's car, he didn't offer his hand to his CO. Clearly, they had ended up on opposite sides.

Parnell felt compelled to reiterate the order to get out of town, but this time Shaw didn't even bother to say anything. He just nodded. Their positions had become clear. Parnell was in. Shaw was out.

Shaw climbed into his Mercury Grand Marquis, shut all the windows tight, turned on his CD player, and headed north. He stopped once for gas and coffee on the Merritt Parkway and to call Jane. He timed his call about fifteen minutes before her regular wake-up time. The way she answered gave him the impression that she had been dead asleep. Could have probably snuck in and grabbed a couple of hours with no problem, he thought. Too bad.

He told Jane that something had come up with the job and he would be gone for a few days. He said it in a way that let her know he didn't want her asking any questions.

As he walked back to his car, Shaw pictured Jane hanging up the phone.

He tried to imagine the look on her face. Would she be concerned? Would she even think about it? Did he give a shit if she did or didn't?

He told himself, not really, as he climbed back into his car.

Shaw sped along as the early morning light came up over the highway, running at about seventy-five mph. He decided he didn't care about a speeding ticket, either.

CHAPTER 9

By the time Archie Reynolds drove the Saab off the Interboro Parkway and hit the bleak streets of East New York and Brownsville, the night had turned into a gray, dull dawn.

He had driven from Saddle Brook, New Jersey, an area comprised mostly of trees and houses, through the Bronx, dominated by apartment buildings, and through Queens, a mix of both. Now he entered Brownsville, much of which was nothing but long stretches of waste and rubble interrupted by structures that had collapsed under the weight of abuse and neglect and the ravages of fire. The houses and apartments and commercial buildings still in use were so run down they seemed to be discarded versions of what the rest of the city used.

There was too much waste in Brownsville, particularly wasted lives. Angry knots of young men collected between the rubble and ruin, standing in front of bodegas or newsstands or subway stations, or roving in bands looking for something amidst the nothing.

As soon as Archie hit the streets of Brownsville, he tuned his radio to 106 and pressed his turn signal switch up and down three times. A hidden door built into the driver's side door popped open. He glanced down to make sure a loaded Taurus .40-caliber PT 101 sat within reach. The gun fit in the car door but could hold an eleven-round magazine with a bullet in the chamber. Plenty of ammo to shoot into the face of any knucklehead who might sidle up to the Saab at a streetlight and try to take the shiny car for himself. Not everyone knew the car carried Archie Ar.

Archie turned the Saab into an alley that ran alongside the elevated Canarsie line tracks. The high-intensity streetlight that should have lit up the area had been broken for years, so the only light that filtered down into the alley came from the overcast predawn glow that made everything look even more dirty and dismal than usual.

One of Archie's gang, a slim, Jamaican youth sporting dreadlocks, stood slouched against the door of a body shop located in the alley. When he saw the black Saab rumble into the alley, he tapped twice on the rolling steel door and it began to slowly winch open so Archie could drive the Saab inside.

There were several cars in various states of repair or reconstruction scattered around the floor of the body shop, including two cars that had been chopped up and reassembled with hidden compartments in the floors, side panels, and inside the trunks to hide drugs and weapons. Opening the secret compartments required a similar series of complicated moves, as with Archie's Saab. Turning the radio to a specific frequency, pushing down door locks, flipping the turn signal.

Along with the cars were sixteen members of Archie Ar's crew, an assortment of angry young black men who had chosen a path nearly guaranteed to cut their lives short. There were enough gold teeth and jewelry, dreadlocks, tattoos, dark glasses, baggy Phat clothes, and quarts of malt liquor for any respectable crack gang. The Blue-Tops differed from other crack gangs only in their degree of viciousness and violence. All but two of the young black men standing around the body shop had killed another human being. Each of the sixteen faces bore a sullen, dangerously aggressive look required to prove to themselves and to each other that they were bad men.

None of the killers appeared happy to be in the body shop. Particularly, Little Marvin, who hung back from the main group.

Reggie Whack stood in the middle of the body shop dressed in his usual attire – black knit cap bearing a New York Knicks logo, sweatshirt, baggy khaki pants, and black boots. Reggie hardly ever smiled or talked. His means of concealing his missing right front tooth and his ferocious stutter. Reggie had earned his street name, Whack, by killing seven men, two of whom died laughing at his speech impediment.

Nobody in Brownsville laughed at Reggie Whack now.

Archie stepped out of the Saab, and Reggie handed Archie a .22- caliber Beretta Model 21 A. The short-barreled, deadly gun weighed just over half a pound. Every member of the gang felt the gun was much too small for a respectable thug. But experience had taught Archie what small bullets could do when fired into a human body.

Archie hardly looked at any of the men except Little Marvin, who was little only in comparison to his older brother, Big Marvin. Archie stepped out of the Saab and motioned for Little Marvin to come over to him, even before he closed the driver's side door.

Archie stepped out quickly, not bothering to pull the keys out of the ignition. With the door open, the car emitted an annoying, incessant, electronic bing-bing sound to remind Archie to take his keys.

Little Marvin did not hurry to reach Archie. As Archie waited for him to come closer, he became more and more annoyed at the electronic bing-bing-bing. Suddenly he pointed the Beretta at Little Marvin and shot him in the head. He had wanted to press the small gun into Little Marvin's head, but he had to forgo that pleasure and fire the Beretta from six feet away so he could slam the car door and stop the damn binging.

Archie said, "Bing that, motherfucker."

Because Archie shot Little Marvin from a distance, the small .22-caliber bullet didn't hit Little Marvin in the center of the head. The bullet hit him just above the right eye, snapping Little Marvin's head backward. The small caliber round tumbled and bounced and ripped around inside his skull, turning his brain into a useless, bloody, ten-pound piece of meat.

Little Marvin's legs twitched in a short, spastic little dance, then crumpled underneath him. All his nerve impulses shut down except for a few basic ones that kicked and twitched for a while. In two seconds, Little Marvin's brain died. The rest of his body died shortly after.

Archie turned to his men, now acknowledging their presence, and said, "That motherfucker was already dead even before I got here. I just put him out of his misery. Point being, any motherfucker in charge of an operation like we got, don't see when someone is planning to hit you, anyone don't see when somebody scoping you out so damn close that everybody all at once is under the gun? They be dead and don't know it. Fact is, right now, you all dead. You all be motherfucking walking dead men. Somebody comes up and puts a gun to your heads, and you don't see it coming? They do that to you last night; they can do it tonight. They can do it tomorrow night. Any motherfucking night.

"So you boys better find out who the fuck these guys are, then git yo' asses out there and put a bullet in their heads before they put one in yours."

End of speech. Having told them why Archie did not need to tell his gang of murderers how.

CHAPTER 10

LESS THAN FIVE BLOCKS FROM WHERE LITTLE MARVIN'S CORPSE dropped to the concrete floor of the body shop, Whitey Williams sat at the window of his New Lots studio apartment in Building D. Whitey, one of the original tenants in the complex, puffed on his morning White Owl cigar and watched. Like most senior citizens in Brownsville, safety dictated that Whitey spend most of his time in his apartment. Whitey had made an art of being inconspicuous. Although he was in decent shape for an eighty-two-year-old, Whitey moved his wiry, five-foot-eight frame slowly and methodically. When he was outside his apartment, Whitey did nothing to attract attention. The fewer who noticed him, the better. There wasn't much to notice except perhaps his close-cropped white hair.

The morning after Rachman's raid on the Blue-Tops crack apartment provided Whitey with a great deal more to watch than the usual. Change had come to New Lots, hauled in by two five-ton trucks loaded with prefabricated sections of iron fencing. Serious fencing consisting of square iron rods an inch wide and ten feet high joined together by thick horizontal bands of iron.

A Case 580K backhoe roared and shoveled and scraped out trenches between each of the five buildings in the complex. A concrete-mixer truck sat on New Lots Avenue, its massive drum turning, ready to pour concrete into the trenches. Even from his fourth-floor perch, Whitey could tell this was a major installation. By the looks of it, once the work crews scrambling around the perimeter of the complex sunk that iron fence into the trenches, nothing would get through except a tank.

Whitey had already heard about the shooting in Building A. Now, the next part of the plan became clear to him. Not only had the management decided to do something to get the Blue-Tops out. Management had decided it was time to keep them out.

Whitey sat and watched New Lots change. He watched a squat, agitated white man wearing a rumpled brown suit and a knit yarmulke standing near a burly black man wearing combat boots, camouflage pants, an army field jacket, and a Kinte cap.

A white man with a black bodyguard, thought Whitey. Damn. Bad as New Lots be, it's gonna get a lot worse around here.

✳

Leon Bloom and Rachman Abdul X stood near the main entrance to the complex where the iron fencing would be turned into the new main gate for New Lots Apartments.

Despite the chilly midmorning April air, Bloom perspired profusely. Not because Bloom carried an extra fifty pounds on his short, squat frame, not because the fifty-year-old man was in terrible physical shape. Bloom dripped with sweat because he knew how dangerous it was to be standing in front of New Lots the morning after Rachman's warning attack.

The fear made him anxious to get the fencing job done quickly. Bloom kept telling the workmen around him to keep moving, to work faster.

Between bothering the workmen, Bloom rushed around, shooing away the dozens of kids who were a perpetual presence at New Lots. Most of the kids barely listened to the portly white man, but Rachman's baleful stares kept them at a distance.

Bloom pushed and yelled. Rachman stood where he was, kept his mouth shut, and watched.

Mostly, Rachman watched the street. Even when Bloom bothered him with nervous questions, he kept an eye on the street. There were no gunmen on the premises, only two of Rachman's regular, unarmed security guards. No police had responded to the early morning shooting because no one in New Lots had dared to report it.

Rachman, too, wanted the fence up as soon as possible, but he knew bothering the workmen wouldn't help.

Rachman kept his distance from Bloom. His questions annoyed him. As did the faint odor Bloom exuded. Rachman's strict vegetarian diet made him particularly sensitive to Bloom's body odor. Bloom ate meat – fatty, heavily seasoned meat. He also smoked at least two packs of filtered Camels every day and drank – mostly gin. Cheap, back-bar gin sloshed with cheap vermouth to make the three double martinis Bloom consumed every day with lunch.

Bloom did not fit the stereotype of the Orthodox Hasid. Not in habits or appearance. Bloom had red hair and freckles and a scraggly red beard much too sparse for his moon-shaped face.

Bloom, of course, didn't care at all about Rachman's desire to keep his distance.

For the second time that morning, Bloom asked, "So, you did what you said?"

"Yes."

"Everything went all right?"

"Yes."

"Your people got out okay?"

"Yes, Mr. Bloom."

"Anybody hurt?"

"Maybe. They shot back at us."

"They what?"

"Shot back at us."

"How? From where?"

"From inside the apartment."

"And you shot at them? You said it would only be a warning. Nobody hurt."

"We will always defend ourselves."

"Ach, this I don't need."

"I explained our methods to you, Mr. Bloom."

"All right, all right. I don't want to hear about it. Let's hope, God willing, it doesn't happen again."

"It will. Be sure of that, Bloom. Before this is over, it will."

"At least that place is cleaned out, right? They left?"

"Yes."

"Out of the complex?"

"No, Mr. Bloom. Not out of the complex. Just out of their poisonous crack den. Just out of one place in one building. You know it's going to take more than warning them."

"Okay, okay. Just keep moving them out of any apartments they use until there's no more of them left."

"Do you know how many empty apartments they use?"

"How many? *Vay iz mer,* how the hell do I know? Who can tell in that dark? They're in, they're out, like rats in a hole. One day you see some bum in one place, the next day he's gone, the next day you got some dreck doing drugs, some street whore doing her business in there, who knows? I got more people wandering those hallways than walking on Atlantic Avenue. You got to get 'em out."

"We'll start getting squatters and wanderers out tomorrow. The Blue-Tops won't be as easy. You have to board up the empties as soon as we clear them out."

"Tomorrow. We start first thing. I bring workmen in tomorrow. But once you get 'em out, you got to keep 'em from going back in, Mr. Rachman, or they just tear off the plywood and throw it out a window where it lands on some poor schmuck's head."

"I know that, Mr. Bloom."

"I have two crews coming in tomorrow to start boarding up empty apartments."

"Doors and windows, right?"

"That's what you said, Mr. Rachman, that's what I'm doing. You have men to go with the crews?"

"A team of three with each crew."

"Armed, right?" asked Bloom.

"One armed and two regulars. But they're not shooters, Mr. Bloom, not gunmen."

"You said you'd have a given percentage of men with arms."

"Licensed men with the regulars, Mr. Bloom. But remember, they're legal. The legals don't want to lose their licenses. They won't shoot unless someone shoots at them."

"Yes, yes, Mr. Rachman. The ones who have the guns legally won't shoot them. The ones who aren't supposed to have guns, they shoot."

"We've been through all this."

"I have to pay extra for people with guns who won't shoot them."

"They don't want to lose their licenses."

"Yes, yes."

"They're worth the price, Mr. Bloom. They'll discourage arguments and intimidate most of the people who want to cause trouble. We don't need the gunmen for that."

"I know, I know. I don't want to know. The rest is your business. Start with the squatters and keep the crackheads out."

Rachman simply nodded this time because he didn't want to discuss it further, and because he saw a five-year-old Lincoln Town Car turn onto New Lots Avenue up the street to his left. The car appeared to be filled with passengers. Rachman moved two steps away from Bloom to get a better look at the car. For a brief moment, he felt sure it was a drive-by but hesitated because the car moved toward them so slowly.

Rachman's experience told him the driver should be too excited or too nervous or too ready to kill to keep coming at them so slowly. But he didn't know that the driver had been smoking marijuana and drinking malt liquor since the dawn gathering of the Blue-Tops at the body shop. The alcohol and pot made him too stoned to care or worry about the fact that he drove at ten miles per hour.

It wasn't until Rachman saw the first shotgun barrel poke out of the rear window that he shoved Bloom to his right and yelled for the others to get down.

Most of the workmen heard him yell, but few understood him.

Bloom hit the ground just before the first loud bang and blast of shot cracked into the iron fence and bricks of Building A. The first solitary blast stunned everyone into a deadly instant of paralysis. And then the entire area around the front entrance erupted as the slow-moving car drifted past. Shotgun blasts intermingled with the popping of 9mm handguns. Dozens of bullets slammed into the welder's truck, the concrete sidewalk, the fencing. Glass broke, chips of brick and pavement zinged through the air. Rachman just managed to dive behind the welder's truck. So many bullets and buckshot hit the generator bolted to the truck bed that it exploded in an eruption of sparks and smoke.

Rachman pulled out one of the Glocks he had kept from the early morning raid, braced the gun on the fender of the truck, and shot back at the Town Car.

The gunfire from the drive-by never even paused. Rachman unloaded five shots at the flashing windows of the Town Car to no effect. He realized that with all the gunfire and spent cartridges that must be flying around inside the car, the Blue-Tops probably didn't even realize someone had returned fire.

Rachman heard someone behind him grunt and gag.

The welder's truck dropped as bullets blew out both front tires. Rachman kept his gun braced on the fender and emptied the Glock at the Blue-Tops car.

And finally, finally, the shooting stopped, only because the Blue-Tops ran out of ammunition.

The Town Car rolled down New Lots Avenue at the same slow speed it had rolled past the complex. The driver made a lazy left turn at the next block as if he were driving his elderly mother to church.

They had executed the drive-by as if they owned the street. If Rachman's bravery had accomplished anything, it might have only been to prevent them from stopping the car, getting out, and emptying their weapons from a standing position.

For a few moments after the explosive chaos, a stunned silence reigned. And then it seemed everyone alive was yelling and shouting for help.

Two of the workmen had been hit. One of them knocked onto his back, his chest blossoming blood, his head thrown sideways. He appeared to be dead. Shotgun pellets had sprayed the face, neck, and shoulder of another worker. Shredded skin hung off his jaw. The man kept screaming about his eyes.

Rachman's first concern was his guards. He had expected them to be hit because they wore dark blue MS-2 jackets emblazoned with the word "security" in gold letters across the back.

Both guards lay on the ground behind a pile of iron fencing, one still covering his head with his hands. No sound came from them. At first, Rachman feared they were both dead, but he saw no blood. And then, slowly, they started moving, cautiously lifting their heads. Rachman muttered a brief prayer of thanks to Allah, acknowledging his will. But in the next instant, Rachman's prayer turned to a curse when booming shotgun blasts and the chilling crack of automatic-weapons fire exploded on the other side of the complex.

Rachman turned and looked past The Pit toward the back of the complex. A second Blue-Tops car had stopped in front of that worksite. Shooters in the front and back seats blasted fire and shot at the workmen. A third shooter on the far side of the car had leaned far enough out the window so he could rest an automatic rifle on the roof of the car and fire streams of bullets toward the complex.

Rachman saw one of the workmen absurdly standing up on the back of his truck, trying to see what was happening. Rachman turned back and saw Bloom on his knees frantically trying to pull a cell phone out of his suit jacket pocket that was too small to accommodate both the phone and his fat hand.

Rachman had expected Bloom to be too terrified to do anything except soil himself. His respect for Bloom increased as he watched him struggle to his feet, cursing, concentrating on getting his phone out so he could call for help.

Rachman shoved a fresh clip into the Glock. As he ran toward the gunfire, he yelled at Bloom, "Call for ambulances first, then the cops."

The assault in the back of the complex raged even more furiously than the attack at the front. There were more workmen back there, but, fortunately, the two trucks and backhoe provided more cover. Most of the men made it behind the vehicles. Then, just as suddenly as the second attack had started, it ended, and the second Blue-Tops car roared away. One workman had been hit in his shoulder; the high-velocity bullet had destroyed the joint. Miraculously, no one else had been hit.

The Blue-Tops shooters, of course, had not aimed carefully. They had simply pointed their weapons in the general direction of the complex and pulled the triggers until their guns were emptied. The bullets could have hit anyone or anything – cars, walls, women, children, dogs, anything, innocent or guilty.

Since Rachman's gunmen had left the complex hours ago, there were no guilty people in New Lots that morning. That fact didn't even begin to bother Archie Reynolds.

He had sat in his black Saab about a half block from the entrance to the New Lots Apartments back parking area, sipping coffee and watching his men drive by and shoot. He had watched the workmen drop to the ground so quickly that it seemed like all of them were hit. Their desperate attempts to avoid the gunfire had amused him.

Beyond instant retaliation, Archie had had another reason for ordering the drive-bys. Archie wanted the shooting to cause enough chaos and commotion so that he could slip out of his car and duck unseen into a narrow gangway that led to The Pit. From there, he had walked ten yards and entered the lobby of Building D.

CHAPTER 11

By the time Rachman Abdul X reached the scene of the second drive-by, Archie Reynolds was strolling past the out-of-service lobby elevators in Building D headed for the stairwell door. As he opened the door, the full stench of New Lots Apartments hit him – urine, excrement, cat spray, and rancid cooking smells. And garbage. Garbage at the rotting stage, a magnet for rats and cockroaches. New Lots Apartments swarmed with both. Archie heard them scurry as he walked up the dark stairwells.

Archie breathed through his mouth and sprinted up the stairs, light-footed, sure of himself, taking the stairs two at a time.

"Now we see what the fuck is going on here," Archie told himself.

He pounded on Whitey Williams's door. From inside, he heard Whitey's old-man voice ask, "Who is it?"

Archie said, "Open up, goddamn it. It's me."

It took Whitey a bit of time to shuffle over to his door and unlatch all the chains and locks.

He pulled his door open and slowly walked back to his chair by the window, not bothering to greet Archie. He picked up his dead White Owl cigar and gazed back out the window as if to demonstrate his devotion to his lookout post.

Archie stood near the doorway and watched Whitey watching, sitting near the window in an old green cardigan sweater with the elbows worn out and a faded canvas work shirt buttoned to the collar.

"You get your checks this month, old man?"

When Whitey answered, he spoke quietly, revealing a country Southern accent. "You mean my government checks?"

Government came out sounding like guvmint.

"Yeah."

"I got 'em."

"How much that amount to?"

"One thirty-six social security, plus one eighty-six from dis-ability."

"Shit, Whitey, you a rich man. That why you don't need my money?"

"Who said I don't need it? How's a man supposed to live on three hundred dollars a month?"

"Three hundred twenty-six dollars, motherfucker. Yeah, that's why I be so surprised that you quit your job."

"Not me. No, sir, I never quit."

"Then how come all this shit come down last night without me knowin' it was gonna happen? How come they be putting up this goddamn fence around my place and I don't hear shit about it?"

For the first time, Whitey looked away from the window and faced Archie.

"No way to see this comin', Mr. Archie. Nobody knew 'bout it until it was here."

"Who's behind all this shit?"

"Far's I heard it's a new security company the complex hired."

"They brought in a security company?"

"I heard it be Muslims."

"Muslims? What fucking Muslims? No Muslims come along and shoot shit up like they did here last night. Who the fuck are these guys?"

Whitey turned back to his window as if gazing out might bring in the answer. He saw the first flash of emergency vehicle lights coming up Rockaway Avenue. Police and ambulance sirens sounded, forcing Whitey to speak louder.

"I don't know. Some kind a hardcore bunch. Take a look out here and maybe you see who it is. A burly fella run through there jes' after you come in. Look like he runnin' toward the trouble in the back while everybody else runnin' away. Had on military-type clothes, field jacket and all, combat boots and one of them skull caps the Muslim brothers wear. Had a gun in his hand, too."

"This is bullshit, man."

Archie walked over to Whitey's window and bent low so he could see out. The angle gave him a clear view of the parking area. He could see that at least one man had been shot. Other workmen surrounded him. Even from the fourth-floor window, Archie could see the dark pools of blood slowly spreading near the fallen men.

He picked out Rachman based on Whitey's description. Watched him check to see how many men had been shot, directing the others back away from the street, holding his handgun pointed up, ready to shoot if the Blue-Tops decided to come back.

While Archie watched Rachman, Whitey checked the apartment windows facing The Pit. More faces were peering out than he had seen in a long time.

Archie followed Whitey's gaze and yelled at the people across The Pit, "Get the fuck away from the window. I'll come over there and kick your fuckin' eyes out yo' heads."

Nobody heard Archie, but if they had, they would have instantly disappeared from their windows.

Archie stepped back and asked, "What else you see?"

"Not much. That fence they puttin' up is gonna make a difference."

"How long you live here, Whitey?"

"Since they opened the place."

"How much rent you pay?"

"One-eighty a month."

"You still pay it?"

"Yes, sir."

"Shit, you must be one of the only ones. How many regular people you figure still left?"

"Maybe half of what used to be. Not counting the squatters and riffraff and such that come in and out."

Archie turned away from Whitey, chewing on his lower lip, thinking. Whitey didn't interrupt him. Finally, Archie spoke.

"Motherfuckers who got this place now can't wait to make their money off the ghetto. Fill up these empties."

Whitey nodded, "I'd say so. Might be time you picked an easier place to work out of."

Archie turned back to Whitey. "That's what you think, huh?"

Whitey shrugged. "I don't know. Seems like it might just be easier for you to avoid all this mess. You hit 'em back for last night. Showed 'em they can't push you around. Might make sense to take the easy way for a while."

"Just pack up and leave."

Whitey shrugged again. "Alls I'm saying is, it ain't easy runnin' your business with all this trouble around."

"You never mind about my business. I'll find a way to run my business, trouble or not. And where I'm going to go, old man? How many niggers I got to kill to get another setup like this?"

Whitey knew better than to respond.

"You want to kill 'em for me?"

Whitey didn't move. Archie stepped over to the window and looked out again. He seemed to calm down a bit.

"That's what's wrong with you nappy-headed, old motherfuckers. Always ready to put your damn head down and shuffle off."

Archie turned back to Whitey, "You keep your goddamn advice to yourself, old man, and just find out who the fuck is in this security company. How many, where, when, whatever."

"Yes, sir."

Archie shouted, "Don't fucking sir me. Just fucking do it."

Whitey realized he should never have told Archie to leave New Lots. Archie ranted at Whitey, "You know how I started in this neighborhood? Huh, old man? Do you know?"

Whitey knew quite well how Archie had started in his neighborhood, but he just sat at his table, head down, silent.

"That bodega across the street on the New Lots side. That little piece of shit corner. I had to buy that fucking spot in my own fucking neighborhood from the Terell brothers three years ago. You know how much it cost me?"

"No."

"Everything I had, old man. All my time scrambling and hustling and selling on every fucking corner in Brownsville to get my stake. Looking over my shoulder, ready to shoot any motherfucker who come after me. And even after I paid for the corner, Reggie and me had to kill three motherfuckers before they let us have the goddamn corner. Took our money, piss all over us, try to kill us, and tell us it wasn't them. Bastards."

Archie bent close to Whitey. His voice dropped from a shout to a whisper. His face twisted into an ugly, evil grimace.

"You know how long it took me to kill that last Terell?"

"No."

"Almost two years before I got the last one. Two years, old man."

"I understand."

"You understand? I hope you fuckin' understand, Whitey, cuz if you want to fuck with me, I'll kill you right now and save us a lot of time and trouble."

"I ain't fuckin' with you, Mr. Archie."

"Goddamn right, you ain't."

Whitey turned back to the window, looking, watching the police and ambulances arrive, hoping Archie would see that he was doing his job. Hoping if he didn't move or speak out of turn, the storm would pass without hurting him.

Archie paced the small apartment, seeming to calm down a bit.

"May be time to leave here, may not be, but I goddamn guarantee you one thing, Whitey, I'm gonna kill that burly Muslim motherfucker you talkin' about before I do go. Yes, sir, *salaam aleichem,* my ass, motherfucker. Gonna be hell to pay around here for some other people, too, before I go anywhere. If I go. You hear me?"

"I hear you."

"You fuckin' right, you hear me."

Whitey sat in his place, making sure he didn't move. He felt a single droplet of sweat slide down the right side of his ribcage. It made him feel like shivering, but he held himself still.

Whitey knew the blood in the street outside had ignited something in Archie. The silence from Archie unnerved him even more than the rants and threats.

But then, just as suddenly as the murderous aura around Archie Ar had emerged, it faded away.

Archie began to walk around the room, looking carefully at everything in Whitey's small apartment. The place was clean and simply furnished. It seemed to amuse Archie that an apartment as clean and neat as Whitey's could exist within the filth and chaos of New Lots. But Whitey knew there was more than one apartment like this in New Lots, some occupied by old people like Whitey, others by women and children. Some even occupied by families struggling to stay together. Islands of civility in the midst of degradation and danger. Apartments hidden away, locked up, and used carefully by the people who lived there. People who still worked or quietly collected their welfare checks and tried to keep their children alive in the Brownsville/New Lots world of sudden death and danger and grief. People who could have easily been hit by one of Archie's drive-by bullets.

"You said you still pay rent, right, old man?"

Whitey nodded.

"So, you'll be a keeper, right?"

"I suppose so."

"And you gonna stay right here, ain't you?"

"I ain't goin' nowhere."

"And you clear about who you workin' for?"

"I'm clear."

"Okay, good. So how you gonna find out what I need to know?"

Whitey said, "Just about everyone aroun' here talk to me. I'll find out whatever there is to know about these security fellas. You know these Muslim boys believe in what they be doing. They be talkin' to people, I suspect. They think it's a divine mission or somethin' to clean up their neighborhoods."

"I give a shit what they think. Let's see how divine they think it is getting they ass shot up."

"Okay."

"Damn right, okay. You just get the information I need."

"I'll find out. Lots a people with eyes and ears around here."

Archie dropped one hundred dollars in tens and twenties on Whitey's kitchen table. The money collected from the ravaged hands of the New Lots people. Crack money.

"Don't forget who you workin' for, Whitey."

Whitey nodded.

Archie turned toward the door, but Whitey interrupted his exit. "I'll tell you something you ought to know right now."

"What's that?"

The old man had a trump card, and he decided now was the time to play it.

CHAPTER 12

JUST ABOUT THE TIME THE FIRST BLUE-TOPS DRIVE-BY HIT NEW Lots, Loyd Shaw made it to his renovated barn, situated on a twenty-five-acre farm in Massachusetts. The trip had taken under three hours. Enough time to bring Shaw to another world. Instead of bloodshed and bedlam, Shaw only heard the sounds of birds and the occasional bark of Mrs. McGovern's black Labrador as he walked into his country home.

The caffeine he had consumed during the drive from Brooklyn didn't have a chance against his fatigue. Shaw walked straight into his bedroom and laid down. He felt grungy and out of sorts from his night in the precinct house, but he didn't bother to shower or change clothes. He just wanted to rest awhile with his eyes closed and try to dispel some of the tension that had seeped into him during the night's events and long drive north. Within minutes, Shaw fell dead asleep.

Mrs. McGovern owned the twenty-five-acre property surrounding Shaw's renovated barn. She had seen Shaw arrive but wouldn't think of intruding on him. Her staid New England personality, poor Irish background, and eighty years of hard times made her a very private and reserved person.

Shaw had met Mrs. McGovern on a chilly September Sunday evening a year and a half before. For two months prior to that, he had been taking weekend excursions trying to find a country place he could afford. Finding a retreat out of New York City had been the second step in constructing a life after the NYPD.

The first step had happened two years before that when Shaw began to pursue one of his dreams – learning to paint.

During the last few years, besides being a police detective, Shaw had spent almost all of his free time either trying to create art or looking at art. He took drawing courses at the Art Students League, spent hours laboring over live figure studies in a basement studio in Soho, and haunted art galleries and museums from one end of Manhattan to the other. During the last year, Shaw had finally begun putting paint to canvas.

The weekend Shaw met Mrs. McGovern, he had already spent all of Saturday and most of Sunday looking at places that either didn't fit his needs or cost too much. Before he headed back to the city, he decided to check in with a real estate agent. He stood at a highway payphone, the sun low in the sky, the engine of his Mercury running, expecting the call to be a short one, just to tell her he would be leaving and returning the following weekend.

But the agent told him not to go before he saw one more place.

"She must have just gotten home and heard my message. You should see this place, Mr. Shaw. I think it could be exactly what you want."

Shaw checked his watch and figured, what the hell.

After three or four wrong turns trying to follow the real estate agent's directions, Shaw finally found the farm, a small one situated on the edge of a scrub forest. As soon as he saw the modest, partially renovated barn, even before walking inside it, Shaw knew he wanted it. The barn sat off in a corner of the property bordered on the west by a dirt road and a scrub forest, by tall pine trees on the north side and a big open field on the south and east sides, separating the barn from Mrs. McGovern's old farmhouse.

When he drove up, he saw his real estate agent standing near the owner's front porch waiting for him.

Shaw reached out to shake her hand.

"Hello, Joan."

Joan Cummings was a petite woman who looked even smaller next to Shaw.

"Hi, Loyd. So here's the situation. Mrs. McGovern is getting on. Her husband died about four months ago. She loves this place, but she needs cash for probate expenses and taxes. The price is right. Not a steal, but fair. It's in your range. You get the barn, two surrounding acres, and an easement for access. The place needs some work, but you said that's okay. The main thing, it's a beautiful setting."

"So, what's the downside?"

"She's a little stubborn. Mostly she's choosy about who she sells this to."

Shaw shrugged. "I'll be nice."

"Well, just be yourself. There's no telling what she likes."

"Okay."

Shaw never decided why Mrs. McGovern had sold it to him. Joan introduced them, then left them alone on the front porch while she sat in her car. The old lady didn't invite him inside, giving Shaw the impression that she didn't like him at all.

She stood at her front door, dressed in what looked like men's clothes: a plaid flannel shirt, corduroy pants so worn out that the cord was gone at the knees, and suede Birkenstock sandals over wool socks.

"What do you do for a living, Mr. Shaw?" she had asked.

"I'm a cop."

"I'm sorry, I'm hard of hearing."

Shaw raised his voice, trying not to shout at her.

"I'm a detective. NYPD."

"Oh," she said. "In New York?"

"Yes."

"In the city?"

"Yes."

"Are you married?"

"Yes."

Shaw didn't say anything else. He knew Jane wouldn't be coming up to the country with him, but he couldn't see why that would matter to Mrs. McGovern. Shaw let her assume whatever she wanted about his marriage.

"My husband died four months ago," she said.

For a second, Shaw felt like congratulating her, but instead gave the usual, "I'm sorry."

"Any children?" she asked.

"No."

"Ah."

Shaw had a feeling that *ah* was meant to communicate sympathy that they were supposed to share about being childless, but he didn't feel he needed sympathy on that score. He wasn't about to tell her that Jane had long ago made it clear she didn't want any children and that he had conceded to it without nearly the fight he should have waged. Nor did he want to mention his belief that if he and Jane had become parents, he would have never saved the money he was going to use to buy the barn.

"So, it's a weekend place you're looking for?"

"Yes."

Shaw didn't mention that he planned on living full time in Massachusetts after he retired from the force, because he wasn't sure if the barn would work as a full-time place.

McGovern suddenly stopped talking. She stood there looking at him. Most people would have been uncomfortable with Mrs. McGovern's silent stare. Most would have needed to fill in the silence. But Shaw knew the silence came from her attempt to make a decision. Shaw knew as long as she didn't turn and walk back in the house, there was a chance.

Finally, Mrs. McGovern spoke, but not the words Shaw expected.

"Do you carry a gun?" she asked.

Instead of asking why she cared, Shaw simply said, "Yes."

"Is that legal for you in Massachusetts?"

"I don't think it would create any problems for me here."

And then she waved her freckled hand, as if to say it was a stupid question. She looked out at the barn, then back at Shaw.

"All right, you might as well take a look at the place. It's solid. My husband started a renovation back there. Never finished it, but it's got new wiring and new roof and all. I expect you'll know more about that than me. He never wanted me back there. If you want it, talk to Joan. She knows the price. I suppose I'll bargain a little since it's expected, but not much. And I won't take a mortgage. Get your money from the bank. Joan will help with all that."

When Shaw looked inside the barn, he saw the skylight on the mezzanine running along the south side of the barn. That's when he knew for sure he wanted to buy the place. It took another week of haggling and a month to get a mortgage. Not all that long for Shaw to secure his safe haven.

Once he had his country place, Shaw looked forward to his retirement more than ever. He poured the rest of his savings and most of his free time into finishing the renovation of the barn's interior. It took longer and cost more than Shaw had budgeted. Now it looked like he might lose the pension he'd planned on having after he quit the force.

When he woke from his long nap, he stripped off his clothes, which still smelled of gunpowder and cigarette smoke, showered, shaved, and scrubbed his teeth for a good long time. As he cleaned his body, he tried to clear his mind of any thoughts relating to his life on the job.

He dressed in his comfortable, paint-stained country clothes, loaded his CD player with music, and took a few minutes to sit and gaze at the sun as it slowly settled down behind the trees and mountains in the distance. Then he poured about four ounces of Jack Daniel's over ice, took the first sip to banish the taste of toothpaste from his mouth, and began working on the painting he had left propped up on an easel, positioned under his skylight to catch the changing daylight that poured into his renovated barn.

For the next two days, Shaw's activities remained much the same. He only added eating an occasional meal and taking a few walks to the drinking, painting, and listening to music. Sometimes he slept in his bed. Sometimes he simply sat in his chair, looking out at the changing light of day, and napped.

The routine would have been nearly perfect if Shaw had been doing it voluntarily.

CHAPTER 13

Archie Reynolds turned to Whitey Williams and said, "What's that? What you saying I ought to know 'bout, old man?"

Whitey motioned Archie to come back to the window. "You see that lady out there by all the mess?"

Archie peered out. Cops and EMS personnel swarmed around the drive-by victims. Amidst all the uniforms, crackling radios, and flashing lights, Archie picked out a young black woman dressed in a dark blue business suit and white blouse. Her height nearly matched that of the men surrounding her. She had an air of authority. Despite the emergency situation, several of the policemen on the scene stopped to respond to her.

"Who's that mouthy bitch? And why those cops listening to her?"

Whitey said, "Cuz, that mouthy bitch is the police commissioner's daughter."

Archie turned to Whitey. "Fuck you say."

"It's true."

Archie looked back down. "What the hell she doin' in New Lots?"

Whitey pointed into the distance, "You see that set of trailers they put up over there?"

"What? Those prefab things they dump down on empty lots?"

"Yeah, they use 'em for temporary classrooms and such."

"What about 'em?"

"That's some kind of shelter for homeless women and kids. She's runnin' it."

"She is?"

"Uh-huh."

"For women? What women? Ain't nothing around here except a bunch of worthless crackhead bitches and whores and shit."

Whitey didn't respond.

Archie stood back from the window, shaking his head, talking more to himself than to Whitey.

"I see it now."

"See what?"

"Why they cleanin' this place up now. What the fuck she think she's gonna do in New Lots, man?"

"I s'pose she figures she's doing some good out here. Make a reputation for herself."

"Let her do good in her own motherfucking neighborhood, 'stead of bringing her Uncle Tom ass out here and mess with my shit."

Whitey turned back to his window. Five seconds later, he heard his front door slam as Archie left without another word.

Three minutes later, Archie crossed the street behind the complex and stood in front of five prefabricated trailers Whitey had pointed out. They were no-frills, one-story structures that had been hauled into an empty rubble-strewn lot, set up, and placed end to end, creating one long, narrow temporary building. In front of the line of prefabricated trailers, a large sign announced: Caring Community Center. Executive Director, Justine Burton.

Archie gazed at the sign for a few moments. Then he looked behind him at the police and emergency vehicles clustered around the scene of the shooting. He looked past the emergency vehicles and personnel, stared at the New Lots Apartments complex, and then back at Justine Burton's center. He spit on the ground once and turned away, walking toward the far side of the complex.

Archie had figured out who his enemies were. By the time he walked around to the front of the complex, he had come up with a plan to hurt all of them.

When Archie reached the New Lots Avenue side of the complex, he crossed the street and entered the bodega he had told Whitey about. By then, he knew that the police commissioner's daughter, Justine Burton, had finished her head-to-head with the police and had returned to her Caring Community Center. He knew that two workmen had been shot in front of the complex and one behind. And he had looked closely enough at the burly guy in the military garb and Muslim skullcap so that he could identify him later.

Inside the bodega, Archie picked up the phone behind the counter. As he began dialing the first number, he mumbled to no one in particular, "Shit, fucking drive-bys be a picnic compared to what I got for you next."

At the same time, across the street, Rachman Abdul X had finished making his own set of phone calls.

Leon Bloom saw him, broke away from the group clustered around the dead workman, and walked over to Rachman as quickly as his short, fat legs would allow without running.

He hissed, "What the hell is this?"

Rachman looked at Bloom, narrowed his eyes, and said, "What do you think? It's payback for last night."

"Last night was supposed to intimidate them."

"Hey, you think they'd be doing this if we didn't shake them? But it's not going to be easy to teach them what they have to learn."

"Easy? You want to talk about easy. How easy do you think it's going to be to get somebody to work on this job now? Who's going to risk getting killed to put up this damn fence now? I can't have this."

"Don't yell at me, Mr. Bloom. You want us to leave, tell me now. This is just the beginning."

"Leave? You start this mess, and you want…"

Without warning, Rachman grabbed Bloom by the lapels of his jacket and turned him away from the others, nearly lifting him off his feet. He put his face down close to Bloom's and spoke softly but intensely.

"I told you not to yell, Mr. Bloom. We don't want people to hear our business, do we?"

Bloom swallowed once and took a deep breath.

"No. We don't. Sorry. I apologize. But we can't have this."

Rachman slowly released his grip on Bloom but kept his face close to Bloom's and his body between him and the others.

"Every man, woman, and child in New Lots lives in danger. A bullet can hit any of them almost anytime. Now every one of them is under the protection of MS-Two. We didn't put them in this situation. But we will help them get out of it. This is war, Mr. Bloom. Do you understand? Don't play innocent or surprised. You know damn well more people might die here before this is over. We either turn back now or see it to the end. Tell me now if you want to quit. Don't pull out on me later."

"Can you do this, Rachman? Can you handle these animals? These killers?"

"Do you think anybody else can?"

"I don't know."

"We'll handle them. They will learn, Mr. Bloom. They will learn that if they spill one drop of our blood, we will spill a gallon of theirs. They will learn."

"Then do what you have to do. Just do it."

Bloom turned away from Rachman and walked out of the complex.

Rachman turned in the other direction looking for his guards. He walked past the dead workman. Someone had covered the corpse with a green jacket. A bloom of red had already seeped through the cloth. Rachman never understood why people covered dead bodies like that. Out of respect? Or simply because the living didn't want to see the faces of the dead? Rachman thought it much better to look at the faces of the dead, whether they were friends or enemies or even strangers.

*

Across the street, Archie Ar finished his phone calls. He sidled up to Oscar, who stood at the doorway of the bodega watching the cops and EMS personnel. Archie stood with Oscar, calmly gazing at the scene across the street.

"Lazy fucks. Look like nothing but dead meat over there. Nobody worried about rushin' that to a hospital."

Archie turned back into the bodega.

"Okay, Oscar, my man, I'm going to catch some z's back in the storeroom. When Reggie come in, tell him to wake me roun' lunchtime. Make us some sandwiches. No bologna and cheese shit. I want turkey on whole wheat. You got it?"

"Yes."

Oscar headed back to the counter, wondering how Archie could sleep after what had happened.

Archie turned and called out, "And we ain't moving nothing but groceries today, Oscar."

Oscar had already hidden the crack stash into the floor safe behind the counter. He knew the cops would be coming in to ask questions or, if not that, to get coffee. The image of policemen in his bodega made Oscar's stomach turn sour. He walked behind the counter, looking for his bottle of Maalox.

*

Rachman had no more interest in talking to the police than Oscar. He reached the spot where his regular guards stood and motioned for them to follow him. He led them away from the police toward The Pit. Once they were off by themselves, he took a moment to see how the drive-by had affected them.

One of the guards, a short, stocky boy, just eighteen years old, stood hunched over looking at the ground, his hands thrust deep into the side pockets of his MS-2 jacket. The shooting had so unnerved him that he could not stop his teeth from chattering.

The other guard, an older, thin, balding man, seemed to Rachman to be a harder case. He didn't display any outward signs of fear, but Rachman sensed that, given a chance, the man would walk away from New Lots and never return.

Neither one of the guards was Muslim. They were just black men looking for a job. Some of the legitimate people Rachman used for the day-to-day security work.

Rachman stood close to them so they couldn't avoid the power of his physical presence. It wasn't Rachman's thick muscular body that intimidated as much as his demeanor. Rachman always appeared to be seconds away from lashing out with a blow or a gunshot. He didn't look at someone, he glowered. When he spoke, he made sure to lock eyes with that person.

As long as Rachman stood in front of them, neither guard had any thoughts of walking away.

Rachman spoke to both men but concentrated on the younger guard.

"You're all right now. It's over."

He waited for a response, but neither guard agreed with him.

"Allah protected you. You weren't hit. You made it. Didn't you? Didn't you?"

Rachman waited, staring at them until they both nodded.

"You stood up to the evil around you. Allah protected you. You're blessed. He will continue to protect you. You've done a good act. Goodness will come to you. Don't turn your back on it."

The younger guard's teeth stopped chattering as he spoke, but his voice shook from the fear and shock.

"I can't do this, Mr. Rachman. No disrespect, but I just took this job cuz my momma got on me to get some work. I know she didn't think I'd be getting shot at."

Rachman cut him off. "That's over now. By the end of the week, you'll be inside a bulletproof guardhouse. Right over there. Behind an iron gate. Nobody will get near you unless you push a button to let them in. There'll be a phone in there, too. Phone for anything you need. You won't have to go out. You'll be safer here than at home."

The other guard spoke, "Then I'll be back when you got that built."

Rachman stepped in front of the older guard. "No, you stick it out. You don't let evil drive you off. You've got to earn the right to be here and be protected and earn clean, honest money, and do good work."

The younger guard looked over at the older man, waiting to see if he would argue with Rachman. The guard acted as if the young man weren't even there. He shook his head and turned away from Rachman but did not say anything.

Rachman let the man move away, knowing he had probably lost him anyhow. But he didn't want the younger one to succumb to his fear.

"Stop worrying," he told the young guard. "You're under the protection of righteous men. Men who will give their lives for you and for others. Our men. Our gunmen. Who else will do that for you?"

The older guard turned back to them and said, "I don't see no gunmen around here."

"Then stand there and wait and see. The gunmen are coming. Stay here and do your job. Don't let those crack-dealing scum drive you off. Don't let them take this job from you. I promise you; you'll be safe."

Rachman told them, "Go stand by the entrance there. Talk to the police. Tell them what you saw. Then stay until your shift is over. My people are on their way."

The two guards walked off, following Rachman's instructions. Rachman did not delude himself. He assumed they would both disappear the first chance they got. But for now, they kept their MS-2 jackets on and stayed.

CHAPTER 14

THREE HOURS LATER, ARCHIE REYNOLDS, FRESH FROM HIS NAP IN the back room of the bodega, finished his turkey sandwich and chased it with the last swallow from a sixteen-ounce can of Ballantine Ale.

He sat with Reggie Whack in the bodega's backroom. Archie had assumed a new identity. Over his good clothes, he wore a jumpsuit-style set of overalls, the kind car mechanics and janitors wore. On his head, he'd placed a black knit ski cap.

Reggie had on the same clothes he had been wearing at the body shop – a blue knit cap with a New York Knicks sweatshirt and baggy pants.

Archie asked Reggie, "Our guys ready?"

"Yuh, yuh, yeah, Arch."

"Everything set up like I said?"

"Ju, just like you said."

"Any problems inside?"

"Nope. Those muth, muth, motherfuckers be runnin' around outside, we do what we want inside. Couple a cops maybe in there try, trying to find out if anybody seen anything. But no more'n that. No, no, nobody comin' in there after us."

"Not yet, anyhow," said Archie. "Okay. Just you make sure you be ready where you supposed to be."

Reggie nodded, "Fu, fu, fuckin' count on it, homes."

Reggie pulled out a 9mm Smith and Wesson semiautomatic, chambered a round, and gently clicked the hammer back into position. "Any motherfucker get clo, clo, close, I kill 'em."

*

By the time Archie and Reggie had finished eating, New Lots had almost returned to normal. All the emergency medical service people had left and nearly all the police. Most of the tenants remained indoors except for a few of the older kids drawn to the possibility of further violence. They stood in clusters near the doorways of the five buildings in case they had to duck inside. Most of them watched Rachman and his two nervous regular guards. It was clear to everybody that if the Blue-Tops came looking for another target, it would be Rachman and his guards.

Outwardly, Rachman Abdul X didn't show it, but each minute he waited for reinforcements to arrive seemed like ten. When the two cars filled with MS-2 gunmen finally screeched to a halt in front of the complex, Rachman displayed no sign of relief other than taking his hand off the butt of his Glock stuck in the waistband of his pants.

Five gunmen and two legals, guards with gun-carry permits, quickly piled out of the two MS-2 cars. John X and three of the gunmen from the morning raid had returned along with a fifth gunman, Walli X, a man who displayed a nearly constant smile, brought on by tension rather than any jovial nature.

All the gunmen were Muslim. All sported dark beards except for Walli X. All five wore skullcaps and military-style garb, camouflage pants or field jackets, and combat boots. The two legals were not Muslim, and, like Rachman's regular guards, they wore conventional street clothes and MS-2 jackets with the word SECURITY across the backs and the MS-2 logo on the fronts.

Rachman pointed to John X and one of the legals named Solomon. "You two, go over to the east corner and stand guard. Anybody you see headed for the entrance, you call in."

Rachman paired Walli X with another legal and told them, "Go into the courtyard. Keep watch on the back. I'll watch the front." To the other three gunmen, he said, "You three circle the complex. If they come back, it could be from any direction. Keep moving. That way, at least one or two of you will be close to a possible trouble spot. Call in if you see anything. Anyone shows up looking for trouble, anywhere in or around this complex, shoot first."

Rachman nodded once for emphasis, then said, "Go."

Rachman remained standing in front of the entrance to New Lots with the two regular guards as the others headed off to follow Rachman's orders. All three gunmen carried two-way radios.

Rachman held up his radio and said, "Call me every five minutes. I'll be walking around every so often to check on you. If these infidels return, I want to see them before they get near this entrance. Stay alert."

*

As Rachman dispersed his gunmen outside, inside the complex, a team of two detectives from the 73rd Precinct went about the thankless task of trying to find witnesses to the drive-by shooting.

Detective David Rampton, a big, blunt Irishman who favored cheap sports coats and slacks, led the way through the dark, foul-smelling hallways. Rampton did his job and complained just enough to be one of the guys, but not enough to anger any of his bosses. He carried about thirty extra pounds on his six-foot frame, not including his snub-nosed .38 revolver.

His partner, a whip-thin black detective named Jimmy Silver, always dressed meticulously in one of his six suits carefully acquired at the Sy Syms discount outlet.

The two detectives knocked on every door they passed, but only about one in four opened to them. Jimmy Silver tried to be polite; David Rampton tried not to insult anyone. It didn't matter. People either claimed not to have seen anything or asked more questions than they answered.

After about the twentieth door, Rampton asked Silver, "Hey, Jimmy, you think if this had been some crackheads or dealers got shot, we'd be doing this?"

"Probably not for this long."

"Then why don't we get the fuck out of here?"

"I don't know."

"Come on, the hell with it. We ain't going to learn anything in this shithole."

"All right. Finish this floor, and we're out of here."

✳

Archie Reynolds, dressed in his mechanic's overalls, stood just inside the bodega watching the entrance to the complex and tracking Rachman's gunmen on patrol. He waited patiently, picking turkey meat from between his teeth with a toothpick until Rachman set out on his route to check his men.

Nobody noticed Archie cross New Lots Avenue and head for the front entrance. Not even the two regular unarmed guards posted near the unfinished gate, who were just standing, wearing their MS-2 jackets, trying to make it through the rest of the afternoon. They didn't notice Archie until he approached them, and even then, they took Archie dressed in his blue jumpsuit for an ordinary working man, maybe coming home from his job for lunch, or maybe a quick midday visit with a girlfriend.

As Archie approached the entrance, the older guard stepped in front of him and asked, "Sir, can I help you?"

"Help me do what?" asked Archie.

"Are you a resident, or are you visiting someone?"

Archie smiled, checked the MS-2 logos on their jackets, and gave them a quizzical look.

"A resident? You mean, do I live here?"

"Yes, sir. Do you live here?"

"What's this? You some kind of guards or something?"

The guard answered, "We work for the security company that's watching the building. What apartment are you in?"

Archie noticed the younger guard coming over to stand on his right. Archie looked at him, then back left to the older guard. He cocked his head and smiled at them both.

"You guys really security guards?"

"Yes, sir," said the younger guard.

"Whoa," said Archie. "Since when did anybody give a shit about guarding this place? You gonna keep all those nasty crackheads and drug dealers out of here?"

✳

A block away, Rachman finished checking with John X and turned back onto New Lots Avenue. He looked toward the entrance a block away and noticed the two guards talking to Archie near the entrance to the complex. Rachman watched them, but the three men seemed to be having a normal conversation. A conversation that would take place over and over as his regular guards explained the new security procedures at New Lots Apartments.

✳

Archie said, "So, what'd you say the name of this security company is? Muslim what?"

"Muslim Security Two," said the younger guard.

"Two? Why two?" Archie smiled, "What the fuck happened to one? When did they tell you to come in here?"

The older guard put on a hard face and again asked, "Sir, which apartment are you in?"

Archie turned to the older guard and pointed at him, "Yo, man, what you getting an attitude for? Don't be interruptin' me. I asked a question."

"Sir, do you live here? If not, I'm going to have to ask you to leave."

Archie snapped his head around and looked at the older guard.

"What the fuck did you say to me?"

"You'll have to…"

"No, no, motherfucker, I don't *have* to do anything."

The younger guard instinctively took a step back from Archie and the rage that had sparked in him without warning.

"Anybody gonna get the fuck out of here, it's gonna be you assholes. You think some shuffling house nigger like you gonna tell *me* to leave? I want to see you reach up your hand and put me out of here. Pull this phony *sir* bullshit, on me. You gonna sir *me*, motherfucker? You know who the fuck I am?"

Rachman couldn't hear Archie, hadn't ever seen Archie Reynolds before, but he didn't have to be any closer than a block away to see that the conversation had turned ugly. Rachman headed for the entrance, moving quickly, trying to attract the attention of the man giving his guards a hard time. And then it happened without nearly enough warning.

Archie pulled his .22-caliber Beretta from the back pocket of the overalls and shot the older guard in the middle of his fore-head. This time, unlike with Little Marvin, Archie shot with the gun inches away from the man's head, just the way he wanted to, just when his anger flared to the right pitch. This time, the bullet blew right through the back of his victim's head, spraying a fine mist of red blood against the unfinished, black iron fence.

For a moment, Rachman thought Archie had punched his guard's face, hoped Archie had, but the snapping crack of the exploding cartridge, the sudden puff of smoke, and Archie's extended arm told him differently. Rachman reached for his Glock and broke into a run.

The younger guard, the eighteen-year-old who Rachman had promised would be safe, flinched and ducked from Archie's gun, turning away, covering his head.

From a block away, Rachman yelled, "No!"

Archie glanced at Rachman, turned back to the young guard, and said, "Little punk bitch."

He pulled the trigger three times. Three quick cracks without even a second thought and three bullets exploded into the boy's back, burning through skin, muscle, and bone. The last bullet tore into the boy's spine, severing it just below his neck, instantly condemning the young man to a life of paralysis from the shoulders down. Eighteen years old and in one second, the young man whose mother had sent him to work that morning faced a lifetime of pain and heartbreaking disability.

Archie didn't waste any time viewing his carnage. He glanced to his right at the onrushing Rachman. He held his position, waiting insolently as if he were daring Rachman to catch him. Then, seemingly without effort, Archie bolted, gliding away from the scene of blood and mayhem he had created.

Archie still held the Beretta in his right hand. With his left hand, he pulled down on the knit cap he wore. There was enough material to cover his face, except for the holes he'd cut for his eyes and mouth.

Rachman roared after Archie, his combat boots pounding on the pavement, his bulky body straining to close the long distance between him and the arrogant, murderous enemy who had dared to shoot his guards.

✳

Inside the complex, Rampton and Silver had heard the first shot. They knew that sound; a faint, sharp pop. They looked at each other. Rampton cursed. Silver frowned. They headed as quickly as they could in the dimly lit hallway toward a stairwell, listening for more shots but not wanting to hear them. Then the three fast gunshots echoed in the courtyard, and the two detectives ran for the stairs, pulling out their guns, their hearts suddenly pounding.

✳

Outside, Archie had disappeared from view, but Rachman estimated the shooter had to still be in The Pit. He yelled into his radio, "Close the courtyard. Everybody head for the courtyard."

Rachman charged ahead. Everything in him concentrated on catching and killing whoever had shot his guards. When he reached the front entrance, he ran past the fallen guards. Rachman had to trap the killer in the courtyard. If the killer made it into one of the buildings, it would be nearly impossible to find him in the dark maze of apartments. If he made it to the street behind New Lots, they could easily lose him.

✳

In the back of the complex, Rachman's shout squawked over Walli X's radio. The licensed guard, the legal, immediately handed his weapon to Walli X and ran for cover. Walli X moved quickly into The Pit, saw Archie running with a mask on his face and a gun in his hand, and opened fire with both his weapon and the licensed guard's gun. At the same time, John X on the eastern corner out front and the three gunmen patrolling the perimeter ran for The Pit in response to Rachman's command.

✱

The sound of Walli X's gunshots told Rampton and Silver they were now rushing toward multiple shooters. Silver fumbled for his radio. Rampton continued pounding down the last set of stairs. Silver yelled into his police radio a report of shots fired at New Lots Apartments and called for backup.

✱

Archie continued running, angling away from Walli X, who tried to run and shoot at the moving target even though he knew he had little chance of hitting the shooter.

Archie ran quickly, moving with the light, quick strides of a man who carried no excess weight. He never even looked at Walli X or the gunman who appeared in the back parking area, or at Rachman charging after him from behind.

Rachman entered The Pit, taking in everything at once. Walli X shooting from the far side of The Pit, his gunmen closing in from the back, John X and the last legal coming up fast behind him.

He watched Archie run past the entrance to Building A, heading for Building E at the north end of The Pit. The gunmen emerging from the parking lot should cut him off. If so, the shooter wouldn't be able to turn back without running into Rachman's gun. They had the bastard trapped.

And then the trap snapped shut, not on Archie, but on the Muslims.

From the top floors of the buildings on the east and west sides of The Pit, the barrels of two fully automatic AK-47 rifles emerged from open windows. Just then, Detective Rampton shoved open the lobby door of Building B, ducked behind it, and held his shield out, yelling, "Police! Put down your guns."

Rampton's command meant nothing. Both Blue-Tops shooters opened fire from up above, and the crackling sound of automatic rifles filled The Pit.

Half-inch projectiles of pointed steel screamed into the courtyard at eight-hundred feet per second. Walli X turned toward the sound of Rampton's voice just as a stream of bullets ripped through his chest, neck, and head, sending fist-size chunks of flesh, blood, and bone flying away from his body. He died before his remains dropped to the ground.

Rampton jerked back behind the door, yelling to his partner, "Fuck, Jimmy, they got automatic weapons. Get back. Tell 'em they got fucking heavy weapons out here."

A spray of bullets ripped into the heavy door that Rampton leaned against. He felt the door buck and shatter as rounds blasted through above him, plowing into the lobby floor. Rampton twisted away from the door but not in time to avoid a bullet that barely caught the top of his left shoulder, tearing out a finger-size groove of flesh.

Jimmy Silver dove away from the door, banged his head into the wall, and dropped his police radio.

The first of three Muslim gunmen who had been patrolling around the complex ran into the rear of The Pit. He moved fast, hunched over, making himself a more difficult target. The Blue-Tops shooter in the west window of the courtyard took lazy aim in his direction and squeezed off a burst, missing him. A second gunman appeared close behind the first. The shooter aimed more carefully this time, tracking the running man. The second stream of bullets hit his legs, shattering both below the knees.

The first gunman dove for cover behind the remnants of a wooden bench set on a concrete stand. He landed on his back and fired blindly in the direction of the fourth-floor window in the west building. In response, the Blue-Tops shooter emptied the rest of his clip at the bench and concrete stand. The faded, green, wooden slats exploded. Chunks of concrete flew. The gunman stayed down on his back. The shooter in the east building also aimed a spray of bullets at him, but the angle was too acute. He gave up and raked a stream of fire at Rachman, who continued charging after Archie.

One gunman, Walli X, lay dead. The second remained motionless behind cover. The third had turned into an inert heap, legs shattered and bleeding. In a split second, they had changed from shooters to victims.

Rachman, however, had never taken his eyes off Archie, had never hesitated one step in his mad dash after the killer. He saw Archie run into a narrow gangway opening at the ground floor of the far north building, Building C. Despite the wild bursts of fire from the assault rifles, Rachman had managed to stay close enough to the east building that the shooter on that side hadn't spotted him. The second Blue-Tops shooter on the west side ran out of bullets just as he had figured out the range between him and Rachman. He immediately grabbed another full magazine, but in his excitement for the kill, he fumbled as he tried to shove it into his automatic rifle.

Rachman did not know or care how close to death he ran. He would kill Archie or be killed trying. Either way, it would be Allah's will.

The last of Rachman's gunmen who had been patrolling the perimeter came running around to the north side of the complex just as Archie emerged from the gangway onto Rockaway Avenue.

The Muslim was not sure if Archie was the one they were after. Archie skidded to a stop and looked back at him, giving the gunman a chance to see him. Then he raised his Beretta and pegged three shots at him. The gunman threw himself on the ground and fired back at Archie as he ran across Rockaway Avenue.

Rachman just made it into the gangway tunnel as Archie's shooter on the west side of The Pit finished loading the AK–47 and opened up at him. The shooter had the rifle on full automatic. The bullets seemed to hit everywhere around the gangway entrance, chipping brick, breaking windows, tearing up dirt from the ground, but Rachman was gone. He charged into the gangway just in time to see Archie fire his third shot at the last gunman.

As Archie broke into a run, Rachman raised the Glock and fired. The booming explosion inside the gangway deafened him. He had to aim low to clear the ceiling of the gangway near the exit. His bullet zinged off the street and angled past Archie's hip.

Archie turned and fired his last shot on the run, aiming for Rachman as the big man emerged from the gangway. The bullet screamed past Rachman's left ear. Rachman didn't even flinch.

The last gunman jumped to his feet and ran for Archie, too. He and Rachman were almost twenty yards behind their target.

Archie never ducked or dodged or changed directions. He headed straight for the front door of Justine Burton's Caring Community Center.

He burst through the double doors, turned right, and ran down a corridor. One of the women who worked in the center stepped out of her office. Archie rammed a forearm into her chest, knocking her down hard enough that she cracked the tip of her tailbone when she hit the floor.

Archie ran over her body, stomping on her shoulder. The woman screamed. He never even looked at her. He knew the Muslims were close now. Too close.

Archie skidded into the center's main waiting area as Rachman and his gunman thundered through the entrance behind him. Two women and five children sat against the far wall of the waiting room. They all cringed at the sight of a running man, gun in hand, face covered by a black ski mask.

An intake worker sat at a desk to Archie's left, in front of the only window in the area. Justine Burton came storming into the waiting area from her office located through an archway across from where Archie stood.

"Get out of here!" she yelled.

Archie aimed the Beretta at her, yelling back with such fury that Justine felt his spit spray her face.

"Fuck you! *You* get out of here."

Archie aimed the Beretta at Justine's face. She raised her hands, turned away from the gun, and screamed. Archie pulled the trigger. Nothing. Justine continued screaming, and Archie kept pulling the trigger of the empty gun, each time cursing the police commissioner's daughter.

Finally, infuriated that he couldn't kill her, Archie smashed Justine with the back of his hand. His time was up. The Muslims were seconds away from him. He turned from Justine, picked up a folding gray metal chair set against the wall behind him, and heaved it over the head of the woman sitting at the intake desk.

The heavy chair smashed through the double-pane window behind her. She dropped to the floor.

Rachman and his armed gunman, pounding down the narrow corridor, had almost reached the waiting area. Rachman, running hard, raised the Glock and yelled, "Don't move!"

Archie turned, grabbed Justine's arm, and spun her toward the corridor opening just as Rachman burst into the waiting area. Rachman crashed into Justine, knocking her off her feet.

Archie jumped up onto the desk and dove headfirst out the broken window.

Justine landed with a sickening thud and slid across the floor, right into a shard of glass which tore a groove of flesh out of her chin.

The collision with Justine knocked Rachman off balance, but he stumbled forward and banged into the wall next to the broken window. By the time he twisted back around and looked out the window, Archie had already landed on the sidewalk, rolled over once, and jumped to his feet. He ran toward the passenger side of his Saab. The convertible top was down. Reggie Whack sat in the driver's seat, gunning the engine, his Smith & Wesson in his free hand. Archie jumped in.

Reggie floored the accelerator, and the car roared down the street, tires squealing, rear-end fishtailing, Reggie blindly shooting behind him to cover the escape.

Rachman recovered his balance and fired two shots at the fleeing Saab. Too late. He would not shoot at a target he could not hit. He forced himself to stop shooting, pointed the Glock up, and roared in frustration and rage.

CHAPTER 15

On Saturday, the day after the ambush in New Lots, Loyd Shaw rolled out of bed shortly past noon, relieved his full bladder, skipped the shower and shave, and decided it might be time to cut back on the Jack Daniel's. The hangovers were becoming bothersome.

He stepped out to a cloudless blue sky and determined to sweat out the remains of the alcohol in his system and pump fresh air through his fuzzy brain. A three-mile jog should do it.

He headed toward the main house, angling toward a dirt trail across the road that led through a forested area to a small lake about a mile and a half away.

As soon as he came within a hundred yards of the farmhouse, Mrs. McGovern's black Lab came bounding toward him.

Shaw waved at the dog and called out, "Ellie!"

Shaw had grown fond of the Lab, as she had him. Her owner wasn't able to take her on long walks, so whenever the Lab spotted Shaw, the dog bounded out, ready for an outing.

Ellie would run ahead of Shaw, searching and sniffing, but she never let Shaw out of her sight for long. Every few minutes, Ellie would run back to check on him. Shaw found the dog's attention endearing.

By the time they returned from their walk, both felt better.

Shaw had worked up a decent sweat. Ellie bounded up onto Mrs. McGovern's porch and inhaled her bowl of water, then stood on the porch panting, looking, waiting for her mistress to bring her food.

The elderly widow came out of her kitchen, holding the dog's kibble in a chipped brown bowl, and waved Shaw up onto the porch.

Mrs. McGovern rarely engaged Shaw in conversation. She surprised him even more when she motioned toward her kitchen and asked, "You have breakfast yet?"

Shaw checked his watch. Breakfast time had long passed. It never occurred to him that Mrs. McGovern would have known he hadn't eaten, much less invite him in for breakfast.

"No, thanks."

"Well, suit yourself. You came up early this week."

"Yep."

"Everything all right?"

Shaw didn't mind when the friendly Labrador checked on him, but he wasn't comfortable with Mrs. McGovern's attention. It hadn't occurred to him that the older woman kept an eye on him.

"Why do you ask?"

She waved a hand as if to apologize for being nosy.

"I'm not trying to pry, Mr. Shaw."

"Okay."

"Well, you know, at my age, I get up two or three times a night. Couldn't help noticing your lights on."

"Just caught up in my work, Mrs. McGovern."

"Oh. Well. That's good."

Shaw didn't feel like offering more but tried to be polite.

"Ellie and I had a nice walk. I'm going to clean up."

"Oh, hell, I'm too old to be coy, Mr. Shaw. Fact is, you look awful. Haven't ever seen you look this way or stay up to all hours and sleep until noon. It's none of my business, of course, none at all, but I just thought I'd inquire. Say what's on my mind. In case you…"

She left whatever offer she had in mind unspoken.

Shaw rubbed the stubble on his chin, wondering just how much his appearance had deteriorated. He realized he hadn't done much to ameliorate a long night in the Brooklyn precinct three days ago. Did he look the way he did because he had been more shaken by his exile than he realized? Had he fallen into a depression aggravated by too much bourbon?

"I'm fine, Mrs. McGovern. Fine."

He knew even as he said the words that they sounded like an attempt to convince both himself and Mrs. McGovern.

"But it's nice of you to ask. It's just as well that you did because you'll be seeing more of me for the time being. There's…well, it's a little complicated. But I'm fine. Thanks for asking."

"Listen, Mr. Shaw, you can tell me whatever you want, or not tell me. But don't tell me you're fine because you're not fine. You're a long way from *fine*. If you don't know that, then me telling you so is about the best I can do for you. If you do know, well then, you'll do what you can, or you won't. That's up to you."

Mrs. McGovern closed the issue with a half-wave of her hand. The dog had watched her short speech and knew that her mistress was done talking. She barked sharply once to remind Mrs. McGovern she was still holding her bowl of food.

"Oh, look at me," said Mrs. McGovern. "Forgot about you, didn't I, girl?"

Mrs. McGovern bent down quickly and placed the bowl on the wooden floor of the porch. The Lab set about wolfing down her food.

Mrs. McGovern looked at Shaw but said no more. Shaw knew she didn't have to.

"Thanks, Mrs. McGovern. See you later."

She nodded and allowed Shaw his quick exit, but he had the feeling the old lady would be keeping tabs on him whether he liked it or not.

Shaw began to wonder what she might be speculating. He told himself she's probably decided it had to do with his marriage. He had never brought Jane to the see the place, and he never intended to. They had both accepted the flimsy excuse that the renovation wasn't complete. It provided a reason to avoid admitting that neither of them wanted to spend a weekend together in the country.

Thinking about it, Shaw winced at the discomfort he might have had to endure if Jane had forced the issue.

"Fuck it," he said out loud. "Fuck all of it."

But, despite his attempt to dismiss his situation as he walked back to his studio, Shaw found himself making a mental list of things he would do over the next couple of days. Check with Jake Bennett to see if he had run down the punks who had attacked him in Flatbush. Call the union lawyer Siegel. Contact a few people he knew who would sniff around and give him the word on the assistant district attorney, Johnson.

Maybe he wanted to prove Mrs. McGovern wrong. Maybe the thought of Jane viewing the demise of his career with one more galling ounce of pity drove him. By the time he returned to the studio, Shaw had almost convinced himself that he might be able to hang on to the tatters of his career for the one final wretched year he needed to make his twenty.

CHAPTER 16

By Sunday, Rachman's rage over the Friday afternoon ambush had settled into a persistent, festering wrath. Almost every thought he allowed himself centered on vengeance.

On Saturday, Rachman and the MS-2 members had attended to the dead and wounded. Now, Sunday morning, one of the quietest times in Brownsville, the three top-ranking members of MS-2 – John X, Youssef X, and Rachman Abdul X – sat around an old Formica-topped kitchen table in an unoccupied apartment on the top floor of Building A planning vengeance. Three hardened felons with minds bent from years in maximum-security prisons and without futures in a normal society sat planning the next move in their holy war, a war they felt entirely justified in waging. A war that now had obligated them to avenge the deaths of Walli X, the regular MS-2 guard shot through the head, and the brutal wounding of two others.

Rachman and John X were warriors. John X was taller and thinner than Rachman but nearly as strong and maybe even more intense. He had a full beard and shoulder-length dreads.

Youssef X was a small man. He functioned as the group's intelligence officer. He wore an old black suit a size too big for him, a white shirt buttoned to the neck, and the requisite Kufi skullcap. There was a sparseness about the man, as if prison and hate and fanatical discipline had excised everything extra. Youssef carried no extra baggage, no fat, no sympathy, no softness, no affectations. Even his skullcap had been knit out of simple, unbleached cotton string.

The only things Youssef X held in extra measure were fanaticism, intelligence, and hate.

Rachman opened the meeting.

"Tell us what your people found out."

Youssef lit a cigarette with the burning stub of another as if taking that time to organize his thoughts. Rachman and the others tolerated his chain-smoking, a violation for most Muslims. But Youssef X was not most Muslims. Their disapproval did not make the slightest difference to Youssef.

"We know most of what we need to about their operation. First point, they're more organized than most scum like them who deal in poison and intimidation."

Youssef reached into his breast pocket and extracted a photocopy of a map showing the section of Brownsville surrounding the New Lots Apartments complex. He had enlarged it to the point where the lines and letters had turned grainy, but it was easier for everybody to see the street names and landmarks.

He laid the photocopy on the table, and the MS-2 inner circle leaned toward it. Youssef pointed out areas on the map he had circled with a red pen.

"This is their headquarters. It's a body shop in the alley that runs alongside the elevated tracks behind the New Lots stop. They keep weapons and at least one of their stash cars in there. It's also the main supply point for their poison. It goes from here into various apartments. Then from those apartments into whatever hole they are selling out of. So they always have people in there. Four or five, sometimes more.

"Also, there are usually two lookouts guarding the outside, here and here. They will be armed."

Youssef pushed the map toward the others and sat back.

"Friday and Saturday are their biggest selling days. Today, most of them and their customers will recover from the weekend. Monday, they start to gear up. It's the day they bring in their biggest supply."

Youssef leaned forward and pointed to a red X on the map. "They'll have the most people in there, the most supply, tomorrow."

Rachman and John X nodded. They had no questions.

Youssef returned their nods as if to confirm their understanding, and then described what tomorrow would bring. For a few moments, no one spoke. Even Rachman seemed to be taken aback by the brutality of it. Youssef knew there would now be questions. He sat back, legs crossed, hunched in his chair, smoking, ready to provide answers.

CHAPTER 17

LOYD SHAW HAD SPENT THE REST OF SUNDAY AFTERNOON PAINTING. When the daylight dimmed, he switched on artificial light and kept daubing at the canvas, laying on different tones of acrylic red. Over the last months, Shaw had become intrigued with the color. No matter what he painted, even the shapes suggested by the deep dark greens and grays of the forest around him, it all came out red.

The painting kept his mind off what the NYPD had in store for him, but by the time the Massachusetts moon rose high enough to shine above his skylight, Shaw's anger and dread seeped into his consciousness like an annoying stain reappearing after yet another coat of paint.

Night was a catalyst for his anger. It used to be that on Sunday evenings Shaw would be packing up and getting ready to drive back to the city for work on Monday. With his seniority, he generally avoided work on weekends. Each Sunday, when he left his painting and returned to the job, his level of discontent crept up another notch. His resentment grew another degree.

But now, the department had told him *not* to come back. Now, Shaw felt even more resentful. Now, he wasn't even good enough for one of their stinking Mondays.

Shaw dropped his paintbrush into the coffee can filled with thinner, walked to his kitchen area, and filled a glass with four fingers of Jack Daniel's.

Once again, he told himself, "Fuck it."

✳

Youssef X sat back in his chair, having answered the questions John X and Rachman had asked. His plan was brutal, efficient, and deadly. Its success depended on timing and the veracity of information Youssef had gathered.

Rachman Abdul X trusted that Youssef's information was correct. After all, who better to gather information on the dealings of a black ghetto drug gang than black ex-convicts, many of whom had committed the same crimes in the same types of neighborhoods? As to the timing, Rachman trusted only himself and the will of Allah.

CHAPTER 18

At six o'clock Monday morning, all was quiet in the alley where the Blue-Tops body shop was located. As usual, two members of the gang guarded the outside. One of them, a gangly young man with bad skin and a worse attitude named Nelson, slouched against the brick wall next to the large steel garage door. The other guard, a squat, muscular type called Beal, sat on the step that led up to the door next to the big rolling garage door. Beal cradled a loaded Uzi in his lap. Both of the men were alert, watching, mindful of the fact that a shipment would be arriving soon.

A mongrel dog entered the west end of the alley, loping toward them with a sideways gate. About ten feet before the dog reached the guards, he lifted his head in the air, sniffed, then abruptly turned, disappearing between two ramshackle buildings.

Behind and above them on the elevated platform, the subway pulled into the New Lots station. The old tracks rumbled under the weight of the train, the shrieking steel wheels and squealing announcing the arrival.

Between the dog and the train, the guards didn't see the hunched-over bum enter the alley at the west end. He wore a long raincoat bearing stains and dirt that looked as if it had taken years to accumulate them. The bottom of the coat had reached the shredded stage. Under the raincoat, the derelict wore a filthy hooded sweatshirt despite the warmth of the April morning. Behind him, the bum dragged a banged-up shopping cart jam-packed with assorted junk: a milk crate, broken pieces of iron pipe, a black plastic bag filled with soda cans, more dirty plastic bags wrapped in tape, and an old quilt.

Nelson noticed him first. He sneered at the human wreck, another loser in Brownsville looking for worthless shit in a back alley.

Beal cradled the Uzi and told Nelson, "Go tell that old motherfucker to get the hell out of here. I don't want him close enough I can smell the piss on him."

"What makes you think I want to get close enough to smell him?"

"Go on. Get him out of here."

Muttering to himself, Nelson headed off. The bum stood at the wall of an abandoned building, feeling the edge on a piece of tin that had been nailed over a busted-out window. He seemed to be trying to figure out how to pull it off so he could add it to the collection in his cart.

Nelson yelled, "Yo. Old man."

The bum kept looking at the sheet of tin.

Nelson pulled out his gun and walked closer.

"Yo. I'm talking to you."

Nelson had closed the distance to five yards and kept coming. "Hey!"

Finally, the bum turned.

"Get the fuck outa here, man."

"What?"

Nelson raised the gun, pointing it at the bum, coming close enough so that he could aim the barrel in front of the filthy face buried inside the hood of the sweatshirt. He extended his arm but kept his head back from the bum, not wanting to smell him.

"I said…"

Nelson never really saw the club come out from under Rach-man Abdul X's filthy raincoat. He just caught a flash of it before the wood shattered the left side of his skull and cracked his eye socket. After an instant of intense pain, everything went black. Five seconds later, the boy was dead.

Beal had been watching it all, impatient, a scowl on his face, the Uzi cradled in his lap. And then, inexplicably, suddenly, the bum had Nelson in his arms.

"What the fuck?"

Beal stood, gripped the Uzi, and moved toward them quickly as Rachman bent Nelson over the shopping cart.

Beal thought, what the fuck had that bum done? It was the last thought he would ever have.

John X stepped out from between two buildings just as Beal passed him and swung a baseball bat at the back of the guard's head. The hollow crunch of the bat connecting against the skull was loud enough for Rachman to hear it at the other end of the alley.

From between the decrepit buildings, gunmen materialized, gathering around the two fallen guards. No one spoke a word. Rachman shucked off the filthy clothes. The gunmen stripped the Blue-Tops down to their underwear. Two of the Muslims pulled on the clothing while the others loaded the inert bodies into Rachman's shopping cart.

Within minutes, two of Rachman's gunmen had replaced Beal and Nelson, dressed in their clothes, holding their weapons, standing guard at the entrance to the body shop.

Rachman, John X, and the others disappeared. Thirty min-utes later, the car pulled up to deliver the Blue-Tops' weekly shipment of processed crack cocaine.

The gunman who had taken Nelson's place banged on the steel door. An electric winch kicked in, and the rolling steel door slowly rose. The car entered. The rolling steel door immediately began to close. Rachman and John X were standing at both sides of the rolling overhead security door with short sledgehammers and coal chisels. Two blows from each of the sledgehammers jammed the chisels into the door's tracks, stopping it a foot above the ground.

Four gunmen appeared, each carrying two five-gallon plastic jugs filled with gasoline. They slung forty gallons of gas under the jammed door in seconds. Another gunman jammed an iron bar across the regular size entrance door next to the rolling door.

Voices inside began shouting. Someone inside lifted the steel door, trying to free it.

Calmly, Rachman took the Uzi from the gunman who had replaced Beal. He bent over and unleashed a spray of bullets under the jammed door. Red-hot lead skimmed and skipped on the concrete floor, ricocheting off the hard surfaces and cars inside. Bullets hit two of the eight jugs. Gasoline burst out of the plastic jugs. Outside, John X lit a gasoline-soaked rag stuffed into the neck of a forty-ounce malt liquor bottle filled with gas and threw it under the door.

With a muffled whump, the gasoline ignited. Within seconds, a series of concussions erupted and instantly built into one long, horrible, rolling blast.

The screaming started before the last jug of gasoline ignited, continued, and rose as billows and plumes of the deadly black smoke rose from under the jammed door. One of the gang members managed to squeeze his head under the door, clawing with bloody hands on the concrete, trying to pull himself outside and tearing the skin off the back of his head to escape the flames that were burning the flesh off his back and legs.

A single gunshot exploded his skull, ending his misery.

Rachman had already motioned for his gunmen to leave the scene. He stood outside the burning massacre listening to the last screams, letting the heat from inside sear his face, hoping that the one they called Archie Ar was inside burning.

All that was left to do now was to walk to the empty lot where his men had taken Beal and Nelson and supervise the final task—beating the corpses bloody and putting their broken bodies on display. Rachman wanted the residents of New Lots to see what happened to those who harmed members of MS-2.

Youssef's plan had worked. All praise to Allah.

CHAPTER 19

When the phone rang at nine on Monday morning, Shaw was not ready to answer it.

He wouldn't have, except that the phone line did not have call answering, and the ringing went on and on as if the caller on the other end knew Shaw was lying there, stubbornly refusing to answer. Finally, Shaw leaned out of his bed and snatched the receiver, yelling "What!" into the mouthpiece.

Shaw heard Richard Parnell's voice, undeterred by his bellow.

"Shaw."

"Yeah."

"Parnell."

"Yeah?"

"Report to the chief of D's office, today, noon. Suit and tie."

"What?"

"You heard me. Chief's office. Noon."

"What time is it?"

"Nine."

"Are you crazy? I'm up in Massachusetts."

"The chief of D, Shaw. When can you get here?"

Shaw tried to focus, to concentrate.

"What the hell does he want with me?"

"Shaw, you got 'til one o'clock. You have to speed, show 'em your badge. Be there. Suit and tie."

The line went dead.

The chief of D's office. Just like that. No explanation. Only a flat-out order.

Shaw yelled into the dead mouthpiece, "Fuck you, Parnell, you stiff-ass shanty Irish bastard!" Then slammed the phone down.

Shaw sat on the edge of his bed, deciding if he dared defy the chief of detectives. He knew it would be tantamount to defying God. Parnell, sure. The district attorney's office, why not? But the chief of detectives? He had the power to decide his fate more than anybody.

Shaw looked at his watch. If he waited five more minutes, he'd never make it.

∗

At precisely two minutes to one, Shaw walked into the foyer of the chief of detectives' office at One Police Plaza, adjusting his best tie. He wore his last clean dress shirt and his second-best suit. He ran his fingers through his thick hair, still damp from the quick shower he'd taken at his loft.

Shaw announced himself to the administrative assistant guarding the entrance to the office of the person Shaw considered the most powerful man in the NYPD – Chief of Detectives Albert J. DeLuca.

Most people assumed the police commissioner held the most powerful position. Shaw believed that on a day-to-day basis, the chief of D played a more crucial role. He controlled the investigative arm of one of the world's largest police forces operating in one of the world's most important cities. No crime in New York City could be solved or prosecuted until investigated. Police commissioners set policy, commanded tens of thousands of men and women. But only the detective division could investigate and gather evidence. Without investigation, there could be no prosecution, no punishment, no justice. Controlling that process made Albert J. DeLuca a force to be reckoned with.

When the administrative officer told Shaw to take a seat, he studiously avoided making eye contact with Shaw. It reminded Shaw of how jury members avoid looking at a defendant they are about to send to prison.

After a ten-minute wait, Shaw heard a small speaker on the assistant's desk emit a soft tone. He looked up at Shaw and said, "Okay."

Shaw walked down a short corridor. He caught the rich aroma of cigar smoke. At the end of the hallway, a door opened onto an office designed to impress. Shaw entered the office, his footsteps muted by thick, blue carpeting. Chief of Detectives Albert J. DeLuca sat behind a massive wooden desk, hunched over a pile of papers like a turn-of-the-century scrivener. The office walls were crowded with police insignia, memorabilia, and pictures of DeLuca at various ceremonies with police and public officials. There was even a section of the office set up for photos with the chief.

DeLuca did not bother to acknowledge that another person had entered the room. He continued reading pages spilling out of a red folder. Shaw watched, noticing that DeLuca seemed to be reading two or three pages at once. Shaw wondered if the red color of the folder meant anything significant. Top Secret? Beware? Or maybe red was DeLuca's favorite color, too.

Without raising his head, DeLuca reached over and picked up a Churchill-size Cuban El Rey del Mundo from a massive marble cigar ashtray. He puffed thoughtfully while he perused his papers. Two kings, thought Shaw – DeLuca and the El Rey.

The cigar had the rich, deep, earthy aroma of a Cuban. Shaw suddenly had a fierce desire for one. And four fingers of bourbon to go with it.

When DeLuca finally looked up at him, Shaw was reminded of DeLuca's nickname, The Shark. DeLuca's pale skin blended in with steel gray hair, slicked back tight on his big skull. His head, neck, and shoulders all tapered into a thick body. DeLuca had a piercing gaze, yet his eyes were strangely lifeless, as if he could not afford to display the slightest emotion. At public affairs, DeLuca tended to flash a smile intended to charm but mostly just revealed a brutal set of brilliantly white teeth. Shaw didn't expect any smiles from The Shark today.

DeLuca pushed the papers aside and looked up at Shaw, staring at him as if he had just finished reading about him.

"What are you, Shaw, some kind of psycho?"

"No, but if I were, I suppose I would know it, would I?"

DeLuca looked at Shaw to make sure he wasn't being flip, decided he wasn't, then told Shaw, "Sit down."

Shaw sat.

"What prompted you to shoot up a car full of African-Americans at three o'clock in the morning while on restricted duty?"

Shaw looked at DeLuca for a moment to see if he were asking a serious question or just baiting him. Bait from The Shark? DeLuca's deadpan stare revealed nothing. For a moment, Shaw considered answering, I don't know, but he wasn't ready to play games with the chief of detectives.

Shaw told the chief his version of what had happened without exaggeration or affectation.

"So you shot up the car to stop the music."

"Right. And drive those guys off."

"Sounds foolish. Why not just shoot the pricks who jumped you? According to your record, you don't mind shooting people."

Shaw decided not to rise to that comment, keeping his face deadpan, too.

"I figured it would cause me less trouble if I shot the car."

"Uh-huh. And what was this *look* you gave them?"

"I looked at them like they were assholes."

"Assholes? Or criminals?"

"Both."

"Right. So you were pissed off?"

"Very."

"At them and their music."

"Yes."

"Black guys."

"Yes."

"Black music."

"I suppose. I guess some white people listen to it, too."

"And you're seeing Psych Services. What's the problem, Shaw? You got a thing about black people?"

"What do you mean by 'a thing'?"

DeLuca's chin lifted just a few degrees. His eyes narrowed slightly. Without saying a word, Shaw knew that answering a question with a question would not be tolerated.

DeLuca's tone hardened slightly.

"Detective Shaw, are you a racist? Do you hate blacks?"

"No."

DeLuca stared at him, not responding. After several moments of silence, Shaw asked, "Are we finished?"

"You're finished enough, Shaw. Your whole career is finished."

"Then why am I here?"

"Because I say so. And I'm the one asking the questions, Detective. Don't think because your career is over, you have nothing to lose. And I'll tell you when you've given me enough answers. Or do you want to say fuck you to me and get up and walk out of here?"

The hard words were said without DeLuca raising his voice but with a clearly higher level of intensity.

"I want to find out why I'm here more than I want to say fuck you. At least so far."

NEW LOTS | 113

"We'll get to that. Couple more questions. Anything more you want to say about the black issue?"

"Not really. Ask some black people who know me if they think I'm a racist."

"So, some of your best friends are black?"

"Some good friends."

"All right. Were you drunk when this happened?"

"No. I'd had a total of one drink. I didn't feel much like drinking that night."

"You have any trouble with alcohol? Are you an alcoholic?"

"No. I like to drink, but not when it's going to get in my way."

"You went all the way out to Bushwick for one drink."

"I went out there to wish someone a happy birthday. The drinking was incidental."

"You must have really hated those guys who jumped you."

DeLuca's sudden change in topic gave Shaw pause. What was DeLuca trying to do? Catch him at something?

Shaw did not respond for a few moments but decided he didn't care to attempt figuring out what DeLuca was up to. He did, however, find it interesting to gauge the amount of anger in DeLuca and what had caused it. DeLuca didn't wait for Shaw to finish his introspection.

"All right, never mind. I don't think you're a racist. Nothing in your record indicates it. I don't think you have a thing for blacks. I'll tell you why you went after three black guys in the middle of the night, two of which, according to your testimony, had guns."

"Okay." Shaw was interested to know himself.

"You did it because you were scared shitless, or close to it. You did it because you were scared of those murderous bastards and you didn't want to die. And you got angry, not at them, but at yourself because you were so terrified. So you had to risk your life with that crazy move you took."

Shaw realized that DeLuca might be right but didn't feel like admitting it.

"I had no choice."

"Nonsense. You could have run. Run like hell. You know how damn hard it is to shoot a running target. Those guys might not have even run after you."

"No, just gotten back in their car and run me down."

"I don't think so. I think running was an option."

"Maybe you're right, Chief. Maybe you got it right."

"Are you patronizing me, Detective Shaw?"

"I don't think so."

"Don't avoid the truth here. It's important. Don't concede if you think I'm wrong. Of course you were afraid of them, that's the easy part. The harder part is admitting that your fear made you angry. That's what was going on out there."

Shaw said, "Sounds right," and tried to sound like he meant it.

DeLuca nodded, picked up his fat cigar, blinked at Shaw a few times, and rewarded himself with a couple of puffs. "Okay. Next question. Any ideas on how you're going to save your pension?"

"Excuse me?"

"You heard me."

After a few moments, Shaw said, "I guess that depends on what my lawyer and the union guys tell me."

"Your lawyer and the union guys?"

"Yes."

"Fuck your lawyer and the union."

Shaw hadn't expected that. Hadn't expected any of this.

"Detective Shaw, have you done the numbers?"

"The numbers?"

"Do you know how much your pension decreases if we throw you out before you make your twenty? Do you know how much you lose?"

"No. I haven't gone over the numbers."

"Why not?"

Shaw started to answer, but DeLuca kept talking.

"I'll tell you why not. Because you think we'll just suspend you. Shove you off behind a desk in the property office or somewhere horrible for…" DeLuca looked at the papers in front of him. "…What is it? For sixteen months. Counting your accrued vacation time. That's what you have left. You figure they'll hide you for sixteen months, make your life miserable, take away vacation days, then let you out to pasture. But if they don't, if they strip you and throw you out, it means you're too old to start a career, assuming a cop like you has another career possibility, which you don't, but if you did, now you have to do it without your base, without your pension. With nothing. You're out, and you have nothing but your savings and your infinitesimal chance of getting a job that pays enough to keep you solvent. Do you have any savings, Shaw?"

"Isn't that somewhere in your pile of papers."

"No. Just your credit history. I didn't bother to get your financial status. I think I already know it. I think even with a pension and a few odd jobs, you're going to live a very simple life. Without it, you're going to be a poor old man."

Shaw thought to himself, what about Jane? He must know I'm married to a lawyer. A successful lawyer. How the hell does he know that she and I are quits? How is he so certain that I couldn't lose my pension and still live on Jane's salary plus whatever I pick up on my own? How does he know Jane is gone from me?

Shaw did his best to keep his thoughts hidden and simply said, "I guess I'd better look at the numbers." But he felt himself losing his usual control and perspective. Somehow DeLuca had overwhelmed him with his quiet, monotone delivery, his unblinking gaze devoid of emotion, his horrible barbs discharged between puffs on his fat, expensive, illegal Cuban cigar.

"Yes," said DeLuca, "But that's not what the real problem is."

Shaw yelled to himself, *that's not the real problem. I'm going to be stripped and left with nothing? That's not the fucking problem? What the hell is the problem, you prick?*

"The real problem is, once we throw you out, nobody else will hire you. Not even to watch a damn candy store."

"Why is that?"

"Because when we throw you out, we'll make sure to label you as a rogue cop, a psycho, racist, rogue cop who got tossed off the force. It'll ruin you forever."

Shaw felt a constricting feeling in his throat and chest, a kind of sickening, paralyzing heartburn that had nothing to do with anything in his stomach and everything to do with the knowledge that, even though DeLuca had delivered the threat without a hint of emotion, his ability to make good on it was undeniable.

DeLuca puffed and squinted, looking as if he had effortlessly engineered the meeting to a point where he could deliver his coup de grace.

"I'll compliment you on your ability to keep your mouth shut. Not acting stupidly. Arguing about any of this. I only hope you're not sitting there thinking this is an empty threat."

"Absolutely not, sir."

"Good. Good. So the only thing left for me to say to you, to drive this painful reality home, is this – you might walk out of here and call the lawyers and the union rep and hear the line, 'they can't do that to a twenty-year, first-grade, veteran detective.' Now, normally, *normally,* they would be somewhat correct."

DeLuca looked at Shaw, making sure he followed.

"But in your case, no. It doesn't apply."

"Why is that?"

"Well, there's your record. You had that crazy shoot-out a few years back that made you notorious. You're off-center enough to need a shrink. Now you're shooting up cars in the middle of the night. We could spin that so the union would back off. But here's the bitch, Shaw. Even without that, I don't think you'd be much of a problem to get rid of and blackball."

Shaw swallowed hard, fighting off the anger and nausea. He didn't want to hear this, but DeLuca kept right on rolling.

DeLuca leaned forward. "You see, you never fit in here, Shaw. I know you. I don't know you as well as some, but I know you. I know the men you worked with and the people you worked for. You never fit in. You were always above it. You stink of an above-it-all attitude. An attitude that says, I don't want to be here because I'm better than the rest of you. I can do exactly what I described to you and not demoralize anybody, not start any grumbling or worry in the division. I could ruin you because nobody gives a shit about you."

Shaw nodded. He knew DeLuca was right, but something about this meeting was wrong. DeLuca was too high up and too busy to take all this time to beat him down, threaten him, demoralize him. If he wanted to, the chief of D could ruin him without the sermon.

Shaw decided he wasn't going down without a fight.

"Nobody gives a shit about anybody on this job, and you know it. All you're saying is it would be easier with me."

"Okay. If that's the way you want to look at it."

Shaw said, "The fact that I'm sitting here listening to all this from you — and trust me, I believe you — gives me the feeling that there's a possibility you aren't going to do any of that to me, are you?"

DeLuca said nothing, didn't move, but he kept his shark eyes on Shaw, watching him carefully.

Shaw continued, "Not only that, I suspect you're about to tell me you can make it all go away. The departmental stuff, even that asshole ADA Johnson, all of it."

Finally, DeLuca nodded.

"I haven't said I can make it all go away."

Shaw said, "You don't have to. There isn't a district attorney's office in the city that can get very far without the cooperation of the detectives' division. Everything else is just a couple of phone calls."

DeLuca nodded. "That's good."

Shaw asked, "What's good?"

"That you're smart enough to see what's going on here."

"So, what do you want from me?" Shaw asked.

DeLuca leaned back, picked up the El Rey, blinked, and puffed. He pushed his chair back from his desk and half turned away, puffing, thinking. He crossed his legs and absentmindedly flexed his ankle, twisting his foot counterclockwise.

He said, almost as much to himself as to Shaw, "It's much easier working with smart people. I've always said that."

As DeLuca turned his ankle, Shaw caught glimpses of the bottom of DeLuca's shoe. Hardly a scuff marred the surface of the leather soles. It was as if DeLuca had spent all his time walking on carpet. But DeLuca's access to privilege hadn't dampened his ability to put Shaw exactly where he wanted him.

"So we agree that A, I know you better than you know yourself, and B, I control your fate." DeLuca swiveled around on his chair and faced Shaw again. "That's clear?"

"Clear."

"And do we agree that you are willing to help me out so that I will not do the terrible things that will ensure a life of poverty and subsequent misery for you?"

"Yes. Providing we agree that 'helping you out' doesn't get me sent to jail. I'll be poor on the outside before I'll be anything on the inside."

DeLuca puffed on the El Ray and dipped his head slightly to the right.

"That's certainly not my intent. I don't want to see you locked up. I intend to do the right thing here, not the wrong thing, but how you do it is up to you. You may have to cut a few corners. I'll cover for you as much as possible, but, obviously, I can't guarantee immunity. You go too far, you'll have to live with the consequences. We still on the same page?"

"Yes."

"You want to say fuck you and walk now?"

"No."

"Okay, you'll have to sit there and listen to me for a few minutes."

CHAPTER 20

ALBERT J. DELUCA SPOKE WITHOUT INTERRUPTION, WITHOUT emotion, reciting the story as if he were dictating facts to a stenographer, even through the worst of it – the slaughter at the Blue-Tops headquarters. He puffed his Cuban cigar and dispassionately related the details of a community deep in the process of destroying itself.

Shaw sat and listened without interrupting, trying to picture the New Lots Apartments complex, the Blue-Tops crack gang, the Muslims. His years on the force had exposed him to enough situations so that he could understand what DeLuca's words conveyed, and yet he still had a hard time understanding why the chief of detectives was taking such a special interest in the situation. As DeLuca talked, Shaw tried to figure it out. Were there political contributions coming from the real estate company that took over the project? Or was it simply too many bodies falling in Brownsville too fast? Had the press gotten wind of it?

When DeLuca casually mentioned that the woman injured at the community center was Justine Burton, Shaw asked his first question.

"Did you say, Burton?"

"Yes."

"The same Burton? You're talking about the commissioner's daughter?"

DeLuca nodded.

Shaw sat back in his chair and scowled.

"Shit. That's why I'm sitting here? That's why you're threatening to ruin my life? Because the fucking commissioner's daughter got her chin cut?"

DeLuca watched Shaw's reaction without commenting on it.

"That's part of it. The commissioner is naturally upset."

"Then why doesn't he tell his daughter to get out of there? What the hell is she doing out in Brownsville anyhow?"

"Maybe she's trying to help some people? What's the matter, Shaw, don't you think she should be able to help people who need it?"

"Not if she's going to get killed doing it. Sounds like she's in a war zone out there."

"That's nothing new. The area has had a war zone mortality rate for years."

Shaw asked, "What did the Muslims do about the drive-bys and the other shooting?"

"Oh, that's right, you've been hiding out up in Massachusetts. You didn't see the papers today."

"No. I came straight here."

"Didn't listen to the news when you drove down?"

"No, I prefer driving to music."

DeLuca reached over and dropped the morning editions of *The New York Times* and *Daily News* in front of Shaw. Both headlines screamed: SEVEN DIE IN BROOKLYN ARSON FIRE.

Shaw scanned the front pages.

"How'd that happen?"

"I haven't gotten full reports yet. Apparently, the Muslims went in, shot up the place, locked the doors, and set everything on fire. That's not all of it. Just before you walked in here, I received a report of two bodies found propped up on benches in a little triangle park across from the complex. The victims appeared to have been beaten to death. Last Friday, the precinct out there investigated a report submitted by a funeral home about a corpse killed by a single gunshot to the head. The family denied knowing anything about the murder. Refused to cooperate."

DeLuca dropped a red folder on top of the newspapers.

"That folder contains copies of all the reports I've received. You'll get more details from reading them. That's all I know so far. Obviously, it's not all of it. Bottom line, this has to be stopped."

"So the commissioner's daughter can play Mother Teresa in Brownsville."

For the first time in the meeting, DeLuca raised his voice. "For a lot of reasons, Detective. She's just one of them. Some of us still think that people don't have the right to kill each other whenever they want to. Some of us still think the police department should do something about this. Maybe other people think blacks should just have at it out there and kill each other off. Save us a lot of trouble. I don't think so. What do you think, Detective?"

"I think you're right. I think people shouldn't be allowed to kill other people."

"Good." DeLuca pointed his cigar at Shaw. "So now we move from thinking to doing. You're going to shut this war down, Shaw. Now. Whatever it takes. Or you're going to live to regret it. Regret it in more ways than you know. Is that understood?"

"Yes."

"From this moment, you're under my command on special assignment. As far as everybody else in the department knows, you're still suspended. But now you have a chance to get yourself back in good standing and deserve the life you want." DeLuca dropped another folder on the pile. "You're going to need help, get it from the men on that list but keep it limited. Decide who you want before you leave headquarters. Then talk to Lieutenant

Conklin two doors to the left, down the hall. Anything you think you'll need, get it through him. Don't waste his time. He has your gun, badge, and ID. Do you have any questions?"

Shaw had plenty of questions, but he knew DeLuca didn't have the time or inclination to answer them.

"No."

"Then I suggest you get on with it. I want this fixed yesterday. I'll expect to hear from you soon."

DeLuca turned to his desk and put his head down. The meeting had ended.

Shaw walked out of the chief's office, his folders and newspapers in hand, and wandered to Conklin's office.

A police lieutenant in his officer's white shirt and insignia looked up at Shaw as he entered. Shaw looked at the older cop thinking if Fred Gwynne had a brother, this guy would be it.

Without a word, Conklin pushed Shaw's ID, gun, and badge at him, along with a form to sign. Shaw scribbled his signature without reading the form.

Shaw said, "I need an office. A place to sit and read. Make some phone calls."

Conklin pointed out his door and said, "Across the hall. Keep the door closed."

Shaw found the office and dropped DeLuca's reports on the desk, but he couldn't bring himself to sit down and begin. Suddenly breathing felt difficult. He loosened his tie and unbuttoned his collar. He needed air.

The ride down in the closed-in elevator and the walk through the lobby, past the security turnstiles, seemed to take twenty minutes instead of five. Finally, Shaw strode out into the cool air and sunshine. He took several deep breaths.

He walked through the empty plaza and sat on a bench. He muttered to himself, "Shit. What the fuck have I gotten myself into?"

He watched his fellow New Yorkers stroll by, thinking they didn't have a clue. Not a goddamn fucking clue. And then Shaw thought about killing or being killed, about violent young black men shooting and burning one another.

Shaw sat deciding whether or not he would walk back into One Police and do what he said he would. DeLuca had tried to make him feel as if he had no choice and done a damn good job of it. But Shaw knew full well he could walk away. Just stand up and walk away. Leave those reports in that empty office and simply walk out of the plaza. Hail a cab, go back to his place, and get in his car. Just head up the West Side Highway. Call the lawyer or Parnell, or not call. Just go. Take his chances. Certainly, DeLuca would do what he said. But he could still survive. It wouldn't cost much to live in his barn in Massachusetts. Maybe he would sell a few paintings. Hell, maybe he'd sell a lot of paintings. Not likely, but he could still survive. Somehow.

Shaw knew he could have said, fuck you. And if, at the very worst, it didn't work out, he could always drink a half bottle of good bourbon, stick his Glock in his mouth, get it positioned just right – pointing up so that it would blow his brains out the top of his head – then squeeze. One last, dramatic, messy red painting. At the very least, Shaw knew he could determine how and when and who would kill him. He could have said fuck you to DeLuca and walked out.

But he didn't.

Why? Because Shaw knew DeLuca had told him the truth. Somebody had to shut down the war. Somebody had to stop the mindless murderers. Civil society required civilized killers to keep the uncivilized killers at bay. And Albert J. DeLuca, the closest a detective gets to God on earth, had just told him he had been picked to do the killing.

Shaw stood up and walked back into One Police.

CHAPTER 21

LOYD SHAW PICKED FOUR OTHERS. FOUR AND NO MORE. FOUR who might be able to provide what he needed.

He walked across the hall and stepped into Conklin's office, handed him the list.

"Do you think you can get all of them together for a meeting tonight?"

"What time?"

"Let's say eight o'clock."

"Where?"

"Restaurant in Tribeca."

"Yes."

Shaw gave Conklin the address of the restaurant and left.

✳

At five after eight, Shaw sat alone, waiting in the place he had chosen, a bar-restaurant selected because it offered a quiet back room. And also because it had aged into a comfortably rundown state long before the neighborhood gained its trendy name, Tribeca.

He checked his watch. All four were late. Was this a show of independence? Shaw decided to believe they were having trouble finding their way in the confusing downtown streets.

As Shaw waited, he drank a Bass Ale, spicing it with sips from a double shot of Jameson Irish whiskey.

The first of the group arrived at eight-fifteen: Detective Anthony Impelliteri, a nine-year veteran who worked homicide out of the 75th Precinct in East New York, neighboring Brownsville.

Impelliteri looked much as Shaw imagined he would from reading his file – early thirties, six-foot, slim, well built. He wore black jeans, a black t-shirt, and a dark green vest. Impelliteri's thick black hair was cropped short. He needed a shave, but Shaw decided the dark stubble looked good on him. Shaw noticed that Impelliteri carried his Glock shoved into a pancake holster behind his right hip and didn't seem to care that his vest didn't cover it very well.

To Shaw, Impelliteri looked like a cop the average citizen would think was a criminal, and the average criminal would make as a cop immediately.

Impelliteri gave Shaw a half-wave instead of a handshake and said, "If you're Shaw, this must be the place."

"I am, and it is."

Impelliteri looked out at the bar assessing the possibility of getting a decent drink in the place. He told the barmaid who had followed him into the back room, "I'll take a glass of red."

Once that was done, Impelliteri ignored Shaw and busied himself with looking at the menu.

Shaw wasn't interested in any small talk, either. He took another sip of his Jameson and chased it with ale.

A few minutes later, two more detectives walked in behind the waitress bringing Impelliteri's wine. Shaw knew one of them very well. The other he had never met. One was black, one white. One big and meaty, the other not much more than a frame for his clothes.

The black detective, the bigger and the older of the two, was Orestes Mason. The younger man was James Sperling.

Shaw couldn't help but notice that the gaunt Sperling had no expression on his face. Shaw couldn't tell if Sperling had achieved a Zenlike calm or if he had arrived at a deep state of depression. Considering the circumstances, Shaw decided Sperling's appearance might be due to depression.

Mason's big, broad face spoke volumes, even with his mouth shut. At the moment, Mason's face said he was not happy.

Sperling nodded at Shaw and took a seat. Mason stood pointing a large finger at Shaw and asked, "What the hell have you gotten me into, partner?"

"Have a seat, Mase. I'll tell you when the last of our group gets here." Mason sat next to Shaw at the round table. Sperling sat between him and Impelliteri but seemed to be sitting all by himself. Impelliteri and Sperling nodded to each other but didn't bother to introduce themselves.

Shaw said, "We've got one more coming. What're you guys drinking?"

Mason asked, "Who's paying?"

"The department."

"I'll have what you're having."

Sperling said, "Club soda."

Before the drinks came, the last member of the crew arrived, Walter Wang. At twenty-six, he was the youngest in the group. Impelliteri and Sperling were in their thirties. Shaw represented the forties. Mason hovered somewhere on the other side of fifty.

Shaw had heard of Walter Wang even before his name appeared on DeLuca's loser list. Wang had run a particularly audacious scam using NYPD personnel records.

Walter fit the image of the archetypal Asian, straight-A, math-computer whiz right down to the cheap suit, white shirt, and wire-rimmed glasses. But Shaw knew that Wang was a scammer, a con artist, someone who would not be constrained by rules and regulations. Shaw decided the clothes and the nerd act were a front.

Wang quickly took a seat at the round table to Shaw's left. He bobbed his head up and down and said, "Sorry, sir. I had a few last minutes things to clean up."

Shaw didn't take to the con. He waved off Wang's excuse.

"What are you drinking, Wang?"

"Uh, Rolling Rock, sir."

Shaw snapped, "Hey, drop the fucking act, all right? Don't call me sir, and don't come in here trying to bullshit me about taking care of last-minute job obligations. You want to be late, just fucking be late and take the consequences." Shaw looked around the table and said, "Same goes for the rest of you. I'm not your boss. This thing we're involved with is way past rank or any normal command structure."

Shaw paused to see if any of them had something to say. They didn't.

"Okay, we all know this is not a normal situation here, so for the next hour or so, leave the bullshit at the door."

Wang lifted his head from its half-bowed position and dropped most of his Asian act.

"I'll hear you out but reserve the right to step left of whatever this is."

"Fair enough. Check the menu, fellas, and order some food, and whatever else you want to drink. I don't want any interruptions once I start."

Shaw watched each man give the waitress his order. Impelliteri couldn't resist flirting. Sperling, looking more like a prep-school teacher than a cop in his button-down white shirt and khaki pants, didn't seem interested in either the food or the waitress. Mason, dressed in the tried-and-true detective uniform of a sports jacket, tie, and slacks, displayed his usual politeness and attention to detail. He looked at the menu with his reading glasses propped on the end of his broad nose, asked the waitress a couple of questions about the menu, and ordered a sizable amount for his sizable appetite.

Wang didn't ask any questions but made two specific requests about how his hamburger should be prepared.

Shaw gave his order last and asked the waitress to keep everybody's glass full so they wouldn't have to bother calling for her. Once the waitress left the drab back room, Shaw addressed the others.

"All right," Shaw said, "I'll speak for myself. I'm about to get kicked off the force, lose my pension, and have Albert J. DeLuca do whatever he can to make my retirement years painful."

Mason asked, "What happened?"

"Past sins, plus a run-in I had while on restricted duty."

Mason asked quietly, "You shoot somebody?"

"No. If you want the gory details, Mase, I'll give them to you when I have time. Let's just say the chief of D has me where he wants me."

Impelliteri chimed in, "Sorry for your troubles, Shaw, but why should we give a shit?"

"Because, according to DeLuca, all of you are in similar situations. Your names are on a shit list he told me to recruit from. He threw me a lifeline. Told me he'd give me a chance to redeem myself. He's throwing you guys the same line. If you don't think you need it, I'd advise you to leave now."

Mason said, "What's the deal, Shaw?"

"The deal is, if we do his dirty work, we get a clean slate. All sins forgiven. If we don't, he shits on us from a very high place. Needless to say, what he wants done before he extends us absolution is not going to be easy to deliver. Still interested?"

Impelliteri said, "It ain't just what he wants us to do, which I figure you'll tell us. It's also who we do it with. I take it we aren't the most respectable cops on the force."

Shaw said, "All right, let's just get it out on the table. Then you guys can decide if you're in or out. Since you came last, we'll start with you, Walter."

Wang shrugged and said, "Fine."

"Walter is one of the department's resident computer geniuses. He works in Operations. Personnel Division, right?"

"Right."

"You pulled a scam that shows me you know your way around the bureaucracy. What buttons to push where. What form you need for what. How to access personnel records, among other things. According to DeLuca's file, Officer Wang used his talents and NYPD records to sell a shitload of disability and life insurance to fellow police officers."

Wang interrupted, "Which, by the way, is something each of you should look into. I've figured out a very easy method to finance the—"

"Hey!"

Wang stopped. Shaw glared at him for a second.

Mason asked, "So what's so bad about that? You could survive that."

Shaw said, "Not if you fiddled the payments and skimmed extra commissions from the premiums."

"They'll never prove that."

Shaw responded, "Maybe. I don't care. DeLuca's file says you're looking at the possibility of criminal, civil, and departmental prosecution. But, as you say, maybe DeLuca can't prove it. At the very least, you won't be a cop for much longer."

"Big deal," said Wang.

"Apparently, you must be considering this offer, since you're still here."

Wang said, "Tell me what I'm going to have to do? Presumably, fill the role of the smart Asian geek nerd."

Shaw said, "Call it whatever the hell you want. If you sign on, I want you to be our operations manager. If we need equipment, you get it. If we need computer searches, you do them. Requisitions, liaison with other elements of the department, out-of-state databases, whatever we need, you're the man. Bottom line, you're our inside guy. You work the system. Your contact is one of DeLuca's people, a lieutenant named Conklin. You organize it, find it, arrange it, get it. If you get jammed up, work it through this guy Conklin. That's it."

"Doesn't sound too tough."

"I don't think it will be. For you. Plus, one other thing."

"What's that?"

"I want you to keep the activity reports for us. You write our fives based on what I give you. I want a tight paper trail covering all our asses. We'll give you enough information to pull something together, but you make up the rest. I don't trust DeLuca. This gets shitty, and it will, nobody is going to cover for us. I want a record that says what we want it to say."

"How's your English?" Impelliteri asked.

Wang answered, "Fuck English. I speak Police as good as anybody."

"Fine," said Impelliteri, "but listen, Kung Fu, just because you write it don't mean I ain't gonna read 'em. Don't fuck me up if I'm in on this."

Mason broke in. "That goes for me, too. Nobody files a five for me until I see it."

Wang shrugged. "Whatever."

Shaw nodded toward Impelliteri.

"Detective Impelliteri is from the Seven-Five out in East New York. He works homicide there. I'm sure you have a full plate since East New York usually has the most murders in the city. Homicides are part of the problem that we'll be dealing with, so I figured Tony – is it Tony or Anthony?"

"Either one."

"I figure Anthony will be helpful to us. His arrest record indicates he's good at what he does. Homicides are a big part of this situation. I need you to investigate with the maximum amount of efficiency."

Wang said, "What did Anthony do to deserve this fucked up detail, Shaw?"

Shaw said, "Detective Impelliteri has a major problem."

"What's that?" Mason asked.

"A sexual harassment charge filed by a female officer."

"How bad can that be?" said Wang.

"There's more," Shaw said. "Turns out, the female officer is the wife of a deputy inspector."

"Oh Lord," said Mason.

Impelliteri spoke up. "You assholes don't know anything. You have no idea the shit that's going on. That lady didn't get sexually harassed. She and her dumbass husband know it. I banged her three times a week for over a month, and then her damn husband found out about it. He's the one who forced her into that sexual harassment thing so he could save face and get revenge on me. He keeps up this shit, he's going to find his head in his fucking lap."

Mason said, "Then DeLuca will have you for murdering a deputy inspector. That don't sound like a plan."

"My lawyer will beat this bogus harassment shit. C'mon, she got harassed for over a month? It's bullshit."

Shaw commented, "I'm sure you know that doesn't matter, Detective. You admit to consensual sex with a superior officer's wife, and DeLuca will have Commissioner Burton fire your ass in about ten seconds. On the other hand, if you keep your mouth shut and take the harassment charge, it's over, too. So, either way, you're screwed."

Impelliteri sneered. "And DeLuca can wave a magic wand and make it all go away?"

"If he wants to, without a doubt," said Mason. "Without a shadow of a doubt."

Impelliteri turned to Mason and said, "I hope you're right. So what's your deal? Why is your ass in a sling? You must have fucked up pretty bad. Black cops really have to fuck up to get nailed."

Mason's face turned hard. "Mind your manners, son. You don't know me well enough to talk to me like that."

"All right, all right. No offense. All I'm saying is, a guy your age and seniority, the force being run by a black commissioner, how bad could it be for you?"

"You got a problem with there being a black commissioner?"

"Not really," answered Impelliteri. "You still haven't answered my question. What'd you do?"

"Mason doesn't have a deal," Shaw said. "He's not in danger of getting thrown out like the rest of us. In fact, his name wasn't even on DeLuca's list. Mason and I worked as partners a while back. He got caught in the middle of an operation that I fucked up. He ended up being associated with a disaster he didn't create. He became damaged goods. He's still riding a desk. I know it's driving him nuts." Shaw turned to Mason, "I figured I owed you a shot to make that mess go away, Mase. It's your call if you want to take it."

"What happened?" asked Impelliteri.

Shaw told him, "Never mind." He turned to Mason. "Like I said, it's your choice, but we could use you. Finding guys is part of what we have to do, and you're about the best at that out of anybody I know."

Mason nodded as if he understood, but he didn't tell Shaw he would accept the opportunity.

Impelliteri interrupted. "All right, so Detective Mason here is squeaky clean, huh? Fine. We're the scumbags. But just for the record, that deputy inspector's wife was a lousy piece of ass. Unless she was drunk. Then she could be lots of fun for the ten or fifteen minutes before she passed out."

Sperling finally spoke up. "Thank you for sharing that with us, Detective Impelliteri. I think that should cover it."

"No problem. Speaking of sharing, it's your turn."

"What do you want to know?"

Shaw spoke first.

"Detective Sperling is a specialist formerly with the Emergency Services Unit. Started out in the old Neighborhood Stabilization Units, then Narcotics, then a stint with a Federal Task Force. Trained at Quantico. I assume that's when you got deeper into weapons. Now assigned to the shooting range in the Bronx."

"Sounds like Siberia," Impelliteri said.

Sperling said, "It is. I'm not interested in who did what to get in trouble with DeLuca. I think it's irrelevant. And I don't believe it's anybody's business what I did or didn't do. What I want to find out is exactly what we have to do to get out of it."

Wang said, "He's right. What's the story, Shaw?"

"I can't tell you exactly what we'll have to do. We won't know until we get into it. But I can tell you what's going on."

The food came. Shaw waited until everyone had their plates in front of them and started talking. He kept talking throughout the meal, telling them about New Lots Apartments, the Blue-Tops, the Muslims, and the police commissioner's daughter. And how the Muslims had responded to Archie Reynold's ambush in The Pit.

When he got to the part about Rachman's revenge, Loyd Shaw hesitated. He finished the last finger of Irish in his glass and downed the dregs of the Bass Ale. The waiting made his audience restless.

Orestes Mason finally asked, "So what did they do?"

"I don't know all the details. Apparently, it made the headlines today. I just got back in town."

Anthony Impelliteri spoke up. "That body shop thing in Brownsville. That was those Muslims?"

"Yeah."

"Christ," said Impelliteri. "That was a fucking mess. What'd they do, drive 'em into that place and burn them up?"

"Basically. Read the reports. I don't want to go into it."

"How many died?" asked Mason.

"Nine altogether. Seven in the body shop, plus two they beat to death and left in a park across the apartment complex to send a message."

Impelliteri added, "Sounds like those boys don't play around."

Mason wiped his broad face. "Lord Almighty."

James Sperling asked in a tone devoid of emotion, "And what are the five of us supposed to do about this insanity?"

"Stop it," said Shaw. "Shut it down. Both sides. And make sure nothing happens to the commissioner's daughter."

"Christ," said Impelliteri. "I might take my chances with the deputy inspector and that bitch wife of his."

Without warning, Sperling announced, "I'm in."

Impelliteri looked at him, "That was quick. What, you got some sort of death wish?"

"No."

Shaw turned to Mason. "What about it, Mase? You want in?"

Mason hesitated then answered, "I'm in unless I hear some crazy scheme you got cooked up."

"And you, Walter? You with us?"

"Didn't I already say yes."

"Fucking aye right, Fu Manchu, what have you got to lose? Doesn't sound like you're going to be anywhere you can get shot at."

Wang didn't bother to respond to Impelliteri.

Shaw said, "All right, Anthony, that leaves you. In or out?"

Impelliteri shrugged, "Fuck it. Why spoil the party? I'm in."

Shaw pushed on.

"All right, that's settled. Now, getting back to Mason's question about how we should do this. Obviously, I don't have all the answers. I'm sure things will change once we get into it. Right now, I want to do three things. See what the hell the deal is with the police commissioner's daughter. Then shut down the bullshit Muslim security operation. Probably do that through the real estate management company. Last, dismantle the crack gang."

Sperling asked, "How're you going to make the Blue-Tops gang disappear?"

"Take out the leaders, the rest will disappear. Or at least go fight with somebody else and sell their drugs some other place. We start with Archie Reynolds. He's the top dog. There's a second in charge, two managers, a couple of enforcer types. We take them out, the rest should fold."

Mason said, "I don't think we'll have to worry about the commissioner's daughter. Intelligence Division takes care of security for his family. Probably got a squad of three around her twenty-four-seven. Plus uniforms from the precinct. I don't know about the Muslims and the crack gang. You're looking at some violent people."

"I didn't say it would be easy. I'm just laying out my rough plan."

Shaw looked around the room to see if anybody had any comments or questions. There were none.

"Okay, good. Next step —we meet tomorrow at the Seven-Three out in Brownsville. I'll give everybody specific assignments. It's on East New York Avenue."

Mason asked, "That's the new Seven-Three precinct house, right?"

"Yeah. We have an office there we can work out of."

Shaw reached beneath his chair and picked up four manila folders. He slid one of the folders to each of the others.

"These files give you more background on the Blue-Tops gang and the real estate management company. Let's meet at noon tomorrow. That should give you all time to read this file and get at least one night's good sleep before we start."

Shaw turned to Wang.

"Walter, in that report, you'll find four names, including Archie Reynolds. According to the information DeLuca got from Gangs, those are the four top guys in this Blue-Tops outfit."

Impelliteri said, "The four top Blue-Tops?"

"Exactly."

"Sounds like a fucking singing group."

"I didn't name them, Anthony. Anyhow, Walter..."

"Yes."

"Before you come out to Brownsville tomorrow, I want you to stop off at Central Records and check for any outstanding warrants on those four. If you find any, get copies of them."

Mason asked, "You gonna use the warrants squads to serve 'em?"

"No. We keep control. The fewer people know about what we're doing, the better."

"I hear ya."

"Also, Walter..."

Wang seemed to have drifted off into his own thoughts.

"Walter."

"Yes?"

"Inside your packet is a list of supplies. I want two unmarked cars in good shape. I want shotguns, vests, cellular phones, portable radios, scanners for each of us. And a few other things I've listed."

Impelliteri said, "Yeah, how about a tank with a flame-thrower?"

Shaw ignored Impelliteri and said to Wang, "Organize it, find out where we can get everything. Then let Conklin know and find out when he can procure everything for us. Other than him, we keep this to ourselves."

Wang looked at Shaw's list.

"It's not going to be easy to find all this."

"If it were easy, I wouldn't need you."

"I'll see what I can do. I know some guys at Emergency Services who find most of this for us."

"Don't see what you can do. Do it. Okay? I'm not going to wait for DeLuca's guy Conklin to locate everything."

"Okay."

"Good. Next, what guns are you all using?"

"Glock," said Impelliteri.

"Seventeen?"

"Yeah. I carry a nineteen for a backup."

"Sig," said Mason. "I don't carry a backup."

"Thirty-eight. Revolver," said Walter. "No backup."

"Okay, before you all go, have a quick conversation with Detective Sperling to make sure your shit is up to par. And I want everybody to carry a backup. Wang, Mason, fill out forms tomorrow. Make it simple. Just get another of the same gun you use now. Sperling, can you get weapons for them quickly?"

"If I have the right paper."

Mason said, "Hell, man, those forty-nines take weeks, months."

"Not for us, Mase," said Shaw. "Walter, work that one through Conklin, too. Sperling, get the weapons as soon as Walter gives you the approvals."

The dinner had reached the coffee stage. Impelliteri drank regular with Sambuca. Shaw had a Grand Marnier with black, decaffeinated coffee, and Mason, Remy. Sperling stuck with just black coffee.

Mason fired up a double-corona size cigar. Impelliteri dropped a pack of Marlboro Reds on the table and lit up. Shaw bummed one from him, wishing he had a decent cigar, knowing that whatever Mason smoked wasn't.

Nobody bothered with after-dinner small talk. No one had any interest in being cordial, and all of them already had too much to do.

Impelliteri tossed down his Sambuca. He said, "See ya," and left.

After a quick discussion about firearms with Mason and Wang, Sperling left without saying anything.

Shaw told Wang to get some sleep, and he took off.

The waitress looked in and brought Shaw and Mason one more round and the bill. Shaw knew the night wasn't over yet.

Mason finished his first snifter of Remy and waited for the second. He seemed just as sober as when he had entered the restaurant. Shaw was feeling the liquor but liking it. He rolled a little of the Grand Marnier around his snifter and took a sip, waiting for Mason to start in on him. It didn't take long.

"You realize how crazy this thing is, don't you, Loyd?"

Shaw shrugged and said, "It is what it is."

"What the hell does that mean?"

"I don't know. Isn't that what you say in a situation like this?"

"All right, between us, Loyd, what's so important we got to go out there and risk our necks for it? End up killin' people for it?"

"Nobody said anything about killing anybody."

"What you think is gonna happen when we go up against those maniacs? The drug gangs out there are the worst of the worst. Most of them knuckleheads don't expect to ever see thirty. Hell, twenty-five. Even if they know you're a cop, they'll shoot you as soon as look at you. You think there's any way we can get out of this without killing somebody?"

"Maybe. Look, Mase, I don't know where all the pressure is coming from. But the goddamn chief of D doesn't pull a move like putting together a team of fuckups without a reason. How much pressure you think the commissioner is putting on this with his daughter being involved?"

"That's it? The commissioner's daughter?"

"A good part of it. There's the money, too. You know how much money is at stake here?"

"How much?"

"Millions. Before I came here, I called a friend of mine works in NYCHA—"

"This a public project?"

"No. It's private. Private companies are eager to take over public housing. Especially this complex. The place got built with HUD money. The original group couldn't run it. Rents went down. The place went in the shithole. HUD foreclosed. They ate most of the loss. My friend figures the bank just about gave the place away. There's no debt. This company that took it over, Arbor Realty, if they clean it up and fill it with people getting subsidies, the rents are subsidized so there's little risk. The usual overhead is much lower without a big mortgage underlying it. Mase, they stand to make millions. That much money at stake, who knows what kind of money is being promised in campaign contributions? Not to mention DeLuca also gave me a pretty decent version of the thin-blue-line speech. Maybe he really believes that. Whatever the reasons, the powers that be want this done. If that helps us get out of the shit, so much the better."

Mason nodded, sipped his cognac, and puffed on his cigar.

"So what you think of this crew of yours?"

"You should have seen the others on that list. Impelliteri seems like a wild man, but he could be just what we need. Whatever is going on with Sperling, he knows more about firearms than the rest of us put together, and his record says he knows how to shoot."

"Shooting at a target is one thing. Shooting at armed bad guys is a whole 'nother deal."

"I know."

Mason said, "What about Wang? That boy looks like he's in another world."

"Yeah, but he could be just what we need. Someone to handle the bureaucracy, get us supplied. You know the department runs on paper. Always has."

"I suppose."

Shaw asked, "Did you tell Muriel about this?"

"No way. She'll start buggin' me to turn in my papers and go find that house in South Carolina she wants."

"So why don't you?"

Instead of answering, Mason asked, "Is what you told them really the plan?"

"At the moment."

"If we find these crack guys, how long you think we can keep them off the street even if there are old warrants out on them?"

"Hey, they're young black men. Locking up young black men for long sentences isn't a problem in this city. Most of 'em I'm sure have records. Most of 'em are probably already predicate felons on probation. We get them with drugs or parole violations or violating any terms, they go away for a long time. And if any ADAs have a problem with our arrests, I'm counting on DeLuca to grease the path with the Brooklyn District Attorney's office."

Mason shook his head. "I don't know. Five guys against how many? And with the commissioner's daughter in the middle of it?"

"Hey, Mase, I'm just going step-by-step on this. I got my ass in a ringer, and DeLuca's turning the fucking crank. He gives me a shot at retiring with a shred of dignity and my pension. I don't think I'll make it with Jane. I'm on my own here.

"I realize I'm working with a bunch of ringers. I know I'm going up against some vicious criminals in Brownsville who'll shoot me in the face without even breathing heavy. Not to mention what these Muslim guys are capable of doing. From what I can tell, they're worse than the crack gang. The word is they're ex-cons who got the faith in prisons all around the state. They killed nine guys in one morning, Mase. Beat two of them to death up close and personal. You think I want to walk into this shit storm? If you want out, I understand. Completely. Like I said, I thought I'd give you a shot. I couldn't not give you the option, Mase. It's up to you."

Mason took a long pull off his cigar. He looked at Shaw and said. "I wish it was, brother."

"What was?"

"My call. It ain't."

"What do you mean, Mase?"

"DeLuca ain't leaving anything up to chance."

"What do you mean?"

"You went off his list. I guess you told his guy Conklin about it."

"Yeah. Told him there wasn't anybody on DeLuca's list as good as you."

"Yeah, well, Conklin obviously checked with DeLuca to make sure it was all right. Conklin didn't call me, DeLuca called me himself. Said I had to step up. Didn't ask me, *told* me. Said I'm supposed to watch you. Make sure you don't go off like last time. Said I'm the only one you'd listen to."

Shaw looked at Mason and shook his head. "I should have figured that. What a prick."

"Yeah. Workin' all the angles."

"Shit."

Shaw drained his snifter. He looked at Mason and said, "You still don't have to do it. Listen to Muriel."

Mason looked straight at Shaw. "You really think I can tell the chief of D no? All this talk about what's he got on me and how much he knows and what do we have to do – it's all bs. Everybody sitting here knows they gonna do what the man wants. Nobody wants to deal with the consequences of *not* doing it."

Mason pointed an extra-large finger at Shaw.

"And the other side is obvious, too, Loyd. Everybody wants the juice they gonna get if the chief of detectives owes 'em. Guarantee you, they all thinkin' about gettin' upped in rank and pay."

"I suppose."

"Either way, the chief of D wins."

"What do you mean?"

"You know what I mean."

"I do?"

"Yeah, you do. You know damn well how DeLuca has this figured. He's got a big problem out there. He throws you and the rest of us into it, maybe we stop it sooner than it would be otherwise. He wins. Maybe we don't stop it. He tosses us out. Maybe we get shot up and disappear from his police force. He don't have to do a damn thing. We're gone. What the hell has he got to lose?"

"Nothing."

"Right," said Mason. "And what do we have to lose? Chances are, everything. And if we survive, we end up with nightmares for the rest of our lives. How long it take you to stop thinking and dreaming about the last thing?"

"The dreams are almost gone. I still think about it and get sick. If I'm not really goddamn careful, I sink into obsessive thinking about it that can go on for days. Shrink says that's a sign of depression."

"They give you drugs for it?"

"At first. The stuff didn't seem to do much. Doctor kept telling me it could take time before they kicked in. I said the hell with that. The goddamn stuff interfered with my drinking, too. What about you?"

"God and Muriel helped me out of it more than anything. That and time. I don't want to go through anything like that again, Loyd."

"You think I do?"

Mason sat back and finished his drink. Shaw started to feel the effects of the booze and the late hour.

"We're in for a war, Mase."

"I expect so."

"Well, war has its spoils. We come out of this alive, I'm going to make sure we get all our veteran's benefits, you know what I mean?"

"Oh yeah, how are you going to do that?"

"You know how, Mase."

"How?"

"We don't just have to beat the killers in Brownsville. We have to beat The Shark, too."

CHAPTER 22

By the time Loyd Shaw shook Orestes Mason's hand and walked out of the restaurant, he was grateful that his apartment was only three blocks away but uneasy at the realization that Jane would be home and certainly be annoyed at him for coming in so late, once again smelling of whiskey and cigars.

Ah, yes, thought Shaw, can't upset the big breadwinner. The big-time lawyer who made it to the big law firm despite all the odds. Made it the hard way. Yeah, Jane made it all right. Not like you, asshole.

Thinking about his wife, thinking about going home, an image popped into Shaw's mind, a picture of him standing at his front door, sticking his key into the lock and discovering that it no longer turned. He supposed that someday it might come to that. He believed that Jane had it in her to change the locks on him.

It was not the kind of thing he wanted to imagine while he walked through the streets tired, angry, tense, and half-drunk on Irish whiskey.

He suddenly had a nearly overwhelming urge to keep on drinking. He pictured it, sitting at some dive bar, drinking by himself, brooding about the mess he was in.

He turned into a deli on Hudson Street and bought a pack of Marlboros, lit one up, and took a deep drag. It tasted just as good as he wanted it to.

Shaw knew every bar in the neighborhood. He thought about an old Irish joint within walking distance and even thought about which bar stool he would occupy, seeing himself having two, maybe three more drinks, then saying screw you to all of them, getting in his car and driving all night, zooming along nearly empty early morning highways all the way up to his barn studio. Drive until he sobered up; then sleep with the phone turned off for as long as he wanted; then, get up and paint red paintings for as long as it took to lose himself in the color, the texture, the smell of acrylic paint.

He pictured it all as he walked along the night-filled streets of the city. But instead of a bar, Shaw found himself standing outside his front door, turning familiar keys in familiar locks that still opened for him.

He stepped into the loft apartment and quietly closed the door behind him. Shaw knew that sound. He knew how loudly the hinges squeaked and how much the wood floors creaked, no matter how quietly he tried to move. And he knew there was no way he could keep the sounds from waking Jane. She slept too lightly.

When Shaw climbed into bed, she kept her back turned to him as she asked, "Are you in trouble?"

Although Jane's question revealed her usual perceptiveness, the question didn't carry her usual accusatory tone.

"Yeah. Probably."

"Probably?"

"Well, definitely, but I've got a way I can work it out."

"Really."

Skepticism had leaked in. With one word, the slight glimmer of warmth and concern she had conveyed disappeared.

Shaw answered, "Yeah. Really. One way or another."

Jane sensed something in his tone. Without judgment or reproach, she said, "Okay."

And, at that particular moment, some part of the Jane that Loyd Shaw had once loved emerged. Shaw knew it would not last, and he knew that would be more his fault than hers. He would be gone long periods without explanation. She would be hurt. He would be angry, short, tense, unable to deal with her. Shaw knew it would soon get bad. But for that one brief moment, her "okay" felt like a sort of blanket absolution. Like the kind priests give to assembled troops before they run off to get shot. No recitation of specific sins required. No queries as to the exact level of guilt. No acts of contrition needed.

She simply said, "Okay." And that was it.

CHAPTER 23

SHAW SLEPT FITFULLY, WAITING FOR THE FIRST CITY LIGHT TO LEAK under his window shade. He wanted to be up, to begin facing what lay before him, but he waited until Jane left the apartment. She was always up and out early.

He went through his morning routine. Trying to shake off the loneliness that suddenly surrounded him, and the slight achy hangover from too much liquor the night before. He stared in the mirror, razor in hand, looking past his face into the crevices around his mouth, examining the crow's feet around his bloodshot eyes. Shaw knew that what he would do this day and the next day and the next until it was done would change him. Even though Shaw had come to resent everything the job had taken out of his life, he had tried to follow the rules. But now, what he was about to do in Brownsville would change all that. The irony stung him. To stay on the job until he could leave with what he had earned over twenty years, he and his crew of outcasts would have to work like outlaws. The regular precinct detectives assigned to the case would proceed in their customary, plodding fashion, according to the rules. Following procedure. Shaw and his men wouldn't even think about the rules. They would go after everybody at once, any way they could, as fast and hard as they could.

Time to start. Shaw knew where. With the commissioner's daughter, Justine Burton.

Shaw had an appointment to meet her at nine o'clock at her community center. Since the department's cars were going to be sent to the Seven-Three, and Shaw had no intention of driving his own car to Brownsville, he took the subway. He figured it would also give him a chance to walk the neighborhood a little.

According to the street and subway maps he'd checked, the New Lots subway station was closest to Justine's community center. About four blocks away. So Shaw rode the A train uptown to Fourteenth Street, a multilevel hub where several train lines interconnected and the Brooklyn L train terminated. He walked down the grimy concrete stairs to the lower platform and stepped into the waiting L train.

After a few minutes' wait, the train lurched once and pulled out, sliding across Manhattan, rumbling under the East River, and then finally up into the early morning light of Brooklyn.

The train traveled against the morning commute of passengers into Manhattan, so Shaw's subway car wasn't very crowded, but with each successive stop in Brooklyn, the passengers became less white, less Manhattan. More black, more Brooklyn.

Until that morning, April in New York had felt more like March, as if the city were unable to leave behind a winter that had buried it in snow and ice. But today, the first trace of warm air floated into the city.

As the L train creaked along the elevated tracks, Shaw suddenly spotted a massive bank of fog off to the north. Fog? For a moment, he assumed he must be near water. Couldn't be, he told himself. He was traveling right through the center of the borough. What the hell is this fog doing here? His already unsettled state became more unsettled and disoriented.

As the train rounded a bend, he peered deeper into the mist and finally saw what was causing the strange phenomenon. They were passing a large tract of open land covered in the remnants of snow and ice still remaining from a series of winter storms. The warm air passing over the cold ground had created the unsettling bank of fog.

But what was this open tract of land in the middle of Brooklyn? Shaw knew he wasn't near Prospect Park. As the cloud bank thinned out a little, he saw a scene out of a Dracula movie. The open land was a cemetery. Actually, not just one cemetery but a jumble of interconnected cemeteries: Cemetery of the Evergreens, Trinity Cemetery, Mount Judah Cemetery, Salem Field Cemetery, and on and on. There seemed to be a million old graves, headstones, and mausoleums in there. Crypts from way back. Shaw began to picture heaps of dead bones rotting in the ground under a cold blanket of acid fog. Death was the last thing he wanted to be reminded of that morning. He knew black men were killing each other in New Lots. Shooting, beating, burning each other. But he hadn't let the images fill his mind. Up to that point, it had all been told to him, or he had read about it in DeLuca's reports. Somehow the acres of graves acted as a catalyst, triggering a dread in Shaw. He asked himself if it was a fear of dying or killing. Or both.

If the cemeteries were the final resting place of the dead, Brownsville seemed like the last stop for the living. As Shaw's train creaked along heading into Brownsville, his view from the elevated track revealed a neighborhood in which nothing seemed new or alive or vibrant. No new cars, no new buildings, no new streets. Even the paint on signs and stoplights seemed old. And what wasn't old was dead or dying. Buildings abandoned, left to fall into ruin. Others simply burned out and left to crumble. There were small pockets of life amidst the ruins. A food store, a car repair shop, a used furniture store, all poor neighborhood businesses. And everything in between was old, ruined, dead space.

The subway pulled into the New Lots station. Shaw stepped out, alone, onto the elevated platform. Welcome to Brownsville. Even the air seemed dead.

And it didn't take long for his discomfort to increase. From the elevated tracks, he could see the burned-out body shop. It looked like an open black sore back in the alley that ran parallel to the elevated tracks. The westbound train on the other side of the tracks screeched into the station, sounding like a scream, but this time it seemed to Shaw as if he heard the screams of burning men. Despite the warm air, Shaw felt a shiver run from the back of his neck down his back. He rolled his shoulders and shook his head, trying to banish the feelings that had suddenly gripped him.

"Shit," he muttered to himself.

He moved forward, heading for the exit. Trying to just get on with it. He didn't get far. The moment he reached the top of the stairwell leading down to street level, he saw an angry face at the bottom step turn toward him. One of the neighborhood homeboys staking out the station for marks.

He glared at Shaw the entire time Shaw walked down the steps. Shaw knew that the young man was deciding whether or not to make a move on him. A fast mugging, and he might have what he needed for the day.

After his episode with the gangsta rap boys on Tilden Avenue, Shaw was in no mood to mix it up again with a young black man. He ignored him, but when Shaw stepped through the turnstile and into the station, there were three more angry young black men just like the one he had passed. They stood inside the station house, which was so old, beat up, dirty, and neglected that the only thing new was the bullet-proof booth that housed the token clerk. And even that was covered in graffiti.

Now the entire situation became clear. The first one back in the stairwell was the lookout. He would pick the mark, follow him into the station, and give a sign to the others. They'd either take him in the station or follow him out onto the street.

Shaw felt a sickening mix of anger and fear seep into him. Here we go again, he thought. Fuck it. Look right at them. Right the fuck at them.

There were three of them clustered in the station wearing puffed-up down jackets, baggy clothes, hoods, heavy boots, and over-priced basketball shoes. They seemed to Shaw more like a three-headed beast than three young men.

Shaw didn't try to look tough or angry. But he did concentrate on looking right at them, carefully picking out their faces, their eyes. He kept his expression neutral, not challenging them so they would have to go for him as a matter of pride. No, just look at them, Shaw told himself. Even though he could feel his heart pounding, just look at them so they know you're not to be played with. Don't even think about walking by quietly with your head down, Shaw told himself. Think about the Glock on your hip and the backup under your left armpit. Think about drawing it quickly, pulling back the slide, and pointing it. Don't think about them.

They glared at Shaw, not wanting to lose the opportunity to terrify him, even if they decided not to mug him. They let Shaw pass. Better to pick somebody easier.

Shaw pushed open the swinging door, noting that the glass had been bashed out, and stepped onto the sidewalk.

Outside wasn't much better than inside the subway station. Shaw felt as if he'd stepped out into an abandoned no-man's-land in the middle of a war zone. He stood in the dim morning light under the elevated train viaduct looking to his right and left, trying to get some sense of where he stood. There was nothing much to see. No people, no busy commuters rushing to work, no street signs. Nothing but a few one- and two-story buildings that might or might not have been unoccupied, along with boarded-up buildings, burned-out buildings, and rubble-strewn empty lots.

Within his range of vision, only two places seemed to be in use. On a short block to his right stood a street-corner bodega. To Shaw's left, he could see a newsstand-candy store. So where the hell was New Lots Apartments? Four stories, five buildings, hundreds of people?

Shaw's memory of the map he'd studied told him New Lots Apartments was to his left, so he set off in that direction, hoping he was heading toward the complex. That meant walking past the newsstand-candy store where another group of neighborhood toughs had gathered.

Shaw thought about the constitutional right to assembly. They had that right, didn't they? But they weren't assembling for morning prayers or peaceful protest, or to discuss the events of the world. They were just waiting. Hanging out. And now they had something to do – check out the white man and give him a hard time.

Shaw wondered the difference it would make if he were black, a person who lived in this neighborhood. He thought, yeah, it'd make a difference. At least he wouldn't be looking around for street signs that weren't there. If he lived in this neighborhood, at least he'd know where the hell he was.

The usual litany of silent curses filled Shaw's head. He knew standing under the subway tracks looking lost wasn't going to make getting through this gauntlet any easier. He stomped off toward the newsstand, heading for the bad boys hanging out.

As he walked toward the intersection, Shaw finally spotted the first sign of normal life in the neighborhood. A gypsy cab turned toward him and headed for the station entrance. The cab stopped, and Shaw watched an older man, his wife, and their adult daughter step out of the car. They were black, neatly dressed, obviously on their way to work. And obviously experienced enough to know that walking to the subway was not a good idea.

So what the hell am I walking around for? Shaw asked himself. Because you've come to save guys like the ones ready to jump you from killing themselves.

Shaw didn't make it even halfway to the intersection before five pairs of eyes were on him. By the time he came parallel to the newsstand-candy store on the opposite side of the street, one of the homeboys had already peeled away from the group, falling in behind him.

Shaw unzipped his leather jacket so that it would be easier to reach the Glock. Christ, he thought, this is ridiculous. I've been here five minutes and I'm ready to pull my gun for the second time.

He heard the footsteps trailing him. He told himself, come on, this guy knows you're a cop. He has to know. Why the hell is he doing this? And then Shaw imagined the other four falling in behind him. And Shaw pictured them swarming him. And one of them getting his gun. And not being able to get to his backup before one of them punched his face or kicked his head. And if he did get his weapon, then what? A close-range shootout on the street?

No way. Shaw suddenly turned around, and the guy behind him stopped short. He was way too close to Shaw. Less than six feet behind.

Shaw figured him for no more than sixteen. A teenager, old enough to intimidate, too young to know better. Shaw's sudden move surprised the kid, but he lifted his chin and looked at Shaw with his version of a badass stare. He was dressed homeboy style: baggy blue jeans, unlaced sneakers, a black leather coat. Everything so big on him, he seemed like his clothes belonged to someone else, his head down inside the high collar of his jacket, half-hidden, feral.

Shaw took a step toward him and pointed a finger at the boy. "Get the fuck away from me. I'm a cop. You don't want anything to do with me."

The bad-ass glare flickered a moment, then came back, not quite so bad.

Shaw didn't wait for an answer. He didn't want one. He turned and walked away, listening for any sudden movement behind him, listening for the footsteps to start up after him. But he heard nothing. He had won.

The gypsy cab driver who had let the family off at the subway station drove back in Shaw's direction and passed him. The driver looked at Shaw, waiting for Shaw to wave him down because he knew it was crazy for a white man to be walking alone in this Brownsville neighborhood. But Shaw waved him off. Fuck that, nobody's driving me off. Not their way, not your way, buddy.

Shaw reached the corner and finally saw a street sign. He'd been walking on Van Sinderen Avenue. The cross street was Hegeman. Farther up Van Sinderen, a ghetto supermarket slumped in the middle of the block. Shaw caught sight of a woman with three young children exiting the supermarket. The mother carried two brown bags of groceries. The oldest child, a boy about six, carried a third bag. His two little sisters, three and four, tagged behind the mother.

Shaw estimated the mother couldn't have been more than twenty-five years old. He watched the young woman head in his direction. Probably toward New Lots, since there wasn't much else around him.

Shaw crossed the street diagonally, and there it was, sitting in the middle of Brownsville like a squat red-brick fortress. No wonder the Blue-Tops had taken it over. The five buildings comprising New Lots Apartments were the only structures of any substance within sight, obviously the major enclave in the neighborhood. If you wanted to sell anything to anybody, this was the place to sell it. If a crack gang had established itself in that complex, nobody was going to get them out of there without a fight.

As Shaw approached the buildings, he saw two blue NYPD sawhorses set up in front of the gated entrance to the complex and one squad car parked out front on New Lots Avenue. Inside the blue and white sat two cops. One drank coffee. The other had his head down, studying the word jumble puzzle in the *New York Post*.

The woman and three kids with their groceries walked toward the new iron gate. The older girl ran ahead into the courtyard, defined by the five buildings that surrounded it. Shaw's eyes followed her as she met up with a group of girls about her age. He noticed dozens of kids ranging from toddlers to teenagers inside the open space between buildings. He could make out only one cluster of three mothers sitting on a bench. For a moment, New Lots seemed almost like a school. The courtyard almost like a playground.

Shaw turned right and headed for the community center. He spotted no more cops on the street. No police presence away from the front entrance. But as he came parallel with the eastern building of the complex, Shaw saw a pair of black men coming his way. They both wore black pants and combat boots. One man wore a military field jacket, the other a long, black leather overcoat. Both had full beards. Both wore Kufi skullcaps. One of them carried a radio unit. Muslim security guards. Shaw immediately felt safer. The Muslims were on the street, not sitting in a squad car.

By the time he walked to the north side of the complex and turned onto Rockaway, Shaw didn't feel so foolish about his decision to walk alone on the streets of Brownsville. In ten minutes, he had learned a great deal.

As the Caring Community Center and Shelter came into sight, Shaw quickly learned even more about the police department's priorities with regard to New Lots. Four hundred tenants got two cops sitting in a squad car. Justine Burton got five uniformed cops standing guard outside her center, on their feet on the street; plus two squad cars parked at the far end of the block with more cops inside; and an unmarked car parked in front of the center occupied by three detectives from Intelligence, the commissioner's personal security people. Blue sawhorses extended along the entire length of the four prefab trailers that comprised the center.

Shaw flashed his ID wallet and shield at the cop standing outside the front door to the center. The policeman checked the credentials more carefully than Shaw expected he would, then stepped aside. Yet another officer standing inside opened a second door after Shaw displayed his ID.

Shaw started to reformulate the goal of his meeting. He had come to convince the commissioner's daughter to get out of the neighborhood until the troubles were resolved. But now, he thought, this is probably one of the safest spots in the city right now.

Inside the center, quiet reigned. Shaw checked his watch. Three minutes to nine. Nobody was around to give directions, so he walked down the same corridor through which Rachman Abdul X had chased Archie Reynolds, checking out offices as he passed them. In two of them he saw sleeping bodies laid across plastic chairs, all women and children. He wondered why they didn't just sleep on the floor, and the answer came to him quickly. Something other than women and children might be using the floor.

Shaw reached the waiting area. A mother and three young children were just waking up out there. The young woman was dressed in baggy jeans and a powder blue sweatshirt, but the bulky clothing still couldn't hide how thin and frail she had become. Her hair needed combing. Her skin looked sallow and ashen. The kids seemed normal enough. Shaw estimated they were about three, four, and six. All boys, all dressed in jeans and t-shirts, still sleepy and a little cranky. Their ordinary aspect seemed to heighten their mother's plight. Shaw felt she might as well have had a sign on her that said, LOST IT ALL TO CRACK. She seemed embarrassed to have her plight be witnessed by Shaw. He tried to act as if it were completely normal that a young woman with three kids began her day waking up on plastic chairs in a homeless shelter.

An intake worker sat at a battered desk in the waiting area. Despite the early hour, the young woman looked bright and alert, her hair pulled back into a tight bun, her neat clothes complementing her trim body. Shaw had the impression this was her first job. And here she was, ready for work, even though men with guns had recently invaded this space. Good for you, thought Shaw. Don't let the murderous fuck run you out.

A sheet of plywood had replaced the broken window behind her, making the area more gloomy. But, on the plus side, more conducive to sleeping, thought Shaw.

He quietly asked the young woman, "Is Ms. Burton in? I'm Detective Shaw. I have an appointment at nine."

She responded with a nod and pointed to a connecting doorway on the right. Shaw thanked her. A couple of steps past the doorway, he reached an open door on his left.

Justine Burton sat at her desk silhouetted by the morning light, speaking into her phone. Shaw had been looking forward to seeing her. He had heard that the commissioner's daughter was a beautiful woman. But Shaw decided beautiful was a lazy way to describe her. Justine Burton was beyond beautiful. Shaw stopped outside her office so he could have more time to look at her.

At first, even though she was sitting, her height and bearing reminded Shaw of an imperious, black supermodel. But he quickly discarded that first impression. There was more to Justine Burton. She was older than a model, which gave her stature beyond the physical. And her voice imparted additional status. It sounded soft, refined, and engaging, but suffused with directness and confidence.

After a few moments, she noticed Shaw in her peripheral vision, turned, and motioned him in, pointing to a chair next to her desk. Then she turned away from him to finish her phone conversation. Shaw didn't mind waiting. It gave him more time to look at her.

He started with her left hand, holding the phone receiver to her ear. In the morning sunlight, Shaw decided her hand looked like an elegant, burnished piece of renaissance sculpture. Something labored over by an artist who wanted to render one simple perfect piece that would embody beauty, grace, and femininity. The skin was smooth. The fingers long. The wrist delicate but imbued with strength. The color of her skin, a creamy light brown, seemed to absorb the glow of the early sun.

After the hand, Shaw wanted more but satisfied himself with the silhouetted profile. He could just make out the strong lines of her forehead and cheek.

Then, without any warning, no preamble to her goodbye, she ended her conversation, hung up, and turned much too quickly for Shaw to prepare himself.

"I take it you're Detective Shaw?"

Shaw simply nodded, still trying to formulate the right word for her. Stunning? No. Beautiful. He kept coming back to that simple yet inadequate word.

Shaw hoped her looks hadn't made her insufferable. Not to mention her position as the daughter of a powerful man. But even if she did turn out to be spoiled, he decided he could still enjoy himself gazing at her.

He found that he had to clear his throat before he spoke.

"Yes, Loyd Shaw, Ms. Burton. Uh, I hope I'm not coming at a bad time."

That elicited no response.

Of course, this is a bad time. Why the hell else would I be here?

A moment of awkward silence emerged. No matter how good Justine Burton looked, she obviously didn't feel very well. Now that she had turned toward Shaw, he could see a surgical dressing on the right side of her face, starting just beneath the corner of her mouth and extending down under her chin and jaw. Her shoulder and arm seemed to be causing her discomfort. She rested her right arm in her lap. She appeared tired. Also uneasy and perhaps a bit impatient.

"I'm sorry. I guess if it were a good time, I wouldn't be here."

"Right."

"Well, I have a few questions, if you don't mind."

She shifted uncomfortably in her chair. "You said it was important that I speak with you, so go ahead."

"Are you in much pain?"

"That's your first question?"

"Well, I guess so."

She frowned at him for a moment, but the frown quickly turned into a rueful smile.

"Well, yeah. My damn chin hurts. The stitches are pulling on my skin. Especially if I smile. Which I'm not doing much lately. And if I move my arm, my back and shoulder hurt like hell."

"You should put your arm in a sling."

"I don't like the way that looks."

Shaw thought, if you don't like the way a sling looks, you're going to be real happy with stitches in your face.

Shaw said, "Uh-huh."

Justine Burton didn't respond.

"So, uh, I was going to ask you a few questions that you've already been asked just to kind of warm up a little, but why don't we skip that and go right to what I want to know?"

"Yes, let's. I haven't been sleeping well lately with my injuries. I'm not in the mood to have another cop ask me if I can identify the man who came through here when you already know who he is."

"Archie Reynolds."

"Yes. Do you know him?"

"Not personally. How is it you know him?"

Justine gave Shaw a look that said, do I look stupid?

Shaw said, "Well, what do you know about him?"

"Detective Shaw, I'm not interested in Archie Reynolds. The only thing I'm concerned about is what his crack business does to the women in this neighborhood."

"And that is?"

"It damages and degrades them to a level that is hardly imaginable."

Shaw said, "And their children, too, of course."

Shaw's comment softened Justine Burton for a moment.

"Yes. You don't see it as much; the children suffer more than anybody."

"At least the adults start with a choice. Maybe not much choice, but…" Shaw stopped himself. "I'm sure you know more about all that than I do."

"I've seen more than I want to, firsthand."

"And that's why you're here?"

"That's why I'm here, Detective Shaw. These women need help. Their children need help. And I'm here to give it to them. Right now, this isn't much more than a shelter for battered women in emergency situations. But I'm interested in providing much more than that."

"Uh-huh."

"The only way these people can survive is with a full range of services – healthcare, jobs, living skills, drug counseling, rehab, shelter. It just won't work any other way."

"That seems ambitious."

"It is. But if I can make it work here, I can make it work anywhere. Anywhere in the city."

"You don't seem to have nearly enough room for all that."

"I don't."

"So…"

"So, where am I going to get it? Is that your question?"

"Yes."

"Where do you think? You seem like an intelligent person."

"For a cop?"

"I didn't say that."

"I know. But what's your opinion of them?"

"I don't like to generalize about anybody. But I will say, most of 'em don't stare at me quite as openly as you do."

"Is that because they're more polite or more worried about your father?"

"I don't know."

"Sorry."

"It's all right. I still find it flattering."

"I'm glad to hear that. You've got a fairly direct gaze yourself."

"I'm not afraid to look."

"Am I holding up okay?"

"Haven't seen anything I don't like, which is usually the case by now."

"I'm flattered."

"So now that we're both flattered, Detective, how about you get to what you really wanted to ask me about?"

"Okay. How much of New Lots Apartments are you getting for your community center?"

"Thank you for getting to the point. Who said I was getting part of New Lots for my center?"

"Well, aren't you?"

Justine paused for just a beat before she said, "Yes."

"How'd you swing it?"

"With difficulty. It's still nimby, nimby, nimby."

"Not in my backyard."

"Right. But this yard is so bad, I finally pulled it all together: the political, financial, and community support. Arbor Realty agreed to give me twenty apartments and the ground floor in Building A. And maybe additional offices somewhere in the complex."

"Uh-huh."

"What's that supposed to mean? 'Uh-huh.'"

"Things are a little more understandable now."

"Why?"

"Well, I don't suppose it's a total secret that you're going to be moving over into New Lots Apartments."

"No. It's not."

"So we can assume Archie Reynolds knows that?"

"Why?"

"Because he came in here and stuck a gun in your face and threatened you."

"What? Like he's gonna run me out of here?"

"He wouldn't have had to run you out if he'd shot you."

"So why didn't he?"

"The report I read said his gun was empty."

"Look, my impression was that people were chasing him. and he simply ran through here."

"No. He came in here intentionally. He planned it."

"How do you know?"

"His getaway car was on the street, ready and waiting. The reports said that he ran through the apartment complex across the street and came out through a gangway onto Rockaway. I just walked past that spot. His getaway car could have been waiting for him right there. Instead, it was all the way on the other side of this set of trailers. He knew where he was going. Right in here. I suspect if he'd had time to reload, you'd be dead."

Shaw watched Justine's face. Some of her bravado seemed to ebb away. He asked, "Where were your security people?"

"I have two security guards. One for the day shift, one for the night shift. The day guard was on his lunch break."

"No, where were your people from the force?"

"I'm not guarded twenty-four hours a day. At least not until now. It's my father who gets full coverage. I don't want that. Up until now, they just checked with me on a regular basis. And there was no indication that there would be any trouble."

"You didn't think there might be problems out here?"

Justine paused for a moment, then said, "They told me I'd be safe."

"Who told you?"

"The realty company said they were taking care of the security problems out here."

"How? With their Muslims?"

"Yes. They are supposed to be particularly good at that."

"Exactly who told you the problems out here would be taken care of?"

"A man named Bloom. Leon Bloom."

"And you took his word for it that everything was fine out here?"

"He seemed confident. Very sure."

"But he was wrong. This time the Muslims didn't scare anybody off. This time the bad guys fought back."

"Apparently."

"But you didn't know that these Blue-Tops weren't running scared, so you didn't make arrangements to have your security people look after you."

"Look, I told you, I'm not normally guarded closely. It's my father who gets the protection, not me."

"Well, your father isn't trying to set up a community center in a housing complex run by a crack gang in a war with an outlaw Muslim security company, is he?"

Justine Burton sat back in her chair and frowned. For a moment, Shaw thought he had overstepped. He thought she was about to tell him to leave.

Shaw didn't want her to feel that he blamed her.

"Your people should have known what you all are dealing with out here."

"Well, they do now, don't they? That's why you're here, isn't it?"

"I'm not with the Intelligence Division. I'm on special assignment here."

"What's your assignment, Detective Shaw?"

"End the situation out here."

"Situation?"

"Shut down the Blue-Tops, and the Muslims, and make sure nothing happens to you."

"I see. And how are you going to do that? You going to tell me to go home and keep my head under the covers until you clean up this neighborhood and make it all safe?"

"I don't get the impression you're going home."

"Not while women and children are streaming in here every day and night. I can't wait for you to *end the situation*. I don't even know how you think you're going to do that. They've already locked up half the men in the neighborhood, and it's still just as bad as ever, maybe worse. What are *you* going to do that's any different?"

"Well—"

"How is it possible to build strong families out here without men? Without the fathers of these children? Not every man in Brownsville is a violent drug dealer who preys on women."

"I'm only interested in the ones who aren't building families. Drug dealers who prey on the weak, like Archie Reynolds."

"So, you're going to lock him up?"

"For the rest of his life, if possible."

"What a surprise."

"You already have me figured, don't you?"

"Well, don't I? What do you see when you look at a young black man? You tell me."

"It depends on the young black man I'm looking at. Hey, I live in America, Ms. Burton. I see a lot—"

"A lot of what?"

"A lot of black people. Seen and heard and read and lived with and worked with. Just because I'm a cop doesn't mean I don't know about Malcolm and Martin Luther King and Miles and Mingus and Mandela. Or my friend Orestes Mason."

"Oh, some of your best friends are black?"

"Just the ones whose last names begin with M. What kind of a question is that? Doesn't it get tiresome assuming every white person you meet is a racist?"

"Not as tiresome as finding out they are."

Justine sat back in her chair, forcing herself to step back from the argument.

"You want to know what's really tired? Constantly seeing white cops come into black neighborhoods under the pretext of law enforcement and all it ends up meaning is more black men get killed, or, if they're lucky, jailed."

Shaw said, "I'm sure you are tired of it, Ms. Burton. I'm sure you're tired of the decades of injustice that caused what's happening in New Lots Apartments. Believe it or not, I don't think every young black man or woman caught up in this situation deserves to be shot or put in jail. But this guy, Archie Reynolds, Ms. Burton, he shot two unarmed, innocent black men trying to earn a living, trying to take care of their families. He shot them in cold blood without mercy, right in that complex. He led a bunch of others into an ambush that killed one and seriously wounded two. He's a murdering psychopath who scarred your face and hurt you and would have killed you if he'd had another bullet in his gun. He belongs in jail. If not, there's no way in hell you're going to be able to do what you want for the women and children who need you."

Justine didn't respond. Shaw couldn't tell from her reaction if he had gone overboard with his speech.

Shaw said, "Sorry. I don't exactly know where all that came from."

"I suspect from a good place. Perhaps I put you in a category you shouldn't be in."

"Don't worry about it."

"Now you've got me worried."

"What do you mean?"

"Now you've got me thinking you might know what you're talking about."

Shaw shrugged. "Well, I do know one thing."

"What?"

"If the reports I read are accurate, and I think they are, Archie Reynolds isn't your usual thug crack dealer. He was smart enough to plan an attack that killed three, wounded two, terrorized the people in this place, and almost took care of you, too. Not bad for about five minutes of work. He's not the kind of person I would want to be targeting me."

"And you're sure he's targeting me?"

"Yes, I'm sure. But even if I weren't, you'd better figure it that way until this gang is out of here."

"Detective Shaw, New Lots Apartments would be changing with or without me. Arbor Realty had possession of that property before I made my pitch."

"You know that. But who knows what this crack gang thinks? And, let's be honest, that real estate company realized getting the place cleaned up would happen sooner and more surely with the police commissioner's daughter working in their property. Archie Reynolds knows it, too. Unless, of course, we've all misjudged Arbor Realty's altruism and sense of community service and they would have turned over twenty apartments and the ground floor to anybody who asked for them."

Justine shifted in her chair, trying to position her arm in a way it wouldn't hurt.

"I don't think you misjudge much of anything, Detective."

"But you're not backing off, are you?"

"Do you have any idea what I can do with that space? I can provide housing, daycare, vocational training, drug counseling, psychiatric services. Get some of these women out from under their addiction. Give them a chance to stop selling their bodies, killing themselves, ruining their children. I might even have enough space for a small clinic."

"At least save some if you can't save them all."

"Exactly. Yesterday we got a call from a woman who said her twenty-four-year-old daughter had disappeared. But it wasn't the daughter the woman was worried about. It was the daughter's four children. She gave us the daughter's address, right across the street in New Lots. We broke into the apartment. Two of the children had been locked in a bedroom for almost three days, six and four years old. The four-year-old was so malnourished and dehydrated they think she might have sustained brain damage. Both kids were filthy, obviously abused. The boy's hands and fingernails were bloody from trying to beat and scratch open the bedroom door. An eight-month infant was lying in a crib, naked, covered in its own mess, wheezing. It had pneumonia, lying uncovered like that. I have no idea if that baby is going to live. They still haven't found the oldest boy. He's all of eight years old. They think she took him with her on her binge."

"Why?"

"Use him as currency. Sell him to the drug dealers so they could use him as a messenger. Or maybe for some other abomination that might suit them. You know where the mother was?"

"Somewhere smoking crack for three days."

"Somewhere? She was across the courtyard from her own apartment in New Lots, not more than two hundred feet from her babies. Does anybody realize how insane that is, or is it just me? Do you realize how easy it would be to eliminate untold misery around here?" Justine motioned with her hand. "I don't have to go outside these four square blocks. I have the resources. I can do something about this. The people who need me are right here. All I need is the space."

Shaw said, "And I believe you should have it. Certainly instead of a vicious crack gang."

"I agree."

"Then I've only got one more question."

"What?"

"How many more people do you think are going to have to die before you get it?"

For the first time in the conversation, Justine Burton looked away. But just for a few moments. Then she turned back and said, "I suppose more than I want to know. I would hope to God, Detective Shaw, that you are not a killer they've sent in. I hope to God you might be the kind of man who could prevent anybody from dying over this."

"You mean anybody else. There are already twelve people who have died over this. You heard what the Muslims did yesterday in response to the ambush, didn't you?"

Justine did not answer.

Shaw's voice softened. "I'm not a killer. But I don't believe anybody is going to stop this without spilling blood."

"Well then, Detective Shaw, let me ask you one more question."

"What?"

"How many more women and children are going to die if I *don't* get New Lots?"

CHAPTER 24

AFTER HE LEFT JUSTINE BURTON, LOYD SHAW WALKED OVER TO the unmarked NYPD car. He spoke briefly to the three detectives assigned to watch the Caring Community Center and Shelter. He confirmed with the detectives that Justine would be watched around the clock. Shaw knew the detectives had no interest in listening to him or he to them, but he wanted to make sure, when they saw his face, they would know which side he was on.

Shaw's meeting with the commissioner's daughter had done nothing to improve his mood, but it had definitely clarified the issues for him. Justine Burton knew what she wanted. So did The Shark, DeLuca. Shaw asked himself, so what the hell do you want? Besides your job, reputation, and pension?

The answer came so naturally to him that he wondered why he had even needed to ask himself the question. Now that he had come into the neighborhood, talked to Justine Burton, seen the people, the mothers and children, watched that family get on the subway and head off to earn a living, Shaw knew that he wanted to stop the killing, to end the terror being unleashed on an entire housing complex.

By the time he had reached the east side of the complex, he had spotted the two-man Muslim security patrol he'd seen earlier. He headed directly for them. They made Shaw for a cop in about five seconds. Shaw made a point of politely introducing himself. He tried to put out of his mind the fact that these men were connected with burning seven human beings to death.

"Excuse me, gentlemen, my name is Loyd Shaw. I'm with the NYPD. I'd like to speak to your boss. Is he around?"

Instead of flashing his gold shield, Shaw folded his ID wallet and showed only his NYPD identification card. It felt less threatening. Less like the usual white cop announcing his authority.

Shaw stood holding his police ID, and the Muslims stood stiffly in front of him, waiting to see if Shaw tried to push them. He didn't. Finally, one of the guards told him, "Ground floor, Building A. Our office is in there."

"Thanks."

The second guard pointed toward the front of the complex around the corner to the right.

Shaw approached the front gate, noticing again how many children inhabited the area in and around New Lots. It seemed as if they were everywhere. Running around. Dodging between cars. Popping in and out of the courtyard. Their presence seemed to be an indelible part of New Lots Apartments. He wondered why more of them weren't in school. He didn't know that the schools in the neighborhood were so crowded the children attended in shifts. In the afternoon, most of the kids he saw would be in school. Then their counterparts would fill the courtyard of New Lots.

The two regular MS-2 guards manning the new front entrance to the complex made sure to check Shaw's ID before they hit the switch that unlocked the new ten-foot iron gate.

Shaw stood for a moment looking at the buildings that comprised New Lots Apartments – five of them arranged into a giant U. Four buildings, A, B, C, and D, paired off facing each other, and a fifth larger building, E, ran between them at the far end, completing the bottom of the U.

Shaw walked into the courtyard, The Pit, wondering how none of the kids had been injured during the two drive-bys and the ambush. Shaw knew that luck wouldn't last forever. If the bullets kept flying, one would find a child.

Shaw found the ground-floor MS-2 office, a mostly bare room. Nothing softened the battleship gray paint and harsh fluorescent ceiling fixtures. The furniture consisted of a desk, two gray metal folding chairs, and a battered file cabinet. One phone sat on the desk along with three two-way radios recharging in a rack.

Again, Shaw found himself standing in the doorway of an office. But, unlike Justine Burton, Rachman Abdul X was not on the phone. He was on his knees, facing east, his prayer rug under him, arms extended, palms up, praying.

Shaw's reaction surprised him. Rachman's praying made him angry. It seemed like an act. A hypocritical mumbling act. He looked at Rachman and thought, Mr. Muslim here is the boss of guys who burn people to death, beat people to death, and propped them up in public for display. It seemed an affront that this same man would engage in prayer.

Rachman seemed to sense Shaw's presence behind him. And Shaw's hostility. He quickly finished his prayers. Shaw waited while Rachman rolled up his rug. When Rachman turned to give Shaw his bad-guy stare, Shaw made sure not to start by apologizing for interrupting.

"Are you done?"

"Yes. Who are you? More police?"

"My name is Loyd Shaw. Yes, NYPD. And you are?"

"Rachman Abdul X."

For a second, Shaw felt like asking Rachman his real name, but he suppressed the urge. Shaw looked at Rachman and again thought about that body shop and its seven piles of human ashes and burnt bones.

"So which do you prefer, Mr. Rachman, Mr. Abdul, or Mr. X?"

Rachman stared at Shaw, waiting to see if there would be any smile or smirk, any sign of disrespect.

Shaw kept his face blank even though he really didn't care if Rachman thought he was disrespectful. In fact, part of Shaw wished Rachman would take offense and try something. Part of Shaw wanted to go at this stolid black man who stood trying to intimidate him with his bad-guy look. Shaw thought about provoking him into taking a swing or making a threat, and then punching him in the throat, putting a gun to his head, cuffing him, and arresting him. Just take him out of the equation right now. Take out one of the killers right now.

Rachman was much too disciplined to rise to the bait. He held his hands in front of him, right hand holding his left wrist, and spoke evenly.

"Rachman will be fine."

"Are you in charge of the security operation here?"

"Yes."

"Then I'd like to ask you a few questions. Is that all right?"

"Why are so many police coming around now?"

"You know, Mr. Rachman, normally I don't mind when I ask someone a question and they answer with a question. It gets the conversation going. But, to tell you the truth, I don't want you asking me any questions. I just want to know if you're going to answer mine."

"I see."

"Yeah, you fucking see. And you see why there are more cops around here, too. There are too many people being shot and burned to death and beaten to death around here, aren't there?"

Rachman's jaw clenched, but he managed to keep his voice even.

"There were too many before you all started showing up."

"Maybe so, but when you get nine at a time, that tends to create a police presence. Do you have an objection to police showing up around here?"

"Not if they are just and lawful. But we don't want police coming down on us just because we are trying to defend ourselves or clean the criminals out of this place."

"I see. And what exactly do you mean by clean out?"

"I mean, do what nobody else will. Nobody else wanted to have anything to do with this place before we got here. No police ever came in here. Not even when they were called."

"So now we're supposed to argue about whether or not that gives you the right to take the law into your own hands."

"Why argue?"

"Right. Why argue? You mind that the police are here now?"

"No. I want the police here. Every day. If you all had been here every day before, there would be no dead bodies now."

"Yeah, it's our fault. I admit it. We forced you into this situation. We should have had a policeman on every block, twenty-four hours a day. Should have thought of that a long time ago. Be that as it may, Mr. Rachman, it still doesn't give you the right to do most of what you do."

"We abide by a just authority in all regards, Mr. Shaw."

"What's the qualifier mean?"

"Say what?"

"*Just* authority. That implies that you consider some authority *unjust*. Just for the hell of it, let me ask you – what authority gives you the right to beat people to death, to shoot them, to burn them alive? What authority might somebody need to justify those acts?"

"It's wrong to take a life for no reason. It's wrongful to take the law into one's own hands. But the greatest wrong is to be oppressed and do nothing. To have your life threatened, to have your own people killed, and then to lay down and submit to your enemies. That is the greatest sin. The world has already seen what happens when a group of people does that. The result is genocide, which is exactly what is happening to my people."

"So, the solution is to kill more of your people?"

"Only those who oppress us. Of any color."

Shaw nodded at the implied threat. "Any color?"

"Any color."

"White or black?"

Rachman repeated, "White or black."

"By any means necessary," said Shaw.

Rachman decided to stop answering.

Shaw said, "I know the excuse, Mr. Rachman. The end justifies the means. The lesser of two evils."

Rachman remained silent. Perhaps more to evaluate Shaw than his question. But, after a moment or two, he simply answered, "Yes."

"Good," said Shaw, "I can relate to that." He took a step toward Rachman, leaning forward to emphasize his point, entering Rachman's space, challenging Rachman.

"Now relate to this – as far as I'm concerned, you and your people are way the hell up high on the list of dangerous criminals. You're murderers. Killers. Bad people. I haven't looked at the details of your police record yet. Or the records of the people you use, but clearly Arbor Realty didn't recruit you out of a legitimate security operation. Most of your previous work experience was in prison. So I don't give a shit how much you pray, you and your people are felons. Many are murderers."

Shaw paused to give Rachman a chance to respond. Rachman stood without moving or talking.

Shaw stepped back and extended his hands, palms up, empty.

"But, hey, for right now, out here, you *do* actually happen to be the lesser of two evils. When it comes to bad guys, amazingly, you come in second. So here's what I propose. I'm going to take care of the worse evil out here. Me and my men are going to hunt down Archie Reynolds and his top people, and we are going to eliminate them from your life and the life of this community. Whatever was done before by the police, or wasn't done, whatever the detectives from the local precinct didn't do or should do or won't do, I don't care. I am going to personally fulfill our responsibility to this community. And I don't want you in my way. You have any problem with that?"

"Why should I?"

"You like answering questions with questions. That's all right. That's close enough. My goal is to stop people out here from killing each other. You have any problem with that?"

"No."

"Good. Now while I do that, I don't want to worry about eliminating *you* from this community. So I'm asking you to keep your guns in your pockets. Stand down. Tell your people to stand down. Otherwise, it will be much more difficult for me. And I may not succeed. And if I don't succeed, that will not help you. I'm not asking you for your help. I'm asking you to stop fighting with the Blue-Tops and let us take care of it."

"Why should I believe you will?"

"Because I'm telling you. But, obviously, that's not enough for you. So I suggest you just agree to wait a few days and see what happens. I don't intend to take very long doing this."

Rachman nodded.

"So, are we in agreement?"

"For the moment."

"Will you honor that agreement?"

"Honor? I have no reason to believe that you're an honorable man."

"Why's that?"

"Because you're police."

"I see. Well, just tell me straight out so I know where I stand with you. What are you going to do? You going to hold off in your vigilante war to see what I'm going to do? Or are you just going to keep on killing people?"

Rachman paused again as if he were actually making a decision. Shaw went along with Rachman's act, but he already knew Rachman's answer. Rachman would wait-and-see because he was already in that mode. Shaw had figured out Rachman's tactics. Go in. Threaten people. If you get any opposition, come down hard and fast on your enemies. Then wait, daring your enemies to strike back. Rachman would lose nothing by agreeing to what he was already doing.

After a few more moments, Rachman made a show of nodding and solemnly uttering, "I'll wait and see."

Shaw couldn't resist pushing him.

"Meaning?"

"I won't go after my enemies. But, if they come after me, I'll defend myself. And I'll defend this property as long as it's under my protection."

Shaw nodded as if he, too, were deciding something. Finally, he said, "Good enough, Mr. Rachman."

"Just call me Rachman."

"Uh-huh. By the way, who is it at Arbor Realty who hired you? What's his name? Bloom?"

Rachman bristled.

"Why do you ask me if you already know?"

"Because I want you to know I'm calling on the guy who's paying you. Where can I find him?"

"His office is in Crown Heights. I've never been there. Check the phonebook."

Shaw smiled. "The phonebook. Will do."

Shaw lay his card on Rachman's desk and wrote down the number of the 73rd Precinct on it. He didn't bother to hand it to Rachman because he wasn't in the mood to see Rachman refuse to touch it. Shaw had what he wanted. For now.

CHAPTER 25

LOYD SHAW LEFT RACHMAN X'S OFFICE AND STOOD ON NEW Lots Avenue until he spotted a gypsy cab. The drive to the 73rd Precinct took five minutes. He found the space that had been set aside for his team. It was small but adequate.

Everyone had arrived on time.

Four desks had been pushed together facing each other, creating an island in the middle of the green cinderblock room. There were also four phones, a file cabinet, one long table against the wall, and no windows. Standard issue.

The new precinct had replaced a crumbling old fortress that had generally been referred to as a shithole. In the new Seven-Three, the plumbing worked, the lighting was bright, and there was room for parking. It would do.

Walter Wang struggled with setting up over twenty thousand dollars' worth of electronic equipment on the long table set against the far wall of the crowded room. Impelliteri sat at a desk with his feet up reading the *NY Post*. Mason was on the phone. Sperling sat quietly, mostly watching Walter Wang.

Shaw said, "Walter, looks like you got everything you need."
"Yeah."
"Did you get that other stuff?"
"In the cars."
"You get everything on my list?"
"Yeah."
"Where are the cars?"

"Precinct lot. Keys are on top of the file cabinet."

Walter wrestled a seventeen-inch color monitor onto the table, shoving it into position between a scanner, fax machine, a tower model CPU, and a laptop computer. He pushed the power cord off the back of the table, adding to a rat's nest of cables, power cords, and surge suppressors.

Shaw took a seat at the desk across from Orestes Mason. James Sperling and Tony Impelliteri faced each other across their respective desks. Just like that, they were partnered up.

Shaw said, "Welcome to Brownsville, boys."

Nobody bothered to respond.

Shaw took a moment to look over his team in daylight.

Impelliteri wore his usual plainclothes cop garb: black jeans and t-shirt, a V-necked cashmere sweater, and a gold chili pepper dangling from a gold chain.

Sperling looked like an aging preppy in his neatly creased khaki pants, loafers, blue button-down oxford shirt, and blue blazer. Mason dressed in the usual senior detective-style – gray herringbone sports coat, shirt, tie, slacks, and sensible wingtip shoes.

Shaw wore black jeans, a blue-striped shirt, and a black windbreaker.

Walter Wang wore an ill-fitting Brooks Brothers suit and a cheap standard white shirt but with a tie that looked as if somebody else had bought it for him. With its interlocking pattern of rectangular shapes in shades of brown that ranged from deep chocolate to copper. Shaw admired the tie. He thought about asking Wang where he got it but didn't bother.

"All right, let's get to it. The object of the game is to get as many Blue-Tops out of commission as possible. Are we clear on that?"

Sperling said, "Define 'out of commission.'"

"That's up to each of you. I'd start with arresting them." Shaw yanked out a page he'd brought from DeLuca's file and taped it on the wall. "This is a list of twelve targets along with their NYSID numbers. DeLuca and his people in Career Criminals and Gangs have identified these twelve as Blue-Tops gang-bangers. This is not a complete list. They estimate the active membership ranges from around thirty-five to forty. But, like I said last night, we're concentrating on the leaders."

Shaw took out a set of mugshots and arrest sheets that Conklin had provided from the Bureau of Criminal Identification and the Photo Division, both at One Police. He began taping them on the wall next to the list of names.

"Here are the top five members of this gang. I want them first. Cut off the head, the rest will wither away. Obviously, we'll take what we can get, but these five are first.

"Number one, Archie Reynolds, a.k.a. Archie Ar. Head honcho. He's the one who shot the two guards outside the complex last Friday and set up the ambush of the Muslim security people. He's the one who terrorized Justine Burton's community center, knocked people down, brandished a gun, and got away clean.

"Number two, Reginal Wilson, a.k.a. Reggie Whack. He's second-in-command. A manager. Apparently, one of three managers. Don't know much about him, but I do have his arrest records and pictures. He looks like the original gangster type to me. Haven't seen any young guys with their hair conked straight like this. Notes from his parole officer say he's got a bad stuttering problem. That might help you find him.

"Number three, Ellard Watkins, street name Weight, as in heavyweight. This guy goes three hundred plus."

Impelliteri piped up, "Looks closer to four hundred."

Shaw continued, "I don't have much on him. Don't have all his records yet. Clearly, he's got to be well known on the street. Assume because of his size that he's one of Archie's enforcers. Shouldn't be hard to find.

"Number four, Ronald Jenkins—"

Mason cut him off. "We got a message ten minutes ago about him. They identified his remains. He was one of the guys burned up in the body shop fire."

"They identified him already?"

They identified all of them except one. They're sending us what they have. Chief's jobs go to the head of the line."

Impelliteri said, "Maybe the last pile of burnt shit is Archie Reynolds."

"Don't bet on it, Anthony," said Shaw as he took down one of the mugshots he'd taped on the wall. "Okay, if Ronald Jenkins is dead, our new number four is Melvin Brown, street name Melly Mel or some such nonsense. He's another one of their enforcers. Maybe the guy in charge of the drive-by shootings."

Shaw returned to his desk and sat down facing the pages he'd taped on the wall. "According to DeLuca, those are the top guys in this particular crack gang. As I said, this gang isn't real big, but it is vicious. They don't negotiate. They just shoot. That's why the other crews leave them alone. Also, they pretty much confine themselves to Brownsville. New Lots Apartments might be their biggest operation."

Impelliteri interrupted again and slid another mugshot and arrest sheet to Shaw.

"Before I came out, I talked to a buddy of mine who works in Gangs. This is from his personal file, so we didn't get it from him. Put this asshole up on the wall. Name's Sanchez. Carmen Sanchez. He's another one of their enforcers. Comes through their Dominican suppliers. He works freelance, but he's definitely hooked in with the Blue-Tops."

Shaw got up and taped Sanchez's picture and sheet on the wall.

"Good. Good work."

Impelliteri continued.

"Not much is known about his background except that he's suspected of killing about twenty guys. My source tells me when things get shitty, the suppliers make him available, or they point him at somebody they want taken care of. I'd say this is one of those times."

"Where's he live?" asked Mason.

"My guy said somewhere in the Bronx. When he's not out of town."

"Then what," asked Mason. "He go hide out in the islands?"

"Exactly. The Dominican Republic."

Shaw asked. "Any warrants out on him?"

"Hell, yes. Federal and state. Both for murder."

"All right. If Sanchez is a hitter, I gotta believe Archie Reynolds will ask for him. He's not going to slink off and let the Muslims get away with burning his meeting place down with seven of his guys inside. They're going to hit back. I want to take them out before they get a chance."

Shaw returned to his desk across from Mason and sat down, flipped open a legal pad, and began making notes.

"Okay, let's just take a second here to get organized. Let me ask you guys a couple of questions.

"First question, Walter, have you found warrants on any of these guys?"

Wang stopped attaching cables and opened a manila folder sitting on his worktable. He turned through the pages he'd compiled. Shaw noticed that Wang became completely engrossed in whatever he was doing. He talked more to himself than to the others, looking at the various printouts he had collected.

"Nothing on Archie Reynolds yet. I only got through like two databases in FATN. Just State and City, and not even all the courts. I still got district attorney warrants to check, motor vehicle, outside agencies, I mean, you know, I only had a couple of hours, and there weren't terminals available right away. Not even talking about out-of-state yet. But I had a good guy I know on it with me, so we got some shit done."

"Understood, you're just starting, but what did you get? Anything useful?"

"Yes. I got some things on the Whack guy, Reginal Wilson, and the fat guy, Ellard Watkins. Nothing yet on Melvin Brown, although I just started one search on him. Course, nothing on Sanchez, but you already got stuff on him, which is good because this fucking city has like a million Sanchezes."

"What? Like there ain't a million Browns out there?" asked Impelliteri.

"There are. And it took a long time."

Shaw asked, "What are the warrants for, Walter?"

"Uh, let's see. Reginal Wilson got one for possession and sale of a controlled substance…"

Impelliteri said, "Bingo, seven to fifteen."

Shaw asked, "What else?"

"Two bench warrants out on him for little shit."

"Anything on the other guys?"

"Got one out on Ellard Watkins for rape."

Again, Impelliteri piped up, "Rape? Fat, four-hundred-pound fuck goes out and rapes someone? How's he rape someone? He probably can't even find his dick under the folds."

Shaw said, "Okay, Impelliteri, let's skip that image if you don't mind. Rape will do nicely. Thanks, Walter. That it?"

"So far."

"Okay, any preference on who wants who?" asked Shaw.

Impelliteri said, "I got the line on him, so I guess me and Sperling should look for Sanchez."

"Okay, but before you go roaming around the Bronx, take your pick on the other two. Reggie Whack or Ellard Watkins?"

"I'll take Whack. I shoot some four-hundred-pound cocksucker, I don't want to get a hernia rolling him over to check him out."

Sperling said, "Good thinking."

"Hey," said Impelliteri. "The man of few words speaks. And when he speaks, he speaks the truth."

Sperling didn't respond.

"Okay," said Shaw, "Mase and I will take care of the heavy-weight."

"Fine with me. I don't picture him running very fast."

"All right, you guys know the drill. Find their cars, find their girlfriends, their ex-girlfriends, find their mothers, their kids, where they like to hang out, buy their gas, get their morning coffee and take a shit, fill their prescriptions, do their laundry, whatever. Just find them. And if you can't find the guys on the top of our list, find the others. And if you find one of the others, use him to find the top guys. But…"

"But what?" said Impelliteri.

"This is important. When you find them, bring 'em into *this* precinct and hold them here. Don't take anyone to central booking until I'm done with whoever you get in here. Don't let the desk sergeant or somebody on the midnight-to-eight shift send them off to central booking until I say so. I don't want these guys whipping through the turnstile and getting back on the street. I want to assign them to an ADA that will do what it takes to keep them locked up until they go to trial. I don't want any of these murderers making bail. We get them, we keep them. Understood?"

"We shoot 'em, ain't gonna be no turnstile to worry about."

"I didn't hear that, Impelliteri."

"Yeah, and I didn't say it."

"Walter?"

Wang was down under the table, looking for a phone jack. He stuck his head out. "Yes."

"Listen up for a second." Shaw turned to the others. "Walter secured a cell phone for each team and a portable radio for each of us. Write down the phone number for this office. Walter, you will be the central point of communications. If we can't get each other, we'll call you. Got it?"

"Yeah."

"The rest of the equipment is in the cars?"

"Yeah."

"Are the radios tuned to our own frequency?"

"Yeah. Don't change 'em."

Impelliteri said, "Probably a million Pakistani cabdrivers on the same frequency."

"No. No way," said Walter.

"All right, guys, when we're on the air, just use first names."

"What the fuck is your first name, Shaw?"

"Loyd, Anthony. With one L."

"And Mason's?"

"Orestes."

"Oh, like those names won't stick out. Tony and James, no problem, but someone hears Orestes and Loyd over the air? Forget about it."

"All right, all right, just use our initials. We don't want any other cops to know who we are and what we're doing out there." Shaw continued. "Walter, while we're gone, keep searching records on those other three Blue-Tops. Then keep adding names from DeLuca's file. And any other names we feed to you."

"Shit. I be here forever."

"Yes, Walter. Don't expect to go home any time soon. And when you do, you'd better bring a change of clothing and whatever toiletries you need. And you don't need to wear a suit, man. There's going to be no time off for any of us until this job is done or DeLuca says it's over. You got everything you need here to do your searches?"

"Yeah, I don't have to be at Central Warrants. I got my own modem, and I got the codes to get into Central from here. But don't tell anyone. You're not supposed to be able to do that."

Shaw said, "That won't be the only thing we'll be doing that we aren't supposed to. And don't forget to bullshit up our fives."

Impelliteri raised his hand. "Question."

"What?"

"You got any money? We're gonna need money."

Shaw knew Impelliteri was right. It was the first thing he had asked of Conklin, and it seemed to be the easiest thing for Conklin to provide. Shaw pulled out a stack of used hundred-dollar bills.

"Each team has a grand."

He tossed a pack of bills to Impelliteri.

"Now you're talking, boss. Now we can make something happen out there, right, Sperl?"

Sperling didn't react to his shortened name.

"Use it wisely," said Shaw. "Every penny."

Wang chimed in right away. "Hey, where's my cut?"

Shaw peeled off one bill.

"Here's a hundred for food. Impelliteri, give him a hundred."

"Fuck that."

Wang frowned. Impelliteri laughed. "Hey, just kidding, Kung Fu." He handed over the hundred. "That'll keep you in chow mein for the whole deal. Enjoy."

"Fuck you, you wop dago bastard."

Wang had stuttered and spit out the epithet so quickly that his underlying Chinese accent popped through. The nerd had turned. Everybody laughed, including Impelliteri.

Shaw said, "That's right, Walter. Don't let him fuck with you. Now get your magic little Asian fingers flying on that keyboard."

Mason raised a hand. "One thing."

"What, Mase?"

"Speaking of everybody else in the precinct. How much we gonna be trippin' over the precinct detectives out there? How much do they know about us? I mean, they know we're here. What's the cover story?"

"I don't think we've attracted too much attention. Anybody asks, we're a special task force looking into drug trafficking. The best way to avoid attention is to get this done before anybody starts wondering about us."

"Good luck," said Impelliteri.

Shaw turned to the others. "Forget about the precinct guys. Forget about everything in your lives except these Blue-Tops bastards. Get the top guys as soon as you can and the little guys while you're developing leads. I don't give a shit if a month from now, your arrests don't stand up. I want these guys locked up, and I want names. Get 'em from people on the street, get 'em from your connections, get 'em any way you can."

Sperling finally spoke. "One question, Mr. Shaw."

"Yeah?"

"I assume the top priority is to get the main man here."

"Archie Reynolds? Yeah."

"Well, if we go after his underlings and managers and enforcers, that's going to send Mr. Reynolds deep into a hole where we can't find him. Or it's going to make him run."

Impelliteri spoke up. "Sperling could be right. Seems like Archie Reynolds has been pretty quiet since the Muslims burned up his buddies."

Shaw said, "Maybe. Or maybe he's meeting with his suppliers and his hitters, planning his next move. Or maybe he's trying to find a way to get his business running somewhere else and then come back after the Muslims. It really doesn't matter. We go for whoever we can get now. If we flush him out and nail his ass, fine. If he runs or hides out, that might prevent him from killing people."

"I'd rather get the man," said Mason.

"So would I. But one thing I want you to remember, this gang is in the middle of a war. They've already gone for cover. Or at least they're going to be goddamn careful about being out on the street. But when you do find them, and I know we will, you make goddamn sure you watch yourself. The first thing they're going to do is shoot."

Impelliteri said, "Fuck 'em. They get the drop on me and shoot first, they deserve to get away. And just remember, Shaw, nobody is gonna mistake me and Sperling for black Muslims. You better make sure your partner there doesn't go around wearing his Kunte robes and Kufi cap."

Mason had been looking at DeLuca's file through his battered reading glasses. He peered over the top of his spectacles at Impelliteri.

"Hey, Impelliteri."

"What?"

Mason said, "It's Kente, not Kunte. And I'm a Baptist," and said it in a way to make it clear he didn't want to hear any more of Impelliteri's misplaced wit.

Anthony Impelliteri raised a fist and said, "Right on, brother." He stood up and said, "Come on, Sperling."

Shaw and Mason watched them go.

Mason said, "Hope that guy is good enough at his job to make up for all the bullshit."

"Me, too," said Shaw. "Before we head out, let's check with Walter for a second." Shaw went over to Wang's worktable. "How long until you're all set up?"

Wang was already making clickety-click noises with his keyboard and sliding his mouse around. Shaw heard the weird echoey noise modems make when they are establishing a connection. Wang's nose was aimed at his screen, and his expression had already turned blank with a far-off gaze. He spoke to Shaw without looking at him.

"I'm set for now."

Shaw squinted at the computer monitor. "What's that?"

"Field Assistant Terminal Network."

Mason and Shaw exchanged looks.

"Mase, did you know that's what FATN stood for?"

"I knew about the TN part," said Mason. "But not the FA."

Wang ignored them.

Shaw said, "Walter, are you listening to me?"

Without taking his eyes off his computer monitor, Walter said, "Yes."

"Concentrate on Archie Reynolds. But get something for us on Ellard Watkins, too. I'll call you in a couple of hours. Have something for me, will you?"

"Yeah, yeah."

"Both of their NYSID numbers are in DeLuca's file."

"I know, I know."

Wang had already lost interest in any conversations. He tapped and clicked his way deeper into the police database.

"Walter, did you get me a phone monitor?"

"Car trunk."

Shaw grabbed the remaining set of car keys and headed out with Mason. On the way to the precinct parking lot, Shaw told Mason what he had planned.

"Before we go looking for Watkins, I want to run down this real estate guy who's paying the Muslims."

"What for?"

"Couple of reasons. You know how to work one of those phone monitor boxes?"

"Not really."

Shaw gave Mason a quick lesson on the way.

CHAPTER 26

JUST ABOUT THE TIME SHAW HAD ENDED HIS MEETING WITH HIS detectives in the 75th Precinct, Reggie Whack got the call to pick Archie Ar up at the Hotel Doral in Manhattan.

After the ambush on Friday in The Pit at New Lots Apartments, Archie had laid low in a Days Inn motel off Cross Bay Boulevard near JFK Airport. He'd spent most of the weekend partying with his managers and planning his next moves. And then on Monday morning, Reggie arrived at the motel stuttering the bad news. Seven of their gang had been burned to death in the body shop by the Muslims. Two more had been beaten to death and put on display across from New Lots Apartment. He watched Archie retreat into a deadly, rage-filled silence.

Archie and Reggie left the motel without a word. Archie moved to a motel near LaGuardia airport. He fought the urge to retaliate against the Muslims, knowing that he could not be distracted from meeting the demands of his drug business – the task made more difficult because Archie knew he had to stay out of Brownsville and New Lots Apartments.

He instructed Reggie Whack to bring his surviving gang members in twos and threes to a motel. Archie gave all of them the same message: Stay off the streets. Don't worry about the Muslims. Keep the crackheads out of The Pit. Move the sales down to the ground floors. Steer customers to windows around the perimeter of the complex. Sell out of the windows. Keep everything moving.

Monday night, Archie moved into yet another hotel, this time in Manhattan.

When Reggie got the call on Tuesday, he knew Archie was ready to move against the Muslims.

Archie climbed into Reggie's Jeep Cherokee and told him to head for Brownsville. Once there, Archie directed Reggie to a series of hardware stores, gas stations, and grocery stores. They ended up behind a salvage yard about ten blocks east of New Lots, unloading five-gallon, red plastic containers. There were ten of them, each containing four gallons of gasoline. Archie set the containers on the ground and screwed off their tops. While Reggie unpacked bags filled with boxes of mothballs, Knox gelatin, and liquid laundry detergent, Archie muttered to himself, "Motherfuckers. Trying to burn me out. Nigger ghetto bullshit. Niggers want to burn out the Jew motherfuckers who ripping you off, go on. Burn up the white man's prison when you riot, I give a shit. Burn out the Blue-Tops? Burn out Archie Ar? No fucking way, man. They want to see something burn? I'll fucking show 'em how to burn."

Archie pulled twenty boxes of mothballs out of the hardware store bags and dropped them on the ground. He methodically stomped on the boxes, motioning for Reggie to do the same.

Archie distributed the crushed mothballs into each of the plastic gasoline cans. Then he divided his supply of gelatin and detergent and poured that into the cans, too.

"So what's this?" asked Reggie.

"My special blend. Ar-Man napalm."

"Nay, nay, napalm?"

"Homemade version."

"What the fuck, man, that shit ay, ay, ain't gonna eh, eh, explode in my Jeep, is it?"

"No, motherfucker. That ain't the point. This shit just makes the gas nice and thick. Like jelly. You pour it on, it stays put and keeps burning."

For the first time since the body shop massacre, Reggie smiled his gold-toothed smile.

"When we gah, gah, gonna do that?" asked Reggie.

"When I say. When the time is right. But right now, we got to take care of other business."

"What business?"

"The crack business, motherfucker. First, we make sure the new system be working. Make sure nobody too fucked up about what happened. *Then* we take care of these Muslim cocksuckers and that Uncle Tom bitch once and for all."

They loaded the cans into the back of the Jeep. Reggie asked, "Na, na, now where?"

"New Lots," said Archie. "Where the fuck else we gonna go?"

CHAPTER 27

LOYD SHAW FOUND LEON BLOOM'S OFFICE ON PROSPECT PLACE in Crown Heights on the ground floor of a commercial storefront. If this is a real estate office, thought Shaw, there's never been one like it.

When he entered, Shaw saw a long, narrow room. A counter across the full width blocked access. The place looked as if it hadn't been cleaned in twenty years. Several large photocopy machines ran ceaselessly. Phones at four desks rang constantly. Piles of paper covered every vertical surface. Shaw counted five men and two women packed into the small space. The men dressed in their white shirts, black vests, and pants, all wearing yarmulkes, some wearing tzitzits, the women in long skirts, blouses, sweaters, and wigs.

Shaw didn't bother wondering how many and what kind of business operated in the small space.

A wholesomely young lady told Shaw that Mr. Bloom was not in his office.

"I assume he's having lunch?" said Shaw.

She nodded and told Shaw he could find Mr. Bloom at an address one block west.

From the look of Bloom's coworkers, Shaw pictured Bloom spending his lunch hour studying the Torah with a minyan of learned rabbis. Unlikely.

As Shaw walked through the relatively quiet Crown Heights neighborhood, Mason followed in one of the dark blue Chevy Caprices that Conklin had supplied the team.

Shaw turned around to make sure Mason wasn't following too closely. He wanted the car out of sight when he found Leon Bloom.

While he walked toward the address the young woman had given him, Shaw thought about the alliance between Leon Bloom, an orthodox Jew, and Rachman Abdul X, a militant black Muslim. Shaw knew a little bit about the Old Testament, but not nearly enough about the Koran to make a comparison.

As soon as Shaw arrived at the location, he stopped worrying about interrupting a lunch hour debate on Talmudic law. Bloom sat in a bar finishing the last third of a three-martini lunch. The only evidence of food in front of him was a small pile of olive pits.

Bloom sat on a stool at the far end of the bar, sipping his gin and smoking filtered Camels. Leon was the picture of a relaxed man. His untied necktie lay draped across his chest and belly, his collar loosened, his jacket hanging over the back of his bar stool. The only trace of religious orthodoxy was Bloom's yarmulke, which he wore faithfully on the top of his large, round head.

Shaw introduced himself and noted that Bloom didn't seem surprised to be sought out by a police detective. Shaw told himself, why should he be surprised with all the dead bodies dropping around him?

Shaw presented his police ID and said, "Mr. Bloom, I'd like to ask you a few questions."

Bloom answered, "Go ahead." But it sounded like "gahed."

"I understand you've taken over the management of New Lots Apartments."

"Not me personally, thank God, but the company I work for, Arbor Realty. We specialize in restoring properties in trouble."

"Trouble?"

Bloom shrugged. "You know…"

"Uh-huh. Now, as part of this restoration, you're employing an outside security company."

"Yes, at the moment."

"And this company is called Muslim Security Two."

Bloom shrugged and smiled.

"Why did you decide on that particular company?"

"Why not? We're not prejudiced against anybody. The people we work with are dedicated individuals willing to help the people of their community."

"What makes them so dedicated?"

Bloom shrugged again. Shaw thought if this fat fuck shrugs at me one more time, I'm going to smack the side of his head.

"Who can say?" said Bloom. "Many of them believe they are doing God's work."

"God works in mysterious ways, huh, Mr. Bloom?"

"Please, I'm not qualified to comment on God's ways."

Shaw had been leaning back against the bar. He turned to face Bloom directly, his voice hardening. "Yeah, well, you'd better comment on why you think you can get away with using a bunch of vigilante felons to kill people you would rather not have occupying your rental property."

This time Bloom did not shrug. Even with three martinis under his straining belt, Shaw's sudden change unnerved him.

"What?"

Shaw resisted the urge to slap Leon Bloom.

"You heard me. Why do you think you can hire people to commit murder and get away with it?"

"What are you, crazy? You expect me to take you seriously with that kind of question?"

"Yes. I expect you to take me seriously. I'm talking about people dying here."

Now instead of shrugging, Bloom started spluttering.

"It's, it's not a serious question, a question like that. What do you mean commit murder? If someone shoots a gun at you and you shoot back, that's not murder, that's self-defense."

"Are you saying the murders these Muslims committed were in self-defense?"

"They have a right to—"

"Shut up. I'm not done. I want to know where self-defense comes in when you drag people out of an alley and beat them to death. How is it self-defense when you lock human beings up in a body shop and burn them to death?"

"I don't know what you're talking about."

"Vaguely reminiscent of shoving people into ovens, don't you think? How does that constitute self-defense?"

"This conversation is over."

"No, Mr. Bloom, it isn't. Don't cloak yourself in some bullshit holocaust outrage. You look at what you're behind and you fucking answer me or you will be leaving this bar in handcuffs."

Bloom dropped all pretext of innocence and offense. His eyes narrowed, and he looked directly at Shaw.

"Who are you?"

"I told you my name, Detective Loyd Shaw. One L."

"You can't talk to me like this. You can't threaten me."

"Why the fuck can't I? You're aiding and abetting murder."

Shaw watched Bloom consider saying something for a moment. And then he pulled back from the anger pushing him and said, "What do you want?"

That hadn't taken too long, thought Shaw. Shaw forced a smile and leaned back again. "Actually, Mr. Bloom. I really don't want too much. Go on, finish your drink." Bloom pushed his martini glass away and waited.

Shaw nodded as if now they understood each other.

"Let's start over. Regarding self-defense. According to the report I read, this all started when you sent your Muslim security company into New Lots to shoot up one of that drug gang's crack apartments. What was that? A warning of some sort? I mean, not that you know exactly what I'm talking about. Hypothetically. Off the record. What would that be? A warning?"

Bloom decided to answer. Or at least tell the man what he wanted to hear until he left.

"Yes," Bloom said. "A warning."

"And after the warning is given, presumably, you have even more right to defend yourself."

"Presumably."

Shaw edged closer to Bloom, but this time he dropped all posturing, spoke very quietly, looking right into Bloom's face.

"Okay, Mr. Bloom, here comes *my* warning. You ready? Because after I give you my warning, I'm going to have more right than ever to wage a vigorous defense, a very vigorous and direct defense. Are you following me?" Shaw looked directly at the fat, disheveled man, staring right into his eyes. Standing right in front of him, not sitting. He wanted to penetrate the gin, and any feeling of protection and complacency Bloom might still possess.

Shaw slowly reached under his jacket and extracted his Glock. He pressed the hard muzzle into Bloom's belly. He held the gun low enough so that the bartender couldn't see it.

"How does it go, Bloom?" Shaw lifted the Glock up a few inches. "I read the report on how they shot up that crack den. A couple hundred bullets and no dead bodies. Is that how it goes? Is that the warning?"

"I don't know."

"Okay, know this. Know my warning, Mr. Bloom. I don't want your vigilantes shooting or beating or burning people in Brownsville. You shut that down, or I will come after *you*. Not that ex-con Rachman Abdul X. Not the usual targets. I'll come after you, Mr. Bloom. Nobody will stop me. Nobody from the police department. Nobody from the Muslims. Nobody. Do you hear me? Do you understand my warning to you?"

Shaw maintained eye contact with Bloom, who had begun to sweat slightly.

"You're crazy."

"That's what they tell me. Do you understand me?"

"Yes."

"You're sure. You're absolutely sure?"

"Yes."

"Okay, then."

Shaw slowly removed the gun from Bloom's ample belly and shoved the Glock back into the holster on his hip. He sat down on the empty barstool next to Bloom.

"Now, I'm going to make this easier for you."

"Meaning what?"

"You tell your little private army to stop their war out there because I am going to take care of their enemies. I am going to eliminate this vicious little crack gang. I already talked to your man Rachman this morning and told him I will do this. Now I want *you* to tell him to stand down."

"Yes."

"That way, Mr. Bloom, you and your Muslims don't have to be the murderers."

"You're going to be the murderer? Is that what you're saying? Because you know as well as I do, Mr. Detective, you know those animals won't stop until they are dead."

"Don't tell me what I know or don't know. Just concentrate on what you need to know. Shut it down."

Bloom asked, "Are you done?"

"Only if you assure me that you completely understand me."

"What's not to understand? I don't think the police department really works this way. If your superiors knew—"

"Shut up, Bloom. Just tell me now. Are we together on this or not?"

"Sure, sure, why not? Anything you say."

"Good. Now, one last thing."

"What?"

"Tell your Muslim boys to give me whatever information they have on the Blue-Tops. Convince them it's the fastest way to end this mess. Tell them they will still get paid even if they stand down. Tell them whatever you have to but tell them to give me information. I want to know everything they know about the Blue-Tops."

"I can tell them, but I can't guarantee they'll listen to me. I can't make them cooperate with the police. They don't really like the police, Mr. Detective. And from what I'm seeing, I can't say that I blame them. You act like some Cossack, coming in here with your threats and accusations."

Shaw nodded.

"I do hope you understand, Mr. Bloom. Cossacks are what it's going to take with this. If I were you, I'd get used to it. Just make sure you do what I tell you."

Shaw stood up and patted Bloom's fat back.

"Talk to Mr. Rachman. Today. I'll be seeing him later tonight. Okay?"

And with that, Shaw turned and walked out of the bar.

Shaw reached the Caprice parked across the street just in time. Mason had the monitor fired up, tuning in, trying to pick up the radio signal from Bloom's cellular phone as it bounced off the cell tower. That's why Shaw wanted to meet Bloom out of his office. He wanted Bloom to use his cell phone.

Luckily, it wasn't one of the newer digital models. The analog transmission was easier to intercept. Bloom hadn't wasted any time making the phone call Shaw wanted him to make. Shaw just managed to place his tape recorder in front of the monitor's speaker in time to pick up the conversation.

Mason had his reading glasses perched on his broad nose, carefully writing down the model number and phone number of Bloom's cellular phone as it appeared on the monitor's LCD readout.

Shaw watched the numbers scroll and listened. The usual bits of static faded in and out, but the monitor snatched the conversation he wanted to hear right out of the air. He listened to the doleful, steady voice of Lieutenant Conklin respond to the tense, exasperated voice of Leon Bloom.

Bloom was telling Conklin all about Loyd, one L, Shaw. Bloom wanted to know what to do. He wanted to be told that someone would make Shaw go away and leave him alone. He wanted to know why Shaw had harassed and threatened him.

Bloom had a lot of questions. Conklin had a lot of smarts. He didn't invoke his boss's name once. And everything Conklin did say was carefully calculated. He told Bloom to consider Shaw part of the solution. He told Bloom that it was always wise to cooperate with the police, but that his concerns were duly noted. Conklin wouldn't speak too openly over the cellular connection, but it was good enough for starters.

Shaw would have liked Bloom to invoke Justine Burton's name. Or her father's name. Bloom had to believe he had a significant amount of protection if he thought he could unleash armed felons to kill the Blue-Tops gang members. Shaw would have liked to hear him invoke that protection so he could capture it on tape, but Conklin cut the conversation short.

Mason switched off the monitoring equipment and gave Shaw a tired, seen-it-all look.

"You really want to step in this shit?"

"You think we have a choice? This guy Bloom thinks he can get away with murder. You think that comes from nowhere?"

"Now you going after the commissioner, too?"

"I'll go after whoever I have to, Mase."

"Jeezus."

"I know. But we're in this now." Shaw held up the tape recorder. "We go wherever it leads us."

"Yeah, and where would that be, exactly?"

"Right now?"

"Yeah."

Shaw rubbed his stomach.

"Someplace where I can get something to eat."

Shaw and Mason hit a McDonald's drive-thru and came away with four bags of food. Shaw ate while he called their office in the Seven-Three.

"Walter, what's happening?"

"I got stuff on Watkins. Turn on the fax in your car and I'll modem it to you."

"A fax? I have a fax in this car?"

"Yeah. See that thing that looks like a keyboard with a screen."

Shaw looked around and saw a piece of equipment where a cellular phone might be hooked up. He had never seen a police car of any kind with a fax machine in it. He realized Wang must have stayed up most of the night getting the array of equipment he had secured. Wang walked Shaw through the steps, and, within a minute, the contraption started emitting a grinding noise as it oozed out a sticky length of fax paper bearing information that would put them on the trail of Weight Watkins.

The printout came through Walter's computer via a database deep in the bowels of the NYPD computer network. Shaw studied the fax carefully and decided he'd made the right choice when he recruited Walter Wang.

CHAPTER 28

By the time Anthony Impelliteri and James Sperling left the temporary office in the Seven-Three, Impelliteri had already taken over making the decisions. He took the wheel of the other Chevy Caprice Wang had procured. Before they even pulled out of the precinct parking lot, Impelliteri started telling Sperling his plan.

"Sperl, you and I have to talk."

"Uh-huh."

"Well, not really. You listen and grunt if you disagree."

Sperling didn't bother to respond.

Impelliteri talked fast and drove even faster.

"Look, my view on this is real simple. I ain't waltzing around the streets of goddamn Brownsville looking for a bunch of crack-dealing moolies. It ain't gonna work. The second our white asses hit the street, the word goes out. They'll be gone before we turn the corner, and for goddamn sure some knucklehead is gonna take a shot at us just for laughs."

Sperling nodded once.

"So, I got a different plan."

"Which is?"

"I'm glad you asked. I prefer we make them come to us."

"Them being these Blue-Tops we're looking for?"

"Who else?"

Sperling asked, "And how will that happen?"

"It's gonna take a little running around, but what the fuck. You'll see. This is one where I call in a few markers. You hungry?"

"Not really."

"Come on, we'll take a little chip out of our expense money." Impelliteri drove east out of Brownsville to an Italian restaurant near Aqueduct Racetrack. Impelliteri walked in, sat at a table for four. Sperling took the chair opposite Impelliteri and settled back. He didn't bother to look at the menu.

Impelliteri didn't ask Sperling what he wanted. He ordered antipasto and fried calamari with Fra Diavolo sauce for starters. Then salad. Then roasted whole red snapper with side dishes of black linguini in garlic and oil sauce. Impelliteri polished off most of a bottle of Chianti Classico Riserva and finished the meal with melon and prosciutto.

Sperling didn't drink, barely ate, and hardly spoke during the meal. Impelliteri left Sperling to his silence while he made a series of phone calls on the restaurant owner's cordless phone.

Nobody brought a bill for the meal, but Impelliteri dropped a fifty-dollar tip on the table and led the way back to the car.

"Okay, Sperl, we gotta make a few stops. Everything is set up except for running down the Kilo Queen."

"Who?"

"Never mind, you'll see. By the way, you mind me calling you Sperl?"

"I prefer James."

"How about Jimmy?"

"Suit yourself."

"Okay, Sperl…just kidding, James, we gotta head over to my precinct and get a bunch of mugshots a pal of mine picked up for us at Photo Division. They match most of the guys on that list Shaw laid on us. Then we make a few stops, and we get to work."

Impelliteri drove the Caprice almost as if the siren and lights were flashing. They made their rounds very quickly.

They picked up copies of ten mugshots at the East New York precinct, then, in quick succession, stopped at two bars, a pool hall, a beauty parlor, and a Caribbean-French restaurant that catered to Haitians. They finally found the Kilo Queen in the back room of a car service company on Dumont Avenue, just over the dividing line between East New York and Brownsville.

As they headed for the car service office, Sperling emerged from his shell to ask, "Do I get to know who this person is?"

"Nope."

"She deals in kilos?"

"Yep."

"Of what?"

"Mostly coke. But she's been known to locate heroin if needed."

"Kilos."

"Exactly. No small deals. But nothing too big. She's right in the middle." Impelliteri paused at the doorway and warned Sperling, "Hey, in case you get a wild urge to suddenly launch into a big conversation, don't. Don't say anything unless she asks you a question."

"Okay. Are we cops?"

"Hell yeah, we're cops. She knows who I am. And one more thing."

"What?"

"She's not exactly a she. She's more of an it."

Sperling's only reaction to that bit of information was a slightly raised eyebrow.

They entered at street level through a reinforced glass door, walked up one flight of stairs, and turned into the expected beat-up, dimly lit, dirty-paint office. A poorly constructed wood and glass partition separated the main section of the office from a small waiting area. On one side of the barrier, three chain smoking car service drivers in cheap suits stood waiting to start their shifts. They checked in with a dark-skinned, Middle Eastern man who stood on the other side of the partition making notes on timesheets. He could have been anything from an Israeli to a Pakistani and looked as if he hadn't slept in about three days.

Another swarthy type sat at a console shouting incessantly into a microphone broadcasting addresses and assignments. The language sounded Arabic.

None of it mattered to Impelliteri, not even the hard stares he received when he entered. He barely broke stride as he pointed to the back and said, "Margo."

They buzzed him in past the partition. Sperling followed close behind. At the far end of the office, they walked through another door more formidable than any other they had passed through. They entered a back office about the same size as the office in front. The only occupants were the Kilo Queen and her bodyguard.

Even Sperling had to admit that the queen did have a somewhat regal presence. Queen Margo was a flamboyant transsexual draped in an androgynous red rayon blouse-shirt opened low enough to reveal a distinct cleavage.

It wasn't clear whether this somewhat impressive décolletage was the result of silicone, saline, hormones, or all three. Her ensemble included bright yellow bolero pants and leopard-skin slippers. Her accessories consisted of fake Paloma Picasso earrings, strings of brightly colored Mardi Gras necklaces, and fashionable barrettes strategically placed in her heavily pomaded, marcelled, reddish-black hair with platinum highlights. Makeup included matching dark lipstick and nail polish, generous mascara, and blue eye shadow.

Margo was a handsome Hispanic man, dressed as a homosexual version of a woman who seemed to be imitating a very effeminate man.

The only part not immediately entertaining was the 9mm Smith & Wesson semi-auto next to the phone Margo spoke into with a heavy Hispanic, decidedly effeminate accent.

The other occupant of the office, a beefy bodyguard, sat against the far wall. Unlike Margo, there was nothing charming about him. His name was Benny. He wore a dark suit too tight for his steroid-built body, a black vest, and white shirt open at the collar. He looked at Impelliteri and Sperling as if they smelled bad and he was getting ready to throw them out with the rest of the garbage.

Margo sat at a neat desk speaking in quick bursts of Spanglish using a combination of code, obscure references, and abstruse analogies.

Margo took due notice of Impelliteri and Sperling, frowning at Impelliteri to convey her displeasure. The chilly reception didn't seem to bother Impelliteri.

Queen Margo finished her conversation, arranged herself, and asked, "So what the fuck is with you, Anthony? I know you ain't coming in here with good news. I already got three phone calls telling me you're looking for me. What do you want?"

"Hey, I would have called you direct, but I don't have your current number."

"Whatever. I give a shit what you don't got." Margo suddenly turned to Sperling. "Who's your friend?"

"This is James."

Margo extended her hand. Sperling took it and received a surprisingly firm handshake instead of something more demure. Margo said, "Nice to meet you. What did you do to get hooked up with him? I know the cops ain't putting no good policeman with that one."

Sperling responded with a shrug.

Margo spun quickly on her swivel chair and told her bodyguard, "Benny, be a doll and go get us some coffee." Back to Impelliteri and Sperling, "You all want coffee?"

Impelliteri said, "Yes."

Benny lumbered off.

Margo said, "Talk to me before my phone starts ringing." She turned to Sperling, pointed to Impelliteri, and said, "Now listen closely to the bullshit this one here comes up with. It's amazing how guys with cute asses think they can say anything and get away with it." She turned back to Impelliteri. "Like I'm one of your chippy girlfriends you can bullshit anytime you want. Go on. What kind of trouble are you in now?"

"Margo, don't be such a hard-ass."

"Come on, baby." She tapped her wrist. "Time is money. Don't take any more of mine than you have to."

Impelliteri pointed at Margo. "Hey, this is worth your time. You want me to leave, just tell me."

"You're here now, talk."

"I'm looking for bad guys. If I find them, I can help solve a problem. I solve the problem, I get a big chip redeemable with powerful people."

"Really. How powerful?"

Impelliteri didn't hold back.

"Chief of D powerful."

"Oh, really?"

"Really. This could be a shot at moving from the shit list to the A-list real quick. But I gotta produce."

"Well, well, well, so what does God want?"

"Somebody is trying to bust up a crack gang that took over a housing complex in Brownsville. A bunch called the Blue-Tops. You ever hear of 'em?"

"Yes."

"Ever do business with them?"

"Maybe."

"Margo, please, don't fuck around now. You want in? You want to help me with this?"

"Why is the chief of detectives interested in this?"

"Why should you care? He is. That's all you gotta know."

The Kilo Queen grew quiet. Impelliteri had brought her an opportunity. A line into the chief of detectives could be extremely valuable. But would it be worth the price Impelliteri wanted her to pay?

"Blue-Tops are the bad guys you're after?"

"Yes."

"You want my help with that?"

"Yeah. No pressure. You want to help, great. If not, no hard feelings."

"Bullshit. I say no, maybe you don't become my enemy, but you won't forget."

Margo and Impelliteri exchanged looks, but Impelliteri didn't say anything.

"If you produce, Anthony, you going to have to be on the good side of one big *pendejo*, sweetheart."

"Exactly."

"But you fuck up, *El Jefe* don't owe you nothing, and I got more bad boys on my sweet ass than I could handle with even two or three Bennys."

"Well, tell you the truth, Margo, it ain't that hard a decision. This particular group is going down. It's goin' down with or without your help and with or without me. The word has come from on high. So the only question is whether or not you and me want to reap some of the rewards or let somebody else come along and take what's ours to get."

Margo looked at Sperling. "What do you say, *El Morté?*"

Sperling answered without attitude or challenge. "Yes or no, and we'll be on our way."

Impelliteri said, "Hey, I've already given you valuable information. You just found out there's going to be a shortage of supply in Brownsville. If you're ready to fill it, that's good for you."

"There's always a shortage in Brownsville, honey. Just depends on how much. I don't time the market, Anthony. I just keep my regular thing goin'. I don't worry about a week from now."

"Right. But it's today you gotta decide. So what's it going to be, Margo?"

"What's the play? Exactly."

"I don't want to be running around out there in circles. I want these cockroaches to come to me, so I was thinking, maybe we have a sale. Something good enough to draw the mutts we're looking for but not so good as to make anybody suspicious."

"Wait a minute, you want me to sell my shit for less?"

"Yeah."

"I'm not losing money on this. My budget does not call for losing money for nobody. Not you, not the chief of D, not nobody, honey."

"Who said anything about losing money? I got you covered. Gimme your best wholesale price, and I'll cover a few hundred off that to make the offer attractive. You won't lose anything."

"Pricing under the market can end up costing me."

"Hey, Margo, nuthin's risk-free. You want to end up on the right side of this situation, you gotta make some investment here."

"How much of an investment?"

"You tell me. How many keys you gotta sell at a discount to attract attention?"

"Whose attention exactly?"

"Listen, the way I figure it, there's got to be guys in this Blue-Tops outfit already smelling blood. There's no loyalty among those ruthless pricks. They see the head guy in the bullseye, some of them will be breaking off to find a new supply for themselves if it all goes tits up. You won't be selling to corner dealers, Margo. Just like one notch down. Guys who want their own thing."

Margo pursed her lips and frowned while she made her calculations. "All right. Maybe there's enough in this for me to fuck with the price a little. Make some new connections. Offering good prices in bad times isn't a totally bad idea."

Impelliteri turned to Sperling, "See, man, that's why they call her the Kilo Queen. She knows how to do business."

"Don't fuckin' con me, Anthony. You leave my business to me. If I get jammed up, I might hit you for a few hundred. Are we clear?"

"Deal. Put the word out."

"How am I gonna know who's who on your hit parade?"

Impelliteri slid the mugshots to Margo.

"Those are the names and faces I'm lookin' for. Tell me when you think you got a line on any of these guys. I'll get the fuck over here and take care of them."

"I don't want you taking care of anybody within two blocks of wherever I'm workin'. You understand?"

"Understood."

"And this doesn't go on for more than a week."

"Hey, I'm not interested in anything that's gonna even take that long."

"All right. I'm in." Margo smiled, revealing a set of gleaming white teeth that looked much too perfect to be real. "Seal it with a kiss, honey."

"Thanks. Okay, Margo, I trust you."

"Come on."

"Hey, you ain't even getting a handshake out of me."

"For such a tough guy, you got no guts."

"You fuckin' got that right."

"All right, Mr. Crime Buster, you run along now with your silent partner here. I'll put the word out…"

"…in the direction of Brownsville."

"Yeah, yeah. I'll put the word out. I'll get some extra. We'll see what happens. But you don't fuck with my regulars or anybody I say don't fuck with. We clear on that?"

"Sure."

"Okay. We'll make it work. I don't mind the chief of D owes you, and you owe me."

"Okay, Margo. Good. One last thing."

"Shit, you never quit, do you?"

"This ain't a big thing. You know a guy named Reginal Wilson? Calls himself Reggie Whack?"

"Reginal Wilson, is that his real name?"

"Yeah."

"Reggie Whack, I know who he is."

"Know where I can find him?"

"He's not a nice person, Anthony."

"Yeah, neither am I. Where can I find him?"

Margo sighed. This was not part of the deal. Impelliteri was asking for more, but it didn't surprise Margo.

"All right. I don't know where he stays. My memory tells me he's one of these dogs fucking women all over the damn city. Who knows where he lays his head? But he's got a sister. Maybe you can work her for a lead. She works over on Sutter. A beauty shop called African Woman. No, it's Afro Lady. Something like that."

"Sutter and what?"

"Uh, 'round Amboy or Bristol. Over from the Tilden Housing."

"Okay, what's she look like?"

"Skinny, no tits, but cute. Light-skinned. Kind of rust-colored hair. Wears glasses."

"How tall?"

"Jeezus, *pendejo,* how the fuck do I know? Average."

"What's her name?"

"Lilly. No, no, it's Milly. Milly. That's it, Milly."

Margo had allowed her phone to go unanswered for two calls. When it started ringing a third time, she told Impelliteri, "I gotta work, Anthony."

"Okay, Margo. Appreciate it. I'll check back tomorrow. You gonna be here?"

"Yeah, but after that, I'll let you know."

And that was it. Impelliteri had his trap set. And he was on the trail of Reggie Whack.

CHAPTER 29

THE PHONE CALL FROM ARCHIE REYNOLDS CAME WHILE WHITEY Williams stood hunched over his two-burner stove stirring a can of Campbell's black bean soup in a stained aluminum pot with a loose handle. He listened to Archie's instructions, turned the burner off, and left, leaving the soup to congeal in the pot.

Five minutes later, Whitey walked into the storeroom in the back of the bodega across from the New Lots complex. Archie sat on a beat-up wooden office chair, the kind with a padded green seat, high-slat back, and big rolling wheels. Archie wore a tight-fitting white tank top under a blue rayon shirt left unbuttoned. His slacks were light wool, also blue. Archie propped his feet up onto a stack of corrugated boxes. Whitey noticed the Gucci buckle on the black slip-ons.

Reggie Whack sat off to the side, chewing a toothpick, his outfit the customary oversized denim jeans, Tommy Hilfiger sweatshirt, and black watch cap with the Knicks logo.

A faint odor of gasoline and mothballs lingered in the air, but Whitey didn't dare ask about it.

Neither of them motioned for Whitey to find a seat in the crowded room. Whitey didn't indicate any displeasure. He had heard about the massacre in the body shop. He wasn't about to do or say anything to set Archie off.

Archie asked his questions without explanation or repetition as if he wanted to get it over with quickly.

"So tell me about these Muslim motherfuckers again? They for real?"

"Real Muslims?"

"Yeah."

"I don't know a whole lot about that Islam stuff, but the ones who are Muslims seem like they take that shit real seriously. Fact is, though, a lot of them guards ain't Muslims at all."

"No?"

"Hell no. Just the heavy hitters. Lots of 'em jus' regular guys tryin' to work."

"So, just the shooters are Muslim."

"From what I can tell."

"Where's their mosque or temple or what have you?"

"Bushwick Avenue is what I hear. Over west near Greene. The brown building with the thing on the top."

"Right. How many of them are there?"

"In the temple?"

"No, motherfucker, in this guard company."

"Altogether, I don't know. I can jus' count the ones workin' round here. Every day I see two guards in the lobby of Building A and B, two at the front gate, and four on outside patrols. But they got three shifts."

"So outside, they work two and two?"

"Outside?"

"Yeah."

"Right," said Whitey. "They always patrol outside in pairs."

"Nothing inside?"

Whitey shook his head. "No, they have some inside, too. At least two in the lobbies like I said, but they be regular guards. Then, ever since they started buildin' that fence, they got a few more roamin' around in A and B looking after the construction workers. Those guys got guns."

Archie interrupted the old man. He had heard enough.

"Yeah, awright. Bushwick Avenue. I know the place. Okay, old man, keep on it."

Archie had finished with Whitey, but Whitey didn't leave. He stood in front of Archie, waiting, suppressing the little bit of dignity he had left in his old bones.

Whitey's lingering set off a flash of anger in Archie. He knew what Whitey was doing. Waiting for his handout, for doing nothing more than report the words that floated freely among the women and elderly residents of New Lots Apartments. Whitey provided nothing more than what gossips talked about, or little kids heard, or what a new guard would tell a shuffling old man who had common questions. It didn't seem like something Archie should really need to buy. But here was Whitey, standing in front of him, waiting, doing everything short of putting his hand out. It was worse than paying off old fool bums who squeegeed the windshield on Archie's Saab. Another drop in the bucket of acid that ate away at Archie's gut.

He stuffed a ten-dollar bill in the old man's shirt pocket.

Once the money was in his pocket, Whitey asked, "Anything else, boss?"

Archie knew the old man used the word *boss* deliberately.

"No, you got nothing else for me, Whitey. What the fuck else can you do for me?"

Whitey took a step back. Reggie stood up as if to signal the old man to move along.

"Nuthin', I suppose," said Whitey. "But, you never know."

"Fuck, I don't know. Go on, old man. Get the hell out."

As Whitey moved on out from the storeroom, Archie called after him, "Hey, what about the pohleeceman's daughter? What the fuck is she doing? She still coming around?"

Whitey turned back and said, "Oh, yeah, she's still around. Every day. Got a whole mess of cops around her. Guess she feels safe now. She's still over there."

Whitey waited for the vitriol that information would bring out of Archie, but Archie would not give him the satisfaction. He simply nodded his head and watched Whitey walk out to buy something in the bodega. He had extra money now. Enough for cheese and bologna and bread to go with his soup. Enough for a can of beer, too.

Reggie asked, "So what we gaw, gaw, gonna do next, Arch?"

Archie grimaced, shifting the anger around inside him so it wouldn't cloud his thinking.

"You got Weight and Melly set up?"

"Yeah, we me, me, meeting them later."

"Good." Archie shifted in his chair, unable to let it go, the last bit of information on the commissioner's daughter. "Goddamn that bitch. Got the fuckin' nerve to be still comin' round here. You know this is going down this way cuz of her."

"I s'pose."

"Fuck her. She can have all the cops on her she wants. We got time to show her who runs this damn neighborhood. Come on. Get your Jeep, bro."

Once in the Jeep, Archie directed Reggie to drive north several blocks on East 98th Street. They came back south on Rockaway Avenue, avoiding the police guarding Justine's community center but still managing to get close enough so that they could see the center's north exit.

Archie smirked at his ability to be so close and yet stay undetected by the police.

Archie and Reggie sat in the Jeep watching. Within fifteen minutes, they had seen two women exit, but Archie waited patiently for what he wanted. Another five minutes passed, and two more women emerged from the back door accompanied by three children between them. Archie recognized both the women, and he knew what they had come out for.

218 | JOHN CLARKSON

As they passed Reggie's car, Archie rolled down the passenger side window and said, "Yo."

They turned, and Archie motioned for them to come to him. They didn't hesitate for much more than a second or two. They were looking at the source of crack cocaine for the whole neighborhood, and crack had brought them onto the street.

One woman was black, the other white; their children were a mix of both. Both women had the tense, bleary-eyed, beaten-down appearance of people feeling the crippling need for crack cocaine.

The white woman hung back behind the black woman, figuring Archie would be more prone to deal with her. But Archie wasn't interested in selling crack. He was interested in humiliation and terror.

"Hey, cracker. Yeah, you come over here. Tell your sister to stand over there and watch them kids."

Her black friend gathered the kids around her. She didn't want to witness whatever was about to happen, so she kept her back to the car, trying to block the children's view. She should have done the opposite – made sure the children were facing away from the car, but she wasn't thinking clearly.

The white woman shuffled to the passenger-side window, her head down. Archie looked at her black roots, revealed by the part in her dirty platinum hair.

"Lift yo head up, honey, and tell me your name."

She looked up, "Lorraine."

"You know my name?"

Lorraine nodded.

"What's my name?"

"Archie."

"That's right, baby, you know what I do?"

Lorraine shrugged. She wore a V-necked sweater that was too small for her, dirty blue jeans, and worn-out tennis shoes.

She wrapped a thin raincoat around her body, trying to hide herself from Archie's gaze and help conceal the slight shaking that gripped her.

"I asked you a question, do you know what I do?"

"I guess."

"You guess?"

"You sell."

"Sell what?"

"Crack."

"That's right, baby. And that's what you lookin' for out here, ain't it."

"Yeah."

"You need some rock?"

Lorraine looked directly at Archie now. She tried to smile, revealing bad teeth along with the tension filling her because she was so close to what she desperately wanted, so close yet afraid of what she would have to endure in order to get it.

Archie reached over and took something out of Reggie's hand. He shifted and raised his left hand to the car window, showing Lorraine three small plastic vials capped with the familiar plastic blue tops. Each vial held a twenty-dollar dose of rock. Seeing them made Lorraine's stomach ache.

"How much money you got?"

"Twenty."

"Between the two of you?"

"Yeah."

Lorraine's nose ran slightly. She sniffed and wiped it with the back of her hand.

"Well, gimme the fuckin' twenty."

Lorraine quickly pulled out a crumpled bill from her raincoat pocket. She handed it to Archie, who snatched it away from her with his right hand as he closed his left hand holding the three vials.

Lorraine shuffled her feet and clenched her jaw. She felt like screaming, *Give me the fucking rock, you asshole.* But she didn't.

"You want the one or all three?"

"You want to give me all three, I'll take 'em."

"But you only gave me twenty."

"Then give me the one."

"But you want the other two."

"I don't have any more money."

"What you got?"

Lorraine paused ever so slightly. There was still a shred of dignity left in her, and her kids were no more than twenty feet away. But she swallowed her dignity and said, "What you want?"

"How about you suck my big black dick and my friend's. Two dicks, two vials."

Lorraine's cheek ticked with tension. Maybe if the kids hadn't been with her, she would have decided more quickly. She looked around behind her, checking to see how close they stood. The boy was eight. The girl five. The boy boldly peeked around her friend's leg, but the black woman moved his head back. Lorraine was getting ready to say "Okay," but Reggie spoke up first.

"Fuck that, man. She's stanky. Ai, ai, ain't gonna let no stank cracker bitch co, co, cop my joint."

Lorraine slumped forward, her shoulders hunched, almost unable to bear the wave of anger and loss that hit her.

Then Archie seemed to offer her another chance. He motioned for Lorraine to come closer.

"Come here."

When she stepped closer, Archie grabbed her throat.

"Open your fuckin' mouth, bitch."

At first, she thought Archie wanted her to show that her mouth was suitable for his penis. She started to open her mouth. But suddenly he squeezed his thumb into her throat, and Lorraine had no choice but to open her mouth wide as she gagged and desperately tried to suck in air. Archie leaned forward, hawked, and spat a load of phlegm into her open mouth.

And still he held her throat, pulling her closer. She could not swallow, could not spit it out. The warm excrescence sat in her mouth, sickening her.

"Now you listen to me, bitch, and you tell your friend and all those other crackhead bitches like you who go into that shithole you came out of, I see any of you in that place you'll never buy another rock in this neighborhood. You go in that place, I'll cut you off. And if I feel like it, I'll cut your fucking throats, too. You understand me?"

Lorraine nodded, crying now, choking, humiliated, burning with fear and hate, hoping her children hadn't seen what was being done to her.

"And you tell 'em who gave you this warning – me, the Ar-Man, Archie Reynolds. You decide what you want more – me, your shit-ass lives, and my crack, or that Uncle Tom bitch letting you sleep on her floor and kiss her light, bright ass. Got it?"

Lorraine didn't even know if she nodded. The pain had made her close her eyes.

"Look at me."

She did, and Archie shoved one vial in her mouth and pushed her away.

Lorraine bent over, humiliated, spitting out the vial and Archie's phlegm, openly crying now, spitting and choking on his slobber, trying to wipe away tears while she wiped off the vial with her dirty raincoat.

CHAPTER 30

THE FAX ON ELLARD WATKINS TOTALED ALMOST FOUR PAGES. BY the time the last page eked out of Caprice's fax machine, Loyd Shaw had given up on the McDonald's food.

The pages told Shaw and Mason just about everything law enforcement agencies had on Ellard "Weight" Watkins. His arrest record went back to 1978, mostly drug-related and assault charges. There was an NYPD career criminal file on him, as well as state and federal records. Shaw noted that Ellard's arrest and incarceration ratio ran about average, which meant he served time for about three percent of his arrests. The pages were impersonal. The facts they showed were interchangeable with thousands of criminals like him. But Shaw knew that if Weight Watkins had risen to become one of the Blue-Tops managers, he must have hurt a lot of people along the way. He certainly had to be capable of killing.

Shaw and Mason sat in the front seat of the parked Caprice reading the pages, shoving the ridiculous amount of wrappings and Styrofoam and cardboard from their drive-thru meal into the stained McDonald's bag.

Shaw rolled down the car window to let out some of the pungent food odors. As Shaw finished one page of the fax, he handed it to Mason.

Mason wore a beat-up pair of tortoiseshell reading glasses. They gave him a professorial air. As he read about Ellard Watkins, he made a few notes in the small stenographer's notebook

he carried around stuck in the side pocket of his gray herringbone sports coat. Shaw kept his thoughts to himself and
let Mason work on the facts in his old-school cop, thorough,
plodding way.

Shaw didn't know who Ellard Watkins was. But from the
facts on Walter's printouts, and the blurry arrest photo, an
image of the Blue-Tops manager began to form in his mind.
Watkins weighed over three hundred pounds, but Shaw did
not picture somebody who was fat. He pictured a big man
who intimidated with his size. When Shaw imagined Watkins
at trial or in his cell at Dannemora or walking the streets of
Brownsville, it was easy to imagine him as hard and mean
and brutal.

Mason finished his last note and pulled off his glasses.

Shaw said, "I want us to take down the first one, Mase."

"Why?"

"I don't know. I just do. I'll bet Walter got us the information
on our guy first."

"You want to beat Impelliteri. Show 'em the old dogs still
can do it."

"Maybe."

Mason shrugged. "I just want this over as quick as possible.
These are bad people. Any ideas?"

"Every time he's been arrested, he's given an address in
Brooklyn."

"Right. But sittin' on those addresses ain't going to make
anything happen quickly."

"No, but those addresses tell me he's a Brooklyn boy. I'll bet
he doesn't go into Manhattan much."

"Maybe."

"What does he drive?"

Mason checked his notes. Then he shuffled through the
fax pages.

"DMV has no record of a car owned by him. Last arrest reported he was picked up driving a ninety-one Lincoln Continental. You want to look for the car?"

"No. No, I just keep thinking about him. Big car. Big guy. Big Brooklyn boy. Weight Watkins." Shaw lapsed into silence, then sat upright and said, "Come on, I got an idea."

"What?"

"I need a Brooklyn Yellow Pages. And I'm still hungry."

"After all that?"

"I can't eat that shit. Come on."

First, they found a Chinese restaurant, then they found a Yellow Pages in the owner's office. Both detectives had to flash their shields at the suspicious owner before he would hand over his copy of the phonebook.

Once they got the book, they sat at a table and shoveled food into their mouths from three plates of Chinese food while Shaw flipped through the phonebook. They'd eaten a late lunch. Now they were eating an early dinner.

As Shaw looked through the phonebook, he remembered an old advertising slogan, "If it's out there, it's in here." It was in there, Shaw just had to find out where. It wasn't under "Clothing." It wasn't under "Apparel." It was under "Men's." He figured there'd be quite a few listings under "Men's."

The Yellow Pages told Shaw what he wanted to know, including the number of Men's fat-man clothing stores were in Brooklyn. The euphemistic descriptions varied: big, tall, portly.

After consulting with Mason, they eliminated the shop in Bay Ridge, figuring their clientele would be mostly Caucasian. They called the other stores and inquired as to the racial mix of their clientele. They decided two of the stores might provide them with a lead. One was open until eight, the other until nine o'clock. It was a little after five. They finished their

Tsingtao beers and were just about to head out when Shaw's police radio squawked.

It was Walter Wang.

"Yeah, Walter, go ahead."

"I got Justine Burton on the line. She wants to talk to you. Sounds like she's on a cell phone."

"Get the number. Tell her I'll call her right back."

Justine answered on the first ring. Her voice mixed with the background noise her cell phone picked up, but Shaw could still hear the anger in it.

"Detective Shaw?"

"Yes."

"I need to talk to you."

"In person?"

"Yes. I'd prefer that."

"Where are you?"

"I'm in my car. I'm heading into Manhattan."

"Where are you going?"

"To see my father. But I want to talk to you first."

"All right."

Shaw didn't waste time asking her what was going on. He exchanged locations with Justine, and they figured out a place where they could meet on Ocean Parkway.

Mason asked, "What's that all about?"

"Commissioner's daughter. She sounds pissed."

"At us?"

"I can't see why. But who knows? She's on her way to complain to Daddy."

"Damn."

"Yeah, that's all we need now. Let's see if I can calm her down."

Shaw found Justine in a quiet Italian neighborhood bar-restaurant waiting for him. She sat at a table in the back. Her three-man security squad from the Intelligence Division sat parked out front. Mason waited in the car outside.

Shaw nodded at the detectives. They looked back at him as if to say, "She's all yours."

Shaw took a seat across from Justine. She sat rigidly on the other side of the checkerboard tablecloth, now wearing the jacket to her suit. With her white silk blouse and a single strand of pearls, Shaw thought she looked like she should be working in a Park Avenue law firm. It occurred to him that her very appearance could set off someone like Archie Reynolds.

There was one other couple in the back of the dining area. Shaw had the impression they were a boss and his secretary. The couple held hands and stared into each other's eyes, sneaking kisses like high school kids playing hooky. Shaw couldn't have cared less about what they were doing, but their adolescent behavior stood in contrast to Justine Burton's angry demeanor.

Even angry, she looked beautiful. For the first time, Shaw noticed her hair. It seemed to him more Hispanic than African American. No, he thought, American Indian. Straight, thick, and black. But she must have permed it slightly since there was a soft wave to it. Or maybe she had straightened it into a soft wave. Whatever she had done, it was perfect for her oval face, straight nose, and high cheekbones. The nose and cheekbones, that's what said American Indian to him.

And then, all those thoughts disappeared when Shaw saw Justine lifting her coffee cup with two hands so that she could control her shaking hands.

Shaw asked, "What happened?"

"Before I tell you, I'm going to warn you that I don't think I have ever been quite this angry or disgusted in my life. So I apologize in advance if you think my anger is directed at you. I'm just livid. I'm sorry."

"At what?"

"At Archie Reynolds. And at you, because you haven't done anything about him, even though that's absurd since it's been less than one day."

Shaw didn't comment. He asked again, "What did he do?"

She told Shaw the story she had managed to pull out of Lorraine's friend after one of her social workers saw Lorraine dragging her kids out of the center. And she told Shaw what Archie Reynolds had promised to do to any woman who dared stay at her shelter.

Shaw listened. Justine's reticence to speak about unspeakable acts made her story even more disturbing to him than if he had witnessed it himself.

By the time she finished, Shaw had noted her tightly pursed mouth and clenched jaw.

"He's a fucking animal, Justine. He's just an animal. No, he's worse. He plans this shit."

The waitress came by to refill Justine's coffee cup, and Shaw told her, "Bring me a shot of Maker's Mark, please. Straight up."

Without prompting, Justine said, "Make it two."

After a few moments of silence, during which the image of Archie spitting into a poor woman's mouth continued searing itself into Shaw's brain, Justine spoke quietly.

"I hardly know this man, and I hate him so much it makes my stomach ache. It's not bad enough what he does to these women with his drugs. It's not bad enough what they do to themselves because of it. Now he tells them they can't even seek a modicum of shelter, a night's sleep in a place where someone isn't going to come home drunk or angry and beat them up."

"Look," Shaw said, "he isn't doing this just to hurt them. He's doing it to send you a message. To show you that you can't come into his neighborhood and take away what's his. He's trying to show you who is in control."

Justine glared at Shaw and said, "I know, damn it. I know. But why doesn't he have the goddamn nerve to come to me and tell me? Why does he have to go through them?"

"Because you've got three detectives with you and a half dozen uniformed cops around you. And he *did* come to you and tell you. He came with his gun in his hand and told you to get out. You didn't listen."

"I can't let that animal run me out."

"I know. I know. Did that woman leave?"

"I tried to calm her down. I tried to convince her to stay."

"Did you?"

"I don't know. She was still there when I left. Could I guarantee her that nothing would happen to her? Could I tell her that the man would be arrested?"

"Yes. That's exactly what you could have told her."

"I can't guarantee her that. You know that."

"Why the hell can't you? You think I'm out here playing a game? That fucking guy is already dead. He's a walking dead man."

Suddenly, Justine grabbed Shaw's wrist. The strength in her long fingers surprised him.

"But you said it yourself this morning. How many people are going to die before he does? How many women are going to get hurt? You understand what I'm dealing with, don't you? I don't mean to put this all on you, but you understand what I'm trying to do?"

"Yes. Of course."

She looked at Shaw as if she wanted to believe him but couldn't allow herself to.

"What are you going to do?" she asked.

"I'm going to track him down, track down his gang, find every lead I can get on him, and keep after him until he's dead, gone, or locked up. I don't know how long it will take or when it will happen exactly, but it *will* happen. If I don't nail him, someone else will."

She released her grip on Shaw's wrist and sat back in her chair. She seemed to fade away, her mind going someplace else. Shaw couldn't tell whether or not she believed him.

Shaw tapped the side of her hand to get her attention. And maybe to see if she would allow him to touch her.

"Justine."

She allowed the touch and the use of her first name. She focused on Shaw, and he said, "Did you hear me?"

And then she surprised Shaw by grabbing his hand, looking straight into his eyes, and saying, "Yes. I heard you."

"Did you believe me?"

"I believe *you* believe it."

She gave his hand a final squeeze, perhaps by way of telling Shaw he had gotten as much agreement from her as he was going to get.

"You're going to see your father now?"

"Yes."

"If you're going to keep those women in your center, ask your father for patrols on the streets around you, not just in front of the center and at the ends of the block. But if you want to be really smart, move them to other shelters. Don't put yourself or them in unnecessary danger. If you could move everything to another locale until this is over, I think you should do that."

"I won't let him run me out."

"I'm not telling you to run. I'm telling you to be smart. Take away his targets. Help everyone survive while we beat him. You and your clients." Justine picked up her bourbon and took a long sip. Shaw drained his shot glass and chased it with lukewarm coffee while she thought over what Shaw said.

"I don't know why I picked you, Shaw."

"You didn't. The chief of detectives did."

"No. He may have given you the job, but I picked you to focus on. There's plenty of uniformed guys and detectives working on this, but I picked you. There's something different about you and about the way you're working. I don't get that usual cop procedure feel about you. You're not in the usual loop, are you?"

"No."

"What are you? Some sort of special-assignment cop?"

"I don't know. I guess so."

"It's not your responsibility any more than anyone else's, but for better or worse, as far as I'm concerned, you're the guy."

"That's fine with me."

"Good. I don't want you to think I'm exerting unfair pressure on you."

"I didn't say it was fair. I just said it was fine. Believe me, there's so much pressure on me, yours doesn't make a whole lot of difference."

"Well, sorry if I'm adding more."

She took another sip of her bourbon while she prepared for her next statement.

"You make a lot of sense, Shaw. You also seem to have the ability to calm me down."

"Maybe it's the Maker's."

She smiled. "No. Not yet anyhow. It's you."

"Well, I take that as a compliment."

"You should. I don't pay compliments to very many men."

"Why is that?"

"There aren't too many I think deserve it. Actually, there aren't very many men who want to deal with me."

"And vice versa?"

"Right."

"And why is that?"

"I don't know. Maybe I make them nervous."

"I can't imagine why. You're only a stunning six-foot black woman who's probably twice as smart as most men, who's got a pair of eyes like lasers, and who happens to be the police commissioner's daughter. Why should anybody be reluctant to deal with you or get involved?"

Justine smiled again. Shaw was beginning to enjoy making her smile. "Involved? You are talking about my social life or professional life?"

"Both. I just threw in the involved part because I was fishing."

"I see. So I don't make you nervous?"

Shaw said, "I'm past nervous."

"What does that mean?"

"I'm not in your league. What do I have to be nervous about?"

"What do you mean, you're not in my league?"

"Well, I'm a cop. I don't imagine you make it a policy to get involved with cops."

"You're right."

"I'm also white. Not implying that you're prejudiced, but I assume your preference is black men."

"Not necessarily. Black men bring their own problems to the equation, believe me."

"And technically, I'm married. You're not married, I take it."

"No, I'm not married. What do you mean, technically?"

Shaw looked at his empty shot glass and resisted the urge to order another.

"If my wife and I weren't so busy, we'd have filed for a divorce quite a while ago."

"Do you live together?"

"We're under the same roof, sometimes."

"I think I've heard this one before."

"I wouldn't be surprised. But why are we talking about this anyhow?"

"How old are you, Shaw?"

"Older than you."

"You don't really look it. You're in fairly good shape."

"Thanks. How old are you?"

"Thirty-four."

Shaw's reaction told her he thought she was younger.

"Yeah, I'm getting up there. The clock is just about ticked out."

"You were never married?"

"Close once. That was enough."

Shaw said, "I'm forty-two. So other than being older, white, a cop, *technically* married, and this being the wrong time... when's our first date?"

Justine answered without skipping a beat.

"When this is over."

Shaw stopped for several beats before he responded. "Did I just hear what I think I did?"

"You're the one who decided to fish."

"You serious?"

"I don't joke around about dates."

"Now I'm nervous," said Shaw.

"Bullshit."

"Well, maybe a little. What's this? More motivation?"

"Take it whatever way you want. When this is over, we go out to dinner and drink as much damn bourbon as we want."

Shaw reached over and offered his hand. He had an urge to touch Justine Burton for real. She gripped his hand and shook it once."

"Deal," Shaw said.

"Deal. But one more thing."

"What?"

"I can't just leave the center, you know. Women come there all the time. I couldn't live with myself thinking someone will come to that door and it will be locked."

"Does it have to be you? Can't you just keep someone there to direct them to another place?"

"It has to be me at least part of the time. I can't let others do for me what I won't do."

"Then keep it to the minimum. Keep a low profile. Get people out of there to other safe places as soon as you can. And tell the women who are there who still need drugs to have someone else get it for them. Have their boyfriends or people who won't be seen coming out of your shelter get it for them."

Justine listened and nodded. She frowned a bit, thinking over what Shaw had said.

"All right?" Shaw asked.

She looked up at him and finally nodded her head in agreement. "Okay, Shaw, I'll do what you say. But please, let me know how you're doing." She pulled out a card and began writing phone numbers on it. "Here's my cell phone and my home phone. Call me if anything I should know about happens."

"I will. Gotta go."

"Okay. Thanks."

Shaw stood up to leave.

"Hey."

"What?"

"I forgot your first name. What's your first name, Shaw?"

"Loyd. With one L."

"That's right. One L. She nodded as if she approved. "Nice. It fits you. Why'd they name you that?"

"I don't know, after my grandfather, I think. Where'd they get Justine? From justice?"

"My father never would admit that to me, but probably."

"Well, it suits you."

"Thanks. Don't leave me wondering about what's happening out there. I know how cops hate to answer to anybody, but please call me."

"I will."

CHAPTER 31

MASON WAS NAPPING WHEN SHAW RETURNED TO THE CAR. The sound of the door opening woke him. He leaned forward and started the car – back on the case, just like that.

As they drove to the clothing store, Shaw told him about Justine's latest problem with Archie. Mason just shook his head and held his comments. He's right, thought Shaw. There was nothing to say. It was now a question of doing something about it.

They arrived at the fat man's clothing store in a no-nonsense mood. Fortunately, there weren't any big boys searching for clothing when they walked in, so it was easy for Shaw and Mason to corner the manager and his two salesmen. All three of them eyed Weight Watkins's mugshot. All three identified him.

Shaw asked, "You have any records on him? Credit card number? Address? Phone?"

The salesman who seemed to know Watkins best said, "He always pays in cash, but I got a phone number to call when his clothes are ready. After we tailor 'em."

He left to get the phone number while Shaw thought about fat men climbing into oversized pants. The salesman returned with a phone number for Ellard Watkins.

Shaw called Walter Wang and gave him the phone number. Within thirty seconds, Wang had contacted Coles Directory Service and matched the phone number with an address in Brownsville.

Shaw asked the salesman if anybody ever delivered to that address.

"No. We don't deliver."

"How often does he buy clothes?"

"Oh, maybe once a month. He shops pretty regular."

"And you always call when the clothes are ready?"

"Sometimes. Sometimes he just comes in."

"Does Watkins answer when you call?"

"Sometimes. Most times it's a woman. I think she's his mother."

Shaw turned to Mason.

"Mase, call up the number and make like this salesman here. See if you can find out if he's home."

Mason asked the salesman, "You don't have anything ready now, do you?"

"Nope."

Shaw could see that the salesmen and store manager were anxious to be done with them. It had dawned on them that there might be terrible repercussions for leading the police to Weight Watkins. Tough shit. That's the price you pay when you sell to fat criminals, thought Shaw.

Mason dialed the phone and got an answer.

"Hello, this is Classic Clothing calling for Mr. Watkins. Is he available? Uh-huh. Uh-huh."

Shaw watched the concerned look on the salesman's face when Mason mentioned the name of the store. He turned back to watch Mason. Shaw enjoyed seeing his old partner at work. He knew Orestes Mason was a tough man. Genuinely tough. Physically and emotionally. Shaw had seen Mason go through bad times and hard guys, not much fazed by either. But Mason intrigued Shaw because, despite it all, Mason maintained a quiet, thoughtful demeanor, and a disarmingly gentle voice and manner, which he put to good use on the phone call.

Shaw could easily envision Mason teaching at a bucolic black college in the South. Running it down in that slow, thoughtful way. Advising slightly militant African American coeds with their firmly politically correct agendas. Gently leading them toward a more realistic view of life.

Shaw suddenly realized that he didn't want the horror and violence of the Blue-Tops-Muslim war to touch Orestes Mason. He wanted the department to owe them. He wanted Albert J. DeLuca to be beholden to this good, honest, forthright black man. But he didn't want Mason bloodied.

The manager came over and handed Mason copies of the most recent sales receipt for Watkins. The second salesman drifted over and decided to eavesdrop on the call. Despite their fears, they, too, couldn't resist watching Mason in action.

"Well, uh, who am I speaking to? Mrs. Watkins? Oh, I see, Mr. Watkins's mother. Well, Mrs. Watkins, we were just going over our records here, and we noticed that on the last outfit your son bought – uh-huh. Right. As I was saying, Ellard was supposed to get half price on his second pair of pants, but we charged him full price. Uh-huh. Right. So when he gets in, just let him know he has a credit here for, let me see, eighty-six dollars. Right. Classic Clothing. When do you expect him in? Okay. Well, ma'am, please give him that message. Thanks."

Mason hung up the phone.

"So?"

"That was his Moms. She says Ellard comes in and out whenever. Can't say when he'll be around again, but she'll give him the message."

Not great, thought Shaw, but considering how much effort they had put in, not bad.

Shaw turned to the salesmen.

"Gentlemen, thanks for your help. I'd like to ask you to keep our inquiries to yourselves. If Mr. Watkins should happen to come in here within the next couple of days, stall him over that refund and call me right away. We'll be here in five minutes. Five minutes tops. It's very important."

Shaw gave the manager one of his altered business cards with the phone number of the 73rd Precinct. He doubted he'd ever hear from them.

By eight-thirty, Shaw and Mason were parked around the corner from Mrs. Watkins's house, right in the heart of Brownsville on Lott Avenue, within walking distance of New Lots Apartments.

It was a long shot that Weight Watkins would be at his mother's, but Shaw didn't have any other shot to take.

They had circled the block once to get a fix on the house. Like most of the residents on the block, Mrs. Watkins lived in a run-down, cheaply constructed, two-story flat. The house was an old box held up by a sagging wood frame covered in plywood and then finished with cheap asphalt shingle siding, top and sides.

There were more substantial houses in the area. And there were worse. But every occupied house, including Mrs. Watkins's, had been augmented with wrought-iron bars covering doors and windows. The iron enclosures were the most substantial structures in the whole neighborhood. And they were everywhere – cut, formed, welded together, and bolted over every window, every door, over all possible points of entry into the little houses.

Some of the houses were protected with iron-bar barricades that extended from the ground all the way up to the roofs, making the houses look like they were in a giant birdcage.

It occurred to Shaw that if Ellard Watkins were inside that house, he was already behind bars.

There were two ways to find out if Watkins was home. Sit and wait for hours or days and hope to see him arrive or leave. Or go into the damn house and find out.

Shaw sat with Mason in the Caprice thinking about how to get into the house. Since the neighborhood was dangerous enough to require a facade of iron bars on the outside, it was a sure bet most of these people had a supply of weapons inside.

Mason waited for Shaw's decision.

He asked Mason, "What's today's date?"

"The fifth."

"Tuesday, right?"

"Tuesday."

Shaw thought it over.

"I want to get that door open without busting it down. How about you go on up and knock on the door and tell them you're from the landlord? Tell them you're collecting this month's rent. I'll bet Mrs. Watkins hasn't paid it yet."

Mason looked at his watch. It was a fairly reasonable hour to collect the rent. A little past eight o'clock.

"What if she already paid it?"

"Just tell her your records say she didn't. Tell her to open the door so you can show her."

Shaw could see his idea wasn't sitting well with Mason.

Mason said, "I don't know. What if the landlord never comes in here to get his money? Let me think. It's too late to be from Con Ed. Nobody in this neighborhood is lettin' the cable company in. I got a feeling she knows who she pays the rent to. She ain't gonna open the door for someone she's never seen before."

"Well, think up something. I don't want to sit here all night."

Mason didn't argue. He wanted to get it over with, too. Waiting on it made it worse.

"Come on," said Shaw. "Let's get the vests on."

They dug two bulletproof vests out of the car trunk and wrestled into them. Shaw zipped up his leather jacket to cover his vest. Mason buttoned up his sports coat but couldn't cover his vest. In the waning light, it almost looked like a heavy sweater under the large man's jacket.

Suddenly Mason announced, "I got it. Come on."

"What?"

"You'll see."

They left the car where it was, knowing that if they pulled up in the unmarked, they would be identified as a police car before they even stepped out.

Shaw waited to take out his Glock until they reached the front door. He pointed it down next to his right leg, blocking it from sight, standing off to the right, thinking weird thoughts about the semantics of backing up his partner while standing next to him instead of behind him.

Mason carefully took out his Sig and knocked gently on the front door with his free hand. There was no buzzer, no name-plate, no way to know who lived in the house. They listened for sounds inside. Shaw wondered how they received their mail without a mailbox or name on the door.

Mason knocked again and said, "Mrs. Watkins. It's the Public Health Office."

He turned to Shaw and shook off the questioning look.

Shaw heard creaking floors, and then an elderly woman's faint response.

"Who is it?"

"It's the Public Health Office, from Kings County Hospital, Mrs. Watkins. We'd like to speak to you for just a moment."

"About what?"

"It's about your son, Ellard."

"What about him?"

"I'd rather not be shouting through the door, Mrs. Watkins. It's kind of personal. I have to speak to your son."

"About what?"

Mason hesitated for effect then said, "It's about a sexual disease that might have been transmitted to him."

Yeah, from that woman he raped, thought Shaw.

The old lady wasn't going to open the door for anybody, but Mason's news hit one of her buttons. She turned away from the door and called out her son's name.

That was all Mason and Shaw needed to hear. Mason laid his two hundred sixty pounds into the door. Shaw added his two-fifteen. Both of them bounced off Mrs. Watkins's door. Shaw slammed into the door again, harder. Mason reared back and kicked just above the door handle. They heard the frame crack, but it took two more hits before they finally busted all the locks out of the frame.

Ellard was not in sight. But they both heard a pounding sound heading up a set of stairs.

Mrs. Watkins stood about ten feet off to the right, angry, defiant. Shaw expected a stout woman. She was thin, with a face wrinkled and ugly as an old Shar Pei.

"Get the fuck out my house," she yelled.

Shaw yelled back "Police, move!" as he ran through her living room toward the stairs. He angled in front of Mason, but his partner wasn't far behind him.

They'd just reached the stairs when they heard the soul-numbing sound of a shell being pumped into the chamber of a shotgun. They both dropped flat on the stairs as Watkins leaned around into the stairwell and fired a deafening blast. Most of the shot stayed in a tight burst, flying over their heads.

Shaw had seen the carnage a shotgun could cause. A blast at such close range could take out entire sections of a human body. Shaw cringed, imagining the top of his head about to be blown away with the next blast.

Fighting the terror to steady his aim, from his prone position, Shaw pointed his Glock toward the top of the stairs and started pulling the trigger. And kept pulling the trigger, aiming at the wall on the right side, blasting out chunks of lathe and plaster, hoping to keep Watkins from chambering another round and this time aiming when he leaned around to shoot at them.

Shaw had seventeen rounds in the Glock. The blasts from his gun blinded and deafened him in the narrow stairwell. After seven shots, he felt the wall next to him shake. Weight Watkins was on the move. Shaw jumped up, almost fell, but Mason grabbed him and steadied him as they ran up the short flight of stairs.

All Shaw could think of was to move fast and get the son of a bitch in front of him so he could shoot Watkins before Watkins shot them.

Shaw reached the top of the stairs. He was ready to shoot anything that moved and hoped there was nobody else up there to get in his way, some kid popping out of a bedroom or a woman jumping out.

Shaw made it to the landing just in time to see Watkins turn into one of the bedrooms and slam the door behind him. He pegged one shot at the doorway just to make sure Watkins didn't pop back out with his shotgun. Mason ran past and pressed up flat against the wall flanking the bedroom door. Shaw took up the same position on the other side. His heart pounded so forcefully in his chest that Shaw feared he might blow an artery and die even if Watkins didn't shoot.

He managed to get enough wind in him to yell, "Watkins. It's the police. Throw the gun down. You can't win this. Come out."

Watkins answered with another blast that exploded a hole in the bedroom door the size of a dinner plate. Then another and another.

Shaw expected Watkins to keep pumping and blasting away blindly, but he stopped. Mason and Shaw had the same thought. He was reloading.

Mason turned and kicked the remains of the door out of his way and immediately dropped down into a shooter's crouch. He still hadn't fired a shot. Shaw leaned in above Mason, pointing his Glock into the room, but there was nothing in sight but a beat-up bed and gun smoke. They saw that the bedroom opened onto a second-floor back porch. Watkins was already out the door and rumbling across the deck.

They ran after him and caught sight of Weight just as he reached a wooden railing. Watkins hoisted one huge leg over the railing, then the other.

Shaw shouted, "Don't move."

But he did. Without even looking back, Watkins jumped over to the roof of a one-story building next to his house. The distance from his porch to the roof spanned no more than three feet, so Weight Watkins didn't have to launch himself far. But the rooftop was seven feet below him. The enormous man landed with such force that the dilapidated structure never had a chance. Ellard Watkins landed with a crashing thud and went right through the roof.

Mason yelled, "Good Lord!"

Shaw muttered, "Jeesuz Christ."

A sickening thud sounded from the interior, and a plume of dust billowed up from the dark hole. Shaw peered over the porch but couldn't see past the hole.

He didn't think it possible that Watkins would survive unscathed, but Shaw wasn't taking any chances that he might get up and stagger out the front door of whatever he had landed in.

Shaw and Mason ran back down the stairs and out of the house. Mrs. Watkins had disappeared. It occurred to Shaw that she might be shuffling out of her bedroom with her own shotgun, but they made it out of her house without her pegging a shot at them. Two reasons to be grateful, thought Shaw.

They didn't get shot, and didn't have to shoot an elderly black woman in her own home.

They hustled around the corner and found the building Watkins had cannonballed through. It appeared to be the remains of an old brick garage, so decrepit that sections of the mortar and bricks had fallen out in various spots. Watkins had shaken a few more bricks loose with his escape attempt.

Rotting wooden double-garage doors blocked the entrance. At one time, they had been red, but now the remaining paint reminded Shaw of a big, falling-apart scab. The old doors were nailed and braced shut. Shaw and Mason heard sounds of pain from inside.

Shaw stepped back to see if there was an obvious way into the structure. Mason stepped forward and ripped a section of the old door off on the first try.

Shaw peered inside. He saw nothing but heard soft grunts. The kind that come from fighting off intense pain.

They entered the dark, musty interior, stepping over rubble and trash. A good portion of the roof had fallen in on Watkins. Mason pushed and kicked open more of the front doors letting in light from the streetlamps. Shaw could see that the Blue-Tops manager had broken at least one leg. It jutted out from under the big man at an acute angle. He hoped Watkins had broken both legs.

There was enough light to see Ellard lying in a pile, much of which consisted of him.

Shaw wanted to make sure Ellard didn't have a gun in his pocket, so he and Mason pulled off enough debris to ask him.

Watkins began cursing the cops in a particularly vile way. Shaw tried to ignore it, but he could see that it was getting to Orestes.

Shaw yelled, "You got any more guns on you, Ellard?"

"Fuck you."

"The hell with him," said Shaw.

He reached under the rubble and found Watkins's right hand, then just managed to fit one cuff around the huge wrist. He pulled Watkins's right arm free. Watkins resisted, so Shaw straddled the meaty arm and attached the other end of the cuff to a water pipe jutting out of the wall. He had no interest in digging out Watkins's left arm.

"Screw it. Let him lay there."

They called the precinct and asked for assistance, then sat on the curb waiting. It took five cops and two EMS workers to free Watkins from the wreckage and roll him onto a stretcher. Mason and Shaw did not help. But Shaw did follow the ambulance to Kings County Hospital and monitored Watkins's arrest and confinement to the prison ward. He conferred with the assistant district attorney who caught the case and made sure that Ellard Watkins was on his way back to prison, broken leg and all. The ADA readily agreed. Felons who shoot at cops don't get bail.

Shaw and Mason one. Blue-Tops zero.

CHAPTER 32

While Shaw and Mason were tracking down Ellard Watkins, Impelliteri and Sperling were parked outside Afro Lady beauty salon.

Impelliteri asked Sperling, "So how we gonna get in there and find out if the Whack's sister Milly is in there? You need a haircut?"

"No."

"How about a bikini wax?"

"No, I hate waxing. I just shave."

"Hey, the Sperl cracks a joke. You comin' around, James?"

"Don't hold your breath."

Sperling settled his painfully thin body into the front seat, positioning himself for an extended wait.

Sperling's button-down appearance and quiet demeanor made Impelliteri think he might be a prude, which was all the incentive Impelliteri needed.

"So what do you think, James? Do most black women prefer to wax or shave their private areas?"

"Surprisingly, I haven't given it much thought."

"Well, thinking about it now, what is your opinion? I would imagine kinky hair is harder to wax."

"Who said I'm thinking about it."

"Well, I tell you one thing. Waxing pussy is a job I think I'd be great at."

"Well then, Impelliteri, maybe that's your ticket into Afro Lady. Go ask if they have an opening for a hair removal expert."

"Nah, I got a better way." Impelliteri checked his watch. "Shouldn't be too long. I reached out a little while back for someone to meet me here."

"Who'd you ask? Margo?"

"Ha-ha. She's probably already been eighty-sixed from there."

"I would think Margo would be very appreciative of Afro Lady's services."

"I didn't think you took much notice of the beauty shop services Margo might need."

"I notice what there is to notice. How come Margo knew so much about the chief of detectives?"

"Who said she did?"

"Nobody had to. And nobody had to say anything about why a cop attached to a homicide squad knows a drug dealer, either. But she did, and you do, so what's the deal?"

"What do you mean?"

"Why do I have the feeling Margo is a cop?"

For once, Impelliteri had nothing to say, which was answer enough for Sperling.

"Interesting," said Sperling.

"That's pretty good, James. You figured that shit out in one shot. Guys out there have been gettin' burned by Margo for years, and they haven't nailed her yet." Impelliteri pointed to Sperling's head. "Damn, James, you don't say much, but you got some shit going on up there, don't you? Yeah, Margo is a cop. Deep, deep fucking undercover cop. I'm not supposed to know about it. Neither are you. I just found out by luck."

"What's her story?"

"Her name used to be Martin Hernandez. He and I went through the police academy together. I just knew him a bit because so much shit is done there in alphabetical order. A couple of years ago, I run into this Margo character. The Kilo Queen. Had to do with a shooting. A drug hit. Margo was just a person who might have information. So I'm doing this interview, and I get that feeling, you know, that I know this person. And I'm sittin' there trying to figure out how the hell do I know this fucking freak. Underneath all the hormones and makeup and shit, she's still Martin Hernandez, but for the life of me, I can't figure it out."

"But you did."

"Yeah. I kept getting distracted by the way she looked. Then I glanced down at my notes and heard her voice. Just the voice. Then it clicked. Martin Hernandez."

"What did you say to her?"

"Nothing. The minute I got it; she saw that I got it. We weren't in a threatening situation. I mean, it wasn't like a buy-and-bust deal or anything, but it was obvious the people around her didn't have the slightest fuckin' idea who she really was."

"And for once, you kept your mouth shut."

"What do you mean for once I know how to play it? Anyhow, I ran her down about a week later. Busted her balls good."

"Metaphorically."

"Yeah, she's still got the plumbing. Chick with a dick for sure. So, I really played it up how she didn't fool me and how grateful she should be that I didn't bust her cover. Believe me, you can't fuck around with Margo too much, she'll shoot you. But she was grateful that I kept it on the down-low, so she filled me in. Turns out, dig this, they took the guy right out of the police academy. They must have known he was on the fence way back then. They never assigned him to a precinct. Put him undercover right away. The guy has never worked a day in uniform. I bet only a handful of people on our side know Margo is a cop. She's put away a lot of bad guys and none of 'em ever suspected."

"Interesting."

"Yeah. Not many like Margo out there. She and I get along. We help each other out.

She's a good person to know."

A police squad car pulled up, and a young black woman stepped out of the passenger's side, ducked down to window level, and made sure it was Impelliteri sitting in the car. Only then did she turn and wave off her ride. As the squad car pulled away, she sashayed over to Impelliteri's car. She had a sexy Tina Turner sway in her walk and a wry smile that revealed gleaming, white teeth. She wore ankle boots, black jeans, a white knit top that showed off her trim figure, and a New York Mets baseball cap. Her hair was tied up in a ponytail that had been pulled through the adjustable band on her ball cap. Over her shoulder hung a handbag that held her police ID and gun.

She leaned down to Impelliteri's window level and said, "So what kinda trouble you gettin' me into now, bad boy."

"Rita! Get in the car."

By the time she slid into the backseat of their car, Sperling had no doubt that the woman knew how to handle herself.

Impelliteri introduced them. "James Sperling, this is Detective Rita Easton. Easton from East New York. One of our best and a close personal friend of mine."

She shook Sperling's outstretched hand and told him, "Emphasis on friend, James. And forget that close and personal part."

"But the best of friends, right, Rita?"

"Oh, of course. Nothing less. So what can I do for you two in exchange for a complete fashion makeover?"

"Come on, Rita, you don't want to mess with your gorgeous looks. Your skin, your hair, everything is already perfect. How about a manicure? Maybe a bikini wax?"

"Gimme the damn hundred dollars you promised, Anthony. I want to see how far a hundred dollars goes in Afro Lady. And tell me what you want."

Impelliteri quickly explained they were trying to find Reginal Wilson, a.k.a. Reggie Whack, by locating her sister, who might be working in the salon.

Rita went in. An hour later, she came out. The hundred stayed.

This time the baseball cap hung from the strap of her handbag. Her hair had been cut and styled. Her nails gleamed with a polish that seemed to match a new application of lipstick.

Impelliteri didn't waste too much time on compliments.

"You look great, Rita, what'd you find out?"

"That's it? I look great? She completely redid my hair, manicure, pedicure—"

"Classic bikini wax? Mini Brazilian? Full Brazilian?"

"Shut up."

"All right, take it easy. What'd you find out?"

Sperling took the time to look and said, "Rita, that cut is very nice. Absolutely complements the shape of your face. And the texture is lovely. Very inviting."

Rita punched Impelliteri's shoulder and said, "You hear that, you moron? Listen to your partner and take a lesson."

"Hey, he's a fag, what can I tell you? Was she in there, honey? Reggie's sister?"

"No. She works there, but she's not working today."

"What?"

"You heard me."

"And you spent all that time in there using up my hundred dollars?"

"You only wish it was your hundred. Now be quiet and let me talk. I gotta get back. It's better she wasn't there. Girls love to talk behind other people's backs. Milly has problems. Crack problems. That's why she's in and out. But the owner won't fire her because of who her brother is."

"Right."

"But you don't need to worry about Milly. The one you want to find is Reggie's girlfriend."

"I'll take that."

"Where do we find her?" asked Sperling.

"The Bronx. She came into the salon a couple of times. She's Hispanic. Name is Angie. Lives in Mott Haven. A hundred fortieth street. Somewhere around in there."

"Oh, that's good. I got a first name and a street."

"So? You lazy? You can't find her with that? You want me to do everything for you?"

Impelliteri said, "What else you got? Tell me you got something else."

"Then be nice."

"Anything for you, Rita."

"That's better. Now, listen up. Reggie Whack drives a Jeep Grand Cherokee. It's green. He also sees a girl named Darleece at the projects over in Fort Greene." She turned to Sperling. "Green Jeep. Fort Greene. See how I make it easy for him?"

Sperling smiled.

Rita continued. "Reggie and Darleece have a baby together."

"Ah, right," said Impelliteri. "His baby-momma."

"One of 'em, anyhow."

"The project in Fort Greene. What's that? The Walt Whitman Houses?" asked Impelliteri.

"Yeah, that's it."

"Darleece?"

"Right."

"How do you spell that, Rita?"

"Who knows? And, last but not least, our dog-boy Reggie has another woman named Tyeesha in Flatbush."

"Flatbush?"

"That's all I got on Tyeesha."

"How many kids has she got?"

"I don't know. Don't start with your racist bullshit, Anthony."

"Racist? I wish once in a goddamn while these assholes would come up with something new. Every one of 'em has five or six women, all popping out bastards in every shithole in New York. Now I gotta drive all the fuck over Brooklyn and the Bronx to find out where this death-dealing cocksucker is parking his dick tonight?"

Rita had a warning note in her voice. "Anthony."

Impelliteri turned to Sperling, "And see? This is all racist, James. I'm a damn racist because I think this guy is a murderous, death-dealing dog that should be eliminated from the face of the earth, along with all his fucking fatherless children before they turn into death-dealing dogs, too."

Rita said, "My, my, aren't we in a good mood."

Impelliteri smiled and said, "Rita, you are one of the most beautiful women in the world, and someone could spend a million dollars on you in that beauty parlor and you'd still come out lookin' like two million. And I know you'll forgive my outburst, but you know and I know that every fucking word of it is true."

She shook her head. A rueful smile passed quickly, but Rita would not comment further except to say, "You take care of yourself, Anthony. You too, James. The one thing I will say is you better watch out for this guy. The way those girls talked in there, you better believe he didn't get his name for no reason. Reggie Whack is a killer. You know the reputation of this Blue-Tops gang, Anthony, and Reggie Whack is one of their worst. So you do what you gotta do but just take care. Find one of those girls, you'll find him. I gotta go. Gimme a ride back to the precinct, will you."

Impelliteri fired up the Caprice.

"You got it."

"And drive like a human being, Anthony."

Rita primped a bit. "I don't want to mess up my new do."

CHAPTER 33

REGGIE WHACK'S GREEN JEEP CHEROKEE WASN'T PARKED NEAR any of his girlfriends' apartments. It sat double-parked outside a Chino-Latino restaurant on lower Broadway near Houston Street in Manhattan.

Archie Reynolds had called in the enforcer his Dominican supplier provided on a freelance basis, Carmen Sanchez.

Sanchez hadn't bothered to double-park. He drove his 1,270-cc Suzuki Katana motorcycle right up onto the sidewalk and parked it in front of the restaurant doorway. He couldn't care less that passersby had to walk around it.

The maître d' saw Sanchez leave the bike in front of his restaurant, half-blocking his front door. But when Sanchez entered, the maître d' took one look at him and decided to keep his mouth shut. It wasn't that Sanchez was physically imposing. He was short, with the bandy-legged body of an Amazon Indian. It was the way Sanchez looked at the maître d' with eyes that said, give me one reason to hurt you.

Sanchez sat at a window table with Archie Reynolds and Reggie Whack. He shoveled beans and fried pork into his mouth, looking at Archie Reynolds with his hooded, menacing eyes. Sanchez nodded every so often at the words coming out of Archie's mouth but barely bothered to listen. Normal, clearly spoken English generally eluded him. Archie's ghetto-speak meant almost nothing to him.

Archie and Reggie sipped Dos Equis beer while Sanchez

ate. They had finished their meals. Sanchez chewed his way through his second helping.

As far as Sanchez was concerned, Archie talked too much. Archie took pride in his plan. Sanchez did not need a plan. Archie enjoyed the anticipation. Sanchez hardly thought about killing people before or after. He used a simple method. He drove his motorcycle up to his victim – on a sidewalk, next to a car window, in the middle of the street. It didn't matter. He pulled out a weapon – gun, machine pistol, shotgun. That didn't much matter, either. He pulled the trigger until he was absolutely sure the victim had died.

Sanchez wore a full-face motorcycle helmet, so nobody ever got a good look at him. He drove his cycle fast, so nobody ever caught him. And every few weeks he changed bikes.

Sanchez had killed so many victims he'd lost count. When too many people were looking for him, he would simply leave for his home in the Dominican Republic until it quieted down. Then he would come back and kill again.

So while Archie described Rachman Abdul X and where he lived and how the MS-2 operation ran and what he wanted to do to the Muslims, Sanchez ate and occasionally nodded, barely listening.

After he washed down his last mouthful, Sanchez wiped the pork grease from his lips and said, "So, Poppy, jus' show me the ones, okay? I take care of it."

"Aaaright, but I want to kill the burly motherfucker myself."

"So kill him."

"I'll set you up for the other ones."

"Yeah, yeah, okay. *A que hora*?"

"My source tells me he usually gets home about one o'clock in the morning. We meet in front of his house at midnight." Archie slid an address to Sanchez. "I meet you there with everything we need."

"Midnight?"

"Yes," said Archie. *"Dos horas* from now, amigo."

Sanchez frowned. "The information is good?"

"Hey, people owe me this information. They give me wrong fucking information, they gonna be dead. Lucky they ain't dead already, all this bullshit unleashed. That's the place."

"Why we wait so long? Go where he at now."

Archie checked his watch. Almost ten o'clock.

"No, no. Got to be at his place. Got to do the other shit, too. You can wait. Hey, I ain't had any good sleep for four fucking days. Motherfuckers burnin' up my headquarters. Police doggin' everybody. I can't go home. I been duckin' and hidin', movin' around. Shit, man, I got all kinds a shit to do before I meet you. Ain't gonna do us no good to get there if he ain't home, anyhow. We do this the way I want, we do it all in one night."

Sanchez caught "all in one night." That sounded good to him. He nodded.

Archie said, "Don't worry about it. We get busy, we do it all, we don't have to be draggin' this out. Go see a movie or somethin', Sanchez. Relax. Have some more beer."

Archie dropped a fifty-dollar bill on the table. "I'll see you over there."

Sanchez bobbed his head up and down once. He watched Archie and Reggie leave the restaurant. He looked at his watch. He had no problem killing human beings, but it annoyed him that he had to kill two hours.

CHAPTER 34

When Loyd Shaw and Orestes Mason returned to the Seven-Three after processing Ellard Watkins, it was nearly eleven o'clock. Tony Impelliteri and James Sperling sat at their desks, peering through printouts listing hundreds of parking tickets. All four men had been working steadily for almost eleven hours. Walter Wang had started right after dinner on Monday. He had been at it for nearly thirty hours.

Walter continued sending bursts of keystrokes into his CPU, staring at the screen, watching for information to flow back to him, but he looked as if he were reaching the end of his endurance.

The small workspace smelled of cold pepperoni pizza and stale cigarettes. Impelliteri sipped a bottle of Budweiser and added more cigarette smoke to the enclosed room.

Shaw picked up a warm beer from a six-pack on Impelliteri's desk and bummed a cigarette.

Impelliteri handed Shaw his cigarette lighter without looking up from his printout of parking tickets. "We almost got it," he said.

"Got what?" Shaw asked.

"A location for Reggie Whack. We found out he drives a green Jeep Cherokee. Walter the Wizard located the goddamn plate number."

"How'd you do that?"

Walter answered, "Did a search for Wilsons and Jeeps."

"You can do that?"

"*I* can do that."

Impelliteri said, "You have no fucking idea how many Wilsons with Jeeps there are in New York City."

"But only one registered to Mildred Wilson," said Sperling.

"Who's that?" Mason asked.

"Reggie's crackhead sister, Milly," Impelliteri answered.

"So, what's that get you?"

"Not much, but if we match the plate number with locations of his girlfriends, we got a shot."

"You looking at parking tickets?" asked Mason.

"Yep. We got two locations. One in Fort Greene, the other in Mott Haven. Walter ran down every parking ticket issued in the last month in those two areas."

"How many is that?" asked Mason.

"Not that many. Couple hundred. Nobody in those fucking neighborhoods pays 'em anyhow." Impelliteri straightened up. "Bingo, we have a match. How's this – one hundred forty-third street, Bronx? That's near the spic bitch he's fucking, right?"

Sperling said, "You mean Hispanic woman he's having sexual intercourse with outside of marriage?"

"Whatever. Look, license number XVR six, seven, nine. Green Jeep Cherokee. Registered to Mildred Wilson. Two parking tickets on that street. We got you, Reggie, you fucking mongrel dog."

Mason asked, "That's where he shacks up with his girlfriend?"

Impelliteri ran his finger along the small type giving the details on the parking tickets. "Yeah, two tickets in the last ten days. Both of them on the same street. Both of them issued between eight and eight-thirty in the morning. Right when they come by giving out tickets for alternate-side parking violations. Fucker is too lazy to get up and move his car."

Sperling looked up from his printout.

"I've got a ticket for the same vehicle near those Fort Greene projects."

"No shit. What time?"

"Says ten a.m. It's for parking in a restricted area."

"Probably a fire hydrant, the fuck. Reggie's a busy man. He's gonna be in one of those two places. I got a feeling about this one. He's fucking the Bronx piece of ass one night, his baby-momma Darleece the next. Dog boy is running to safe places outside the hood to lay his head down. Detective Sperling and I be making an early morning wake-up call."

"Good. Good work. Anything else going?" asked Shaw.

"Yeah, we got something set up. We'll be pulling in mutts right after we get this Reggie fuck. You guys have any luck?"

Mason spoke up.

"We got Ellard Watkins a few hours ago."

"No shit. Did you shoot him?"

"No," answered Mason. "Detective Shaw tried like hell, but big boy escaped. Sort of."

"What's that mean?"

"He tried to jump over onto a roof and went through it."

"Went through it!?"

"Like a giant cannonball dropped from above."

"Shit! Great. Did he kill his fat ass?"

"Not yet," Shaw said, "But he's busted up enough so that he won't be a problem for quite a while. Won't even be a problem in whatever prison they send him to for quite a while."

Shaw checked his watch. Eleven-twenty. It was time to get over to New Lots Apartments and see Rachman Abdul X. Shaw figured that Leon Bloom had put the word out to Rachman by now. Shaw wanted to see what he could get out of him about Archie Reynolds.

"Walter, you find out anything more about Archie Reynolds?"

Wang rubbed his eyes and told him, "I got his arrest records and an address his parole report lists in Brownsville, but I doubt you'll find him there. That's it. No driver's license, no credit card records, no vehicle registration. I got calls into the Career Criminal Identification Unit on him to see if they can give us a lead, but I haven't heard back yet. I also got a call into an FBI guy I know who might have access to information we don't. Haven't heard back from him, either. The Blue-Tops gang isn't the target of any task force or DEA investigations I can find. I checked outside records in six states. So far, nothing."

Impelliteri spoke up.

"I talked to a guy I know in Gangs earlier this afternoon when we were running around."

"He know anything?"

"Nothing that would help us find him. But my contact got pretty serious when I brought up Archie's name."

"How so?"

"Said nobody knows a whole lot about him. Said he doesn't live in the hood. Comes in and out. Not one of the regular homeboy types. Born and raised here. Knows everybody but seems like he's moved up and on. Comes in to tend to business, then goes back out. But every fuckin' body in this hood is afraid of the dude."

"Why's that?" asked Mason.

"Cuz the guy shoots first and asks questions later. He has no compunction about taking somebody out. Doesn't matter who it is. Even his own guys. He gets suspicious. He loses a shipment. Some money is missing. He kills everybody involved. Or has 'em killed. I can't exactly explain everything my contact was saying, but basically, it sounds as if Archie Reynolds runs things like an outsider. Not like a neighborhood guy. Doesn't give a shit about anybody. If you get a line on him, my advice is – shoot him down the second you see him or there's a good chance you'll be going down first."

Shaw didn't comment on Impelliteri's information. He simply took it in and asked Wang, "Anything on this enforcer, Sanchez?"

"I just started on him. If he's Dominican, I figure he goes in and out of the country a lot. Most of those guys go home and hide out when things get hot. So I'm working on visas and passports and customs reports."

"And what about Melvin Melly Mel or whatever the hell his name is?"

Wang saved something in a computer file, sat back in his chair, rubbed his eyes, and turned to face the others.

"I was talking to some of the precinct detectives assigned to the drive-bys and the shooting over in New Lots. One of them said they had a lead on Melvin, so I'm concentrating on the others."

"Okay. That's smart. Your plate is full with the other guys. Let the precinct do their part."

"Yeah," said Impelliteri, "as soon as they assemble fifty fucking guys to surround him and take him in."

"Anthony, if they can get one, that's one we don't have to worry about. Walter, stay with what you're doing. By the way, did you get to our fives?"

Walter's mouth actually dropped open.

"Okay, take it easy, Walter. Just reminding you. Do 'em when you can. Don't let 'em pile up. Here's some notes on what Mason and I did today. I left out pulling a gun on a civilian, firing without filing reports, illegal monitoring of cellular phone transmissions, entering a premises without probable cause, etcetera."

Impelliteri laughed. "Sounds good."

Shaw said, "And today isn't even over. Walter, just write 'em up from what you got there. You're doing great. Why don't you finish whatever you're doing and go home? Grab a few hours' sleep and some clean clothes. Get back by around eight tomorrow morning. And you don't have to wear a suit, you know. Wear something you'll be comfortable in."

"I am comfortable."

"Suit yourself," said Impelliteri. He waited for a reaction from Walter but didn't get one. He said, "Suit yourself. Get it? Suit. Yourself."

"Oh. Yeah."

"Hey, what am I thinking? You hardly speak English."

"Fuck you, Impelliteri."

"Shaw, did you teach him both of those words all at once? You know, fuck…you, or first fuck then you?"

Walter spluttered, "No, asshole, your momma taught me."

Impelliteri laughed. "Whoa, Kung Fu. Way to go, you sound like a—"

"Watch it," said Mason.

"Homeboy. I was gonna say homeboy, Mason, I swear."

Mason dismissed Impelliteri with a wave and leaned back in his chair, folded his arms across his ample stomach, and closed his eyes. Sperling sat without expression, legs crossed, waiting. Even Impelliteri gave it up, leaned back in his chair, and propped his feet on his desk.

Shaw sat at his desk, checking over how he felt. Lousy. The cigarettes didn't help. The McDonald's meal and Chinese food had congealed in his stomach. He had that washed-out sensation that sets in after the rage and adrenaline are gone.

Shaw thought about how hard he had tried to shoot Weight Watkins. How much he had *wanted* to put a bullet in Watkins after Watkins had fired on them with that goddamn shotgun. Hadn't considered not shooting Ellard Watkins, even though Shaw knew that seeing the damage his bullets would have done to Watkins's big, fleshy body would have haunted him for a long time. Maybe the rest of his life.

Shaw thought about shooting Archie Reynolds on sight. He didn't want to live with that image, either.

Shaw suddenly had an urge for a shot of whiskey to go with his beer. He wanted to feel the energy the alcohol could give as well as the numbing insulation from all the mayhem and chaos gathering around him.

"Is there anything to drink around here?"

Everyone looked at Shaw as if he had asked a stupid question.

"Anybody think to buy a bottle for our so-called office?"

Walter said, "Are you nuts? Liquor isn't allowed in the precinct."

Shaw looked at Wang as if he were from Mars. Impelliteri dropped his feet and stared at Wang. Mason shook his head at Wang's comment. Even Sperling looked perplexed.

Shaw said, "Not allowed? Not allowed? Hey, *we're* not allowed in this fucking precinct, the shit we're doing."

Impelliteri started laughing. Then Mason and Shaw. The laughter even infected Sperling.

In about ten seconds, none of them could stop. In one crystal clear moment, it hit them. The exhilaration of it, the absurdity, the danger, the fatigue, and freedom of it. They laughed until tears rolled. Wang started laughing, not really knowing why, since the joke seemed to be on him. The laughter wore them out and lifted them up at the same time. It felt good. Shaw appreciated both the laughing and the sharing of the moment.

The wave passed, finally. Mason wiped his eyes and settled into himself with a few last chuckles.

"Shit," said Impelliteri. "Don't take it seriously, Fu Manchu, we do it because we love you."

"Whatever."

Impelliteri asked, "So what's next, Shaw?"

"I'm going to go over and have a word with the head of that Muslim security outfit. He knows more about Archie Reynolds than we do. I want his help."

"Good fucking luck."

"No, I think he might be in the mood to cooperate. I put a little pressure on his boss earlier today. Maybe he'll listen."

"Who? The Muslims or the boss?" Mason asked.

"Both."

"You want some company?" asked Impelliteri.

"Sure."

Impelliteri turned to Sperling. "We got some time to kill. You want to come with or sleep?"

"Where are we going?"

Shaw said, "New Lots Apartments."

Sperling gave a slight tip of the head and said, "All right. I want to see where all this trouble is happening."

Shaw mustered up what energy he had left and stood up. "Let's go."

Shaw pointed to the papers and files scattered over Walter's worktable.

"Walter, before you go, just make sure nothing is laying out here you don't want anybody to see. Contacts you want kept private. Whatever."

Walter was glued to the screen again, but he nodded and said, "Okay. Don't worry."

They all left the office and headed for their cars.

CHAPTER 35

By eleven, Archie Reynolds and Reggie Whack were back in Brownsville carefully cruising the streets, avoiding the Muslims, trying to make contact with their boys.

At first, Archie thought there had to be something wrong with his cell phone.

"Reggie, where the fuck is everybody? Nobody's answering me."

"Mo, most of the guys is, is in New Lots getting sh, sh, shit together. Who you callin'?"

Archie pointed to a payphone on the wall outside a small grocery on Bergen Street.

"Pull over to that phone and call my number. See if this fuckin' thing is working."

Reggie double-parked. He punched in the numbers, then turned to the Jeep to watch if Archie's cell phone rang. He saw Archie put the phone to his head and heard Archie's frustrated voice.

"Yeah, okay. Fuck it."

Reggie hopped back into the driver's seat.

"Who, who, who'd you call, man?"

"Weight, Melly Mel, Big Marvin, and Toussant. I just need a couple of motherfuckers. Let the rest keep working."

"Maybe they b, b, busy, man."

"Aaaright, fuck it. Come on."

"Drive over to that little park on Stone. Then the pizza place on Linden. Stay clear of those Muslim motherfuckers around

New Lots. Get your piece in your lap. Be ready to shoot anybody gives us any shit. I'll just have to do a little recruiting."

"For what?"

"For some bullshit I want to create over here by the project while we be doin' our thing, man. Don't worry about it. Fuckin' kids aroun' here want to make some money, the Ar man be happy to provide the opportunity. You got those pieces we took out from our stash house?"

"In the b, b, back there, under the spare."

"Das all I need, brother. Be funny watchin' the big bad Muslim boys shooting some ten, eleven-year-old kid."

CHAPTER 36

Loyd Shaw and his men found Rachman X near the New
Lots Apartments' main gate. Rachman didn't appear particularly
happy to see Shaw, much less Shaw with Mason, Impelliteri,
and Sperling.

Anthony Impelliteri and James Sperling stayed just long
enough to make the point that Shaw was not alone. They
drifted off into the complex to have a look around.

Orestes Mason stood near Shaw, projecting his usual calming
influence.

"Mr. Rachman," Shaw said, trying to sound friendly, "How
are you tonight?"

"Fine."

"Any problems today?"

"Nothing unusual."

"Long day."

"I usually leave at midnight."

"Glad I caught you. I have some good news for you."

"What's that?"

"We picked up one of the Blue-Tops managers, Ellard Watkins."

"Good."

"He won't be bothering you or anybody else for a long time."

"Good."

"We've got a line on the last Blue-Tops manager and the last
of the enforcers. I wouldn't be surprised if we don't get at least
one of them in the next day or two."

266 | JOHN CLARKSON

"Uh-huh."

"Maybe a few of the street-level guys, too."

"You want to get them, put your badge on and come into these buildings with us."

"Is that where they are?"

"They're still selling in there."

"I'll be happy to join you for the cleanup. Soon as I get the main guy. He's the one I want. Archie Reynolds."

Rachman nodded his head, saying nothing.

Shaw nodded toward Mason and said, "Detective Mason and I would like to find him."

Rachman looked at Mason, back at Shaw, but didn't offer any comment.

Shaw said, "So I was wondering, have you thought over our conversation earlier? Have you come up with anything that might be of help?"

Rachman frowned. They both knew Shaw had put the screws to Bloom. And they both knew Bloom had passed on the word that Rachman should cooperate with Shaw.

"Well?" asked Shaw.

Rachman appeared to be making a decision. Shaw waited.

Finally, Rachman said, "What are you doing right now?"

"Now? Talking to you. You're what I'm doing. I'm not doing anything else. Don't have anything else that's more important than you, Mr. Rachman."

"I have to go home. See my children and my women. Come with me. We can talk there. And a person who can help you lives nearby."

"Great. Hang on just a second. Let me find out where my other guys are."

Shaw pulled out the radio which had been in his sagging rear pants pocket and called out for Impelliteri and Sperling. Impelliteri's voice came back through the static.

"Yo."

"A, we're leaving now. You staying?"

"Yeah. Me and S want to look around. Probably catch a couple hours sleep back at the place, then go out dog hunting."

"See you."

＊

Impelliteri turned down his radio and looked for Sperling. He spotted him crouched down, looking at various bullet holes scarring The Pit.

Impelliteri told Sperling, "Shaw and Mason are taking off. Jeezus, look at the size of these fuckin' holes."

Sperling said, "Automatic weapons. Probably AK-47s. Even the compact rounds are about the size of half your little finger. That's a lot of steel. Traveling at over two thousand feet per second makes a devastating impact. Ever see a body hit by one of those bullets?"

"No."

"They can easily take the entire top of your skull off. Put a hole in you the size of a fist. Shatters bones. Doesn't break bones. Obliterates them."

"No shit."

Sperling stood in The Pit looking at the bullet holes that seemed to be everywhere. Then he looked up, shifting his gaze from the top floor of Building A over to the top floor of Building D.

"They had two shooters. One on each side."

"Yeah?"

Sperling muttered to himself, "One one-thousand."

"What?"

"One one thousand," Sperling repeated. "That's a second. Those assault rifles fire a little over ten rounds per second.

"Fuck of a lot of firepower. How many in a clip?"

"Varies. Thirty-two is a standard magazine."

Impelliteri said, "Christ. Fuckers probably had no idea the damage they could do."

Sperling shook his head. "No. No way. They were just pointing and pulling the trigger. Look at these spread-out patterns. Just doing what they've seen on TV and the movies a million times. No idea of what it really means."

Impelliteri started counting to himself. "One one thousand, two one thousand, three one thousand. Thirty-two fucking rounds."

Sperling and Impelliteri exchanged looks.

"Let's get the hell out of here, James."

CHAPTER 37

LOYD SHAW DROVE THE CAPRICE, FOLLOWING CLOSELY BEHIND Rachman X's battered Ford LTD, not paying much attention to where they were headed. They drove north out of Brownsville to Bushwick Avenue and turned west. After about five minutes, they arrived in Rachman's neighborhood.

As with most New York detectives, Shaw was accustomed to entering neighborhoods where he felt as if he'd arrived in another country. Chinese, Dominican, Indian, Russians, Venezuelan – every ethnic group had their own community. But this was one neighborhood he'd never been to.

A one-story mosque dominated the area. It was a concrete-block building, completely nondescript except for a rounded roof with the Islamic crescent moon symbol topping it. A sign in Arabic script over the doorway named the place. Most of the buildings in the surrounding two blocks had been painted a dark brown with white trim, designating them as part of the same Muslim community.

Black men dressed much like the ones guarding the perimeter of New Lots Apartments patrolled the streets in teams of two. Shaw saw one woman walking into an apartment building covered from head to ankle in a burka that left only a small opening that revealed her darting eyes.

Rachman and his people had taken over their own small chunk of New York. It was disorienting and yet encouraging at the same time.

Rachman's apartment was located two buildings south of the mosque. A fire hydrant had created enough open space amidst the parked cars in front of Rachman's building so that he could drive his car over the curb and park it in the narrow opening between two apartment buildings. Shaw followed his lead and parked behind him, noting how Rachman had appropriated his own parking area in the crowded neighborhood.

Rachman walked back to the Caprice and asked that Mason stay outside while he and Shaw talked inside.

Mason said, "No problem." He settled back against his head-rest and closed his eyes.

Shaw followed Rachman into a three-story apartment building, up the stairs to the second floor. After just a few moments inside the building, he had the sense that it was filled with women and children. There was a welcoming scent of curry-flavored cooking in the air mixed with a tinge of used diapers. Despite the foreign feel to the people and place, typically American kids' stuff scattered the hallways – a battered big-wheel tricycle, scooters, volleyballs, baby carriages, strollers.

Inside the building, it seemed quiet and restless at the same time. It was time for sleep, but Shaw had the feeling that nobody here rested completely.

Rachman unlocked his front door. It took a bit of time to turn all the keys. When they entered, a small woman dressed in fundamentalist garb stood in the narrow hallway waiting for Rachman. When she saw a white man with Rachman, a stranger, she bowed her head, not out of respect but to hide her face.

Rachman told her, "I'll be up for a while. How are the children?"

"Fine, dear."

"Everyone asleep?"

"Yes."

"Aleya and Darsel?"

"They're in the kitchen."

"Tell them I'll see them later."

"They have food for you."

"Later."

The woman headed off toward the back of the apartment, leaving the men to their business. Rachman hadn't bothered to introduce Shaw or explain his presence. Shaw followed him through a neat living room to a dining room area. Furnishings were sparse and simple. Everything appeared to be well-tended and clean, the furniture protected by plastic covers.

Shaw asked Rachman how many kids he had.

"Fourteen," he said.

"Your wife must be made of iron."

"Wives. I have four wives."

Uh-huh. That made more sense, thought Shaw. Four into fourteen came out to be only 3.5 kids per woman. He felt like saying, Gee, I didn't know you could have more than one wife, but kept his mouth shut.

Shaw said, "You must be a busy man."

"Have a seat," was Rachman's response.

They sat at his dining room table. The moment of slight familiarity had passed.

"Tell me what you want."

Shaw got right to it.

"I want Archie Reynolds. And I want as many of the skels that work for him as I can get. I have a list of names. I need locations."

Shaw pulled out his list of Blue-Tops gangbangers.

"I need to know where I can find these guys, starting with Archie Reynolds. Where they sleep. Where they buy their groceries. Where they hang out. Any place I can find them."

Rachman picked up the page and looked it over. As he read the other names, he started talking about Archie Reynolds.

"Archie Reynolds does not live among those he exploits. He lives in Saddle Brook, New Jersey. The name of the street is Oak or Maple. I forget exactly. The person I'm going to send you to will give you his exact address, but I don't believe it will help you much. Archie won't go to his home. Not now. Not until this is over. We've heard he's been on our streets recently, but nobody has actually seen him. Just before you arrived at New Lots, we got word he was around. I sent people out looking for him. Maybe we'll get lucky, but I doubt it. He doesn't stay in one place for long. The word is he moves around between motels."

"Who's this man you want me to see?"

"Youssef. Outside, two doors to the right. You'll want to stop over there after you leave me. He might be home. Might not be."

Rachman started writing an address in careful script on the bottom of the list Shaw had handed to him. Shaw watched the apartment number appear after he wrote the address. Clearly, Bloom had advised Rachman to cooperate. Shaw wondered if getting Ellard Watkins off the streets had also made Rachman cooperate.

Either way, Shaw didn't care. Rachman was giving him access to information. Information gathered by black men. Former criminals. Men who knew the streets and had access to people who would never speak to Shaw and his men. Information meant everything. At that moment, Shaw felt as if he could win this war. And then they heard the muffled explosion.

CHAPTER 38

They both knew what it was. Loyd Shaw decided it probably sounded very much like the gasoline that had exploded in the Blue-Tops' headquarters. But this time, the fire burned in the Muslims' mosque.

Rachman X jumped to his feet first. Shaw took a second to grab his list before he ran after him, then blew past Rachman and out the door when Rachman stopped to pull a shotgun out of his front closet.

As he took the stairs two at a time, Shaw had an image of black women in Muslim garb covering children with their bodies. This was the attack they had been told would come. This was what united them and bent them to the disciplines and dictates they followed. The holy war had become a self-fulfilling prophecy.

As Shaw banged open the lobby door, he heard the ripping sound of automatic weapons fire and then the roar of a motorcycle engine. Even as he pulled out both his Glocks, he knew he was no match for machine pistols or assault rifles. He hunched over to make himself a smaller target and ran toward the burning mosque.

There was so much black smoke billowing out of the structure that Shaw couldn't see anything near the building. But he kept hearing the sounds of gunfire and a revving motorcycle engine.

Shaw looked for Mason and saw him on the corner across from the mosque. Flames silhouetted Orestes Mason's big frame into one block-like shape. Suddenly, the motorcycle roared louder and came barreling out of the fire right toward Mason.

Two of Rachman's gunmen chased the motorcyclist, firing handguns. Mason was in his path. It looked like Mason was going to either shoot the driver or get hit by the oncoming bike. Suddenly the motorcycle braked and whipped around, facing the opposite direction. The motorcycle driver, Sanchez, pulled out a machine pistol and fired off bursts at the Muslim guards chasing him. Mason aimed his Sig and carefully pulled off two shots. Sanchez twisted around and let a burst off at Mason, who was already diving down behind a parked car.

Shaw raised his guns, ran toward the cycle, and started shooting at Sanchez with both semi-auto Glocks as fast as he could pull the triggers. Shaw knew he'd have to be lucky to hit the assassin nearly thirty yards away while running, but all he really wanted to do was make sure the shooter didn't turn and fire more rounds at Mason. Shaw kept firing until he nearly reached his partner.

Sanchez shoved the machine pistol into his leather jacket, slammed the bike into gear, and revved the engine. There was nothing between him and Shaw, so Shaw continued to fire.

Sanchez popped the clutch and screeched back toward the flames. The front wheel lifted, then dropped, and Sanchez roared off. Shaw's guns clicked empty. He quickly released the empty clips and reloaded.

Suddenly from behind, Shaw heard a series of pistol shots and an almost simultaneous shotgun blast. He turned and saw Rachman go down, a figure standing over him, pumping bullets into Rachman.

Mason, now behind Shaw, was up on one knee, already turning toward the man shooting into Rachman, and aiming his Sig.

Mason fired his gun. Shaw brought his Glocks around, pointed, and fired, but it was too late.

The murderer had already bolted between Rachman's apartment building and the one next to it.

Mason was up and running toward the injured Rachman. Mason was fast for a man his age and size, but Shaw caught up to him.

Mason yelled, "See to Rachman" and veered to the right.

Shaw made it to Rachman just as Mason reached the space between the two apartments where the shooter had disappeared.

Mason stayed back against the wall of the building, composing himself, then carefully turned into the space between the buildings. Bullets immediately blasted into the brickwork near Mason. He ducked back, then leaned over and fired two shots.

Shaw dropped down next to Rachman, shoving one of his Glocks into his waistband.

He bent over to see if Rachman was still breathing. Amazingly, he was. Rachman was down, bleeding, but undeniably alive. He suddenly growled with rage and pain. Rachman tried to sit up, grabbing for his shotgun, grunting again at the pain as he tried to breathe, telling Shaw, "Archie. It was Archie Reynolds."

Shaw gently pushed him back down on the ground and said, "Don't move. Don't fucking move and don't fucking die."

Again, Mason leaned out and fired off two more shots, then spun back as return fire hit around him.

Now Mason's gun was empty. He holstered it and reached for his backup. Shaw ran up behind Mason and yelled, "Rachman is still alive. Get an ambulance and backup."

Shaw pushed Mason down into a crouch, leaned over him, and squeezed off four shots into the area between the buildings. Then he broke out around Mason and ran forward to a place between the apartment buildings where brickwork around a vent stack offered him cover.

Shaw's pupils had contracted from the gunfire, but he was still able to see a figure pop out about fifteen yards in front of him and run. He bolted out after him. It was Archie. He had a good lead on Shaw but was within sight. Shaw didn't care if Archie Reynolds turned and shot at him. He didn't care about anything. All he wanted to do was get close enough so that he could stop, aim, and get one good shot at Archie Reynolds. Shoot him down. Shoot him in the face or in the back. He didn't care.

Shaw knew he had almost a full clip, so he pulled off another three shots, aiming as best he could while running, trying to make Archie dodge and slow down, trying to think straight and make sure he had bullets left when he got closer.

Shaw didn't believe any of his shots had hit the body moving in front of him, but he saw Archie duck, then trip and slide. He was down. Shaw closed the distance between them and saw a green Jeep parked on the street.

Archie scrambled to his feet. Shaw fired once more as he continued running, hoping to hit Reynolds. Archie stumbled, trying to get his footing. Shaw was still at least twenty yards behind Archie, but he stopped, gripped his Glock 17 in two hands, tried to steady himself, and squeezed shots until his gun was empty.

Shaw was breathing too hard. Archie was moving too fast, but it looked like one of his shots connected. Archie ducked, banged into a wall, and went down. Shaw sprinted for Archie. Archie was already starting to get up. In one last desperate burst, Shaw lunged at Archie, grabbed for him, missed Archie's shoulder, gripped Archie's arm, but Archie spun and smacked the side of Shaw's head with the empty gun in his hand.

Shaw went down. Archie tore away from his grasp just as Reggie Whack walked from behind the Jeep and started shooting slow, steady blasts from a 9mm gun.

Archie's blow actually saved Shaw. Reggie's shots went over Shaw's head as he fell back, hit the ground hard, and managed to roll away from Reggie's shots.

Archie ran for the Jeep. Reggie stopped shooting until Archie made it out of the line of fire.

Shaw crawled for cover behind a car. He pulled out his second Glock, leaned out, and fired at Reggie, who had been peering into the dark, trying to see Shaw. Reggie returned Shaw's fire but scampered backward.

Archie had made it into the Jeep. He yelled out at Reggie, "Forget that motherfucker, we got to go do the rest. Come on!"

Reggie jumped into the Jeep just as Archie floored the accelerator.

Shaw spent a moment feeling around for blood on his body, but he knew he hadn't been hit. He got to his feet and hustled back to where he had left Mason.

The street had quickly filled with black men, mostly Muslims, mostly bearded, wearing their skullcaps. All of them seemed to be armed. The fire raged at the mosque, bathing the area in a deadly, greasy firelight. Billows of acrid, black smoke produced by Archie's homemade napalm merged with the dark night sky. Sirens screamed in the distance.

Shaw knew that within minutes the area would be jammed with fire engines and other emergency vehicles. He changed the frequency on his radio and yelled for all units to stop a green Jeep Cherokee, even though he knew there were way too many commands being broadcast for his shouts to get through clearly.

Mason and the Muslims clustered around Rachman. Rachman's blood had flooded the ground under him. Shaw feared that an ambulance would never get to them soon enough. Even if they had already dispatched an ambulance, it could get jammed behind the police vehicles and firetrucks rushing toward the scene.

Shaw yelled at the men nearest him to help with Rachman.

"Put him in my car. I'm a cop. Come on. We'll get him to a hospital. Come on, come on, don't let him bleed to death here. We can't wait for an ambulance. Let's go, goddamn it. Get him off the fucking ground."

The Muslims wouldn't listen to Shaw. He grabbed one man by the arm and pulled him toward Rachman. He was about to get a fist in the face when Mason's big booming voiced broke through the chaos.

"Now!" he yelled while he grabbed Rachman under the armpits and lifted the big man's torso off the ground.

The others could either fight for possession of Rachman or watch him be dragged away by Mason.

One more "Let's go!" did it. The men grabbed for their leader, lifting an arm, a leg, some managed to get their hands under Rachman's bleeding body. Rachman sagged in their arms, grunted, and passed out.

Shaw scrambled ahead of them and pulled open the backdoor of his Caprice. They slid Rachman onto the back seat on a thick smear of his own blood.

Shaw climbed behind the wheel and fired the engine, turned on his siren and flashers. Mason shouldered his way into the passenger seat, and Shaw bulled his way clear, heading down Bushwick Avenue as the first fire engine came into sight.

"This is fucking crazy," Shaw yelled at Mason. "Fucking insane."

Orestes Mason answered with a grunt. Shaw glanced away from the streets hurtling past and looked at Mason, saw his face twisted with pain, his stomach and lap covered in blood.

"Mase. Is that his blood or yours?"

"Mine."

"Shit. Where?"

Shaw reached over to hold Mason's shoulder.

"My left side."

Mason pressed his right hand against the wound while bracing himself against the dashboard with the left.

The Caprice banged into a sewer top, and Mason hissed in pain.

"Shit! How bad is it?"

"I don't know. I'm soaked in blood down to my drawers, and it hurts like a son of a bitch."

"What's the fastest way to Kings County?"

"Turn right on Nostrand up here, then left on New York."

"Who was it hit you? That prick on the motorcycle?"

"No. Idiot spraying bullets around like that. Damn rounds flying everywhere. No, it was that bastard Archie put a round in me when I leaned into that gangway to take a shot at him."

"Damn it. Think you got a bullet in him?"

Mason shook his head no.

Shaw slammed his hand into the wheel. "Fuck!"

Mason said, "Rachman just kept saying, get Archie. Get Archie. That's all he kept saying to me when you went after him. Get Archie, get Archie. You hit him?"

Shaw answered, "I might have. I unloaded everything I had at him, but I was running, and he was running. I'd had to have been real lucky. He made it back to his car."

"I figured."

"Green Jeep Cherokee parked behind Rachman's apartment building."

Mason asked, "Reggie Whack?"

"Yeah. Impelliteri got the car right. Reggie Whack came out blasting. I had to drop back. Archie made it to the car, and that was it."

Mason shook his head. He had nothing more to say. Shaw turned around to take a quick look at Rachman X. He was still breathing but in rasping gasps. Shaw reached behind and grabbed Rachman's shoulder. "Hang on, man. We'll be there in two minutes."

Rachman's eyes were closed. His clothes were soaked in blood.

"You fucking die on me, I'll throw you right out in the gutter. I swear I will."

Shaw pitched the car into a turn too fast, banged into a curb, straightened out, and fishtailed down the street. Mason growled at him, "Slow down, Loyd. You'll kill all of us before we get there."

Shaw slowed down a little, but not for long. He told himself, screw slowing down. There weren't many cars on the street. Nothing to stop him. Shaw believed the only way he could stave off more death and pain now was with speed. Race ahead of it. Outrun the darkness pulling Rachman into death. Speed away from the pain filling Mason.

Shaw wanted doctors now. Doctors and nurses and drugs and transfusions and help.

They screeched into the emergency room driveway, siren blaring and lights flashing. Shaw braked hard. The Caprice almost slid through the wide swinging doors of the receiving area.

Shaw held his shield high and yelled and ordered, but the hospital personnel ignored him. The blood everywhere said enough.

The hospital personnel had both wounded men out of the car, on gurneys, and into the ER in less than two minutes.

Shaw followed behind as a team of doctors and nurses descended on Rachman while a nurse and an orderly wheeled Mason into another section.

Shaw watched the medical personnel surround Rachman in a tightly choreographed assault. One nurse began scissoring off Rachman's bloody clothes. A doctor shoved a breathing tube down his throat, others pushed IV lines into his arms, wrapped pressure cuffs around his legs, plunged syringes into him, attached monitors; moving, pushing, shoving, cutting, bulling their way past all resistance, all the while yelling orders and responses at each other, and, like Shaw, rushing, rushing as if only speed could keep them ahead of the death about to descend on Rachman Abdul X.

There was nothing remotely gentle in their treatment. It was a fight, a battle, a maelstrom of medicine launched against the dirty, deadly little bullets that had blasted out of Archie Reynolds's gun and ripped into Rachman's body.

Shaw edged his way around the commotion to find Mason. His wounded partner sat on a bed in a corner of the ER set off by curtains. A nurse and an orderly were cutting off his bloody shirt and pants. Seeing his clothes destroyed seemed to make Orestes angrier than getting shot had.

Shaw took charge of Mason's belongings. An orderly had put the contents of his pockets in a plastic bag with a cinch cord. Shaw made sure Mason's badge and ID and wallet were in the bag. He jammed Mason's guns into their holsters and wrapped the holster rig around the weapons. He placed everything into the bag, held it up, and told Mason, "I got everything, partner."

Mason nodded without speaking.

At that moment, nobody knew about the shooting. But Shaw knew once the word went out, an avalanche of police brass and questions would descend on them. Shaw did not want that to happen.

Taking charge of Mason's property was about all Shaw could do for his wounded partner. As they wheeled him out, Shaw said, "Take it easy, Mase. Don't worry," knowing that he sounded useless and inane.

At that moment, Orestes Mason looked every one of his fifty-three years. His face had sagged, and his rich brown skin color had turned ashy and dull. Everything seemed to have hit him at once. For a moment, a dread feeling passed through Shaw. What if they couldn't stop the bleeding? What if Mason's heart gave out under the stress and shock? What the hell would he do if Mason died?

"Fuck it, fuck it," Shaw said out loud. Stop thinking about what could happen to Mason. Start thinking again about Archie Reynolds.

Shaw made his way back to his car. He stored Mason's belongings in the trunk, then started making calls. First, he roused Conklin and told him he had to suppress the usual investigation that would unfold as soon as the hospital reported Rachman's and Mason's gunshot wounds. Conklin said, "We're on it," and hung up.

Then Shaw called his team. He used his cell phone, pager, and police radio until he reached them all. He wanted Impelliteri and Sperling and Wang. He wanted them in the hospital, with their guns. Now.

Loyd Shaw found the waiting room on the surgical floor and sat down to wait for word on his friend, Orestes Mason.

The minute he sat down in the quiet room, images of shotgun blasts and gunfire and burning mosques filled his head, interspersed with imagining Mason and Rachman Abdul X laid out on operating room tables bathed by surreal white light. Doctors slicing into them, poking around in bloody, torn-up flesh looking for bullets.

But it didn't take long before he became haunted by the specter of Archie Reynolds. He kept seeing the dark, slim form running ahead of him, feeling Archie's shoulder under his hand. He's actually had his hand on Archie. Had seen him. Had him, if only for brief moments, in his gun sight. He finally knew what Archie looked like, who he was. And Shaw wanted him. Wanted him back in his hands. He imagined grabbing Archie's throat, punching his face, breaking bones, punching him until Archie's eyes rolled to the back of his head, then slapping hand-cuffs on him so fast and so tight that Archie Reynolds would wake up screaming.

Just let me get the cuffs on him, thought Shaw. Let me get him before anyone stops me. Get him before he has a chance to shoot at me, and I have to shoot back at him. Get Mason out of this hospital and Archie into jail before Albert J. DeLuca pulls me off and tells me I fucked up and sends me to another kind of hell.

CHAPTER 39

ANTHONY IMPELLITERI AND JAMES SPERLING FOUND SHAW IN THE surgical ward waiting room downing bitter coffee, waiting on word about Mason and Rachman. Walter Wang was still on his way.

Shaw told them what had happened. Impelliteri started pacing around the room, muttering curses and threats about shooting Blue-Tops. Sperling shoved himself onto in a beat-up, food-stained chair, stared at nothing, said nothing except, "I hate hospitals."

About ten minutes after they arrived, Shaw's cell phone rang. It was Justine Burton.

"Shaw?"

"Yes."

"I need to talk to you. I need you over here."

"Where?"

"My center."

"You're still there?"

"I came back. You said I could call you. I need to talk to you."

"What happened?"

"Please, all hell has broken loose, can you just come over here?"

"Look, one of my men has been shot, I—"

"What happened?"

"He's all right. He's in the hospital. Kings County. We're waiting."

"You're nearby. Can you come over here? Just for a few minutes."

Shaw told the others, "This shit doesn't end. Stay here until you get word on Mason. I should be back before he gets out of surgery."

✳

Shaw saw the flashing lights surrounding Justine's center from three blocks away. He didn't allow himself to speculate about what had brought them. He parked outside the cordon of police and emergency vehicles, leaving his flasher blinking.

Outside, he saw a knot of uniformed cops and detectives checking bullet holes in the wall at the far end of the center.

As Shaw approached Justine's office, he saw two of the three detectives assigned to her sitting in the waiting area outside her office.

He asked one of them, "What happened?"

"It's fucked up. The neighborhood's been going nuts. Another drive-by went down across the street near the entrance to the complex. Random shots fired everywhere. A handful hit this place. Muslims are going nuts shooting back. Seems like everyone's going crazy."

"Anybody hit?"

"One lady in the dormitory section down at the end got shot in the arm. She isn't going to die from it, but it's a messy wound. Bunch of hysterical women carrying on. They won't leave, they can't stay. We're waiting for the Queen of Sheba to make a decision."

Shaw let that remark go and asked, "How is she?"

"Not happy."

He stepped into the office and closed the door behind him. Justine sat at her desk. The tension in her face made her more austere but somehow even more attractive to Shaw.

He said, "I heard what happened."

She focused on Shaw, but instead of her usual penetrating gaze, he saw her mask drop a bit. This wasn't the confident woman Shaw had seen before. This was the Justine underneath Justine Burton, police commissioner's daughter.

"Loyd, thank you for coming. I need someone to tell me when this is going to stop. What do you know? I can't get anything out of the officers assigned to me. I have to know when this is going to stop."

"Did they catch any of the people shooting at your place?"

"Not the police. The word is that the Muslims caught a ten-year-old boy and killed him."

"What?"

"You heard me. A ten-year-old boy. A child. They killed him."

"How?"

"They saw him up on the roof across the street from here, on one of the New Lots buildings. Shooting from up there. They went after him. They said he ran and fell. I heard one of the uniformed cops say they probably threw him off the roof. They found a gun near his body."

"Christ."

"This is insane. Recruiting children. Giving them guns!"

Shaw moved a chair next to Justine's desk and sat beside her. The moment he came close enough, she reached over, grabbed his forearm, and asked, "What the hell am I supposed to do, Shaw? I can't let people keep dying over this, much less a child. I can't let them run me out. What is happening? What should I do?"

Shaw put his hand on top of hers and tried to sound calm.

"Take it easy, Justine. It's just, just…"

"Just what?"

"Look, you have to—"

"They've been shooting all over this neighborhood tonight. What is Archie Reynolds doing? Is anybody close to finding him? Stopping him? Are you?"

"Listen, Justine, he's trying to terrorize you. What he's doing is horrible. Giving a gun to a ten-year-old. It's desperation. We're putting pressure on his hitters. We got one tonight. The precinct guys have another on the run." Shaw didn't dare tell Justine about the attack Archie Reynolds made on the Muslim mosque. "Believe me, Justine, Archie Reynolds is desperate. He's reaching the end."

"So, he uses children?"

"Less likely that the cops or Muslims would suspect them. I'm sorry. I know it seems insane."

"You've got to stop this, Shaw. I tried to talk to my father. He won't come here. Said he can't display favoritism. He said they're doing everything they can. But I don't know if my father is really doing something or if he's just as helpless against this insanity as everybody else."

"He's not helpless. And you didn't call him just to find out what the department is doing. More and more resources are being put on this. You called him because you need to talk to your father. You should go home, Justine. Get out of here. Get some sleep. The neighborhood is quiet now. Come back in the morning and then start getting these women someplace else to stay until this thing is over."

"Shaw, be honest with me. When is that going to be?"

"When I get Archie Reynolds."

"Same question. When is that going to be?"

"Soon. Believe me, it will be soon."

Justine looked away. Saying more to herself than Shaw, "This is insane. Just insane."

"More reason to get your people and your clients out of here."

She turned back to Shaw, nearly shouting, "I can't place twelve women and twenty-five children in a day. After I talked to you, I didn't go into Manhattan. I came back here and met with my staff and clients. I told them not to worry. I told them

I'd find a safer place for them. And then before they could even get to sleep, the shooting started.

"Now they're more terrified than ever. They're afraid to leave. They think the minute they set foot out there, someone will shoot them. They're afraid to stay and get shot through the windows and walls. This place isn't bulletproof, Shaw. It'll take me days to relocate them. What am I going to do? If I keep this center open, it's going to just go on. If I close it, they win."

Justine talked so rapidly, and her emotions escalated so quickly, Shaw didn't attempt to respond. He reached for her shoulder and shook her gently once to get her to stop.

The slight physical jarring stopped her, giving her a moment to gather herself. But not talking allowed the feelings to overcome her. She turned away from Shaw, her chin trembling slightly. Shaw saw the first tear ooze out the side of her eye.

Angrily, she stood up, steeling herself, stepping away from Shaw as she quickly wiped away the tear. She did not want to cry in front of Loyd Shaw.

"Goddamn it," she said, "what the hell have I started here?"

Shaw stood and took a step toward her.

"Justine, don't. You didn't start this."

Justine turned to him now. Feeling his concern and kindness, she came to him, and, without affectation, she put her hands on his shoulders as if to thank him. She lay her forehead against his chest and let out a quivering breath.

"Oh, God," she said. Giving in to it now. Letting the tension, fatigue, and fear bring the tears to her eyes. Letting the emotions course through her now that her face was hidden.

Shaw let her rest her head against him while he gently patted her back, feeling awkward, not quite sure what he should do but very sure that he wanted to do whatever he could for Justine Burton.

Shaw wanted to be the comforting presence she needed. He wanted to do the right thing and help her calm down, but, without warning, she moved completely into his arms. He felt her tall, elegant body and full breasts pressing into him and her arms around him, and that austerely beautiful face pressed against his chest, and he couldn't stop it. The sexual attraction took over. He had to fight the urge to hold her closer, to allow a deeper intimacy between them. He stood still and kept patting her on the back, keeping it neutral, asexual, but knowing it had already gone too far.

He kept saying, "It's okay. It's okay."

And she continued clinging to him, increasing her hold on him. She held him so tightly that there was nothing Shaw could do. He had an insane urge to run his hands up and down her back and caress her, and then, without warning, she relaxed and stood back from him and looked Shaw directly in the eyes. He looked back at her. And then she titled her head and came forward, and she kissed him. Just on the side of his mouth but not entirely on the cheek, either. He felt her soft, full lips on the corner of his and the brush of the bandage on her face against his chin.

He stood still, letting her do what she wanted to. He kissed her back just slightly so she would know he wasn't offended or put off. It must have been the right thing to do because she relaxed more and again stepped back from him. Her left hand remained on his shoulder. Shaw held her by the elbow and looked at her. Justine waited for him to say something.

"It will be all right," he said.

"Why? Tell me."

For a moment, Shaw thought he should tell her how sure he was that Archie would be stopped. How certain he was that he or the Muslims or the cops would soon get him. Shaw knew he could sound very convincing about the forces lined up against

Archie Reynolds. But deep inside, he knew it was a lie. Shaw knew Archie Reynolds had already consigned himself to his fate. Archie Reynolds knew he had lost New Lots. Archie Reynolds knew he would soon die. And therefore, Archie had the one advantage that any terrorist has against a superior force. Death would not deter him. And as Archie Reynolds rushed toward the inevitable end without regard to his life, Shaw was certain his enemy could do terrible damage to others.

Shaw did not want to lie to Justine. But he would not tell her the terrible truth. He didn't even want to admit it to himself.

"We found Archie tonight. He got away. He might be wounded, might not be. But he's on the run now, Justine. He can't go on like this much longer. He can't keep this up. Not now. One way or another, he'll die. Or he'll spend the rest of his life in jail."

Justine took in what Shaw had said.

"I hope you're right."

"I am."

"I'm sorry I insisted you come here. But I can't talk to any of the other cops. Everything they do is because of who I am. I can't trust anything they say. I need you. I need to trust someone."

"You can trust me."

"Don't hold it against me."

"Of course not."

"And don't hold the other against me."

"What?"

"What I did just now."

"Why would I hold that against you?"

"Because..."

Justine hesitated. Shaw asked gently, "Why? Why would I hold it against you?"

"I don't know. Because it's not right."

"Why?"

"Because it can't—"

"Be any more than just that moment?"

"Yes."

"It's still an honor."

Her soft brown eyes widened for just a moment, and, for a second, it looked as if she might cry again. And then she moved forward and kissed Shaw again. This time lightly. On his cheek.

"Thank you," she said.

"You're welcome."

And then she let out a long slow breath and flashed a quick smile and said, "You keep doing the right thing, don't you?"

"Well…"

"Yeah. Well." Justine let it go and said, "All right. I'm okay."

"Good."

Justine rubbed Shaw's cheek and said, "You scratch."

"Haven't had much time for grooming."

Shaw touched Justine's face where his stubble had scraped her, and she let him. She seemed to be happy that he did.

He said, "Sorry."

"Don't be."

She moved back to her desk and started to gather her suit jacket and purse.

"I'm glad I called you. You said I could call you."

"I did."

"You're giving me good advice. I'm no use to anyone here tonight. I'll get some sleep and deal with this insanity tomorrow. Better in daylight than now."

"Exactly."

Shaw walked her out of her office and handed her over to her guards. The third detective had returned. All three of the men stood up when she entered the waiting area. The way they surrounded Justine and their demeanor made Shaw feel that he didn't need to remind them to be careful.

Justine had returned to being Justine Burton. She told the detectives, "Let's go." They headed out. Shaw trailed behind them, watched them escort Justine to her car, and then he got into his Caprice to head back to Kings County Hospital with another load of feelings and emotions swirling in his head.

CHAPTER 40

IMPELLITERI AND SPERLING WERE AS SHAW HAD LEFT THEM IN the waiting room. Walter had arrived.

A minute or so after Shaw joined his men, a nurse still dressed in green surgical garb shuffled in on booties covering her shoes and told the detectives they could see the doctor. All four followed her as she led them to the recovery area.

The surgeon in charge seemed awfully young to Shaw. But at least he spoke English. His name was Fishman. Ira Fishman. For no other reason except crude stereotyping, Shaw felt reassured that Mason had a Jewish doctor.

Fishman told them that the bullet had entered Mason's left side at a weird angle and lodged itself in the fleshy pad of skin above his left hip. He told them he thought the bullet had been deflected off another object, probably the street, which accounted for its strange entry angle and the fact that it hadn't gone all the way through.

"Did you get it out?"

"Of course. Piece of cake. The hard part was making sure nothing important was hit."

"Was there?"

"No. No damage to the patient's ribs, stomach, major blood vessels, or other internal organs. But we had to cut a bit of a path in him to get it out and clean everything up."

"He'll be okay, right?"

"Yeah. If you're going to get shot, that's a pretty good place. Don't you guys wear vests?"

Nobody answered.

Impelliteri pressed. "He's going to be okay, right?"

"As long as nothing gets infected. So if you want to go see him, keep your distance. And don't take too long."

The doctor left. Shaw and the others walked over to the screened-off area where Mason lay in a bed hooked up to monitors and IV lines.

Their wounded partner lay motionless under the hospital sheets in a crowded area of prostrate dark-skinned bodies, medical equipment, sterile smells, and pain. Mason's color had returned, and he seemed comfortable, deep under the after-effects of the anesthesia and whatever else they had pumped into him.

Shaw stepped forward.

"How you doing, Mase?"

Mason responded, his voice raspy and his mouth dry.

"Doing fine, brother. Thanks for getting me here fast. I expect I'll be feeling a lot worse once the anesthesia wears off."

Impelliteri said, "Just keep taking all the pain killers they'll give you."

"Yeah. Probably end up addicted."

Shaw said, "Just rest, man. You earned it."

Orestes Mason paused to look at the others for a moment, then said, "If you gonna ask me if I need anything, don't. I'll tell you what I need."

"What?"

"I need you to get that son of a bitch Archie Reynolds. By any means necessary."

Shaw nodded. "By any means necessary."

Sperling repeated the phrase. "By any means necessary."

And then Shaw said, "I'm going to call Muriel. Don't worry. I'll tell her everything is fine. I'll tell her you're safe. All set until this mess is over."

"Maybe she'll buy that," said Mason.

Shaw knew that a husband shot and lying in the hospital is a disaster to any wife, no matter what anybody says. At least most of what he was going to tell her would be the truth. He decided his explanation as to why the department wouldn't be sending a chaplain or any of the brass to the hospital would also be mostly the truth. Muriel Mason was too smart and too impatient to be bullshitted. Or to wait until morning to see her husband. Shaw knew no matter what he said, Muriel Mason would be dressed and standing next to her husband within the hour.

Shaw told Walter Wang he should go back to the precinct and try to catch some sleep there instead of home.

Impelliteri and Sperling followed Shaw as he searched for the operating room where Rachman was under the knife.

They got lucky and caught a young surgeon coming out into the hallway. This doctor was more what Shaw expected at a public hospital. He was Pakistani. Apparently, he had finished his part of the job. He told Shaw Rachman would be under the knife for at least another four hours.

Shaw identified himself and asked how Rachman was doing.

The young doctor said, "He's still alive. Lost a massive amount of blood. He was shot with twenty-twos, so no big blunt entry wounds, but they spin around and tear through tissue. It creates a great deal of damage to blood vessels, organs, bones. He had at least six bullets in him, maybe more. We do not have them all out yet."

"Will he live?"

"Possibly. If we don't kill him trying to repair everything."

The doctor turned and walked away. He wasn't willing to devote any more time to answering questions.

Shaw knew that even if Rachman lived, he'd be unable to do anything for them now. But it didn't matter. Now that the shootings at New Lots and the mosque were over, Shaw knew the ones he wanted to talk to would be coming soon. That's why he had called Impelliteri and Spalding to the hospital. He wanted his men and their guns with him.

CHAPTER 41

Fifteen minutes after Loyd Shaw spoke to the Pakistani doctor, they arrived.

Youssef, John X, plus four gunmen. All of them in the MS-2 style – beards, combat boots, dark clothing, heavy coats, and skullcaps. All except Youssef, who wore a baggy black suit and looked neither to his right nor left but directly at Shaw.

They walked into the waiting room. Shaw stood up. The Muslims looked at Shaw and stopped. Shaw nodded to Impelliteri, who had positioned himself near the door. Impelliteri kicked up the doorstop. As the door swung shut, James Sperling moved to the other side of the Muslims. There wasn't a trace of emotion on his face as he folded his arms across his chest, hands under his armpits, gripping the butts of his guns holstered under his blue blazer.

Shaw said to himself, God love you, Sperling, you skinny bastard.

They were outnumbered, but Shaw felt secure. Impelliteri stood behind the Muslims. Shaw in front of them. Sperling next to them. As far as Shaw was concerned, they had the Muslims surrounded.

An elderly black couple sat off in the corner of the waiting room. One of their grandchildren had been injured. For all Shaw knew, another casualty of the Blue-Tops/Muslim war. They stayed in their corner and tried to make believe they were invisible, but they never took their wary eyes off the hard men standing in the small waiting room. They knew they were witnessing a showdown.

When Impelliteri pushed the door shut, it seemed as if the confrontation would explode right then and there. The Muslims were just as keyed up as Shaw and his men. One of the gunmen turned and started to go for the closed door. Impelliteri stepped in front of him.

"Back off."

Impelliteri wanted the gunman to try something. Gun, fists, feet, it didn't matter. He was sick of their arrogance and deadly brutality.

Just before they clashed, and everyone started shooting, a voice snapped out, "Wait."

It came from the wiry man in the baggy suit.

Shaw asked him, "Are you in charge? After Rachman?"

Youssef squinted at Shaw for a moment, looking him over through his thick, wire-rimmed glasses. It was clear Youssef and Shaw were the leaders. "Yes. Who are you?"

"Detective Loyd Shaw. And you. You're Youssef?"

"Yes."

"I was with Rachman when they came tonight. Rachman was sending me to talk to you. Two doors right of his place. I was walking to your apartment when they attacked."

"What happened to our brother?"

"Archie Reynolds shot him."

"You saw it?"

"Yes, I saw it. He ambushed Rachman. My partner and I drove him off. He got away. My partner got shot. We brought Rachman here."

Youssef nodded.

Shaw said, "Don't thank us," and meant it.

Youssef snapped back, "What do you want?"

"I want Archie Reynolds."

"So do we."

"Get in line."

Youssef stiffened. He asked Shaw, "Do you know what else happened tonight?"

"Some of it."

"Another attack. Snipers. Our men shot at. Young ones shooting at us from hiding places."

"I know."

"Archie Reynolds recruited them. Gave them money and a gun. Offered a reward."

"How do you know?"

"Because the children told us."

"I heard you threw one of them off a roof. Is that why the other kids talked?"

Youssef did not respond.

Shaw knew it was useless to push it. He asked, "Do you know where I can find Archie Reynolds?"

Youssef dismissed Shaw with a wave of his hand.

"There is no *where*. You won't find him. You want to know where he lives? He lives at eight-four-six-two Sycamore Place in Saddle Brook, New Jersey. So what? You think he'll be there? If he stops anywhere, to eat or sleep, it won't be in Brownsville. He'll never sleep in the same bed twice now. If he comes into Brownsville, you'll never see him. If you were any good, you would have killed him at the mosque."

"How did he know where and when to find Rachman?"

"We're not sure."

"Are you going to help me find him?"

"Why should we? Are you going to help us?"

"What the hell do you think we're doing? You have what, fifty men? A hundred? Two hundred? We have thousands. We have the power, not you."

Youssef dismissed Shaw with a sneer and another wave of his hand. "Yes, now. But a week from now, you'll have a few squads cruising through our neighborhood, never stopping, never setting foot on the streets. You have nothing. You have no idea what's going on, and you never will."

"Then tell me. Tell me what's going on."

"Look to your own for what you want to know. Don't ask me. What did the doctors say? Will Rachman live?"

Shaw answered, "Maybe."

"Good. So will you unless you get in our way. Tell your man to open this door."

"What?"

Shaw moved toward Youssef.

Youssef stepped back. The gunmen reached inside their coats. But before they had their weapons out, both Impelliteri and Sperling had their guns in their hands. Four guns cocked and pointed, just like that. Impelliteri aimed one Glock at Youssef's head, the other at John X. He knew which targets to pick. Sperling aimed his two guns at the four others. The Muslim gunmen froze.

Shaw yelled at Youssef, holding himself back from grabbing his skinny throat, "What did you say? Say it again, you prick. Say it again, and I'll fucking shoot you right now. Say it! Say you'll kill me!"

Shaw knew without any doubt that if Impelliteri and Sperling hadn't gotten their guns out so quickly, they might already be dead now. It made him even more enraged.

And then Youssef slowly raised his hands.

"I meant it as a friendly warning. I meant no disrespect."

"Bullshit, you little asshole. You fucking threatened me, you little vigilante fuck. Fuck you."

Youssef glared at Shaw, but he kept his hands up.

Shaw stood where he was, struggling to control himself.

Nobody moved. Shaw felt his murderous rage ebbing. Shaw would not risk the blood that would ensue if he went for Youssef.

He quietly told the man, "Don't ever threaten me or my men again. You may think you're a fucking hero on a divine mission, but you're just a murderous little ex-con vigilante as far as I'm concerned. And don't you ever fucking tell one of my men to open a door for you. Do you understand?"

For a moment, Shaw thought he might have pushed Youssef too far, but Youssef slowly turned toward Impelliteri and said, "I apologize."

"All right then," Shaw said.

Shaw nodded at Impelliteri. The cop hesitated for just a moment, then shoved one of his guns in his belt and opened the door, never taking his eyes or his other gun off Youssef.

The Muslims slowly moved out. Youssef filed out last. Impelliteri kept the gun pointed at Youssef's head the entire time, but Youssef never blinked. As the small man reached the door, Impelliteri just nodded at him as if to say, I'll shoot you in a heartbeat.

And then Youssef was gone. And the knot in Shaw's upper back slowly began to loosen. But Youssef's words kept pounding in his head, "Look to your own."

CHAPTER 42

It should have been more difficult for Archie Reynolds to find out where Justine Burton lived. He got it on the first try.

After shooting Rachman, Archie had Reggie Whack drop him off on a quiet street in Queens, where he stole an inconspicuous blue Honda Civic. Then he drove back into Brownsville and parked within sight of Justine's community center. With all the police and ambulances and commotion, no one noticed him. He sat low in his seat, gazing just above the steering wheel, waiting, watching, passing the time by guessing where she lived. Striver's Row in Harlem? One of the middle-class black neighborhoods in Queens, like St. Albans? Maybe with her daddy, the police commissioner, wherever that was.

Spotting Justine couldn't have been easier. The four men escorting her out of the center were hard to miss. Especially one of them. Three of the four cops wore suits. Only one wore black jeans and a dark brown leather jacket. That was the asshole who shot at him and Reggie. Archie nearly changed his plans right then and there. He pulled out his Beretta, started up the Honda, and tried to figure out the best way to cruise up to that motherfucker in the leather jacket and put one in his head. Undercover cop, thought Archie. The damn pohleece be working with the Muslims now. Ain't that some shit.

Shaw had no idea he was within sight of Archie Reynolds. He walked away from Justine's security squad to his car.

Archie was nearly certain that he could shoot the undercover cop and get away before anyone noticed him go down. He eased the Honda into gear and rolled away from the curb. But at the last moment, he braked. Archie's need to hurt Justine outweighed his desire to shoot Shaw.

Archie waited for Justine's Ford Taurus to head off, tailed by the unmarked police car. He'd followed them from a reasonable distance across Eastern Parkway onto the Prospect Expressway, then through the Brooklyn Battery Tunnel. When she'd pulled off the West Side Highway into the small streets of West Village, Archie had sneered. Just like this fuckin' bitch to be livin' in a white Yuppie neighborhood.

There were plenty of parking spots legal until eight a.m. on the Village streets. Archie slid the Honda into one of them as Justine parked her car in an open-air lot on Washington Street. The detective riding with her escorted her to their unmarked NYPD car. Then they drove her one short block to a recently renovated building on Horatio between Washington Street and the West Side Highway. A place rather pretentiously named the West Coast Apartments, as if the grimy West Side Highway constituted a coastline.

Archie didn't even have to leave his car to see where they took her.

One detective walked her into the building. The other two remained in their car parked at the curb.

Archie had to admit the location made sense for her. A black woman like her certainly wouldn't stand out in the Greenwich Village neighborhood. As long as she had the money to live there. Archie wondered about that now as he stepped out of the Honda.

He walked over to her building, then strolled up and down the block, checking entrances to Justine's apartment building, looking up at the few lit windows, wondering which one might be hers.

He continued walking around the neighborhood. Took note of the several bars on Washington Street near Justine's building that were still open at this late hour and doing good business. Nearby on Gansevoort Street, the all-night diner Florent attracted customers around the clock. Right on the corner of her building, a twenty-four-hour deli also attracted customers 24/7. And when the bars closed at four in the morning, the meat market district, just one block north, was up and running.

This neighborhood never slept.

Anybody passing Justine's apartment wouldn't cause alarm to the detectives parked in front of Justine's building, not even Archie. Not even when he cruised by the front entrance twice as he made his plans. The guards didn't even notice him when he stood on Washington Street, trying to guess which window on the eighth floor belonged to that bitch Justine, one of the only two lit up at forty-thirty in the morning.

CHAPTER 43

ONLY WHEN THE HOSPITAL WAITING ROOM DOOR CLOSED BEHIND Youssef and the others did Impelliteri and Sperling holster their guns.

As usual, Impelliteri had the final word.

"Assholes."

Sperling dropped back into a chair. Shaw rolled his head, trying to release some of the tension. Impelliteri stood by the door, still not quite able to let it go.

Shaw checked his watch.

"You guys going after Reggie Whack?"

The question brought Impelliteri's attention back to the immediate objective. He checked his watch. Nearly four a.m.

"Yeah. Now is the right time to head out there. We got a whole hour's sleep before you called."

"At the precinct?"

"Yeah. Neither one of us felt like bothering to go home. Figured by the time we got home, we'd just have to turn around and come back. What are you going to do?"

"Try to find out what the hell that little four-eyed prick meant by *look to your own*."

"Good luck. Let's go, Sperl."

Shaw said, "Keep in touch."

✳

Impelliteri and Sperling tried the Bronx address first because Reggie had collected more parking tickets there. They cruised the neighborhood looking for the Jeep but didn't spot it on any of the surrounding streets. After an hour of searching punctuated by Impelliteri's cursing, they drove back into Brooklyn and headed to Fort Greene. After five minutes cruising around the Walt Whitman housing project, they spotted the Jeep. It wasn't difficult. Reggie hadn't parked at a fire hydrant or driveway. He'd left his car right in the middle of the project courtyard.

"Jeezus, can you believe that crazy fuck? Parks it right out in the open like that."

Sperling answered, "Yes."

"People around here have to know who owns that car. Otherwise, it would have been stripped down to the frame. Dude must have a scary rep."

Sperling squinted at the Jeep. "I suppose."

Impelliteri said, "You think the Brownie who wrote him up had the balls to walk in there and do it?"

"Some of those meter maids can be pretty tough."

"Yeah, most of them big mammas know how to handle they selves."

Impelliteri drove the Caprice over the sidewalk and positioned the car, so it blocked one exit out of the courtyard.

"So, we wait for him?" asked Sperling.

"Fuck, no. I ain't waiting for that asshole to wake up."

Impelliteri got out and rummaged around in his trunk until he found a tire iron and headed for the Jeep.

*

Upstairs in a cluttered one-bedroom project apartment, Reggie Whack, Darleece, their infant baby, and Darleece's five-year-old son by another man slept peacefully. The kids slept in one bed. Reggie and Darleece in another. All in the same room. It was five-twenty in the morning. Long before their wake-up time. Even Darleece's pit bull bitch Queenie slept curled up in a pile of dirty laundry that had collected in the corner of the stuffy, dingy bedroom.

Normally, a car alarm sounding in Fort Greene wouldn't wake anybody. But with the car parked right in the project's courtyard, the blaring alarm couldn't be ignored.

Reggie had smoked some weed and downed two cans of malt liquor to calm his nerves and ease his stutter after the mosque ambush. So when the alarm shrieked its repertoire of beeps and wails and bleats, Reggie hardly stirred.

Impelliteri had used the tire iron to shatter the driver's side window. It hadn't made much noise, but it did set off the car's alarm. The alarm continued to sound through a two-minute cycle then ended mid-wail. Impelliteri immediately shattered a headlight and kicked the side of the Jeep to start the alarm again.

Reggie turned over. The alarm finally awakened him, but he had no desire to open his eyes.

It didn't seem possible, but along with the car alarm, someone seemed to be yelling his name. And then, mixed in with the wailing alarm and the yelling, came the sound of a tire iron smashing sheet metal.

Reggie sat up suddenly and looked out the window. Impelliteri whacked the Jeep with another overhand blow that knocked a crease across the entire width of the hood.

Sperling squatted down near the back of the Jeep, his cocked 9mm Sig-Sauer in hand, waiting.

Impelliteri hit the Jeep twice more and yelled Reggie's name again.

Impelliteri was about to ask Sperling if he thought it possible for someone to sleep through the noise when Reggie Whack burst into the courtyard.

He ran with his gun extended, barefoot and shirtless, firing shots at Impelliteri.

Impelliteri had his Glock ready in his free hand, but he didn't beat Sperling, who quickly stood up, mumbled a warning, dropped into a shooter's crouch, and squeezed off two quick shots at his target. His moving target.

Impelliteri had expected Sperling to be one of the best shooters in the NYPD. In fact, Sperling was *the* best shooter. He put two bullets into Reggie Whack's moving head from almost twenty yards. Most of Reggie's face and skull disappeared. His feet flew out from under him. He died before he hit the ground.

Impelliteri hadn't even raised the Glock.

"*Goddamn*, James."

Even more impressive were the shots Sperling fired when the pit bull bitch burst out of the door Reggie had left open.

Reggie had been a hard target. The animal was an impossible target. She streaked across the courtyard, low to the ground, intent on launching herself at Sperling or Impelliteri or both. Sperling's first shot missed, his second caught the dog at the top of its right leg. The dog yelped, skidded, gathered itself, and kept coming, limping, but still on the run. Impelliteri opened up, too, but Sperling's third shot slammed into the dog's chest, and she dropped.

The dog's feet kept moving. Impelliteri had a better chance at the stationary target and finally put a couple of slugs into the dying dog.

"Well," said Impelliteri, "that's that. Too bad about the dog. Damn beast had a lot of heart."

Sperling looked over at Reggie.

"I assume he's the guy?"

Impelliteri walked over and moved what was left of Reggie's head so he could see the remains of his face.

"I don't know. I see a gold tooth in there. He have a gold tooth?"

"He wasn't smiling in his mugshot."

"He ain't smiling now, that's for sure."

From up high came the screams of Darleece, a big woman, leaning out the window, crying and wailing, "Reggie. Reggie. They kilt my Reggie."

Impelliteri looked up at Darleece, looked back at the corpse, and muttered. "I'll call that a positive ID on the deceased. It's him."

"And I assume that's Darleece. So now what?" asked Sperling.

"You've never gone through a shooting aftermath before?"

"No."

"Well, get ready to have your day ruined. If the uniformed guys don't get here soon, we're supposed to call the supervising officer at the precinct and tell him to haul his ass out here. Then we wait for CSU, wait for our supervisors, wait for the precinct detectives, wait for the medical examiner guy, the union, it's fuckin' unbelievable. When they get done with all their bullshit and interviewing us, we have to go to the hospital and get checked for stress and all that shit. I've done it twice before. It fucking takes forever."

"I don't want to do that," said Sperling.

"What, you want to just walk?"

"Well, I don't know."

"It's gonna cause us untold problems if we walk."

"I don't want to go through all that. In fact, I won't."

"So? What do you suggest?"

Sperling thought it over for a moment.

"Call Shaw. Get him to call DeLuca's guy. What's his name, Conklin? Let's see if DeLuca really is God."

Just then, a blue-and-white screeched into the courtyard with two more following close behind.

Impelliteri held his shield up, as did Sperling. They identified themselves, then ignored the uniforms while they talked to Shaw on their radio. Forty minutes later, when the area had become inundated with police personnel, Conklin showed up with a team of detectives from the police commissioner's personal security squad.

Conklin spoke to Impelliteri and Sperling for a couple of minutes. He looked at Reggie. Saw the gun still in his hand. Looked at the dog. Noted it was a pit bull. He asked Impelliteri and Sperling, "How many shots did he fire at you?"

Impelliteri said, "Four," although he remembered only three.

Conklin walked over to the commanding officer on the scene. He spoke for a few minutes, introduced the detectives from the chief's office. Then he came back and told Impelliteri and Sperling they could leave. The case was now officially under the jurisdiction of the chief of detectives. No more precinct cops. No more questions.

Impelliteri looked at Sperling. Sperling smiled for the first time since they had met.

CHAPTER 44

AFTER IMPELLITERI AND SPERLING LEFT, SHAW DROPPED WALTER Wang off at the Seven-Three and decided to check on Justine. He got the call from Impelliteri to see if DeLuca could run cover for him and Sperling after shooting Reggie Whack as he parked on Justine's block. He finished his call to DeLuca's fixer, Conklin, at 5:45 a.m. Conklin responded in his usual abbreviated manner. He said, "We'll take care of it."

Shaw decided he ought to wait for a more reasonable time to see Justine. He set his wristwatch alarm for seven but woke up after an hour of sitting-up sleep. It helped cut his fatigue, but not much more.

He feared he might fall back asleep, so he got out of the Caprice and breathed deeply and stretched. He checked his watch. Looked around. Wednesday morning, six-fifty-five, overcast, and cool. He hadn't made it to seven. The streets were empty of people and traffic, quiet except for a refrigerated meat truck parked about a block away outside a meatpacking warehouse. The truck's engine had been left running to power the refrigeration unit.

Shaw didn't have the patience to wait any longer. He called Justine's apartment on his cellular phone. He expected her to be sleeping, but she answered on the second ring.

"It's Shaw. We should talk."

"Now?"

"Yeah. I'm parked outside. Are you up?"

"Up and down all night." There was a pause before she said, "Okay. You might as well come up. Eight F."

"Do you want coffee or anything from the deli?"

"Coffee. Light."

Shaw thought a light cup of rich coffee would just about match the color of her skin.

"Okay."

While the deli man poured the coffee, Shaw imagined how Justine would be dressed. He figured her for pajamas and a robe. A woman with a body like Justine's would take care to cover it up at night. He entertained himself with an image of her sleeping nude. Then switched to a black lace teddy. Then stopped.

Shaw had felt her body against his. Had touched her skin. It wasn't good for him to think about Justine Burton in bed, dressed, undressed, or even dressed and under the covers.

As he walked back from the deli, Shaw noted Justine's three-man security team parked in front of the entrance to her building. One of the detectives slept curled up on the backseat. The driver sat reading the *NY Post*. The detective in the passenger seat watched Shaw enter the building. Justine's security team let him enter the building without challenge. Shaw hoped it was because they recognized him.

When he entered Justine's apartment, Shaw saw that he'd guessed wrong. He hadn't pictured a nightgown. When she opened the door, she wore a terry-cloth robe and cotton nightgown that reached about midcalf. Shaw still couldn't get over that skin, what little there was showing.

After the nightgown and robe, he half expected fuzzy slippers on her feet, but she wore something that looked like suede clogs with cork soles. Lightweight and easy to slip on. Practical.

"Well," she said, "my image is absolutely shot after this."

"Not really."

"Liar."

Shaw wasn't lying. At home, without the formalities of her work wardrobe and office surroundings, Justine's manner was more relaxed and feminine.

He handed her a brown bag.

"There's some Danish in there, too."

"Thanks. I just need coffee. I didn't sleep much last night."

She took the bag and led him into a simply furnished, one-bedroom, sheetrock-box apartment. The only outstanding features were higher than average ceilings and an interesting view over the rooftops of the low West Village brownstones and townhouses.

They sat at Justine's kitchen table for two.

"So what's important enough to bring you to me first thing in the morning? Tell me you got Archie Reynolds."

Shaw thought about that phrase for a moment, "bring you to me," and then put it out of his mind.

"No. Not yet. I came because I need to ask you a few things."

"It couldn't wait?"

"Nothing can wait."

"What happened?"

"I told you one of my men was shot last night. He'll be all right. I didn't tell you about Rachman Abdul X, the man in charge of the Muslim security company. He got shot six times by Archie Reynolds."

"Good Lord."

"Rachman's a bull. He's still alive. Might stay that way if he doesn't get shot again. The Blue-Tops set fire to the Muslim's mosque on Bushwick, then ambushed Rachman. Then, as you know, they shot up the area around New Lots."

"Including my center."

"Yes. On the positive side, two of my men took out Reginal Wilson. A.k.a. Reggie Whack. He's number two under Archie Reynolds.

Justine didn't comment on the euphemism "took out." She simply nodded.

"Justine, if there's anything more that you know about what's behind all this, I'm asking you to tell me."

"What do you mean?"

"I'm getting some weird feedback out there."

"Like what?"

"Let me ask you something first. What do you know about Arbor Realty?"

"Not much."

"Did they come to you, or did you find them?"

"I found them. I had inquiries into every community and district planning board in the city trying to find a location for the center. I had a federal grant with matching state and city funds, but I didn't have a space. So I put out the word everywhere I could. A woman named Cecily Adams in City Planning told me about Arbor Realty. She knew Arbor Realty from an apartment building they took over in Bed-Stuy, and she knew about their deal for New Lots Apartments. She gave me a lead. I followed it."

"To where? Who did you talk to?"

"Leon Bloom."

"How does an outfit like Arbor Realty acquire ownership of an apartment complex like New Lots?"

"There are a number of companies interested in taking over subsidized housing projects. When a place goes under, it used to be the city took possession in lieu of back taxes. They stopped doing that unofficially several years ago. There were just too many."

"So how does it work? Whoever wants to assume the debt gets possession?"

"Generally, but it's not that simple. There's a lot of negotiating that goes on, mostly with the banks who hold the mortgages.

In this case it was HUD that backed the loans, so they were involved, too. It can get complicated. But the fact is, the city and banks are fairly eager to get rid of these places, and they make the deal attractive so that there's competition for them."

"So who wins?"

"Basically, whoever offers the debt holders the best deal."

"Was there competition for New Lots Apartments?"

"Not much. Arbor Realty doesn't go for the good properties. It goes for the problem properties. The ones very few investor groups want."

"The low end."

"And the cheapest."

"Even considering the cost of paying an outlaw Muslim security force to clean it up?"

"Actually, they almost always get reimbursed for security contracts."

"They do?"

"Yes. Most of the time, HUD kicks in to pay for security. That leaves the takeover entity with more money for renovations. Of course, they spend as little as they can on that."

"Unbelievable."

Shaw sat at the table, absorbing what Justine had told him.

He said, "Bloom knew who you were, obviously."

"Of course."

"Did your father ever talk to him?"

"Not that I know of."

"He didn't exert any pressure on Arbor Realty?"

"If he did, I didn't hear about it. I don't think he had to. And I sure as hell didn't ask him to."

"Is your father going to profit from this in any way?"

"Hey, Shaw, you're…"

Shaw raised a hand. "I'm sorry. I don't know your father. Just tell me I'm wrong, and I'll shut up about it. The reason

I asked, I'm trying to figure out why Arbor Realty thinks they can bring in a criminal group of vigilantes who have no compunction about murdering people and think they can get away with that."

Justine let it go and said, "Maybe because they've done it before."

"In Bed-Stuy?"

"And other places. I know that New Lots isn't their first property that had to be cleaned up."

"Have they used felons to clean out a place before or just in New Lots?"

"I don't know."

"Well, whether they've done this before or not, it's still the same question. Why does Arbor Realty think they can get away with murder? Even if it is drug dealers they're shooting and burning."

"Maybe *because* it's drug dealers they're shooting and burning."

"Hard to believe. I know the chief of detectives is going outside the box to shut down this mess in New Lots, with your father's approval, but still…"

"You mean bringing you in?"

"And four others. We're not working through the regular chain of command. We're not doing things by the book. But when I put pressure on Leon Bloom, the first person he called was DeLuca's fixer, a lieutenant named Conklin. And then tonight, after all hell broke loose, the Muslims told me to look to my own."

"Look to your own?"

"Yes. I'm not a member of the Elks Club, Justine. If some-body tells me to look to my own, I'm gonna look at cops. I'm trying to figure out if anybody in the NYPD is in bed with Arbor Realty."

"You mean DeLuca?"

"DeLuca, your father, both, I don't know."

"As far as I know, my father isn't involved with Arbor Realty or Leon Bloom. I can't speak for DeLuca. But if they are or aren't, what difference does it make?"

"You don't think it makes a difference?"

"Of course. But I'm asking if it makes a difference for you. Does it make a difference why DeLuca put you in this position?"

"Yes. It makes a difference. If I'm going to die out there, I'd like to know what's really going on."

Justine sat back in her chair and looked at Shaw. She sipped more coffee out of the delicatessen cardboard cup.

"All right. What are the possibilities? Let's say for argument's sake that my father and DeLuca are helping this realty company more than they normally would. I'm not saying they are, but if they are, you want to know why. Beyond the fact that I'm involved."

"Yes."

"Maybe my father plans to run for mayor and needs campaign financing from them. Maybe DeLuca wants to retire and be head of their security operation. Or, what the hell, New Lots Apartments has a good shot at being profitable, maybe it's simply payoffs under the table. Cops have been paid off before. If not with money, then jobs, loans, there's lots of ways to corrupt someone."

"You have any ideas in this particular case?"

Justine leaned forward and gave Shaw one of her direct looks.

"Shaw, I don't know. I honestly don't know. I don't think my father ever took a dime in his life. You know more about DeLuca than I do. What's his reputation?"

Shaw didn't answer.

Justine said, "If you're involved in this because somebody in the NYPD has been corrupted, would you get out?"

"No."

"Why not?"

"Besides wanting to save my pension and play the hero?"

"Yes. Why?"

"Because of you."

The words came out of Shaw's mouth almost before he knew it. Before he could stop it, as if the words had a will of their own.

"What?"

"I guess I'm doing it, at least partly, for you."

"I didn't ask for that."

"Not in so many words. But come on, Justine, you've been watching me look at you like I'm dumbstruck. You call, I come running. You shake my hand and propose a date, I say sure. You kiss me, I kiss you back. I'm not supposed to think there's something going on between us?"

After a moment, Justine said, "Yes. You are. There is."

And there it was. Directly from her. Shaw didn't say anything, because he didn't want to give Justine a chance to change or downplay what she had just said. In his silence, Justine kept looking at Shaw, waiting for a response from him to the truth she had admitted.

"Well," he said, "so I guess I can stop acting like there isn't."

"Right. So now what?"

"I, I don't know. I mean – when this thing started out, it was real simple for me. The chief of D had enough on me to end my career, take away my pension, and make good on a bunch of other grim threats. So he gave me a shot at a reprieve. Go out there and stop this thing, and all is forgiven. I figure, with the right guys, a little luck, move fast, work smart, I've got a chance. Get in, get out.

"Then I see that place. New Lots. I see all those children running around in the courtyard, women, regular people trying to get to work. Trying to get by despite what goes on in that goddamn neighborhood. Unimaginable degradation. Overdoses.

Everybody peddling dope. Girls, not even close to grown up, selling themselves. People either just trapped in that mess or trying to live in New Lots like it's a real neighborhood like any other. They don't deserve what's come down on them, so naturally, I want to stop it.

"And then they start shooting at me. At my partner. I want to shoot back. But I'm thinking about you and your anger about more young black men dying. And I picture putting a bullet in somebody. And living with that. And on one side it feels like the last goddamn thing I want to do. On the other, it's like, goddamn it, just get a fucking bullet in him before he gets one in you. Just shoot first and keep on shooting.

"Then this murderous fuck Archie stands over a man and shoots him six times and puts a bullet in my partner, and I want to put a bullet in him so bad my fucking head aches.

"And suddenly one of the Muslim leaders tells me to look to my own. And I'm wondering, how many people do I need to worry about? Who can I trust? And now you're part of it. You're someone I don't want hurt by this. And I know as sure as I'm sitting here, this maniac Archie Reynolds wants to hurt you. Kill you."

Shaw stopped talking, surprised at how much had spilled out of him. Justine just sat, looking at him, nodding as if she understood every word. Shaw took a deep breath and came back to the original question.

"So, what do you and I do now? I'll tell you what we do. Nothing. Not one damn thing until this is over, Justine. Until you're safe. Until those people out there in New Lots and Brownsville get at least some relief from the endless violence and danger that fills their lives every fucking day. So, yeah, the answer is yes, I'm in this no matter what. As long as you're in it, I'm in it. But I'd still like to know what's really going on."

Justine took his hand.

"Loyd, I don't know anything more than I told you. I'll see what I can find out. I don't know if it will help, but I'll do what I can."

"Okay. Good. Thanks."

"If you're doing this, at least partly for me, it's the least I can do." She held Shaw's hand in both of hers and kept talking. "And I know this is wrong. It's the wrong time. You're probably the wrong person. I'm worried I'm clinging to you because I'm scared. You know I'm not some tough ghetto kid. I don't do well with guns pointed at me and getting knocked around and shot at. I'm scared. So I need you. And I'm attracted to you. And I admire you. So even though this is all wrong, I can't stop. I won't stop."

"I don't want you to stop."

"And I can't make any promises. When this mess is over, what's between us might go nowhere."

"I'm not asking for any promises. What happens, happens."

She touched his face and said, "Well then, Loyd… "

"What?"

"You'd better go shave."

"Shave?"

Justine looked at Shaw, giving him time to absorb what she meant. After a moment, Shaw smiled. "Sorry. I'm not exactly at my sharpest."

He shaved and showered and shampooed and scrubbed until he was sure to get the stink of blood and gunpowder and sweat off his body, if not off his clothes. While Shaw stood in the shower, the door opened. Justine entered, set out a clean towel for him, gathered up his clothes, and left.

Shaw stepped out. There was a condom sitting on top of a large, fluffy, pink bath towel. He found it both charming and practical. It was comforting to know the single set had worked out a method for handling such matters.

He dried himself and wrapped Justine's towel around his waist and stepped out of the steamy bathroom. He heard Justine's voice off to his left.

"I'm in here."

Shaw walked down a short hall and turned into her bedroom. She had drawn the blinds and turned the louvers so that just a touch of early morning daylight entered the room. Justine sat up against the headboard, the covers pulled to her waist. There was no terrycloth robe. No nightgown. Just Justine. All of her.

After a moment, Shaw realized he had actually stopped breathing. Her shoulders, long, lean arms, perfect, full breasts, taut stomach, that silky smooth café au lait skin...it all mesmerized him. He just stood for a few moments, taking her in, realizing that Justine Burton didn't mind at all how much he stood and looked at her.

She asked, "Do we have time?"

"Hey, as long as it's been for me, this won't take very long."

And then Justine laughed. A big, bright, beautiful smile lit up her face, and she laughed. It was marvelous.

And it was incredible.

Shaw had made her promise to wake him in an hour. He'd never had a better hour's sleep in his life. Justine had drained him, not only of his lust, but, for the brief hour, she had relieved the swirl of dark emotions plaguing him and taken away his inhibitions and doubts. She had wrung him out and restored him at the same time. And when it was time to wake him, she did it with a hot towel, first wiping Shaw's face and lips, then his chest, and then, very gently, the rest of him. She dried him and kissed him and said, "Time to climb back in those dirty clothes and do what you got to do, baby."

Baby. It sounded good. Especially the way she said it.

Shaw croaked, "Thanks."

When he left, Shaw didn't say goodbye. Didn't offer any more advice or warnings. And didn't tell her about recording their conversation.

He'd switched on the recorder when she turned around to take the coffee and Danish out of the brown paper bag. Shaw assuaged his guilt by telling himself that he left the recorder on because he couldn't risk Justine seeing him turn it off. But that didn't do anything about the guilt he felt for not erasing the recording.

CHAPTER 45

JAMES SPERLING AND TONY IMPELLITERI ALSO DID THE SLEEP-IN-the-car routine. They managed to grab a couple of hours before Margo, the kilo queen, found them parked across the street from her car-service office.

She rapped on the window and yelled, "What the fuck you doing parked outside my place?"

Sperling almost shot her. He had his gun out and pointing at her after the second rap.

Margo jumped back. Benny went for his piece. Impelliteri woke up fast and gently pushed Sperling's gun toward the floor.

"Easy, partner."

Margo told Benny, "Keep your shit in your pocket, damn it."

Impelliteri stepped out of the car.

"Christ, Margo, don't be rapping on my window like that. You'll give me a heart attack with that shit."

"Then don't park outside my place. You think I'm gonna do any fuckin' business with an unmarked and two raggedy-ass cops sitting here. You look like shit. You need a bath."

"Come on, we had a hard night. We were just waiting to catch you, Margo. You never answered any of my messages."

"I didn't have anything to tell you."

"Well, you could call and fucking tell me that, couldn't you?"

"I don't waste my time with shit like that."

"All right, all right. You still got nothing?"

"No. I don't still got nothing. I got something. I got plenty of something, baby."

"What?"

"Shit, you wouldn't believe it, *pendejo*. Like rats from a sinking ship these Blue-Tops *maricons*. I got three fucking calls for dope. That operation is going down, baby, and everybody knows it."

"Yeah?"

"Hell, yeah. All the two-bit, low-rung guys in that gang are striking out on their own. Trying to get a kilo or two to fill the need. Nobody's watching the store in New Lots. No supply coming in. Everything going out."

"That's what you hear?"

"That's what I know, sugar. You stay around today, you'll get some guys."

"Good."

"But not on my fucking doorstep. Park someplace else."

"I'll go around the corner."

"Stay out of sight. I'll call you when any of the morons you're looking for show up. Gimme your cell phone number."

"Right. I'll follow them far enough away from here so they won't think you tipped us off.

"Thanks. But to tell you the truth, I wouldn't worry too much about it. Give them a little room, but believe me, none of these guys will be surprised if they get busted. The precinct detectives are all over that outfit. Plus a bunch from Narcotics and Homicide and Major Case and who the fuck knows who else."

"No shit."

"No shit. You're not the only bad boys in on this."

Impelliteri spoke quietly, even though no one was close enough to hear him.

"So, Margo, anybody else contacting you for help on this?"

"None of your damn business. I'm helping you, ain't I? I told you I would, and I am. Let the others go fuck themselves. Comes down to it, you the one I know will do the right thing when payback time comes, right, honey?"

"Right. Good. Call me on my cellular, and we'll do it neat and clean."

"Ciao."

Margo strode off with Benny swaying along behind her. Just before she entered the car-service office, she turned back to make sure Impelliteri had cleared out.

As they drove around the corner, Impelliteri turned to Sperling.

"Listen, James, we'll spend some time around here, okay?"

"Yeah."

"Let these knuckleheads come to us, okay?"

"Sure."

"But do me a favor."

"What?"

"Don't shoot anybody unless you really, really have to. I don't know how many times we can pull that trick with the chief of D's guy, okay?"

"Right."

"I mean, don't get me wrong. That was a righteous shooting. But it might not always play out like that."

Sperling had used up his spoken word count. This time he just nodded.

CHAPTER 46

AFTER SHAW LEFT JUSTINE'S, HE STOPPED AT HIS LOFT FOR A change of clothes. Jane had already left for work, which made things easier.

The coffee he'd sipped with Justine had turned sour in his empty stomach. He hadn't eaten anything since the bad Chinese meal. He still didn't feel like eating anything. He grabbed a bottle of Maalox from his kitchen cabinet and swigged down a mouthful while he dialed in a page to Walter Wang.

Walter called back. Shaw sipped more of the chalky antacid as he talked to him.

"Walter."

"Yes."

"It's Shaw. What's happening at the hospital?"

"Huh?"

Shaw swallowed.

"It's Shaw, goddamn it. What's happening at the hospital?"

"They just finished with Rachman. He's in intensive care."

"He's still breathing, huh?"

"Barely. Got some of his brothers watching over him."

"That's nice. How's Mason?"

"Looks okay to me. He woke up about a half hour ago, talked to his wife and went back to sleep."

"She's not hysterical or anything?"

"No."

"All right. Any people from the job show up?"

"Just DeLuca's guy Conklin was here."

"Mr. Fix-it."

"He wasn't here long. But he has a message for you."

"What?"

"Call him. DeLuca wants to talk to you. He's pissed you aren't answering your beeper."

Yeah, like I'm going to keep my beeper on while I'm in bed with Justine Burton, thought Shaw.

"I'll take care of it. You go back to the Seven-Three. See what's going on there."

"Okay."

"If Impelliteri and Sperling show up with any bad guys, make sure they get processed right."

"Okay."

"You got a pencil?"

"What?"

"Take the shit out of your ears, Walter."

"I can't understand you. Are you eating something?"

"Yeah, wait a minute."

Shaw gagged down one more swallow of Maalox. Then he rinsed his mouth out with a handful of tap water.

"Okay, listen up. I'm going to catch some sleep. In the meantime, do these things. Get an alert out on Carmen Sanchez. Ten to one, he was the shooter on the motorcycle, blasting away the mosque last night. Make it all points, man. Especially the Port Authority Police. I want them watching for him at every airport and bus terminal and railroad station, including Newark, especially for any flights to the Dominican Republic or anywhere in the Caribbean. There's a guy I know named Josh Dove at the Port Authority Police. He's got rank. Tell him it's for me. I want everything shut down on this guy Sanchez. Make sure he has mugshots or whatever else he needs. I don't want Sanchez leaving the country."

"Okay."

"And put it out over FATN. I want every cop and every detective in every precinct to know about Sanchez. Alert the Feds, too. That son of a bitch does not leave New York."

"Yeah, yeah, okay. I got it."

"Keep searching for anything that will lead us to Archie Reynolds."

"Yeah."

"And when you get a spare moment, I want you to do background checks on Arbor Realty."

"What do you want to know?"

"Who owns it, who runs it, what properties they manage. Can you do that?"

"Take me a long time, but I know a guy who can do it pretty fast."

"Who's that?"

"My cousin, Jimmy Wang. He's a fixer at the Building Department. You know what that is?"

"No. And I don't much care. If he can do it, get him on it."

"We got money for Jimmy?"

"I thought you said he was your cousin."

"Got to take care of cousins, man."

"I'll throw him a couple hundred, but I want to go to the head of his fucking line."

For some reason, the comment made Walter laugh. Which was good. Shaw figured the little guy must be ready to drop. But if he could laugh, he could work.

"I'll be there in a few hours. Beep me if you need me. But only if you need me. I want to clean up and grab another hour of sleep."

"When am I supposed to sleep?"

"You slept last night. I saw you leave. You went home and slept, didn't you?"

"Yeah. Three whole hours."

"You're young. That's plenty. You'd probably feel better if you'd stayed awake."

"Not me."

"Drink coffee. Take drugs. Do whatever the hell you have to do, Walter, but stay on it."

"Okay."

"Okay. And don't forget about our fives."

Shaw hung up before Walter could protest.

He sat back in a reclining chair, looking out a window that faced an open parking lot. Not much of a view, but by Manhattan standards, any view better than an airshaft was a major plus.

Shaw's apartment took up half the floor of a converted loft building. Of course, he had to build the place from scratch, get it before real estate prices exploded and he lived in a neighborhood with no neighbors for about ten years, but he ended up one of the lucky ones. He had space and light. Shaw also had a woman whom he dreaded seeing in the apartment. And now, suddenly, Shaw also had a nearly unquenchable desire for Justine Burton, making it even more painful to contemplate dealing with Jane.

Shaw knew that whatever was going on between him and Justine could burn out quickly. But he also knew he didn't want it to. He knew that as long as Justine Burton would have him, he would want her. And he knew he would continue wanting her, even after she no longer wanted him.

Why? he asked himself. Why risk it? Her looks and her body were almost enough in themselves. But there was more to it. Shaw wanted the woman behind the beautiful exterior. The woman who generated that smart, penetrating gaze. The woman who could go right ahead and treat him like a man without pretense or guile or qualification. Shaw didn't know if that ability came from her black culture or just from her, but it made him want Justine Burton, fiercely.

Which meant Shaw had to deal with Jane now instead of just letting it linger on. Whether Justine Burton lasted or not, Shaw knew the time had finally come to end his dead-end with Jane. He was ruined now. He knew what else there could be for him. If it were going to be any woman, it would have to be a Justine Burton woman.

That was the hard part. Knowing that he couldn't settle anymore. Allowing it to go on with Jane just so he wouldn't have to bother fighting over a desirable Tribeca loft wasn't worth the price anymore. Not that it was going to be much of a fight. Jane had the money and the law. Shaw had sweat equity and a Glock. If he fought according to the system, he was going to lose.

It didn't help his sour mood.

Shaw sat there, looking out at his view, still smelling and tasting and feeling Justine Burton, thinking about the turn his life had taken, knowing that nothing could come of it until he took care of Archie Reynolds and met DeLuca's demands.

DeLuca. He was a dark presence hanging over Shaw. He couldn't put off calling the chief any longer. And besides, Shaw did wonder what the hell DeLuca was going to say over the phone about New Lots Apartments and Archie Reynolds and killer Muslims.

Shaw popped a fresh mini-cassette into his recorder and attached a little suction cup accessory that made it easy to record off the phone receiver.

The first voice over the phone was the Fred Gwynne rumble that came out of Conklin's mouth.

"Conklin."

"Shaw."

"Hold on."

"Okay."

They understood each other.

DeLuca's voice came over the phone. "Shaw."

"Yeah."

"What the fuck is going on?"

"Just what you said—"

"Don't tell me what I said, tell me what you're doing."

"Going after the Blue-Tops. We got one of the managers last night, another one this morning."

"I know about both."

"Good. I hear the precinct guys are nailing up the third manager. The fourth one went down in that body shop fire. Today we move down to the next echelon of guys. Between the Muslim brothers and us and regular cops, in two days, there won't be anything left of the Blue-Tops."

"Yeah, and what about number one?"

"Archie Reynolds?"

"Answer my question."

"I'm on him. He's next. He's history."

"Don't fuck with me on this, Shaw. I want this over. I got reports of all hell breaking loose last night."

"It's a fucking war, Chief, what do you think is going to happen? Nobody is sleeping, nobody is backing off. It's only been a day and a half for chrissake."

"Get it done. I don't want one goddamn more report of shots being fired at that location. Get that guy. Get it over."

"Yessir."

"And stay the fuck away from the woman. You got no business there."

"What are you talking about?"

"You know what I'm talking about."

"If I think she has information, I'm going to ask her."

"She doesn't. And she's out of bounds. Don't even think about it."

Click.

Fucking DeLuca.

Shaw turned off his tape recorder and added the cassette to his collection. DeLuca hadn't really said anything incriminating. He hadn't even spoken his name or anybody else's. But Shaw had him talking directly about an issue he almost certainly did not want to be connected with. It was something.

Shaw turned off his police radio, phone, everything but his beeper, which he sincerely hoped would not wake him. Sitting in his dirty clothes made him want to shower again, but Shaw decided he'd save that to help him wake up.

He closed his eyes and a jarring jumble of images swept through his mind: Ellard Watkins's shotgun exploding over his head, Mason bleeding, Archie pumping bullets into Rachman, streets racing by, flames, a naked Justine sitting up in her bed looking at him, Walter Wang staring at his computer screen, the desolate, burned-out streets of Brownsville filled with drugs and pain and misery, that endless cemetery. The whole dangerous, unruly mess of it. And then he was out.

CHAPTER 47

Loyd Shaw slept. Walter Wang worked. Tony Impelliteri and James Sperling watched and waited. After Queen Margo rousted them, they parked a block west of the car service, facing the entrance. The East New York street looked dismal, even though the sun had finally broken through the overcast sky. Ripped-up plastic garbage bags, broken glass, and scraps of newspapers lay in the gutter, on the sidewalk, everywhere. Even though it was only April, weeds had already sprouted through the cracked sidewalks on the nearly deserted streets. To their left, a long brick wall barely interrupted by doors or windows filled most of the block. On their right, a jumble of run-down, three-story flats filled half the block. An empty lot filled with tall grass, weeds, and garbage took up the remainder.

They waited and watched.

A crack whore so gaunt even a baggy sweatshirt failed to conceal her bony frame led a man into the empty lot. They disappeared in the overgrown grass and weeds and garbage. Neither Impelliteri nor Sperling wanted to imagine what she was doing in there to earn her endless doses of rock.

Impelliteri checked his watch. Nearly eleven. They had been waiting for almost two hours. He thought, maybe it's too early for the dealers to be out and about.

Just then, a baby blue BMW stopped for a traffic light, about half a car length behind Impelliteri's dark blue Caprice.

Impelliteri had been flipping through his pile of crime photos and mugshots for most of the past hour. He knew the faces of the Blue-Tops gang members he was after. Impelliteri knew that BMWs did not fit into the neighborhood, so when he saw the gleaming car, he looked over the passengers very carefully.

Impelliteri quietly told Sperling, "Slide down until these fucks pass us."

The BMW rolled by, and Impelliteri punched in Margo's number.

"Margo."

"Speak up."

"Listen, there's two guys that just drove past us about a block away from your place. I think they're headed for you. They looked like two of my mutts."

"So?"

"So stay on the phone with me until they walk in. If you recognized them, tell me. I'll take 'em out when they leave."

"Why not before they come in here, damn it."

"Hey, we get 'em after they leave, you get an instant return on the merch, and we take care of your price discount."

"Oh. Okay, honey. See, I always knew you were a smart one. Wait a minute."

Margo came back on the line.

"Are they in a blue BMW?"

"Yeah."

"It's parked right outside. They must be coming up now."

"Both of 'em?"

"Uh-huh," Margo's voice suddenly became more businesslike. "Okay then, that will be fine."

"They just walk in?"

"That's right."

"Good. You know them?"

"Uh-huh."

"Blue-Tops?"

"That's right."

"Okay, Margo. Cool."

Impelliteri turned to Sperling. "You want to drive or you want to shoot?"

Sperling smiled.

Impelliteri drove to the Beamer parked outside the car service. The car was unlocked. Sperling got out of the Caprice and slipped into the backseat of the BMW. Impelliteri continued driving about a half block ahead and sat waiting, watching through his rearview mirror.

Two men came out. One carrying a white garbage bag. By the size and heft of the bag, Impelliteri figured it held at least two kilos.

The BMW pulled away from the curb. Impelliteri let it pass and followed them for two blocks. Far enough. He floored the accelerator, hit the lights and siren, and turned the Caprice in front of the BMW so quickly the driver didn't have time to brake before he banged into the side of the Caprice.

The marks took it for a rip-off or at least a carjacking, but before they could pull their guns, Sperling sat up in the backseat of the BMW and pressed a Sig into each of their heads.

Impelliteri swaggered over with a big smile, flashed his badge, and announced, "You're fucking under arrest, meatheads."

The driver turned around and yelled at Sperling, "What the fuck is this? You can't be hiding in my motherfucking car."

"Why not?" asked Impelliteri. "There some rule against that?"

"It's bogus, man."

"Shut the fuck up, asshole."

In three minutes, the two would-be drug dealers were hand-cuffed and sitting in the backseat of the Caprice, waiting with Impelliteri and Sperling at the same spot a block away from the car-service office where they had parked.

After five minutes, the driver of the blue beamer complained.

"Hey, man, when you takin' us in? I can't sit here in these handcuffs like this. Come on, man."

Impelliteri pulled out his Glock and held it two inches from the man's face.

"Listen, asshole. I already told you to shut the fuck up. You say another word, I'll shoot you. I've got your gun. I've got you. I'll shoot you in your stupid head and shove you out in the gutter. Then I'll take the cuffs off, put your gun in your hand, and swear you tried to shoot me. You got that? Just nod."

The Blue-Tops nodded.

"Good." He turned to Sperling. "Hell, James, I think this is going to work."

Sperling nodded.

"Like dropping your line in the water when the blues are running."

"Uh-huh."

"Get it. Blues. Bluefish. Blue-Tops. Get it?"

"I got it."

"What's the matter? You pissed because you couldn't shoot them?"

Sperling thought about that for a moment before he turned to Impelliteri and gave him a thoughtful answer.

"Well, you may be right. We shoot them there's no arrest, no booking, no cocked-up trial where the defendant has every advantage, where our evidence gets thrown out, where every witness lies. Bam! One and done. Finished."

"More like bam, bam," said Impelliteri. "Pity, we can't just shoot them, huh?"

"Yes. A pity."

Just then, another car drove past them. Another pair going for the bait.

Over the next four hours, Impelliteri and Sperling arrested five more would-be dealers responding to Margo's sale and avoided shooting all of them. They didn't have nearly enough handcuffs.

CHAPTER 48

SHAW ARRIVED AT THE 73RD PRECINCT A LITTLE BEFORE THREE o'clock, just as Impelliteri and Sperling paraded their catch into the precinct lobby. Sperling led the line of seven captured criminals. Impelliteri trailed behind, carrying seven pairs of shoes strung together like scalps.

Shaw watched the procession and smiled. He made arrangements with the desk sergeant to divide the drug dealers between the three precinct holding cells until further notice.

Back in their temporary squad room, Impelliteri regaled Walter Wang and Loyd Shaw with his tale of conquest. Sperling said nothing, leaving center stage from Impelliteri and offering nothing that diminished Impelliteri's boasting.

Shaw allowed it to go on for about ten minutes. What they had achieved was damned impressive. Seven collars, with drugs and guns confiscated for each arrest. Six of the arrested were on their list of Blue-Tops.

Shaw told them they had done a great job. And then he said, "Okay, before we celebrate, there's one little thing left to do. Otherwise, the rest of it doesn't mean much."

"What's that?"

"Nail Archie Reynolds."

That ended the celebration quickly.

"I talked to DeLuca this morning. I keep hearing the same message: get Archie Reynolds."

"Okay, okay," said Impelliteri, "let's get the fucking guy and be done with this."

Shaw asked Walter, "You come up with anything helpful?"

"Nothing. I went through just about everything – federal, NY State, every state east of the Mississippi, and California. Only new thing I got is a traffic ticket in South Carolina."

"How old?"

Walter shuffled through a pile of computer printouts until he came up with a piece of paper.

"Two months ago."

Impelliteri said, "He was probably down there buying guns."

"I don't suppose he was driving his own car, was he?"

"Nope," said Wang. "Rental. But he didn't rent it. Reginal Wilson rented it."

"Well, he's fucking dead, and so is that lead," said Impelliteri.

Shaw asked Walter, "Anything happen with that guy Melvin Brown?"

"Yeah. Precinct detectives found him in Virginia. Hiding out at his aunt's."

"Great. When's he coming back?"

"Don't <u>kn</u>ow. Melvin is fighting extradition. They got him for parole violations. He's going back for the last bit on a fifteen to twenty-five."

Impelliteri said, "He won't be back up here for at least a week."

"Screw it," said Shaw. "We work with what we have. We got six guys, right? Six from the gang?"

"Six," said Impelliteri.

"All right. One of those pricks is going to turn. One of them or all of them are going to tell us something, some goddamn thing about how or where we can find Archie fucking Reynolds. Did you keep those mutts together when you arrested them?"

Impelliteri said, "Shit, we had to keep some of them together. We had to stick them in various cars."

"For how long?"

"Hours. Plus, we got 'em all jammed into two holding cells here. What difference does it make? They're going to lawyer up anyhow."

"Not until I say they can. All right, here's what we do. Walter…"

"Yeah."

"Get their arrest records. I want to know who's going to prison for the longest."

"Okay."

"Anthony, how much coke did you find on them?"

"Nothing less than a kilo. They're all looking at major hard time."

"Good. Let's get as much information as we can. Let them marinate in the holding cells. Then, Anthony, you and I take 'em one by one. We won't spend a lot of time. Make it simple. Tell us how to find Archie Reynolds, and we'll put in the word with the ADA."

Impelliteri said, "Okay, but one suggestion."

"What?"

"Let Sperling be in the room."

"Why?"

"They all know he wants to shoot them. I think that will give us a psychological edge."

"Fine with me."

✳

From the time Walter Wang downloaded the arrest records until the interviews were complete took a little under three hours.

Shaw, Impelliteri, and Sperling returned to the temporary office.

Shaw said, "Okay, fellas, here's the next move. I made a call to Central Booking. There's a good supervising ADA working there now so I can get on this. He'll cooperate with us." Shaw looked at a list he had written. "We concentrate on three guys: Marvin, Jacobs, and Mitchell. Book them. Keep them separate. Get what we get about Archie from each of them. Then let the ADA bury them somewhere for the next thirty-six hours or so before he arraigns them."

Impelliteri asked, "Okay, but I gotta clean up, take a shit, get myself together. Any chance we can catch some sleep?"

"Clean up while we're waiting for transportation to take our three mutts to Central Booking. You got clean clothes with you?"

"No. Neither one of us have been home since we started."

"Fuck it. Buy a couple of shirts on the way to Central Booking. Clean up in their locker room. You'll probably have time to catch some sleep in there while I talk to my ADA."

"That place is a shithole."

Shaw said, "Tell me about it."

Impelliteri said, "Okay. We'll see you there. Come on, James."

Impelliteri and Sperling shuffled out. Shaw turned to Walter. His Asian complexion seemed to be turning slightly green. His eyes were hidden behind two narrow slits. Shaw figured he had maybe two or three hours before Walter crashed.

"How ya doin', Walter?"

"Fine."

"Good."

"How are we doing on Arbor Realty?"

"It's coming. I should have all the reports on the properties they manage. I'm doing a Lexis/Nexis search on outstanding liens and lawsuits. My cousin is on it down at Buildings."

"What about their corporate structure?"

"It's a limited liability real estate partnership."

"I want names of everyone who's a partner or shareholder."

"No shareholders. It's a partnership."

"Then partners. Anyone with an interest in it. Anyone who takes money out of the place."

Wang winced. "I don't know. There's a million ways to get money out. Distributions, salaries, kickbacks…"

"I understand. Find out as much as you can about who takes money out of Arbor Realty."

"That could take a long time. You looking for anybody in particular?"

"Yeah. Commissioner Burton, any members of his family including his daughter, Justine Burton, his wife, brothers, other kids, anybody connected to him. And DeLuca. Albert J. DeLuca and anybody connected to him."

"Shit, you crazy, man? Those guys?"

"Yeah. Those guys. Lift off that rock and see what crawls out."

Walter turned back to his keyboard. The possibility of uncovering something about the commissioner and chief of detectives seemed to energize him. He understood the leverage they would gain if they discovered that the police commissioner and chief of detectives had a financial interest in Arbor Realty.

As Shaw got up to leave the squad room, he saw Walter dialing the phone with his left hand as he slid and clicked his mouse with his right hand. Walter was a virtuoso.

Just before Shaw made it out the door, Walter called out, "Hey, by the way."

Shaw stopped and turned. "What?"

"That big guy, Ellis Marvin – one of the guys you picked out of the seven Impelliteri and Sperling arrested."

"What about him?"

"He's the brother of a murder victim in DeLuca's files. Shot in the head."

"What?"

"James Marvin was in one of DeLuca's reports from the precinct homicide detectives."

"Who killed him?"

"Don't know. Seven-Three homicide squad couldn't find any witnesses, no ballistic match. Case is still open." Walter rummaged through a pile of paper on his desk. "I checked. They're brothers. Street names are Big Marvin and Little Marvin. You obviously got Big Marvin."

"Shit!"

Shaw had missed it. Walter, in his dead-tired fog, hadn't. But he'd almost forgotten to point it out. They came that close to blowing it.

Shaw rummaged through Walter's piles of paper until he came up with the original report submitted by the funeral home on James Marvin in DeLuca's files. He sorted through more documents until he found the coroner's report. They pulled a .22-caliber round out of James Marvin's brain. The bullet had entered just above his right eye.

Twenty-two caliber seemed too small for a gang-related murder. Higher caliber guns were more in vogue in Brownsville. Forty-fives or nine millimeters.

Now, who put that 22. In James Marvin's head? It reminded Shaw of something else in the reports.

Another raft of papers took Shaw through the first shooting at New Lots Apartments. One of the MS-2 guards had been shot in the head. And yes, there it was. A .22 caliber round. Also a headshot. Dead center.

Shaw didn't need forensics to tell him anything further. He knew who had shot James "Little" Marvin. And now he knew how he was going to find Archie Reynolds.

"Hey, Walter."

"What?"

"Good work."

"Thanks."

Shaw didn't think Walter even knew what he was thanking him for. He'd explain it to him later.

CHAPTER 49

Archie Ar's final conversation with Whitey Williams took place over the phone. By the time Archie called him from his room at the Vista Hotel, he knew it would be suicide to come into New Lots to talk to Whitey in person.

"Old man."

"Yeah."

"What took you so long to answer the damn phone?"

"Can't hardly hear it, boss. Cops and yelling and all kinds of nonsense going on aroun' here."

"Yeah, what's happening? Can't get any callbacks from in there."

"Looks like they be tryin' to clean out New Lots today, Archie."

"Who?"

Whitey shuffled over to his window. The cord on the old wall phone in his kitchen just about reached his window overlooking The Pit. He watched the activities in the courtyard as he described it to Archie.

"Got a whole mess of them Muslim security dudes all around the complex and in the courtyard. Got a shitload of cops going in and out of everywhere, too. A bunch of 'em in damn riot gear. Vests and big plastic shields and all. Emergency vehicles parked right down in The Pit. Look like a war down there, except no one's fighting it."

"What the cops doin'?"

"They goin' in and out, rousting everybody."

"Sounds more like a shakedown in a prison."

"I guess so."

"Ain't gonna do 'em no good. No way they got search warrants for all those places. Totally illegal. Can't arrest nobody that way."

"Well, I see some guys coming out in handcuffs."

"Any of my people?"

"If any of your boys in there, I'd say they'll be comin' out. One way or another."

"Probably not many of 'em left anyhow. They find any of my stash?"

"I can't tell. Sounds like they tearin' up a few places."

"Sounds like the end of that deal to me."

"Looks like."

"Fuck 'em. I still got you lookin' out for me, right, Whitey?"

"Yeah, Archie, I'm still here."

"So long, old man."

Archie hung up.

Whitey slowly replaced the silent phone. He knew he'd never see Archie Reynolds again. Probably never see any of those Blue-Tops boys again. Word had come down about Weight Watkins and Reggie Whack and Melvin Brown. The rest of the gang was on the run.

Kids all over the complex were yelling, "Five-Oh, five-oh." Between the cops and the Muslims, the Blue-Tops were done with New Lots Apartments. And Archie was done with Whitey.

The old man sighed, wiped a hand over his tired face, and continued doing what he had always done. He watched the world outside from inside. And he thought about getting along without Archie's money.

Eventually, it all came down to money. Drug money or lunch money or rent money. Who would pay Whitey to watch now? Who would make it possible for Whitey to eat three meals a day instead of one? Or pay for the phone next month? Or for decent shoes on his feet when winter came around again? What if they raised the rent once they got the place fixed up? What if? How much? When? Who?

Change. Whitey knew it never ever changed for the better in New Lots. Not really.

*

After his short conversation with Whitey, Archie checked out of the Vista Hotel in downtown Manhattan. He walked across the West Side Highway, continuing a few blocks uptown along the river until he arrived at an open-air parking lot. He paid his parking fee and climbed into his black Saab.

Archie assumed a description of the Saab had been posted in most of the city precincts, but he counted on the cops in Manhattan to be less interested in looking for him than Brooklyn cops. He also knew he only needed to drive up the West Side Highway to the Henry Hudson to a chop shop in Washington Heights. Pretty much a straight line. It was worth the risk. The time had come to cash in his chips, sell the Saab, and make a few last-minute arrangements.

CHAPTER 50

SHAW HEADED TO CENTRAL BOOKING ON GOLD STREET IN downtown Brooklyn. Having avoided booking them in the precinct, this was the last stop in the arrest process of their prisoners. And Shaw's last chance to get a lead on Archie Reynolds.

Shaw believed Brooklyn's Central Booking was the best place to make his play. Most cops figure that criminals who have been through the system aren't affected by the booking process. Shaw didn't buy that. Shaw believed that even hardened criminals going through Central Booking felt the fear and dread because they knew they had arrived at the point where they were facing jail time. The average, straight citizen who's never done jail time can't imagine what it's like. But a criminal who's been in prison knows entering that facility could well be the first step leading to weeks or months or years of being surrounded by dangerous, violent criminals, strict regimentation, and soul-numbing degradation.

Shaw turned the Caprice into the narrow alley that led to Central Booking's entrance. He sat for a moment staring at the bleak, heartless doorway; not a front entrance, not a doorway leading into an institutional lobby, just a dark, back-alley doorway in the corner of a cramped asphalt parking lot. A single door set in a ragged brick wall. A metal-clad door that was open, revealing another door made of thick iron bars and reinforced blocks of glass. A single lightbulb burned 24/7 over the entrance.

That door in that back-alley parking lot said it all. Walk through here, your life changes.

Shaw stepped out of the Caprice, then walked across the small parking lot and through the dreaded door. He knew he would walk back out, but the sight of it still made him cringe. That door led to a detention cell, then to a holding cell in arraignment court, then to Rikers, and almost certainly for Shaw's prisoners to a prison cell upstate. None of them would set foot on the street for years, if ever.

Shaw wanted his three Blue-Tops bad boys to walk through that door and think about that. He'd seen more than one felon who was supposed to be a tough guy hesitate at that doorway. He'd seen more than one break down right there.

Shaw heard the van transporting his criminals pull into the lot. He stood in the hallway and waited, then watched Ellis Marvin, Toussant Jacobs, and Willie Mitchell cross the threshold with blank looks and hands cuffed. If they felt anything, none of them showed it.

The cops who had transported them deposited Shaw's prisoners with the clerk, who locked them up in separate cells. Shaw went upstairs to find his ADA, a fellow named Charles Edgerton.

Edgerton was a black man who had such strength of character and bearing that he had managed to maintain his equanimity and dignified manner while performing one of the most chaotic, soul-wrenching jobs on earth.

Shaw knew he could never have done Edgerton's job without eventually punching someone, probably starting with lying defense attorneys, ADAs turned into automatons, lazy judges, and remorseless criminals.

Shaw believed that much of the criminal justice system had evolved into contrivances that took their toll. But however mindless and mundane, the system had the power to imprison people, to change their lives forever. That undeniable fact took a massive toll on the people who worked in the system. Somehow, Charles Edgerton had withstood the burdens of his Sisyphean job and managed to remain civilized. Shaw considered him a true gentleman.

So when Shaw dealt with Charles Edgerton, he extended him the highest respect. He spoke and acted carefully. Even when the clerk told Shaw that he would have to wait for Edgerton, Shaw remained respectful. He settled in the waiting area without complaint or comment.

Shaw waited in the police officer's room, a combination locker room, waiting room, bedroom, eating room, smoking, belching, talking, farting, complaining room. There were benches and lockers and a few long tables and beat-up chairs. Cops would do just about anything in that room while they waited for the ADAs to interview them. Some got drunk. Some talked. Some ate. Others smoked. Some did all of it in the hours they had to kill.

Shaw picked a chair back near a window, away from the general commotion, and quickly nodded off. Forty minutes later, a voice yelling into the waiting area roused him. He followed a civilian clerk to Edgerton's cubicle, trying to muster up his energy and wake himself.

The piles of folders and papers on Edgerton's desk and floor told Shaw his workload had not decreased. Edgerton sat amid the piles of paperwork dressed in a white shirt, his tie undone, looking about the same as he had for many years.

Shaw had always figured Charles for an ex-athlete. A football player. A college standout, but too smart to sacrifice his body for the pros. Now in his late forties, his close-cropped hair just beginning to gray, Charles had become an imposing figure with the extra weight that middle age usually brings. His chair creaked as he stood to shake Shaw's hand.

Shaw gripped the meaty hand and returned the firm but cordial handshake.

"Charles, good to see you."

"Thank you, Detective Shaw."

"How's the family?"

"Fine, just fine. Thank you for asking. What can I do for you?"

That was Charles, polite but to the point.

"I know you're busy, Charles, so I'll try to be as brief as possible, but there is quite a bit of background here."

Charles Edgerton sat patiently through Shaw's explanation. He listened. He didn't wait for Shaw to finish talking so he could speak. He didn't allow any phone calls to interrupt. Charles Edgerton sat in his beat-up chair, a chair that seemed to suffer under his large frame, and listened.

When Shaw finished, Edgerton asked, "So what do you want from them?"

"I have to get a lead on Archie Reynolds. I've got to nail Reynolds. Fast."

"What are you going to offer them in return?"

"I'm not totally sure. We'll have enough on each of these felons to put them away for a long time."

"You *will* have? We have to have it right now, Detective Shaw. Not sometime. Have to have all the ducks lined up, or their lawyers aren't going to go for it. Won't go for it unless you have what it takes to nail them right now."

"Charles, let me make the offer. If they refuse to deal with me before their lawyers get here, that'll be the end of it."

"What's your offer going to be?"

"Nothing you can't live with. Just let me do it. I won't offer anything you won't want to give. I'll be straight up. I haven't got time for any back and forth. Either it works first time, or I move on."

"Okay. Go on and make your play. I'll go along unless it looks like it could upset the balance."

"Fine. That's all I need. Just one other thing."

"What?"

"Whatever happens with me, please flag these three so none of them slips out. Hold off the arraignment as long as you can. When you do get to court, some of them might be able to come up with significant bail because there are drugs behind this. But please insist on remand. If a judge screws it up, I'll understand, Charles. But do what you can to keep them off the streets."

"Based on what you've told me regarding their criminal histories, it shouldn't be a problem."

"And Charles, don't let someone screw up the paperwork or make a stupid mistake that springs one of them."

"We'll be careful with them."

Shaw nodded once as if to confirm it.

"Thanks."

They shook hands. Shaw rode the elevator back down to the bowels of the building, formulating his pitch as he stared blankly at the interior walls of the elevator. Somebody had scraped off most of the paint and left it that way, like a wound on the elevator wall that wouldn't heal. Shaw assumed it had been done to get rid of graffiti. The cure seemed hardly better than the illness. The analogy was not lost on Shaw. Shaw knew what he was about to do – something almost as ugly as the crimes he was trying to stop. Like using Muslim ex-cons to eradicate crack dealers. Or Justine dealing in back rooms so she could do good on the street. Or Shaw taking DeLuca's deal so he could go on living and working.

The lesser of two evils. Do what you gotta do. Can't make an omelet without breaking eggs. The moral evasions, the platitudes closed in on Shaw, but he continued to push them out of his mind.

The defaced elevator landed with a thud.

Shaw walked through the cold, narrow corridors, finding Sperling and Impelliteri waiting near the check-in area.

They had stopped on the way to Central Booking to buy clean shirts. Impelliteri had purchased a simple black t-shirt to wear under his cashmere sweater. Sperling had opted for a long-sleeved polo shirt. He wore it buttoned to the top under his blue blazer. It made him appear much more casual, less button-down, more a match in style and sensibility to Impelliteri. They were morphing into a team.

Shaw told them everything was set, and the three proceeded into the first interrogation room.

Shaw asked Impelliteri and Sperling to stay with him. He had to work himself into a rage sufficient to threaten a man with death and really mean it. What he was about to do meant wanting to genuinely kill somebody. Shaw knew that working himself up to that would take a psychological toll on him because he knew he would be calling on the rage that always simmered somewhere inside him. And Shaw knew how close he would come to putting his hands on the prisoners. He wanted Impelliteri and Sperling there to hold him back, as well as infect him with their callous attitude about killing men like the ones he was about to confront.

The three detectives walked into a small locked room where Toussant Jacobs sat dozing. In his disheveled repose, with his long dreadlocks and Bob Marley face, Jacobs looked harmless. Shaw tried to picture him holding a gun or a crack pipe, or hitting his woman, something, anything so that he would deserve condemnation.

Shaw kicked Toussant's chair to wake him. He jerked and woke with a start and looked at Shaw in a way that told Shaw he was rude.

"Cool, mon, jus' dozing, ya know."

Shaw stared at the man. Toussant Jacobs seemed too harmless. Or maybe he simply seemed too useless. Too lacking in force to affect what was happening. Toussant was going away for a long time. That was his life. So be it, thought Shaw. If he lives or dies, it won't be on my head, but Shaw figured he had to try.

"Toussant."

"Yes, boss."

"You're going away for a long time. A long time."

"Yes, boss."

"Do you want to help yourself?"

Toussant took a moment to look at Shaw. He knew the detective was going to offer him a deal.

"Sure, boss. I be happy to do any lickle ting I can do for ya."

"Tell me now, so I don't waste my time – do you know how I can find Archie Reynolds?"

Toussant Jacobs sat up and scratched his head, ran his hand over his face, tried to appear as if he were genuinely giving it some thought.

"Now, Toussant."

"Well, boss, I think I can help you der, but got to have my lawyer here if we be talking a deal."

Shaw looked at the man and decided he wasn't worth another second of his time.

"Okay, Jacobs, go back to sleep."

Toussant frowned as they left him. It didn't usually go that way. What was happening with this cop? Fuck it. He didn't know where to find Archie Reynolds anyhow.

There was no interrogation room available for Willie Mitchell, so the three detectives met with him in his cell. Impelliteri and Sperling stayed back near the entrance to the cell. Shaw stepped forward. Mitchell greeted Shaw with a smirk. The smirk made the rage blossom in Shaw like a devil ascending inside him, and he kicked the seated Mitchell in the middle of his chest.

"Hey!"

Shaw got right up to him and stuck his finger in Mitchell's face.

"Don't fucking hey me, you piece of shit. Keep your mouth shut. You fucking sit there and you listen to me. And you god-damn decide if you believe me. You listen and shut up. Then when I come back in here, you tell me what I want to know, or you tell me to fuck off and take what I swear on the eyes of every person I ever loved I will do to you."

Shaw watched the hate blossom in Mitchell's eyes. Fine, he thought. Hate me. Just make sure you hear me.

"Are you listening? Just fucking nod. Don't talk. Tell me now if you want to hear me out."

Mitchell nodded.

Good, thought Shaw. Progress.

"There are two facts I want you to burn in your ignorant, unused brain. Two hard facts. Number one, you are going to prison for a long time. I've got drug possession of two kilos. That gets me intent to sell. I've got weapons charges, attempted murder, conspiracy, racketeering. I've got more than I need to put you away for a long time. And if you think I don't, just know this – I have every fucking kind of witness I need to say whatever the hell I want them to. I can put you wherever I need you to be. I can eyewitness you at the New Lots drive-bys, the ambush in The Pit, the body shop mas-sacre, the mosque attack, any goddamn thing I want, I got."

Shaw waited for any kind of argument. Mitchell kept his mouth shut. Shaw continued.

"Number two, I will make sure you go someplace where they will kill you. I'll find the prison with the gangs you Blue-Tops fucked with. I'll find the prison filled with Muslims who will take it as a sacred duty to avenge their brethren. If you did wrong to somebody in the sixth grade, I'll find him, too, and put him in a cell with you. I swear to you, I will make sure that the time you serve will be the worst time, the worst hell you've ever faced. If it doesn't kill you, it will maim you first then kill you. You'll be tortured, bitched out, and killed off within a year. You idiots fucked up, and now the heat is on from way high up. I can make all of that happen."

Shaw looked closely at Mitchell, searching for the fear, trying to see if the hate in his eyes had allowed room for doubt. All he could see was hate.

"Now, here's my deal. I can't, I won't do anything about the time they'll give you. But I will do something about *where* you serve your time *if* you give me what I want, which is going to be very simple and easy for even you to understand. But I won't waste my time with you. I'm leaving here now and making the same offer to your pals. First one who says yes and convinces me he can help me gets the deal. You decide. When I step in here again, I want to hear either yes or no. Yes, and we talk. No, you die. Just one word, yes or no. Ten minutes."

As Shaw walked out, he had that shaky, letdown feeling that sets in after the rage wears off. He didn't have much left for Ellis Marvin, except the truth.

As it turned out, he didn't need much.

Ellis had something the others didn't. He had a brain. Shaw could see Ellis Marvin observing him when he walked into the interrogation room.

Shaw sat down opposite the big man, making sure Ellis was securely handcuffed to the bolt welded to the metal table that was also secured to the floor. Impelliteri and Sperling stood on either side of Ellis.

Ellis glanced at them and then back at Shaw.

"Ellis," Shaw asked, "are you interested in a deal? Just tell me yes or no because I'm too damn tired and disgusted to go back and forth. Yes or no?"

"Yeah. Sure."

Shaw waited to hear if Ellis was going to mention his lawyer. He didn't.

Shaw said, "Archie Reynolds shot your brother."

Ellis just stared at Shaw. He didn't deny it or confirm it.

"I don't need you as a witness to that. That's not what this is. There's no lawyer here. I'm not looking for a statement out of you. This is just us, off the record. Archie shot your brother James Marvin in the head with a twenty-two, correct?"

Ellis nodded.

"Okay. Now, listen to me. I want Archie Reynolds. I'm figuring if he shot your brother, you want him, too. You can't get to him now, but I can. He shot my partner. I almost had him, and I lost him. I want to find Archie Reynolds, and I don't have a lot of time."

Ellis said nothing.

"Archie Reynolds has done enough damage. He's hiding now. But I know he's not going away without killing more people. He's going to cause more pain and leave you and all the others behind to pay for it. You're going back to prison. For a long time. In another twenty-four hours, the man who murdered your brother is going to disappear. Don't let that happen, Ellis. Give me Archie Reynolds. I want that murderous bastard in my hands. That's all I want, Ellis. I want Archie Reynolds."

"Uh-huh. And what the fuck do I get?"

"Besides knowing you helped nail the guy who killed your brother?"

"Yeah."

"You get to live."

And so Shaw made his pitch. No histrionics. Just a true promise that he would either arrange for Ellis to die in prison or live in prison.

Shaw already knew that Ellis Marvin was going for the deal. The hard part would come when Ellis had to convince Shaw that the information he was about to give up was true.

Shaw said, "Before you say anything, don't even think about bullshitting me. Don't waste my time. Whatever you tell me, I have to believe it, Ellis."

Shaw sat back and waited.

The expression on Ellis Marvin's face changed to a sly grin. He sat forward and said, "So, you ain't gonna believe some story about Archie needing to say goodbye to some ol' auntie that raised him?"

"No."

"Well, you ain't goin' to believe what I'm gonna tell you. But that's why I know you're gonna believe it when you think about it for a couple seconds."

Shaw looked at the big man. His size and demeanor had fooled him. Ellis Marvin was a lot smarter than he looked. And Ellis was right. What he told Shaw was so unbelievable that Shaw believed him.

Shaw said, "I'm listening."

Ellis said, "If Archie be cashing in and getting ready to run, he's got to go to one person."

"Who?"

"Before I tell you, is the ADA okay with what you're offering?"

"He's already agreed. I walk out of here satisfied, I call your lawyer and tell him to call the ADA on duty right now. He'll agree you get your choice of facilities. Now, what do you have for me? I need it now."

"Guess I got to take your word for it."

"If I don't get Archie Reynolds before he leaves town, there's no deal, Ellis. Talk."

"Okay. Before Archie Reynolds cashes in and disappears, you can be damn sure he's gonna check in with the man he work for, his partner in all of this shit, the man who takes care of his money. He's gonna have to make arrangements with him."

"And who would that be?"

"That would be the Jew boy, Leon Bloom. You find that fat motherfucker, you find Archie Reynolds."

CHAPTER 51

AFTER THREE SECONDS OF SILENCE, LOYD SHAW JUMPED UP SO quickly that he knocked over his chair."

On his way out, he yelled back at Ellis Marvin, "Deal."

Shaw barely spoke to Charles Edgerton as he left except to tell him what he had promised Ellis. Charles agreed with a quiet, "All right."

Shaw hustled out of Central Booking, followed by Tony Impelliteri and James Sperling. As they ran out to the parking lot, Shaw said, "Anthony, we'll take your car. Leave mine here."

"Where to?"

"Crown Heights."

Shaw did not need to tell Impelliteri to drive fast, but, despite Impelliteri's cursing, braking, and accelerating, siren and flashing lights, the congested downtown Brooklyn traffic didn't allow them to make much progress.

This was not a time to be slowed down by traffic. Shaw had to find Bloom – now.

He punched his fist into the dashboard. He could feel Archie Reynolds slipping away. And then Shaw realized that Walter Wang was closer to Crown Heights than they were. He got on his police radio. It took three tries before Wang answered the calls.

"Yeah."

Shaw yelled so loudly that Wang held his radio at arm's length.

"Are you fucking sleeping? You sound like you were sleeping."

"Maybe. I don't know. I guess I closed my eyes."

"Wake up, Walter. This is it. We got a lead on Archie Reynolds. Get in your car. Get over to Prospect Place in Crown Heights. Find Arbor Realty."

"That guy Bloom's place?"

"Yes. I don't remember the exact address. It's on the thirteen hundred block. Just get over there and stake it out. Don't do anything. We got word that Archie Reynolds is going to meet with Bloom."

"With Bloom? The guy who's trying to get rid of him?"

"It's complicated. Go into the office and see if Bloom is there. He's overweight. Reddish hair. Half-assed beard. If he's there, go outside and stake out the place. Watch for Archie Reynolds. If Bloom leaves, follow him."

"That's it?"

"Yes. Keep us posted. Don't do anything. Just stay on Bloom. Go. Now."

Shaw didn't wait for a response.

As Impelliteri bulled his way through traffic, he asked, "So what the fuck is up with the real estate company?"

"Leon Bloom, or whoever he works for, is playing both ends of this. Christ, I tried figuring this every way but that one."

"How?"

"All these bankrupt properties, places like New Lots Apartments, the city stopped taking possession of them years ago. Private investors are going after them. A place like New Lots Apartments would attract a lot of attention and competition, *except* if it's infested with crack dealing scum like the Blue-Tops."

Impelliteri said, "You're saying the real estate company is putting in the dope dealers?"

"That's what I'm saying. Think about it. It makes sense. Arbor Realty puts their own crack dealers in the property. The value goes way down. The drug dealing scares off competitors. Arbor Realty buys it for cheap."

"Very efficient, actually," said Sperling.

"So why the fuck don't they just tell Archie and those Blue-Tops assholes to get out when they take over? And why use the Muslims?"

Shaw said, "It's not that simple. They can't just tell Archie and his boys to leave. It would look suspicious. So they hire the Muslims, which, by the way, costs them nothing because HUD pays for security. In fact, Arbor Realty probably gets the Muslims cheap, so they make money on that, too.

"Think about how it went down. The Muslims gave them a warning. They shot up one of the crack apartments and warned them to get out. All very controlled."

Impelliteri said, "So why didn't the Blue-Tops take a fade?"

"I'm not sure. I have a feeling Arbor Realty got pressure from the commissioner or DeLuca to vacate sooner than Bloom planned."

"Why?"

"Because the commissioner's daughter needed her space in New Lots for her community center. Remember, right after the warning, Reynolds ran through her center, terrorizing everyone."

Sperling said, "Not to mention he executed two of the security guards."

Shaw said, "Which sent the Muslims over the edge – burning up seven Blue-Tops and beating two others to death."

"Insane to think a crack gang and violent felons wouldn't spin out of control."

Shaw said, "Bloom tried to get back control. When the Muslims went off the deep end, I believe Bloom told Archie where to find Rachman. Gave him the green light to kill Rachman, burn down their mosque, and shoot up their neighborhood."

Shaw pounded the dashboard again.

"Shit! Look to your own. That's what Youssef said. I thought he meant the cops. He meant the real estate company."

"Or maybe both," said Sperling.

"Yeah," said Shaw. "Maybe so, James. Maybe so."

Impelliteri asked, "You really think the brass are in on this?"

"Yes. I just don't know how deeply. I don't know if Commissioner Burton was just trying to protect his daughter, putting pressure on DeLuca, whatever. Or if there's more to it. I hate to think Burton and DeLuca are in bed with Arbor Realty."

Sperling said, "There seems to be a lot of money involved. How many properties does Arbor Realty own?"

"I don't know. That's a job for Walter."

Impelliteri said, "What does it matter? Fucking ends up the same. Shit blows up, NYPD has to shut it down. Meaning us."

"A kamikaze squad," said Sperling.

"Fuck that," said Impelliteri. "There's a lot of assholes who're gonna go down before I do."

"Bloom is moving up to number one," said Shaw.

"With a bullet," said Sperling.

Impelliteri smiled. "Nice one, James." Then turned to ask Shaw, "One question."

"What?"

"How long you think Archie Reynolds is going to let Bloom live?"

"At least until he gets his money."

Sperling said, "Assuming the Muslims don't take him out first."

"Or me," said Impelliteri.

Impelliteri drove the Caprice up on a curb to maneuver around stalled traffic.

Shaw said, "Let's hope Leon Bloom stays alive until he leads us to Archie Reynolds. He's at the top of our list. We don't get him, we don't get absolution."

"Roger that," said Impelliteri.

Sperling nodded, saying nothing.

Impelliteri finally made it onto Atlantic Avenue. Traffic opened up and he floored the Caprice. The big engine roared. All three were pinned back into their seats. Shaw caught a glimpse of a street sign that said Vanderbilt Avenue. He checked his watch. At least five minutes away.

CHAPTER 52

It didn't matter how fast Anthony Impelliteri drove. Archie Reynolds was not at Arbor Realty. He was up in the Bronx selling his Saab for cash. The owner of the chop shop would stamp the identification number from a wreck onto the Saab's engine, get new tags and plates, and resell the car for twice the seven thousand he gave Archie.

Archie had his pocket money without needing to risk returning to the safe in his Saddle Brook condo. Now he could take the next steps to put the rest of his plan into action.

He met with his primary cocaine supplier, a Dominican named Ricardo Arcel, who owned a diner in Washington Heights within walking distance of the chop shop. The cocaine shipments fit right in with the bags of produce and other supplies that were delivered daily to the diner.

Arcel knew of Archie's problems. He had arranged for the assassin Carmen Sanchez's services. He was ready to provide more services – for a fee.

Archie's request was straightforward. He wanted Arcel to contact the Colombian group that supplied the cocaine Arcel sold to Archie. That group controlled a small hillside town near Bogota. Archie planned to hide out there under the protection of the Colombian traffickers. Colombia's lack of an extradition treaty with the U.S. would guarantee he would be out of the NYPD's reach.

The negotiation did not take long. Archie was not in a position to bargain. And Arcel was not greedy.

Next, Archie rode a cab to a branch of Chase Bank in downtown Manhattan that provided customers with safe-deposit boxes. It took Archie only a few minutes to retrieve five plastic cards and five keys from his deposit box. The key cards provided entrance to five twenty-four-hour storage facilities in Manhattan and Brooklyn. The five keys opened a small storage room in each of the five facilities.

In addition to the cards and door keys, the safety deposit box contained a valid passport issued to a man named Adam Everett but bearing Archie's picture, address, and signature. Archie had obtained the passport two years earlier for just such an emergency.

All that Archie had left to do was pick up Carmen Sanchez. He wanted Sanchez at his final meeting with Leon Bloom.

Archie knew he couldn't risk hauling his cash to Colombia. Suitcases full of bills don't get through security X-ray machines unnoticed. Archie needed Bloom to handle his payments to Arcel while he was away. But Bloom had already betrayed him once. He needed Sanchez to make sure Bloom didn't do that again. And he wanted the assassin nearby for protection.

Sanchez pulled up outside the bank at the arranged time. He drove a beat-up white 1985 Honda Accord that Archie had agreed to purchase for three thousand dollars. Archie planned to drive the Honda to Boston and fly out of Logan airport, where his name and picture would not be posted at every terminal.

Sanchez drove. He wore jeans and a leather motocross jacket designed in red, white, and blue to suggest an American flag. Sitting next to him was a man Sanchez introduced as his cousin Hector. He wore jeans and a sweater. He couldn't afford an outfit like Sanchez's.

Archie climbed into the backseat, thinking that the guy might really be Carmen Sanchez's cousin. He looked like Sanchez. Or maybe this breed out of the Amazon all looked alike.

"Hey, man," said Archie, "we don't really need two guys for this."

"Don' worry," said Sanchez. "No charge. I break him in. After this, I go back for a while. We need someone from family here to take care of business."

"He strapped?"

"Yeah, yeah." Sanchez pulled out a Smith & Wesson 9mm automatic with a fifteen-shot magazine. He said to Hector, "Show him."

Hector pulled out the same gun.

Archie nodded, shifting in his seat, feeling his Beretta nestled under the belt of his light wool, Jhared Barnes slacks, hidden under his retro-style rayon shirt. The shirt and pants were his last set of clean clothes. Archie flexed his shoulders and settled into the passenger seat, thinking, cops try to stop us, they be in for a shitload of bullets. Not going down easy. Not now.

Archie told Sanchez to drive over the Brooklyn Bridge.

Sanchez asked, "Brownsville?"

"No," said Archie. "Not this time, chief. I'll show you where. Just get over the bridge."

CHAPTER 53

Loyd Shaw and his team were eight blocks away from Leon Bloom's Crown Heights office when Walter Wang's voice came squawking over the radio.

"Shaw, come in."

"Yeah. Where are you?"

"Outside the real estate place. Bloom just came out, going to his car."

"You sure?"

"Yeah, I'm sure. He's a fat, sloppy guy with a scraggly red beard and a yarmulke hanging off the back of his head."

"That's him. Follow the bastard. Don't get spotted. Can you do that?"

"Of course."

"Do it. Let us know where he's going."

Shaw released the transmit button on his radio.

Tony Impelliteri cursed as the traffic brought them to a halt. "Fuck!"

"Don't worry about it," said Shaw. "Turn off the siren. We don't know where we're going yet. Just go with the flow of traffic."

"Like I got a choice."

The police radio squawked, and Walter's voice came over.

"He's heading west on Eastern Parkway. Might be going for the bridge. Can't tell yet."

"Cool," said Impelliteri. "He's headed toward us. We get over to Flatbush Avenue, maybe we can intercept him."

"All right. Go on."

Impelliteri hit the car's siren intermittently until they squeezed through the traffic. It still took them almost five minutes before they approached Flatbush Avenue.

Shaw picked up the radio microphone and called out to Wang. "Where are you now, Walter?"

"We just passed Atlantic Avenue a couple blocks back."

"Shit," said Impelliteri. "Now they're ahead of us."

"Don't worry," said Shaw. "Just head west. We're not far behind."

He pressed the transmitter and said, "Let us know if he gets on the bridge or if he stops anywhere."

"I don't think he's going for the bridge. He turned on Willoughby."

"He's in Brooklyn Heights," said James Sperling.

Five minutes later, Walter's last transmission came over.

"He's parked. He went into a bar called Slades on Montague Street."

"All right, Walter. Pull over where you can keep an eye on that restaurant and stay outside. Don't go in. We'll be there in three minutes. Just wait."

"Slades," said Impelliteri. "Kind of a neighborhood joint. Front part has a long bar, tables on the wall opposite, more tables in the back. Food is shit, but it'll be crowded this time of day. Montague Street. Busy area. Bad place for this kind of thing."

Shaw checked his watch. Nearly nine o'clock. The restaurant would definitely not be empty.

Impelliteri turned a sharp corner, cursing, "Every goddamn street in this neighborhood is one-way the wrong way."

"Ask someone," said Sperling from the backseat.

"I know where it is. I just got to go around here. Every fucking time you ask someone, they give you the wrong directions.

You ever know a New Yorker just say, I don't fucking know? No. They tell you—"

Shaw interrupted him. "It's right there. Turn."

Impelliteri turned onto a tree-lined street, barely wide enough for a single lane of traffic and one double-parked car. Local stores and restaurants lined both sides of the street, plus chain stores – everything from a Waldenbooks to a Starbucks.

They spotted Wang double-parked about a block away in front of a Radio Shack store, across the street from Slades.

Impelliteri pulled up, and Shaw leaned out his window to speak to Wang.

"How long has he been in there?"

"About ten minutes."

A driver, blocked by Shaw and Wang, honked his horn. Impelliteri was about to turn and tell the driver to fuck off, but Shaw grabbed his forearm and said, "Hold it. Let's not start a commotion. Sperling, get out and keep watch on the bar from the other side of the street." He shouted over to Wang, "Walter, follow us and pull around the corner. Let's get these cars off the street."

Sperling faded back near the entrance to a supermarket across from the bar as the cars pulled away.

Within two minutes, Impelliteri, Shaw, and Wang appeared on foot, heading back toward Sperling. Just before they reached him, a white Honda pulled in and parked at a fire hydrant three cars east of Slades. All four detectives watched Carmen Sanchez get out, followed by Hector and Archie Reynolds.

Shaw stopped and turned to face the other way as if he were talking to Impelliteri. Wang kept walking, realized the other two had stopped, then turned around. Sperling stood where he was concentrating on the three men walking into the bar.

Once Archie and the others were inside, Shaw motioned for Sperling to come down the block to where they stood in front of an apartment building.

The first words out of Sperling's mouth were, "That's them. The black guy…"

Shaw finished his sentence. "Archie Reynolds."

"And one of the other two is his shooter, Sanchez," said Sperling.

"Probably."

"No. Not probably. That's him."

"We got 'em," said Impelliteri.

"Not yet, we don't," said Shaw.

Shaw turned to look at the restaurant. Half the sidewalk area in front of the restaurant was filled with tables, most of which were occupied by patrons eating and drinking outside. Flanking the bar's open door were two large plate-glass windows. Despite the large windows, from his angle, Shaw couldn't see very far into the restaurant, but he knew there had to be more people inside.

"Why the hell did they pick this place to meet?" asked Impelliteri.

"Midway between Crown Heights and Manhattan. Close to the bridge," said Sperling.

"It doesn't matter," said Shaw. "He's here now. But there's no way in hell we can take him down in there. Not even until they come past those people eating outside."

"What's the plan?" asked Wang.

"All right, listen up. I'll call for backup. But we can't wait to move until they get here. This guy is not getting away this time. We have to position ourselves now."

Shaw looked around one more time, trying to figure the best way.

"Okay, we can't take them down in that bar. Half the people in there will get shot before it's over. We don't want to move on them while they're past those tables out front, so when they come out, we wait until they reach the street and head for their car. When they get near their car, we should have a clear shot at them."

Sperling asked, "What about Bloom?"

"Forget him for now. Everybody – concentrate on Archie Reynolds."

Shaw looked for reactions. There were nods all around. Impelliteri and Sperling were keyed up for the kill. Walter Wang looked nervous but determined to do his part.

Shaw said. "Okay, listen up. Both Bloom and Archie have seen me, so Anthony, James, you two go inside. Get a table where you can keep an eye on him. Preferably near the front.

"Walter, you wait a couple minutes then go in after them. Get a spot close to the door. If you can't get a seat, stand at the bar. I'll stay out here."

"Then what?" asked Impelliteri.

"When they leave, you and James get behind them, not too close, just follow them out. I'll be positioned near their car. When they get out in the street, you take out Sanchez and the other guy, I'll take down Archie."

"Why don't we all just wait outside?" asked Impelliteri.

"It's better to take them down from two sides, you behind them and me in front. We can't risk them getting to their car. Just make sure we don't shoot each other."

"Easier said than done."

Shaw ignored him. "Plus, I don't know if there's a back exit in that place through the kitchen or something. I doubt it, but I want you in there so we don't lose sight of Archie Reynolds."

Impelliteri shrugged. "Okay. Cool."

"What do I do?" asked Wang.

"You wait in there until they get out of the restaurant, then stand in that doorway. If they try to get back in, stop them. Have your gun in your hand. Hold it down next to your leg so no one sees it. I don't want any civilians flipping out but have the fucking thing in your hand. If any of our three targets breaks and tries to get back inside, you shoot them. Just fucking point and shoot. I don't want any of them getting back in there and taking a bunch of hostages."

Wang grimaced but nodded his head. Shaw's plan gave Wang the least chance of getting into a firefight. But everybody knew Walter might be the last line of defense against seasoned killers.

Shaw pressed him.

"You got it? Can you do that? Just make sure they don't get back inside?"

Wang steeled himself and blurted out, "Yeah. Yeah. I got it."

"Good. Good, Walter. You can do it. All right, everybody clear on what to do?"

The other three nodded.

"Okay. Let's not spook this guy. He's probably way revved up about now. He's been on the run. His whole operation has gone to shit. Just hang in, relax, get behind him, announce yourselves, unless they put their hands up and drop to the ground, shoot. We're done, and DeLuca can kiss our asses. Let's go."

Impelliteri and Sperling positioned their guns so they could reach them quickly. Without another word, they headed for the bar.

Shaw thumbed his police radio and started to call for a supervisor. But then he switched off the radio and pulled out his cell phone. He decided he'd rather not get into an argument with the local precinct about how this was going to go down. He dialed DeLuca's number.

Impelliteri and Sperling walked into the restaurant. They passed Sanchez and Hector sitting near the front door at the corner of the front room bar. They looked past them, trying to spot Archie and Bloom, and saw them sitting against the far wall in the back, Archie facing away from them, Bloom facing toward the front. They quickly took a table in the middle of the front room against the wall opposite the bar. Impelliteri faced Archie's table. Sperling faced the two Dominicans.

"Christ," Impelliteri said, "this place ain't very big."

"It doesn't matter," said Sperling. "This is good. Most of the people are eating outside. I can see his shooter Sanchez and one other guy. You can see our boy?"

"Yeah. I think I could put a bullet in the back of Archie's head from here."

Sperling pictured it. Then said, "Don't."

Impelliteri took a quick look around. A bartender and one waitress stood at the end of the bar near the service area. About half the seats at the bar were occupied. Another waitress entered from outside, carrying an empty tray. Impelliteri pictured her getting in the way just as the bad guys were leaving. Impelliteri noted that out of five tables in the front room opposite the bar, only two were occupied. His, and a table behind them where a young couple sat facing each other. On the side of the table facing the bar sat an eighteen-month-old little girl in her stroller. The baby played with a fistful of plastic keys while her mother patiently fed her bits of grilled chicken.

The back area held six more tables. The space extended around the left, making the room into an L-shaped space. In addition to Archie and Bloom, two of the tables in the back were filled with diners. One occupied by a man and woman, the other by three girls and one guy. Impelliteri had the impression they were coworkers sharing a dinner out together.

Impelliteri looked down, shifted in his chair, and picked up a menu.

"Christ, I hope nothing pops in here. It'll be a fucking mess."

Sperling, as usual, displayed no emotion. He sat back in his chair and stared blankly ahead, keeping Sanchez and Hector in view.

Impelliteri said, "Just so we're clear. You're facing the two beaners, so you concentrate on them. I got eyes on Archie Reynolds, so I'll cover him."

"Understood."

Impelliteri stole a look at Archie. He couldn't see his face or hear what he was saying to Bloom, but from the movement of his head, Archie seemed to be speaking intently. Impelliteri could see most of Bloom's face. The man didn't seem to be too intimidated by Archie Reynolds, answering him with short sentences and shrugs. Impelliteri had the sense that Bloom was trying to placate Archie, but it didn't seem to be working.

✳

In the back of the restaurant, Bloom said, "And how many times do I have to tell you it wasn't my fault?"

"Who hired them crazy Muslims?"

"Who shot two of them out in the open?"

"They wasn't Muslims."

"They worked for them. You started a war, Archie."

"And I finished, too. Fuck that, goddamn it. I held up my end. Went in. Set up my operation. Dealt with all the bullshit and riffraff. Then less than four months later, you shut the whole fucking thing down."

"You think that was my decision? You think I decided when they wanted you out? What am I supposed to do? Tell the community board and all the do-gooders and the police commissioner no? Justine Burton can't move in and pay me rent and set up her center? Once that happened, everything changed."

"Yeah, everything changed. Everything changed, but not for you motherfuckers. You making top dollar coming and going, and I'm the one who gets fucked."

"What's the matter with you?" said Bloom. "It's business. Not every deal makes the same profit. Things change. Sometimes for the better, sometimes worse. Today we have a change. Tomorrow it will change again. There will be more buildings."

"What good will that do me, Leon? I'm busted out. My main guys is all dead or locked up."

Bloom shrugged. "So are you telling me you can't find more guys in Brownsville who want to sell crack? Take a vacation. Come back. There will be more opportunities. You made plenty of money with me, Archie. You'll do it again." Bloom held up his hands, "Excuse me. I have to piss."

"Man, what the fuck you doing? We got business to settle."

"I have to go. It's the drinks."

"You drink too damn much."

"Yes, and I eat too much, too. Maybe I'll take a shit while I'm at it."

Archie leaned forward. "Keep it up, fat boy, and you'll be shitting yourself where you sit."

"All right. All right. Take it easy. Just give me a minute."

Bloom slid his chair back and maneuvered his heft out from behind the table. The bathrooms were located down a short corridor on the far side of the back wall.

Sanchez leaned out from the bar to watch Bloom.

Sperling watched Sanchez.

Impelliteri caught the slight change of focus as Sperling watched Sanchez watching Bloom.

Sperling asked Impelliteri, "What's he looking at?"

"Bloom just slid his fat ass out from the table to hit the shitter, I guess. Take it easy. Don't attract his attention."

Sperling settled back as the waitress approached them.

"What can I get you? You here for dinner?"

"Yes, dear, we are," said Impelliteri.

Sperling frowned at the notion of ordering food.

Impelliteri smiled at the waitress and said, "We're in a little rush. We'd like to order everything at once. We'll have a couple of Bass Ales and two burgers. How are your burgers?"

"Very popular. How do you want them?"

With fucking Uzis, thought Impelliteri.

✳

Archie turned to check on what was happening behind him. The movement caught Impelliteri's attention, and he inadvertently looked at Archie. Their eyes met for just a moment before Impelliteri quickly looked back at the waitress.

Archie became more restless. He stood up and walked out to the front room.

Impelliteri moved his hand under the table and gripped the butt of his Glock. Archie passed their table, and Impelliteri relaxed slightly.

The waitress finished jotting down her order and left.

Impelliteri quietly asked Sperling, "What the fuck is he doing now?"

"Talking to his buddies."

✳

Archie asked Sanchez, "You get a good look at him?"

Sanchez nodded.

"That's Bloom. Make sure you remember him."

Archie began to turn back to his table just as Walter entered, and just as the waitress serving the outside tables approached the door with a tray full of drinks.

For a moment, Walter, Archie, and the waitress had to move side to side to get out of each other's way.

Sperling watched Walter's awkward attempts to get around Archie and couldn't help but grimace. Walter almost bumped into Archie. Archie looked at him for a second, turned away, and headed back to his table.

Sperling made a point to look at Impelliteri as Archie passed.

"So how about those Knicks?" said Sperling.

"What about 'em?"

Archie passed by.

Walter quickly took the last bar stool near the doorway.

Bloom came out of the bathroom. He seemed surprised that Archie was walking back to the table.

"What are you doing?"

"Just shut the fuck up and sit down."

Archie and Bloom took their seats.

Bloom said, "So, why are we here?"

Archie took out an envelope.

"Thanks to you and all this shit with the cops and them Muslims, it's too fuckin' hot for me around here. Couple more little details, then I'm gone until this shit settles down."

Archie slid the envelope to Bloom.

"Now, you're being smart, Archie."

"In that envelope is five pass cards for five storage facilities and five keys. Inside the envelope is a piece of paper with five addresses. Keep that separate. Cards let you in the places. Keys open the storage room doors. You'll figure out which cards and keys fit which places and doors."

Bloom took the envelope and slipped it into his breast pocket without saying anything.

"My money is divided up in those five locked rooms, Leon. Anybody got those cards and keys can get it. You got to handle my cash for me while I'm gone. I'll call you and tell you who to pay, when and where to send money. Once I'm set up, you do it."

Bloom rolled his eyes. "This I need. You never heard of a bank?"

"What the fuck bank is gonna deal with me? Listen…"

Bloom held up a hand to mollify Archie. "Don't worry. I got it. I understand. I'll take care of it."

"You goddamn right, you will." Archie pointed over his shoulder to Carmen Sanchez sitting at the end of the bar. "You see that guy at the end of the bar? The one who looks like he wants to shoot you?"

Bloom looked over Archie's shoulder and saw Sanchez, his dangerous animal eyes staring right at him.

"Yes. Ever since you walked in with him. Why is he here?"

"To get a good look at you, Bloom. He knows your face now. He been staring at it long enough. Any more shit out of you, any more fuckups, him and his partner there will send your fat ass to hell. And believe me, they don't hear from me regularly, they will fucking find you and shoot you."

"What is this? Now you threaten me? You think I should do this because you threaten me? Is this how you do business?"

Archie snarled, "You fat Jew motherfucker, where you get off coming at me with an attitude? You fucked me out of the deal at New Lots. You get those Muslim killers to shoot and burn my people—"

Bloom raised his voice, interrupting. "That wasn't my idea. I had nothing to do with that. I told you where to find their leader, Rachman. I wanted that stopped as much as you."

Archie talked right over him. "And you sit there, giving me shit! Me?"

Archie's voice had become loud enough so that everyone in the restaurant could hear him.

Impelliteri muttered, "Christ, that fucking maniac is losing it."

Sperling gripped the butt of his Sig Sauer.

Sanchez stood up to get a better view of Archie, reaching for his gun.

Archie pulled out his Beretta, shouting now, yelling at Bloom, "Give me back that fucking envelope."

Bloom pressed his suit jacket to his chest, protecting the envelope. "No. I said I'd do it, I'll do it."

Archie reached out. "Give me the fucking envelope!"

Bloom held on tight.

"Give it to me!" yelled Archie.

Sanchez was coming around the corner of the bar.

The bartender moved toward the liftgate to come out from behind the bar. Impelliteri stood and pointed at the bartender. "You, don't move."

Archie and Sanchez heard Impelliteri yell at the bartender and both turned toward him.

Bloom tried to scramble out from behind his table.

Sanchez had his gun out. Sperling pulled his weapon and stood up.

Hector reached for his gun.

Impelliteri stepped away from his table, pulled his Glock, and yelled in Archie's direction, "Police, drop your weapon. Now!"

Sperling yelled at Sanchez. "Police!"

Archie turned to Bloom, who was now almost clear of the table. "You fucking set me up?" He raised the Beretta and shot a bullet into Bloom's left eye.

Impelliteri aimed at Archie and squeezed off a shot just as Archie turned and fired at Impelliteri. Impelliteri's shot went high. Archie's twenty-two hit Impelliteri in the left arm, spinning him back against the wall.

Sanchez turned and aimed at Sperling.

Sperling opened fire. Turning saved Sanchez from catching the bullet dead center. It hit his far shoulder, and he slammed into the bar as Hector opened fire at Sperling.

The restaurant exploded into chaos. The people inside dove to the floor, screamed, clutched their heads. The woman near Sperling fell on top of her baby and stroller.

The people outside panicked, knocking over tables, pushing, and crashing into each other as they tried to flee the area.

Walter pulled his revolver and stood by the front door, facing outward. He had his orders. Nobody gets into the bar.

Impelliteri righted himself to fire again at Archie. One of Hector's wild shots hit his left leg, knocking Impelliteri down.

Sperling put three bullets into Hector, dead center, blowing him backward. Sanchez had recovered enough to shoot at Sperling. Sperling dropped to the floor and pulled his table down for cover. Sanchez scurried around the corner of the bar, firing blindly at Sperling. Both men kept shooting at each other.

Outside, Shaw had positioned himself near the Honda. When he heard the first shot fired, he pulled his gun and ran toward the restaurant, yelling into his police radio, "Ten-thirteen, ten-thirteen, officers under fire! Multiple shooters. Slades restaurant. Montague Street. Slades, Montague Street."

Shaw collided with a large man fleeing the outside dining area. He shoved him aside, yelling, "Police, police, move!" He knocked over a woman, then ducked as one of Slade's front windows shattered, spraying glass out onto the sidewalk.

Even from outside, the gunfire in the restaurant deafened Shaw. The bar was so filled with smoke he could barely see inside.

Archie had taken cover behind a section of the wall that divided the dining area from the front of the bar.

Impelliteri's shots had driven Archie away from Bloom's dead body, but Archie still wanted that envelope. Impelliteri was down on the floor, unable to move, braced against the wall, partially protected by an overturned table. He kept his Glock pointed in Archie's direction, struggling to stay conscious, fighting off the pain from the gunshot wound in his leg, keeping his gun held in two hands, ready to shoot.

Amid the screams and cries, Shaw finally burst into the bar, ducking, squinting under the smoke, gun held in front of him. He ran into Walter, who stood in front of the door, almost knocking him to the ground.

All firing had ended except for another shot from Impelliteri, aimed where he thought Archie crouched.

Shaw cursed, reached out for Walter, and pushed him behind the bend in the bar. He saw the dead bodies of Sanchez and Hector. There was blood everywhere.

"Stay down, Walter. Stay down."

"Shaw," yelled Impelliteri. "He's in the back."

Archie leaned out from his cover. Despite the gun smoke and chaos, he recognized Shaw. He pegged two quick shots at Shaw. Impelliteri fired at Archie, but Archie was already moving, launching himself into the corridor that led to the bathrooms.

Impelliteri fired again.

Shaw yelled to Impelliteri, "Hold your fire."

Shaw reached Impelliteri, saw blood all over him, and reached down instinctively for him. Archie disappeared into the kitchen.

"Go," yelled Impelliteri. "Go. He went out the back. Get him, goddamn it."

Shaw sprang up and ran, stumbling over a woman on the floor. He cautiously entered the kitchen. The cook and two kitchen workers were crouched down. A back door was open. One of the terrified kitchen workers pointed to a cluttered courtyard behind the restaurant.

Shaw ran outside. Archie was nowhere in sight, but Shaw thought he heard a noise from the other side of a wooden fence, set high up on a brick wall, dividing the restaurant's back courtyard from the garden of the townhouse fronting the next street.

Shaw looked to his right and left, more walls topped by cyclone fencing surrounded the courtyard. An airshaft, assorted clutter and junk, an old sink, and stove filled the courtyard. Both fences to Shaw's right and left were topped with razor wire. He heard the sound of a gunshot and glass shattering on the other side of the fence. He shoved his Glock into his belt and ran toward the sound. He had to climb the chain-link fence to his right, lean over, and grab for the top of the wooden fence.

The wood slats were pointed on top, cutting into his hand, his stomach, and the side of his leg as he pulled himself up and over. The drop to the garden below was fifteen feet. Shaw hung off the wood fence, kicked away from the wall and let go, falling, not clearly seeing the ground, landing awkwardly. His right ankle felt as if it had been lashed with a whip. His foot turned under and he went down hard, smashing his right knee, smacking his right hand into the slate stones lining the backyard patio.

He managed to get up, ignoring the pain, limping toward a sliding glass door that had been shot open. He ducked through the opening, sliding awkwardly on a hundred pounds of exploded Thermopane glass covering a terra-cotta floor. He fell, feeling the sting of glass chips cut into his hands and knees. He slid and crawled off the glass until he could stand, breathing heavy, hurting, bleeding, but moving, moving forward after Archie Reynolds.

He was in a kitchen. The room was dark. He pulled out his gun, half expecting to be confronted by a shotgun-toting homeowner. He heard sounds ahead of him, moved forward, and banged his hip on the side of a countertop. He spun to his left, just as Archie leaned around a corner and fired at Shaw's head. The flash from the barrel of Archie's Beretta blinded Shaw. He jerked back, fell, and fired off a shot, barely able to see anything. His shoulder hit the stone floor. He thought he heard footsteps, a door slamming.

He rolled onto his hands and knees, blinking, still half-blinded from the gun flash, trying to see, trying to stand. He managed to rise, staggered with vertigo, reached out blindly for a wall in the dim room. He felt his way forward, moving toward where he imagined the front door to be.

He saw a dim light ahead of him. He reached a door, half-opened, pushed it wide, and stepped out into a common hallway that led to the front door of the townhouse. Shaw bent low, looking for Archie, hoping he wasn't running into another ambush. The hallway was clear. He ran for the front door, shoved it open, and ran up a short flight of stairs to street level.

He looked to his left, saw nothing. Then to his right. Archie, running full speed, had almost a block's lead on him.

Elegant brownstones and townhouses lined the narrow, quiet street, illuminated by streetlights at the corners. The sudden calmness of Brooklyn Heights disoriented Shaw as he ran, limped, pushed on, watching Archie nearing the intersection.

Shaw could hear sirens. It seemed as if police vehicles were arriving at the restaurant one block to his right. Up ahead, a cab had stopped at a red light. A blue-and-white screamed through the intersection in front of the taxi, heading for Montague. The light turned green. Archie ran for the yellow cab. Even though the traffic light had changed, the cab did not move. Shaw wanted to yell for the driver to go, pull away, but the driver was too afraid to venture out into the intersection with all the sirens sounding around him.

Archie veered into the street, heading for the driver's side of the cab. Shaw raised his Glock, aimed, and fired at Archie, who never even turned in Shaw's direction.

Archie reached the door of the cab, his Beretta still in his hand. He raised the gun and shot the cabbie as he turned to look at a man who had suddenly appeared outside his window. No arguing, no fighting, no pulling open the door. One shot. The driver's foot came off the brake. The taxi lurched forward and swerved into a car parked at the curb. The taxi banged into the door of the parked car, and the engine died.

Shaw ran with everything he had. Archie pulled the dead body out of the cab, jumped in, and tried to start the cab. The starter ground as Archie kept turning the key, not realizing the cab's engine had started.

Shaw ran into the street. "Stop."

Shaw raised the Glock. Archie shoved the cab into gear. Shaw slid to a halt and aimed at Archie Reynolds's head. Shaw heard brakes screech behind him and tires sliding on the asphalt. Shaw turned. A blue-and-white skidded toward him. He put his free hand out, moving back, but not fast enough. The squad hit the side of his left leg, sending him up onto the hood, banging into the windshield. Shaw, the wind knocked out of him, rolled off the hood and dropped on the street. He tried to stand as he heard Archie's cab roaring away.

He heard the cops open their doors.

He gasped, "I'm a cop. I'm on the job. I'm on the job," trying to get to his feet and pull out his badge as the two uniformed cops surrounded him, guns drawn.

Shaw desperately held up his badge, hoping they wouldn't shoot him, remembering the night that seemed like an eternity ago when other cops had nearly shot him on a Brooklyn street.

He heard one of the cops yell, "Don't shoot. He's a cop."

Shaw felt hands lift him.

He grunted, pointed. "He's in that cab. Get that cab."

"Are you all right?" the cop asked him.

"Get in the squad." He pointed. "Get that fucking cab."

It seemed to take forever to get back in the squad car. Archie's cab had already sped three or four blocks down Henry Street before the cop took off after him.

Archie heard sirens. He kept his foot on the accelerator, not distinguishing between the sirens around him and the siren behind him. His only thought was to get out of the area, put distance between him and the sirens. He checked his rear-view mirror and saw the flashing blue-and-red light closing in behind him.

"Shit!"

He pounded the steering wheel. And then he saw the girl. About a half-block ahead. With a backpack. Gliding along on her inline skates, maneuvering down the far side of Henry Street, free from the narrow sidewalks and curbs.

Archie smiled and stomped on the accelerator.

Shaw and the cops heard the thud and the scream at the same time. A second later, they saw the limp, bent body fly up in the air, hit the roof of the taxi, sail over Archie's cab, bounce on the trunk, and land in their path with a sickening thud.

The cop driving the squad car slammed on the brakes. The sudden deceleration threw Shaw into the barricade between the front and back seats. The tires shrieked. The squad car shuddered and stopped two feet from the broken body.

Shaw righted himself just in time to see the last glimpse of the yellow cab as it turned right onto Atlantic Avenue.

Both cops jumped out to see to the girl.

Shaw reached forward, fumbled for the squad car radio, thumbing the mic, croaking a plea to stop all cabs in the area. Trying to get through the cacophony of static and babble of police transmissions. He tried. Repeating the message over and over again, knowing it was useless but doing it once more before he finally gave up and slumped back in his seat.

CHAPTER 54

Tony Impelliteri sat on the floor, propped up against the wall. He held a bloody napkin to his face. Two medical personnel tended to him, wrapping the bullet wounds in his arm and leg.

It had taken Loyd Shaw ten minutes to limp back to the nearly destroyed restaurant. In that time, the area had filled with cops, paramedics, and detectives tending to the injured and the dead.

Shaw made his way over to Impelliteri.

"How bad is it?"

"Fucking bad enough. Tell me you got him, Shaw. You got him, right? Somebody got him. Tell me somebody got that cocksucker."

"No."

"Jeezus fucking Christ!"

Shaw turned away from Impelliteri and looked for Walter Wang. He sat in a chair, still in a daze. Shaw saw no blood on him except for a few specks of red on the collar and front of his white shirt.

The room stank of gun smoke, blood, and excrement. At least one of the dead bodies had evacuated. As if it weren't sickening enough, Shaw heard someone behind him vomiting.

Shaw still hadn't found James Sperling. He peered into another clump of cops and medics and saw Sperling's slight body, crumpled between two tables. A tall man in a suit seemed to be examining him. Shaw pushed his way closer. Sperling looked more dead than any corpse Shaw had ever seen. James Sperling hadn't been very expressive when he was alive. Now that he was dead, all the muscles in his face had gone slack, and his mouth had dropped open as if he had emitted one last "oh."

Shaw stared at the dead man. He didn't say anything or attempt to move closer. He didn't feel as if he had the right to alter anything about the death James Sperling had suffered.

Shaw pulled a chair over and sat near the body. He looked around, trying to discern if anybody else had been killed. He'd already seen the dead bodies of Sanchez, Hector. He saw another cluster of police and medical personnel near the back. He assumed they were tending to one of the patrons, not yet knowing that Leon Bloom lay dead back there.

Someone helped Walter to his feet, and he came to where Shaw sat. He dropped into a chair next to Shaw, looking as if he had forgotten his own name. He blinked and swallowed, but he continued to stare off into nowhere, saying nothing.

The paramedics had stabilized Impelliteri and lifted him onto a gurney. As they wheeled Impelliteri past, he saw Sperling, arched up against the straps holding him down and began yelling, "James! James!"

It occurred to Shaw that Impelliteri hadn't realized until that moment that Sperling had been gunned down. As the gurney rolled closer, Impelliteri reached out for Sperling. The paramedics tried to restrain him. He leaned off the gurney, grimacing in pain, yelling, "James, James."

Impelliteri had blood all over him. Sperling was covered in blood. Shaw sprang out of his seat and grabbed Impelliteri's arm, saying, "No. No, Tony, don't. He's gone."

Impelliteri fought against Shaw with his remaining strength.

"Let me go. Let me go, goddamn it."

"Easy. There's nothing you can do."

Impelliteri yelled at the paramedics. "Wait, goddamn it, wait!"

Shaw stood unmoving, blocking the way to Sperling. Impelliteri looked at Shaw, realizing that Shaw purposely stood between him and his dead partner. He clutched at Shaw's arm. Shaw pushed his arm down and gripped the side of the gurney, helping the paramedics wheel him away.

"What the fuck are you doing, man?"

"It's over, Tony. Let it go."

Impelliteri looked back at Sperling one last time, then closed his good hand around Shaw's arm. He pulled Shaw down close to his face, staring at him, digging his fingers into Shaw's biceps, staring into Shaw's eyes with his one good eye, burning with anger and hate.

"You get that fucker, Shaw. You get him, and you kill him. Do you hear me? Just fucking kill him."

Shaw gripped Impelliteri's wrist. Impelliteri finally let go and fell back onto his stretcher.

Shaw stood near the doorway to the restaurant, watched them wheel Impelliteri away, grimacing, wanting to tell Impelliteri why he couldn't let him touch Sperling but knowing now was not the time.

Sperling's name had appeared on DeLuca's list of detectives because James Sperling had AIDS. James had known full well he didn't have much time before his fellow detectives found out about his infection. And he had known when that happened it would be the end. There had always been gay men on the force. And Sperling had known he wasn't the only cop with AIDS. But he had known full well what would happen once the word got out. He had already endured the transfer to the shooting range. It would have only gotten worse. Nothing would've been said. Nothing overt would have happened. But the isolation and rejection would have continued. Slowly, inexorably, almost like the disease itself, Sperling knew he would have eventually found himself alone, working somewhere in an administrative job that had nothing to do with being a real detective.

So Sperling had taken DeLuca's offer. Only Shaw knew the real reason why – because it gave Sperling a chance to die a cop's death. Die in the line of duty. With his fellow police officers fighting next to him.

Shaw took one last look at the mess behind him, then stepped outside. He lifted a fallen chair and sat. Impelliteri's words echoed in his brain, but something had gone out of him, replaced by cold indifference mixed with utter deflation. He imagined pulling the trigger on Archie Reynolds and felt not even a ripple of remorse, not even a speck of reluctance.

Impelliteri was out of action. Mason, too. Sperling was gone forever. And Walter looked to be so used up as to be as good as gone.

They had been so close to getting Archie Reynolds. And now everything had turned into a disaster.

As if it couldn't be any worse, a black unmarked Ford Crown Victoria pulled up, and Albert J. DeLuca stepped out.

Shaw sat and watched him approach.

The chief strode forward, wearing a dark suit, white shirt, and a blue patterned tie accented with yellow, letting his barely scuffed leather soles touch the pavement.

Albert J. DeLuca, king of all he surveys, thought Shaw. Even this bloody, stinking mess.

DeLuca spotted Shaw as he passed by, looked at him briefly, and said, "Don't move."

Shaw noticed how white DeLuca's shirt looked and how stylish his tie seemed, perfectly pinched under the knot so that it would lie straight and handsomely against his bright white shirt, a shirt much too perfect and clean for this place, a place where something nasty could easily stain it.

Shaw sat thinking – DeLuca is going to scuff the leather soles of his shiny shoes. Maybe even cut the bottoms on all the broken glass. Certainly stain them with what he's stepping in. Won't that be a pity?

Shaw waited outside while DeLuca did his chief of detectives act. The walking cadaver Conklin hung back by the doorway monitoring who could come into the restaurant while the exalted DeLuca graced the wounded and dead with his presence.

Shaw figured it was too late to get up and leave. Just as well. Conklin would have tried to stop him, and he would have punched Conklin's face and shoved him out of his way.

Something about the sad-faced, officious old cop intensely annoyed Shaw. The invisible fixer. The facilitator. The enabler of all that flowed around Albert J. DeLuca, the man who had made the things happen that had resulted in the carnage inside Slades restaurant.

Shaw thought about the bloody mess behind him. Thought about the double-dealing of Leon Bloom and Arbor Realty. About DeLuca's demands. The pressures, the ebb and flow of interests. Thought about how all of it eventually meant that cops like Sperling and Impelliteri and Mason paid for it – caught the bullets and bled when it all went to hell.

At that moment, Shaw could probably have shot Conklin if provoked. He was ready to shoot just about anybody now.

He forced himself to look away from DeLuca's henchman and watch the CSU personnel, medical examiner's people, and uniformed cops milling about.

And now Shaw watched DeLuca head his way. Now The Shark was going to come over and tell Shaw that he was used up and done. Fuck that, Shaw said to himself. Fuck that and fuck him.

DeLuca must have seen it on Shaw's face when he sat down across from him. He saw a man who had arrived at the edge of not caring what he said or to whom he said it. Or who he would shoot after saying it.

But DeLuca didn't make chief of detectives by being inept or easily intimidated. DeLuca had the instincts and perceptions to understand he should speak quietly to Shaw.

"You all right, Detective? Did the paramedics see you?"

"Just banged up. Nothing they can do for me."

"You should go home now, Shaw."

"What's that mean? I'm getting tossed in the shit pile? I'm history now?"

"Take it easy."

"Why should I take it easy? Is that your next move, DeLuca? You're done with us now?"

"I said, take it easy. I can see what you've been through. I'm not here to add to it. I've covered you and your guys behind a trail of dead and wounded all over Brooklyn. Don't get stupid on me now, Shaw."

Shaw pictured burying his fist in the middle of DeLuca's face. But suddenly a moment of grace shone somewhere in his brain. It was the obvious moment for Loyd Shaw to revert to his typical behavior. But for once in his life, for one piercing moment of lucidity, Shaw succumbed to a better instinct. He kept his hands down and his mouth shut. Shaw realized that DeLuca's considerate manner had been extended for a reason– to get him to talk. DeLuca did not know everything Shaw knew.

Shaw breathed slowly, realizing how close he had come to blurting everything out – all the accusations, all the suspicions, all the anger. He swallowed hard, determined not to give The Shark what he had come to get. Instead, Shaw repeated his question.

"I'm just asking. Am I history?"

DeLuca sat back in his chair and looked Shaw over. He tried a different approach.

"How's Impelliteri?"

"Don't know. Two gunshot wounds. Don't appear to be fatal. But something hit his eye. Could be glass, a splinter. I don't know."

DeLuca feigned concern.

"I'm sorry about Sperling."

Shaw nodded, saying nothing.

"I hear Mason is okay. He'll be discharged tomorrow."

Like a fucking politician, Shaw thought. Conklin must have prepped him with important facts just before he sat down to talk to me.

"That's good," Shaw said. "I haven't had a chance to catch up with him."

"I know."

Shaw asked, "What about Archie Reynolds? Anybody find him?"

"I don't think so. I doubt he got out of the area. We'll find him. What happened here, Shaw? Why was Leon Bloom here?"

"Ask him."

"He's dead."

DeLuca watched Shaw's reaction.

"How?"

"We're interviewing witnesses. At the moment, it looks like Archie Reynolds shot him."

Shaw thought about asking why but decided not to push it. He simply nodded.

DeLuca asked, "How'd you know he was meeting Archie Reynolds here?"

"We staked out Bloom's office. Just covering bases. Thinking Archie might go after him. We followed Bloom here and got lucky. Why are you taking me off?"

DeLuca leaned back.

"Why am I taking you off? Look at you. I'm taking you off because you're done, Shaw. Your team is done. I guess you got close, but it turned into a bloodbath. Go home. Go sit in the woods until I tell you to come back."

"Come back to what?"

"I'll let you know."

DeLuca didn't want to risk pushing Shaw over the edge now. Not while he sat in front of him. Shaw had just been through a gun battle and seen one of his men wounded and the other one killed.

Shaw didn't press DeLuca for an answer. He was just as much done with DeLuca as DeLuca was done with him.

DeLuca said, "So, what happened to Archie Reynolds?"

"He got away in a cab. I radioed an alert. Did they find the cab?"

"I don't think so."

"Then Reynolds could be anywhere."

DeLuca sat for a moment, staring at Shaw.

Shaw returned his gaze. The Shark looked like he was trying to come to a decision. Shaw kept his mouth shut and waited.

Finally, DeLuca dropped a bloodstained envelope on the table next to Shaw.

"I don't think Archie Reynolds is going to go too far."

Shaw eyed the envelope. He looked inside and put it back on the table.

DeLuca said, "That was in Bloom's pocket."

Shaw said nothing, keeping his thoughts to himself.

"You know what that stuff is?"

"I'd only be guessing," said Shaw.

DeLuca stood up and took one last look at Shaw.

"Goodbye, Detective. Go home."

Home, thought Shaw. Now where exactly would that be?

CHAPTER 55

BEFORE HE LEFT, LOYD SHAW WALKED BACK INTO THE RESTAURANT and grabbed a bottle of Jack Daniel's from the back of the bar, one that didn't have a bullet hole in it.

Nobody tried to stop him. And nobody stopped him from sipping on it as he drove back to Manhattan. But when Shaw walked into his loft, he saw something on his recliner chair that stopped him mid-sip.

She knew just where to put it so he would see it.

It was one of those legal documents, the white pages stapled onto a blue cover so it all folds up into a tidy package. Shaw hated those blue covers. They only meant trouble.

Shaw didn't bother to read the legal pages. He didn't even want to touch them. But Jane had left a note on top of them. He read the note.

Dear Loyd,

It's been on my list for so long. You know I'm a list maker. That's how I do it. First, it was on a mental list. Then, months ago, it made it to a paper list. Kept rewriting it again and again, list after list – file the divorce papers. It took a long time to finally do it. Maybe it was this last week that finally pushed me to get it done.

You've either been gone or acting like you weren't here even when we're in the same room. I can't continue to worry about you anymore, Loyd. It doesn't work for me. It's not a productive part of my life. It's a part that has to end. For both of us. I suppose I would have preferred giving you the papers myself. But, as I said, you haven't been around much lately. And apparently, you're not working at One Police anymore so I couldn't reach you there.

We'll have to discuss the loft. Legally, (I know you hate that term) it's pretty much all mine since most of the money was mine. But I know all the work you put into it, and that counts for something. Sweat equity and all, so we should talk about it. My understanding is that you probably can't make the mortgage payments on your own, so as of now I'm assuming I'll have to buy out your interest. When this one point is agreed on, we can move forward. Let's talk.

Jane.

Shaw held the note in his hand but refused to look at it any longer than it took to read.

Not a productive part of her life, huh? My work was worth *something*. Something? What?

A note. She didn't even have the guts DeLuca had. At least he told me face to face that I'm used up and useless.

Shaw shook his head at the arrogance of it. She was so convinced she had the power to dictate and direct him. Or perhaps, in person, she would have spoken those things she had written, and it wouldn't have sounded nearly as heartless. Shaw knew he would have nodded and agreed. And gone up to Massachusetts and settled into the calm and quiet and painted red paintings with his glass of warm Jack Daniel's.

Everybody wanted him to go away.

He placed Jane's note on top of the heartless blue bundle. He thought, poor Jane. Such a burden I've become. Hanging around on that to-do list for so long. Hanging around her life. She'll pay me to leave. How good of you, Jane. That will make it all right. More fair. The lesser of two evils. That same goddamn rationalization linking all the evil shit from my broken life to my broken marriage to the broken lives of New Lots.

Shaw turned away from the blue and white pages, not wanting to think about what he would need to do in order to sign that evil little pact.

He headed for the bathroom, stripping off his clothes, leaving them where he dropped them.

Under the clean spray of the shower, he told himself, fuck this loft. Whatever it was, it isn't us anymore. Let her have it.

Shaw stood wrapped in a towel, looking through his wallet until he found Justine's card. He called her apartment. No answer. Not even a machine. He checked his watch. Nearly ten. He called the community center. The person answering told him Justine was on another call. Shaw told the woman who answered that it was important that he talk to Ms. Burton. Very important.

After a few minutes of waiting and grinding his teeth, Justine came on the line.

"Hello?"

"It's me, Shaw."

"Yes, sorry. I just got off the phone with my father."

"You heard."

"Yes. I'm so sorry. One of your men…"

Shaw interrupted, changing the subject. For some reason, he didn't want Justine to talk about it.

"Yes, yes. You're still at the center?"

"I'm almost done. I've been at it all day, trying to get these people placed. It's done now. The last ones will be out tomorrow."

"Look, Justine, you should leave now. Archie Reynolds is still out there. I doubt if he'll go near your center, but he might be over the edge now. They're going to find him. It won't be long, but I want you out of there. You should get out of New Lots until this is over."

"I am. I'm just going over details with a few of my people before I send them home. We're closing down now. I'm leaving soon. I'll be fine."

"All right. Just be careful. Stick with your security detail."

"Don't worry. I will. When can I see you? What's happening with you?"

"I don't know. I'm...it doesn't matter. When are you getting home?"

"About an hour."

"Okay. Call me when you get home."

"Okay, baby. I'll call."

Shaw hung up, walked to his window, ignoring the pain in his ankle and leg. He stared out at the nearly empty parking lot. He felt unbalanced. In between everything, and yet near nothing. Everything felt unresolved.

DeLuca had told him he was finished. Refused to say what he was going to do with him. But why had DeLuca shown him those pass cards and keys? Shaw was sure the contents of that envelope provided access to storage facilities. What was in them? Archie's cash? Drugs? Weapons? If DeLuca really thought Shaw was done, why show him that Archie Reynolds was stuck here?

Jane had drawn a line. Filed for divorce. But they had yet to cross it. However, his marriage was going to end, they still had to talk.

Justine was between one version of her community center and whatever form it would take when she moved to the New Lots complex. The future was unresolved, including their relationship.

Shaw knew none of it would be determined until he dealt with Archie Reynolds.

"Where the fuck are you?" he said out loud. How do I find him? How do I end this?

Shaw grabbed his phone and dialed in a page. He still had Walter Wang. He still had himself. He wasn't giving up.

While Shaw waited for Walter to answer his page, he carefully thought through what had happened and where he was at. DeLuca knew Shaw had lost his men, and with that most of his chance to bring Archie Reynolds to justice. So DeLuca had cut Shaw loose. Why risk being connected to a lost cause? But DeLuca still wanted Shaw in the game. That's why he'd shown him the envelope. DeLuca had given Shaw the key to finding Archie Reynolds.

It all came down to money. Archie needed money. He was going on the run. He'd killed his business partner and lost access to his cash, but he still had to finance his escape and pay for a new life.

Shaw's phone rang.

"Walter?"

"Yeah."

"Are you all right?"

"Yeah. Yeah. I guess so."

"Where are you?"

"In a hospital near that restaurant. Off Atlantic. Waiting to talk to a doctor, I think. I don't know."

He still sounded dazed.

"Walter, did they give you any drugs. A sedative? Anything?"

"No. No. I'm just—"

"I know, you're beat. But I need you."

"What? What for?"

"I need you to get ahold of your cousin in the Buildings Department and ask if he got that information on Arbor Realty."

Shaw listened to a long moment of silence. He thought Wang might have fallen asleep. Or might be building up to tell him to fuck off because it was over.

Finally, Walter answered. "What the hell, Shaw? What for?"

"Bloom's dead. I think Archie Reynolds was setting Bloom up to handle his money for him. He lost it and shot Bloom, but he still needs somebody to handle his income while he's on the lam. I think Archie might try to find somebody else at Arbor Realty, or whoever is behind Arbor Realty to take Bloom's place. They owe him. It's all I've got, Walter."

"We got nothing."

"Walter, just do this one last thing for me and you're done."

"I don't even know if I can find my cousin."

"Reach out. Try his home. Get in the car and look for him. I don't care how you do it, find out whatever he knows about Arbor Realty."

Walter asked, "What did DeLuca say?"

"DeLuca is playing it both ways. He told me I'm washed up. And then he gave me a lead on how Archie might have stored his cash. Fuck DeLuca. We're doing this for ourselves, Walter. Don't quit on me. Finish up with Arbor Realty."

Walter shot back, "I'm not a quitter."

"I know you're not. You never stopped, Walter. You never let me down. Don't do it now."

"Okay. Okay."

"Call me with whatever you get."

"Okay."

Shaw hung up.

What the hell am I doing? he wondered. Can't you just let this go? The answer was no. Everybody might be done with me, thought Shaw, but I'm not fucking done with Archie Reynolds.

He fell back onto his bed, aching for the sleep he needed to keep going. He closed his eyes. In a minute, he was out, his feet still on the floor.

When a ringing phone startled Shaw back to consciousness, it could have been ten minutes later or ten hours. Shaw had no idea of the time or even where he was. He fumbled for the phone, expecting to hear Walter's voice, Justine's voice, any voice but the one he heard.

CHAPTER 56

ONCE HE WAS ON ATLANTIC AVENUE, ARCHIE REYNOLDS zigzagged on the downtown Brooklyn one-way streets until he found a place to ditch the cab. Cops would be stopping everybody driving yellow cabs for sure.

He parked the taxi at a meter, paid for two hours, and walked one block to Court Street. He asked a woman for directions to the nearest subway station. She pointed north.

"How far?" asked Archie.

"About five blocks. Joralemon Street."

Archie smiled and thanked the young woman. It was back in the direction of Slades restaurant on Montague Street, but Archie figured Joralemon Street was far enough away from the shooting that he could make it. He had no choice. Every second he spent in the neighborhood increased the chance he would be caught.

Except for a barely noticeable smear of the cabdriver's blood on his dark pants and a scratch on the right side of his head, Archie appeared normal. He walked quickly but not so fast as to attract attention. In five minutes, he was descending the steps at the Borough Hall station.

Now that he was off the streets, Archie began thinking about what had happened in the restaurant. Obviously, Bloom had set him up. He went over what happened. Picturing it. Archie realized that he had seen the cop who chased him all the way until he jacked that cab before. That cop had been with Rachman when he shot down the Muslim. Archie pictured Shaw. Nodding. Telling himself if that motherfucker shows up again, it'll be the last goddamn time he shows up anywhere.

Archie bought a token and made it through the turnstile, checking the signs, deciding to head into Manhattan. Brooklyn was way too hot now.

He took the nearest flight of steps down to the subway platform. He leaned out over the tracks peering into the darkness, willing a train to appear.

From far off, he saw the headlights of a subway approaching the station.

"Come on, motherfucker. Come on."

Suddenly, Archie heard the crackle of police radios overhead. On the far side of the station, he heard footsteps descending and more radio communications. Four cops appeared across the tracks on the other platform.

Archie put his head down and walked away from the steps he had descended toward the approaching train. He made sure not to turn his face toward the other side of the station. Out of the corner of his eye, he could see the cops walking along the platform, checking waiting passengers. The train coming in on his side had almost reached the platform. Another few moments, and it would block him from the police.

"Come on, goddamn it."

And then, just before the train entered the station, it veered off to the left as if playing a bad joke on Archie, heading off on another set of tracks.

Archie cursed and ran to the end of his platform, watching the train swerve toward another section of the Borough Hall station. A passageway met the end of his platform. Archie turned into the connecting walkway. He heard more radios and knew another group of police was entering the station down the same steps back where he had descended.

Now that he was out of sight for a moment, Archie burst into a full run. The train that had veered off was pulling into the platform fifty feet ahead. He could make that train. He didn't care where it was going. The subway screeched to a halt. He was twenty feet away. The doors opened. He ran full blast and just managed to get an arm into the closing doors. The conductor quickly opened and closed the doors. Archie jammed the rest of his arm and shoulder into the subway car. No way this train was leaving the station without him. He tried to push the door open. It wouldn't budge. The conductor finally relented and let him in.

Archie almost fell into the subway car. The train pulled out, heading for Manhattan. He slumped onto the bench seat, trying to get down beneath the window so he couldn't be seen.

Archie found that he had boarded the Seventh Avenue IRT train. By the time he pulled into Manhattan's Fourteenth Street station, it was almost midnight. He emerged on Twelfth Street, got his bearings, and walked west to Justine Burton's apartment building on Horatio Street. He looked to see if Justine Burton's security squad was parked outside her building. There was no sign of them. Good.

He continued toward West Street, head down, making sure he didn't attract attention. He had been thinking about posing as some sort of delivery man to gain entrance into the building. But getting in was only half the problem. And then, almost as if on cue, a delivery truck from All-Season Dry Cleaners appeared, heading Archie's way on Washington Street. Archie smiled.

As the truck slowed to make the turn onto Horatio, Archie simply stepped in front of it, put his hand up, and smiled again.

Maybe if Archie had been uglier, bigger, darker, the young man behind the wheel of the truck would have ignored Archie, driven around him. But Archie Reynolds appeared to be well dressed and friendly. The blood on his dark pants did not show. So Eddie Yung stopped.

Eddie prided himself on being polite as well as hardworking. He made it a point not to be abrupt or tough like many of the other Koreans who worked at the dry cleaner. None of the doormen ever had any problem with Eddie. Neither did Archie. He sauntered over to the driver's side window. Eddie Yung thought the man needed directions. People often got confused about the jumble of West Greenwich Village streets.

Eddie lowered his window. Still smiling, Archie Reynolds fired one shot into Eddie Yung's forehead. The single, sharp crack of the small caliber Beretta didn't attract any notice. Archie opened the driver's side door, released Eddie's seatbelt, and pushed the dead body out of the way. The bullet had stayed inside Eddie's skull, so there was very little blood spatter inside the van. Archie searched the dry cleaning items in the delivery truck. There were four pieces of clothing for West Coast Apartments. Beautiful.

It was a two-block drive to the meatpacking district where Archie stuffed Eddie Yung's body into a large metal drum marked REFUSE.

He drove the truck to Justine Burton's apartment building, double-parked it across the street, then wheeled out a large canvas basket laundry cart with an overhead rack. He had carefully picked out the cleaned items for the West Coast Apartments as well as a few extra pieces for other addresses. He hung everything on the cart's overhead rack.

As he unloaded his rolling cart from the delivery truck, there was still no sign of Justin's security squad. She wasn't home yet. No problem.

The doorman saw the dry cleaning cart. He expected the night delivery. All-Seasons Dry Cleaners offered same-day service. The catch was that All-Seasons considered any time before midnight the same day. The doorman buzzed Archie in.

He'd expected delivery but not Archie Reynolds. The doorman had never seen anyone but the Korean delivery man. He asked, "Where's Eddie?"

Archie smiled his charming smile and said, "Eddie be sick, man. They called me from the other store to fill in."

"They have another store?"

"Yeah. Two others. One up in Washington Heights. And one in Midtown."

The doorman frowned but hearing about a Washington Heights store seemed to explain why a black man could be filling in for the Korean Eddie Yung.

He checked the dry cleaning hanging from the rack over the delivery cart. The tenants' names and addresses were correct.

Archie picked out three hanging items and one box of shirts from the cart. The doorman stored everything in the closet behind the front desk. He brought out two bags of dirty laundry, and Archie loaded them into the cart's canvas bin. Then Archie dutifully headed off to the service door exit, which took him right past the set of elevators that led to Justine's apartment.

If the doorman had been paying attention, he would have looked at the closed-circuit television screen and spotted Archie riding the passenger elevator up to the eighth floor instead of exiting out the service entrance. He never even glanced at the screen. And there were no cameras in the building's hallways.

Archie knew the odds were good that Justine lived on the eighth floor. He remembered lights shining on that floor the night he followed her home. But he had to know for sure.

He arrived on the eighth floor, grabbed a hanger of clothes, and knocked on apartment doors until a voice answered. Archie knew the occupant of the apartment was looking at him from the peephole on the other side.

"Dry cleaning for Burton."

A woman's voice on the other side of the door said, "This isn't Burton's apartment. Isn't it late for a delivery?"

"This is when we deliver the night load. The doorman said she needed this tonight."

"Burton is across the hall. Eight F."

"Oh, okay, thanks." Archie pretended to look at the receipt stapled to the plastic bag covering the clothes. "Sorry."

Archie found apartment eight F and rang the doorbell, even though he knew that Justine was not home. He wanted the neighbor to hear him trying to make the delivery. He hung the dry cleaning on Justine's door handle and headed back toward the elevator where he'd left his cart. He stood left of the elevator and waited.

Twenty minutes later, the eighth-floor elevator doors opened. Justine stepped out, escorted by one detective from her three-man security squad.

Like most working women returning home, Justine had her hands full. She carried a briefcase, a purse, a small bag of groceries with her mail stuffed in it, and her apartment keys.

To make it even worse, she had her head down, trying to pick out her front door key. She didn't see Archie. The detective stepping off about one pace behind saw Archie standing in the hallway with his dry cleaner's cart. The cop eyed him suspiciously. Not for long. Archie raised his right hand and shot the highly trained detective just above the bridge of his nose.

That's when Justine turned, hands full, confused, startled. Archie drove his fist into her solar plexus with enough force to incapacitate a two-hundred-pound man. On Justine's female frame and body, the blow had enough power to stop her heartbeat for two seconds, paralyze her diaphragm, and knock her unconscious.

She collapsed. Archie kicked the back of her head for good measure, then grabbed her around the waist and pulled her up off the floor. Her weight made Archie curse. He shoved his knee under her hip and left thigh raised her off the floor until he had her high enough to dump her into the laundry cart.

"Fucking bitch."

He punched Justine's head and spit on her.

His rage satisfied for a moment, he gathered up her briefcase and fallen keys, groceries, and mail, and threw all but the keys into the cart, aiming so that most of it hit Justine's face and head.

He dragged the dead cop to Justine's apartment, found the key that opened the door, and dumped him inside. He tossed the dry cleaning on top of the dead cop. Just then, the detective's radio crackled.

"All set, Phil?"

Archie pulled the radio out of the dead detective's jacket pocket, held the send button, and said in his best imitation of a white voice, "Yeah. All set."

The answer came back, "Okay."

"Dumb ass," Archie said to himself. He turned down the volume on the radio and shoved it in his back pocket.

He closed the apartment door and hustled back to his cart. Justine had landed in the cart on her side and back, her legs thrust up, her skirt falling to her waist, revealing her long legs sheathed in sheer pantyhose. Archie pulled her left leg over and stared at her crotch. It was worse than if Justine had been naked. She was helpless and grotesquely exposed.

"Gonna get me some a that shit, too, bitch."

He shoved and folded Justine's long legs into the cart, covered her with bags of dirty laundry, and wheeled the cart onto the elevator.

The elevator took him to the ground floor without stopping. Archie and his dry cleaner's cart were around a bend, down a corridor, and out the service entrance in less than one minute.

The remaining two cops parked outside Justine's entrance barely noticed Archie coming out of the service entrance up the street. Archie Reynolds drove off with the police commissioner's daughter, her security detail watching him absentmindedly.

CHAPTER 57

WHEN THE RINGING PHONE FINALLY PULLED SHAW OUT OF HIS exhausted sleep, he expected to hear Justine Burton's voice or Walter Wang's. Instead, the doleful tones of Lieutenant Conklin rumbled in his ear.

"Hold for the chief."

The unexpected voice so disoriented Shaw he thought he heard someone say, "hail to the chief." Even after waiting for The Shark to come on the line, Shaw hadn't awakened enough or focused sufficiently to deal with him.

"Shaw, DeLuca."

"Yeah."

"You awake?"

"Barely."

"Report to the commissioner's office now."

"What?"

"You heard me. Get down to One Police. Come up to the commissioner's office."

Shaw suddenly became fully awake. "Why? What's going on?"

"Just do it. You'll find out when you get here."

Shaw stood up, focusing now, taking in what he had heard. "Wait a minute, wait a minute, what the hell is going on?"

"You'll find out when you get here. Hurry."

"Tell me why I'm coming up there or fucking forget it."

"Shaw—"

"You told me I was used up. Sent me home. What the hell is going on?"

"Shaw, just get up here. Now."

"Do I need a lawyer?"

"No, you don't need a lawyer." There was a pause. Then DeLuca said, "Archie Reynolds kidnapped the commissioner's daughter. You're on the list of demands. There's a blue-and-white waiting outside your building. Get up here. Now."

The phone went dead, and so did something inside Loyd Shaw.

His chest constricted all the way up to his throat. An icy shock hit his stomach, spreading down to his scrotum. Shaw suddenly had difficulty breathing.

He rubbed his hands over his face to break the hold that had suddenly gripped him. Shaw sat down, then forced himself to stand, and his heart pounded at the effort.

He muttered, "No." then it turned into a shout. "No!" and he felt a rush of fear and anxiety and anger rise in him. He concentrated on moving, finding his clothes, getting dressed, grabbing keys and money and his guns, arming himself, grabbing his cell phone and police radio, beeper, equipping himself, trying to move fast and remember to take everything he might need. Extra ammunition, he thought. No. No. They'll have anything I need. But he found himself rummaging in the bottom drawer of his dresser trying to find a spare magazine for his Glock.

He gave up trying to find the clip. There was no time for anything but to just move and keep moving so that he didn't scream.

The blue-and-white, lights flashing, stood parked outside his entrance. He slid into the front seat, still unable to speak, but finally able to think. How did he do it? What happened? How long ago? What the fuck happened to her security detail?

Questions flooded Shaw's mind, each one pushing up his anger and fear one more notch.

Ten minutes later, Shaw walked through the turnstiles in the lobby of One Police. An administrative assistant, his identification hanging from his neck, met Shaw and escorted him into the elevator that led directly to the commissioner's floor.

Shaw finally felt he had control of himself. He began concentrating on *not* thinking about Justine. He tried to force her image out of his mind. To squelch his feelings about her. It was either that or become paralyzed by emotion.

Shaw checked his watch. Nearing midnight. He had slept for barely two hours. He realized he should have been with Justine by now. The image of her standing at her apartment door smiling at him, waiting for him, ripped through his mind. Shaw stopped picturing her.

By the time he entered the police commissioner's large outer office, Shaw felt focused and in control. Not much else seemed to be. Chaos reigned. The area teemed with police personnel, civilians, and outside law enforcement people. Bosses shouted questions or commands, sending people hurrying about. Others stood around doing nothing. Nobody seemed to be in charge.

Shaw spotted Captain Parnell and two of his former partners from the Major Case Squad off in a corner. Major Case was always called in on kidnappings. Shaw assumed they were still waiting to be briefed.

Two crews from the Technical Assistance Response Unit moved about the outer office hooking up their traps and traces and recording equipment and installing extra phone lines.

The supervisor in charge of security for the commissioner stood scowling near a group of his men. White-shirted uniform brass and civilian assistants moved throughout the office. A couple of SWAT commanders from ESU hung out, waiting for the call to swoop in and shoot somebody.

Shaw even spotted a few federal agents, the assumption being that Archie might have crossed a state line, making the kidnapping a federal crime.

He looked around for DeLuca and the commissioner, but they were not present.

Shaw stood on the edge of the mess, thinking, this is wrong. This isn't going to work. Too many people here, too little command control.

It seemed to Shaw that no one had dared to usurp the commissioner's authority, so no one took over.

There was not a scintilla of doubt in his mind that Archie intended to kill Justine Burton, and there wasn't much doubt that the out-of-control operation in front of him wasn't going to do much to stop him.

The assistant who brought him up reappeared.

"Wait here. They'll be calling you in soon."

Shaw nodded, not paying much attention.

The assistant walked off, and Shaw felt his beeper vibrate on his hip. He squinted at the small LCD screen, recognized Walter Wang's cell phone number, and immediately pulled out his own phone to call him.

He stepped out into the hallway and stuck his finger in his other ear, trying to block out the commotion going on behind him.

He barely made out Walter's voice.

"Hello."

"Walter, Shaw. Where are you? What's up?"

"I'm heading back over to the Seven-Three. My cousin called me. He got a bunch of shit on Arbor Realty."

"What?"

"I don't know. He didn't even print it. He just downloaded some files and modemed it to our computer in the Seven-Three."

"When?"

"He's doing it now."

"When will you have the information?"

"It should be there when I get there. I don't know what he found. I don't know how long it will take to print it out. I'll be there in about fifteen minutes."

"Okay, call me when you get there."

Shaw felt a tap on his shoulder. He turned to find Conklin staring down at him.

"This way."

Conklin motioned him away from the outer office. At the far end of the hall, they entered a side door and stepped into a large conference room that had been turned into a command center.

There were fewer people in the conference room, less noise, less commotion.

DeLuca appeared at Shaw's side and led him toward the commissioner.

William Burton, the NYPD Commissioner of Police, sat behind at the far end of the conference table. A phone and a yellow legal pad had been placed near him. Shaw had seen and heard the NYPD Commissioner on many occasions. William Burton, handsome, dignified, dressed in a gray suit, blue shirt, striped tie, looked like a police commissioner. But Shaw had no idea if William Burton had the wherewithal to act like one now.

At the moment, William Burton seemed to be busy looking through a file. Shaw assumed it was his personnel file. Two more men in suits stood off to the side of the large conference table, both of them leaning against a radiator cover, arms crossed, mouths shut tight. Shaw recognized one of them as an FBI agent attached to the New York office. He assumed both were feds.

Another tech crew consisting of three cops worked in front of a long credenza along the far wall. They'd set up two speakers that suddenly crackled with static. One of the crew immediately turned down the volume. A civilian with headphones sat at the far end of the credenza, fielding transmissions from somewhere outside.

No one else was anywhere near the phone on the commissioner's desk, the designated phone, the one hooked up to all the traces and traps and recording devices in the commissioner's office. The phone that would bring Archie Reynolds's calls directly to William Burton.

In every kidnapping, Shaw knew that a negotiator was a crucial element. The family member would speak but with the negotiator's words. No family member could be in the right emotional state to deal with kidnappers. It appeared that William Burton had already broken the first rule.

Without explanation or introduction, DeLuca presented Shaw.

"Commissioner, this is Detective Shaw."

Shaw stepped forward.

The commissioner looked up. He didn't stand or offer a handshake. Neither did Shaw.

Commissioner Burton got right to it.

"You've been dealing with this man, Reynolds."

"Yes."

"He has my daughter. Do you know what he wants?"

"Not all of it, no. I assume he'll ask for money. Maybe some sort of safe transit. But if he has your daughter, sir, I know that Archie Reynolds will put a bullet in her head the instant he decides he doesn't need her. Assuming he hasn't done that already."

By the look on the commissioner's face, Shaw could tell no one else had dared to give the head of the NYPD such a blunt prognosis.

Shaw didn't care.

"You sound very sure about that."

The challenge made Shaw jerk his head back. He looked right at the commissioner. Right in his eyes.

"I am absolutely sure about that. Archie Reynolds is a murderer. A monster. He will pull a trigger without hesitation. Not even a second's hesitation. I know of five victims he's shot without a second thought, including a veteran police officer, Orestes Mason."

The commissioner grimaced. Shaw wasn't sure if the expression was directed at him or his answer.

Shaw asked, "You're sure she's still alive?"

"That's our assumption."

"Your assumption? Have you spoken to him? Has he given you his demands?" Shaw turned to DeLuca. "Don't tell me you negotiated without proof she's alive?"

No one answered Shaw's question. Shaw turned back to the commissioner.

"Sir, we all know the procedure. Did you…?"

The commissioner raised a hand.

"Don't raise your voice in here, Detective. And don't ask me any questions. I'll ask the questions."

Shaw ignored the commissioner and kept talking, moving forward, hands on the desk.

"The minute he can't produce her, put her on the phone, assume she's dead. I hope you're not negotiating with him, sir. It's not possible for a parent to do that. Even a professional."

The commissioner's voice remained calm, but Shaw could hear the anger in it.

"Are you done?"

Shaw stepped back.

Burton continued. "It appears you are part of his demands. He wants you to deliver money. You are to wait in the corridor outside my office. Stay on the premises and be ready to follow my instructions."

"When is he supposed to call back?"

"Soon. Go outside and wait."

The commissioner turned to DeLuca, assuming Shaw would follow his order. Shaw did not move. Burton began to speak to DeLuca. Shaw interrupted.

"No," said Shaw.

The commissioner turned back to him as if he hadn't heard him. "What?"

"You heard me. I said no."

Now it was Burton's turn to raise his force. "You're refusing my order?"

"You're going to ensure her death. I won't participate in that."

Shaw turned to leave. DeLuca grabbed his arm.

"Shaw."

He turned to face the chief, his arm tense, left hand balled into a fist at his side. The look in Shaw's eyes made DeLuca loosen his grip. The commissioner's voice broke the tension.

"Chief!"

"Yes, sir."

"Get him out of here. You're right. He's a loose cannon. I don't want him involved. He's fired. Get his gun and badge on the way out."

DeLuca released his grip and motioned with his head for Shaw to leave.

Shaw took one final look at the commissioner. He knew in his heart that the man had decided to preserve his power and image at the expense of doing the right thing. For a moment, Shaw thought he should try again, but DeLuca quietly told him, "Come on."

Shaw shook his head, half in disgust, half in sympathy, then walked out, DeLuca trailing close behind.

When they reached the hall, Shaw turned and continued walking, heading for the elevator, not looking back, not caring about DeLuca or the commissioner or any of it anymore. He reached the elevator and mashed the down button, feeling as if he wanted to bang his head into the wall.

He heard DeLuca say his name.

"Shaw."

He turned and faced the chief.

"You want my gun and badge? Fine. You gonna throw me out? Come on. You wanted me to tell you, fuck you. All right. Fuck you. Fuck all of you. You're going to kill her. Him, you, all of you."

The elevator arrived; the doors slid open. DeLuca shoved Shaw into the elevator, stepped in after him, and yelled, "Shut up!" The doors closed. DeLuca turned to him, "Shaw, you're right, okay. You're right."

Shaw's anger dissipated.

DeLuca asked, "Do you have anything, Shaw? Any leads? *Anything!*"

Shaw stammered, "I, I don't know. Maybe. Not much. Maybe."

DeLuca reached into his pocket and pulled out a plastic card and set of keys. He handed them to Shaw.

"My car, downstairs, take it. That card will let you out of the parking area. Sublevel two. My parking space is marked."

The elevator doors opened. Shaw stepped out. DeLuca yelled, "Go. Do what you can."

Shaw ran for DeLuca's unmarked.

CHAPTER 58

"Come on, bitch. Wake the fuck up."

Archie Reynolds slapped Justine Burton's face.

The pain brought her back to consciousness. The searing pain on her right side as she took a breath shocked her into complete attention. Archie had broken a rib with one of his kicks.

"Get the fuck up."

Archie grabbed her wrist and dragged her across the floor of the dry cleaner's truck, pulling her out onto the street. She landed hard on the pavement, bruising her hip and skinning her knee.

Archie stepped closer and kicked her backside.

"I said, get the fuck up."

A yellow cab stood parked next to the dry cleaner's truck, engine running, back door open. Justine struggled to stand up. Archie shoved her toward the cab.

"Get in the cab."

The shove sent her toward the open back door. Justine put out both hands to prevent her from falling against the cab, but she could not stop her momentum. Her forehead hit the top edge of the door. For a moment, everything went black, then more pain brought her back.

"Goddamn it."

Archie pushed her into the backseat of the taxi. He grabbed her right arm and pulled it behind her. She felt cloth wrapping around her wrist, then around her left wrist until both arms were immobilized behind her back.

"Get down on the floor."

Before she could comply, Archie pushed Justine onto the floor, wedging her between the front and back seats. He slammed the back door and told her, "Stay down. Don't fucking move, don't say anything."

Archie sped off as Justine lay helpless on top of the cab's transmission hump, her full weight on her bound arms. She tried to sit up. The taxi hit a bump; she let out a short cry of agony.

She turned slightly on her side, gasping for breath, grunting as the taxi hit another bump.

She heard Archie dialing a cell phone from the front seat. She tried to listen to the conversation.

"Let me talk to him. Now." Less than five seconds passed before Archie continued. "You got my money? Good. You got that cop? Good. Chain the fucking money to his wrist and get him ready. I'll tell you where to bring it."

She heard a slight beep as Archie turned off the phone.

Justine shifted her weight, again and again, trying to get into a position that would allow her to endure the ride.

Suddenly the cab pulled over and stopped. The back door opened.

The first kick struck the top of her head. Then more kicks hit her shoulders, face, chest. With her arms bound behind her, she was helpless to block any of them.

"You need to learn a fucking lesson right now, bitch. You keep your ass still and your uppity mouth shut until I tell you to talk."

He punctuated nearly every word with a kick.

"You understand me?"

"Yes, yes," she sobbed.

"You sass me, and I'll kill you right now. You got that?"

"Yes."

"I'll fuckin' kill you. You fucked up my thing. You're the reason all this shit started. So you shut the fuck up and stop moving."

"I'm sorry."

"Not as sorry as you gonna be."

Archie was out of breath by the time he stopped kicking her.

"Now, get the fuck up on the backseat and keep your head down, or I'll beat you to death."

Justine didn't dare stay on the floor. But she hurt so much, she didn't think she could move.

He yelled, "Get up! That's what you want, so do it."

She managed to maneuver herself onto the backseat where she curled up and descended into her private agony, not daring to cry.

He had broken her nose. Her right eye was almost swollen shut. Now two ribs were cracked, and her jaw felt as if it had been dislocated.

If Justine could have willed herself to die, she would have. But even dying wouldn't have assuaged Archie's terrible murderous rage. Justine Burton had become the target of everything that made Archie Reynolds hate. She was the black person he could never become. She was privileged, educated, protected, and powerful enough to take from him what he had fought and killed to get. And she was a woman.

Archie Reynolds would hate Justine Burton even after she died. He would hate Justine all the way to his own grave and beyond.

CHAPTER 59

THE SPEAKERS IN THE COMMISSIONER'S CONFERENCE ROOM WENT silent, but Archie Reynolds's voice seemed to echo in the room.

The commissioner slowly put the phone down and looked up at the men assembled in the room.

Calmly, as if it were part of his everyday routine, he asked the questions he wanted answered.

"All right. How are we organizing the teams here?"

Head of the Police Intelligence Division Walter Peterson responded. It was not lost on DeLuca that the man in charge of the detectives who had allowed the kidnapping in the first place had been put in charge of the field operation.

Peterson tried to sound competent.

"We have approximately twenty teams with trackers assembling in two locations. One in Manhattan, the other in Brooklyn, the two boroughs where we assume Archie has contacts. We also have approximately thirty teams with scanners taking positions on all major highways within the five boroughs trying to pick up any transmission from the kidnapper's cell phone. All teams will coordinate with our squads here and ESU personnel. We've got more people ready to go in, when and where we tell them."

Go in where? DeLuca asked himself.

Burton asked, "What about aerial surveillance?"

"We'll have two helicopters standing by at high enough altitude so that it won't be spotted. Also unmarked cars on the ground."

Burton pointed a finger at DeLuca and said, "I want an experienced man from Major Case the same size as Shaw. Make him available. Have him dressed in similar clothes to what Shaw was wearing when he came in. Dark pants, leather jacket."

DeLuca said, "Archie Reynolds has seen Shaw. He knows what he looks like, sir."

"He'll never get close enough for Reynolds to spot the difference." Burton turned to Ricardo Mendez, head of his technical division.

"You have the transmitters ready?"

"Yes, sir."

"Make sure DeLuca's man is wired."

"Yes, sir."

DeLuca stopped listening and left the room, trying to imagine who the hell he would pick to send on a payoff to a homicidal maniac.

✳

Shaw parked DeLuca's unmarked Impala in the 73rd Precinct's lot. He took the stairs to the small office on the second floor two at a time.

Wang sat in front of his computer screen, shaking his head, silently muttering to himself in Chinese.

"What do you have?" asked Shaw.

"Thirty, forty pages of shit."

"Shit? What do you mean?"

"I don't know, the text format came over fucked up. It's running all together like one big block, all mixed with symbols and shit." Wang turned to Shaw. "I've tried reformatting this text three different ways. It's still a mess. It could take hours to fix this."

NEW LOTS | 423

"Tell him to print it and fax it."

Wang shook his head. "I don't know. He's already pissed off. It would mean going back to his office. He's not answering his phone."

Shaw dropped into a chair. He tried to tamp down his rage. He would not yell at Wang. Could not. He had tried his best. Was trying his best.

"Don't you have anything? There's nothing?"

Wang pointed to the screen. "You want to try and pick out the sentences in this mess? You can see some of it."

Shaw looked at the computer monitor. There were sections on it that bore lines of words, sections that flashed, sections of the screen that were nothing but a mix of symbols and letters and bars of color.

Shaw stepped back and dropped into his chair. He had defied the commissioner of the NYPD and bet Justine's life on the hope that some bureaucrat he knew nothing about might come up with a lead. He felt as if something inside him had shattered.

＊

Archie Reynolds drove the taxi he had car-jacked into a McDonald's parking lot in East Flatbush. He had been sitting, parked, for about ten minutes, thinking.

Absentmindedly, he picked up a steering-wheel lock called the Club from the floor on the passenger side of the cab. He had to pull the device out from under the body of the dead taxi driver. Archie had kept the body in the taxi. He didn't want to take a chance that the cops would find the corpse and locate the cab by identifying the driver.

Absentmindedly, he began tapping the long bar of steel with its sliding U-shaped lock against the steering wheel.

Justine Burton lay in the backseat, concentrating on fighting the pain that tormented her. Her broken nose had swollen so severely that she had to breathe through her mouth. Her tightly bound hands were beginning to swell, adding another unbearable measure of pain.

Archie dialed his cell phone. The commissioner came on the line.

"Get your cop and the money. Send him over to that plaza by the river down near Battery Park, across from the Vista Hotel. Have him stand out there, alone. Near where those boats are. Nobody else. No wires, no surveillance, no bullshit. I see anybody but him, she's dead."

The commissioner answered, finally demanding to know if Justine were alive.

"I need proof my daughter is alive."

"You do, huh?"

"Yes. I do."

"Hey, no problem."

Archie held the phone up and jabbed the end of the steering lock into Justine's pubic bone.

She let out a short shriek of pain.

"Say your name, bitch."

Justine complied instantly.

Archie spoke into the phone.

"Do it," he said. "Don't fuck up, or you'll find her on the bottom of the river."

Justine's cry of pain had clearly unnerved her father. He struggled to maintain his composure. He looked over to the tech crew, asking, "Did you pick up anything? Anything?" A note of pleading had crept into William Burton's voice.

The tech supervisor shook his head.

Somebody began laying out maps of downtown Manhattan at the other end of the conference table.

The commissioner turned to DeLuca, who had returned with the best substitute for Shaw he could find.

"Get your man ready, but don't send him until I give the order."

Burton turned to the others, "Gentlemen, how is he going to make the exchange and get away with the money?"

Somebody said, "Boat? He's right near the water."

Burton said, "Notify Harbor Patrol."

Somebody else in the crowded conference room said, "He's right near the Brooklyn Battery Tunnel and the West Side Highway."

Someone else said, "So he could go uptown or downtown, or head for Jersey."

DeLuca said, "I don't think he's dumb enough to go into the tunnel. If he does, we've got him. He's near the World Trade Center. Lots of connected buildings. Lots of PATH and subway lines that converge underground."

The Commissioner said, "I want men undercover in every connected building, subway platform, and PATH station."

William Burton tried to sound as if he were in command. But the more he heard from his subordinates, the more he realized that none of his orders would ensure the safety of his daughter.

✳

Again, Archie shoved the steel bar into Justine, this time hitting her abdomen. Again, he poked, this time viciously aiming between her legs.

"They gonna try to kill me, ain't they?"

Again, he bruised her.

"Ain't they?"

Harder.

"Ain't they?"

"Yes. Yes!"

"Right." Archie pointed the Club at Justine. "They gonna try. But you remember one thing, bitch. Ain't nothing more dangerous than a nigger don't give a shit if he dies."

Archie started the taxi and drove out of the parking lot, and nobody else breathing on the earth had any idea where he was going or what he intended to do.

While helicopters, boats, mobile units, detectives, highway cops, and patrol cops organized themselves to close off downtown Manhattan, Archie Reynolds drove for five minutes before reaching his destination. He parked the cab between two ramshackle buildings, hiding the yellow taxi underneath an overhanging roof. Then Archie walked between the two-story houses, pulling Justine Burton over the rubble and garbage that seemed to collect in every open space in Brownsville. He waited until there was no one on the street, then crossed quickly and entered the one place where nobody would think to look for Justine Burton – New Lots Apartment Complex.

Archie had made it to where he wanted to be, ready to cause the last heaping measure of pain and loss that his mean soul required before he left New Lots for good.

✳

Desperation drove Loyd Shaw. He sat at Walter Wang's computer, scrolling through the maddening text, picking out words, lists, names, addresses, trying to make sense out of the jumble of letters, numbers, and symbols on the computer screen. The more he tried, the worse he felt. Nothing made sense. The hope that he might pick out somebody in charge at Arbor Realty who could substitute for Leon Bloom had evaporated long ago.

Wang made call after call trying to get his cousin on the line.

Finally, Walter reached his limit. Shaw watched him lay the phone down, close his eyes, and drop his head in his hands.

Shaw pushed his chair back from the computer screen. He stood up, grimacing. He hit his forehead with a closed fist as if that could jar an idea or a thought or a piece of information from somewhere deep in his brain.

The mix of rage, fatigue, and frustration finally sent him down into a chair. He put his feet up on his desk, his elbows on his knees, and his head down on fisted hands.

Shaw felt as if his head would split open. His marriage, over. His home, gone. His job, gone. Everything he and Mason, Impelliteri, Sperling, and Wang had done, everything they had risked trying to meet DeLuca's demands, had all been for nothing.

But none of it meant anything compared to the possibility of losing Justine.

Shaw didn't know if it was love or lust or longing. Didn't know if it was battle fatigue or merely the result of a desperate need to have something in his life above and beyond the dark, debilitating mess he had been living in for what seemed like years. Shaw didn't know why, didn't know how, all he knew was that if Justine Burton died, he would have finally and utterly lost everything. It would be time to eat the Glock. Go up to Massachusetts and paint his last red painting with his own blood blown out of the back of his head.

CHAPTER 60

Out on New Lots Avenue, Archie guided Justine along the sidewalk bordering Building B until they reached a ground-floor window hidden behind a scraggly bush. A wooden shipping flat lay propped up against the wall. Archie stepped up on the makeshift ladder, opened the window, and stepped back down. He placed his Beretta at the back of Justine's head and said, "Get in there."

Archie held her bound arm as Justine climbed awkwardly into the empty apartment. He quickly followed after her, closing the window behind them. From there, they walked out into the hallway and exited out a side door into The Pit.

Newly installed high-intensity lights illuminated the area, but they were far away from the guardhouse at the main entrance. Archie moved quickly across the courtyard, pulling Justine along with him, and entered Building E.

The Blue-Tops had been cleaned out of Building E, but none of the renovation efforts had started. The hallways were still dark. About a third of the apartments were still vacant, wretched, unlocked, and empty. The rest of the units on various floors were still occupied.

As Archie pushed Justine ahead of him up the dark stairwell, she could feel empty crack vials crunch under her shoes, smell the rank odors, and hear the rodents scurry out of their way.

They quietly entered an empty apartment on the fourth floor, Archie pushing Justine ahead of him with the muzzle of his gun still pressed against the back of her head. Sufficient light from outside bled through the windows in the living room area so that Archie could locate a beer bottle with a candle stuck in it. He lit the flame, and the flickering light illuminated the room enough to see but not enough to attract attention from outside.

In the dim candlelight, Archie pushed Justine against a wall. He reached under her skirt and grabbed at her crotch, but Justine squeezed her legs together, preventing him from getting high enough between her legs to grip her. This seemed to amuse Archie.

"You know you're gonna get me hot doin' that, don't you? Gonna get yourself wet playin' like that, too. Right, honey?"

Justine didn't answer.

Archie shoved his hand at her vagina twice more, laughing, then suddenly turned mean and grabbed the waistband of her pantyhose, pulling it down off her waist and over her bottom.

Justine continued to keep her legs together, trying to cover her pubic area. Archie held his Beretta in his free hand but continued to awkwardly pull and tear off the pantyhose.

Justine's hands were bound, but her legs remained free. She steeled herself, ready to kick at him, fight him, determined not to let him rape her without a fight. But Archie was not initiating a rape. Not yet. He shoved his gun under his belt and stuffed part of the torn pantyhose into Justine's mouth, then he wrapped the legs of the hose around her head and tied them into a tight gag.

He pulled Justine's belt off her skirt, shoved her to the floor, and wrapped the belt around her ankles.

He stood back from her. "There. Don't need you trying anything stupid while I'm busy."

Archie moved away from her, disappearing into the shadows beyond the candlelight.

Justine immediately rolled over and got herself into a sitting position. She slid back toward the wall. The movement helped push her skirt down over her and allowed her to rest against the wall. She tucked her legs back and sat on her hip, trying to avoid putting any pressure on the bruised and painful areas where Archie had beaten and kicked her.

Her efforts didn't help much. Both arms were bound behind her in an awkward position, and she hurt just about everywhere. Her right eye had swollen shut, her jaw ached, and, worst of all, the swelling and the blood in her nostrils made it almost impossible to breathe with the pantyhose gag in her mouth.

She looked around the room. It seemed empty of any furniture except for a wooden table against the wall to her right.

She struggled with her bindings but rapidly found herself out of breath. A cycle of panic started in her. Needing more air, she breathed harder, which made it more apparent to her that her nostrils were nearly closed, which caused her to become more fearful and panicky and need more air. She started to cough, then choke. She began suffocating. She desperately struggled to suck air into her nostrils, felt her heart pounding, felt the fear overwhelming her. She began to lose consciousness.

And she could not stand to let that happen. She would not allow herself to die that way.

She focused her will, concentrated, forced herself to calm down and breathe slowly, to slowly pull in air through her blocked nose, to live on that thin stream of life, to calm down and survive.

She bit down on the nylon material in her mouth and flared her nostrils in defiance. She told herself, goddamn it, girl, you do not let that animal beat you. Slow down. Concentrate. Don't you dare make it any easier for him to do this.

And slowly, slowly, Justine used her anger and her will to steel herself against the pain and the fear. She gathered air into her lungs bit by bit, enough so that she could blow once violently through her nostrils, painfully expelling blood clots and mucus. It helped, and she did it again, feeling the mess on her lips and chin. She didn't bother to wipe it off on her shoulder. Good, she told herself, good. Let him see that. Make a nice sight when he tries to rape me.

Then she remembered the rape advice she had once heard. She had plenty of fear available to help her evacuate her bladder and bowels if the monster came to assault her. See how he likes that next time he touches me.

The vertigo and panic subsided, but she still had to struggle for air, so she began to bite and compress the synthetic material filling her mouth. Every movement of her jaw sent searing pain all the way up the side of her head, but Justine kept at it, compressing the material and shoving it to one side of her mouth with her tongue. She managed to open a slight space at the corner of her mouth and greedily sucked in air.

Her head began to clear. Her strength and resolve built moment by moment. She made up her mind to fight him. When he came at her next time, she would use her long powerful legs. Or her head or shoulders or hands or teeth if she could get them free. She was going to kick and hit and lash out at him until she either beat him off or he killed her. Justine had endured enough. Maybe she knew she didn't have a chance against him. Maybe she didn't know. Maybe what she really wanted was to provoke him into killing her sooner rather than later.

And then Justine heard a noise out in the hallway, a splashing, sloshing sound, and even through her broken, clogged nose, she could smell it – gasoline mixed with naphthalene and gelatin.

CHAPTER 61

During that last hour or so Loyd Shaw had spent agonizing in the precinct squad room, he might have actually prayed between muttering curses. Whether it was a curse or a prayer that summoned the answer, it came in such an ordinary way as to seem even more miraculous. A miracle born of dull, ordinary, grinding police work.

If anybody deserved credit, Walter Wang did.

Because he had spent so much time around the Seven-Three, everyone knew that Walter was working on the New Lots Apartments/Blue-Tops thing. At five minutes after one in the morning, a detective named John O'Dwyer ambled into their temporary room with a scrap of paper in his hand.

Shaw's first thought on seeing O'Dwyer was that they had sent him to get the squad room back. Shaw steeled himself for the final insult, the order to leave.

But O'Dwyer asked, "I know it's late, but are either of you interested in talking to somebody from that New Lots place?"

Shaw looked up.

"About what?"

"I dunno. Some old guy is on the phone. He has one of Jimmy Silver's cards. Jimmy was over there after that drive-by shooting. The guy says someone should talk to him."

Walter said, "The drive-bys?"

"Yeah."

Shaw almost told O'Dwyer to tell whoever it was that Silver would call him back if he needed anything. But it seemed simpler to just pick up the phone and do it himself.

"All right, put him through."

"He's on the third line."

Shaw pressed the blinking light.

"This is Detective Shaw. How can I help you?"

"My name is Williams. I live over here at New Lots Apartments."

Silence.

Shaw said, "Yes. Is there a problem?"

"Well, you know I used to do some work for one of the guys who kind of ran things over here."

"Ran what things?"

"You know. With the selling and all."

"Selling?"

"Uh-huh."

Shaw was already sitting up straight, his attention focused.

"What kind of work are we talking about, Mr. Williams?"

"Well, not me, you know. Not with moving or selling…"

Shaw understood the man on the phone didn't want to say anything incriminating, so he said it. "With selling crack."

"Right. I don't mess wit' any of that business."

"So, what exactly did you do for him?"

"Well, you know I was paid for it."

"Right. You worked for him. He paid you."

"And now that type of work is pretty much gone."

"Yes."

The elderly voice said, "I thought maybe you all could use my services."

Shaw sat forward. "Well, maybe we can. But I'm not quite sure what you're selling."

"Is it Detective Shaw, you say?"

"Yes. Loyd Shaw."

"Are you in charge?"

"Yes, Mr. Williams. I'm the one in charge."

"Whitey. They call me Whitey. I guess because of my white hair."

Shaw wanted to yell, yeah, yeah, but what do you want to say? But he kept his cool. There was cunning and wisdom in the old man's voice. And he was sober and cautious.

"So you've been around awhile, Mr. Williams."

"Yes, I have."

"I suppose you've seen a lot over there."

"Seen just about all there is to see, Detective Shaw."

"Is that what you provided to your employer? Information?"

"Yes, sir. I did."

"And who was that you worked for?"

"Well, you know, I'd rather not say over the phone. The top guy, though, you know?"

"You're talking about Archie Reynolds."

"Well, I won't say yes, but I won't say no. You understand?"

Now Shaw couldn't help himself. He began talking faster, pushing Whitey.

"And he's not around to purchase your services?"

"Not exactly."

"Whitey, if you've got information to sell, I'm buying."

"Should we talk about price?"

"I'm buying. Don't worry about the price. You'll be happy with my price, I guarantee it. But I don't have time to discuss it. What do you know about Archie Reynolds?"

"I know where he is."

Shaw stood up.

"Now? You know where he is right now?"

"Yeah."

"Where, Whitey?"

"Well, now, you know…"

"Mr. Williams, I give you my solemn word as a man, I will take care of you. Trust me and tell me. Right now."

Walter was on his feet now, too. Shaw was already reaching into his pocket for DeLuca's car keys.

The voice of the elderly savior came through the earpiece. "He's in New Lots. Archie Reynolds walked into Building E about fifteen, twenty minutes ago. That's the last building, you know. The one at the back of The Pit."

"Twenty minutes?"

"Well, I been tryin' to get through to someone—"

"Was he alone?"

"No. He had someone with him."

"Who?"

"It was kind of dark. Couldn't make out exactly who it was, but if I was going to guess I'd say it was that woman who runs the center across the street. She's the police commissioner's daughter, you know. I don't know if you know that."

"Yes. Yes, I do. I'm going to put you on the phone with one of my detectives now. He'll get your exact location and phone and so on. I will see you soon, Mr. Williams. You're in your apartment now?"

"Yes, sir."

"You stay there. You stay on this phone and keep watch and don't move. Do not move."

Shaw handed the phone to Walter.

"Get everything you can from this guy."

"What are you going to do?"

Shaw realized he had to make a life or death decision. No going back. And he had to decide in seconds.

Shaw looked at his watch. If he alerted the brass, he knew they would come full force. Archie would hear them. He couldn't risk that. But could he possibly take this on by himself?

He told Walter, "You wait twenty minutes. Twenty minutes. Then you call One Police. Tell them you just found out that Archie Reynolds was spotted in Building E, New Lots Apartments, possibly with Justine Burton. Twenty minutes from now." Shaw shouted the last words as he ran down the stairs.

＊

Archie walked backward into the apartment, pouring out gobs of gelatinous gasoline. He splashed the reeking solution on the floor and walls of the room.

All of Justine's resolve disappeared. Deep, implacable fear took over.

She pulled her feet back and cowered away from the splashing liquid, but a cold, sticky blob of it splattered across her legs and thigh. She could already feel the searing pain, could imagine her skin bubbling and burning when Archie ignited it.

He set down his five-gallon can and turned to her.

"Had this shit stashed up here for a while now. Got a nice can full of it emptying down the stairwell. Outside hall is wet down real nice, too. Gonna be hell to pay soon. You people gonna wish you'd never messed with the Ar-Man."

Justine could do nothing but stare back at him, her mind too blank and numb to allow her to nod.

"I take that shit out your mouth, you gonna scream?"

Justine managed to shake her head no. Anything to be able to breathe again. Anything to delay the match.

"Okay, now, don't fuck with me, bitch. Don't move while I cut this shit off you."

The wing knife opened in Archie's hand with a snap.

He came within striking range, but Justine remained motionless as he sliced through the pantyhose. Justine spit out the gag. She didn't scream. She didn't say anything. She just sat there against the wall breathing through her mouth, practically tasting the noxious, flammable liquid.

Archie cut the belt off her legs then deftly stepped back as if expecting a kick.

"You gonna die over this thing, you know. Was it worth dying over? That stupid-ass community center of yours?"

Justine cleared her throat, responding, "What about you? Is it worth you dying over it?"

"Shit. Who says I'm gonna die? I got some cash in my pocket. Boost another car, drive on out of here when this place goes up. They catch me, fuck it, I won't die alone like you."

Justine didn't comment.

"So? Was it worth it?" he asked.

"Yes," she answered.

"Why? To help a bunch of crackhead bitches and their crazy fuckin' kids they don't even give a shit about anyhow. Most of them whores'd let their kids starve in rags if it means another hit on the pipe. What the fuck you think you were gonna do for 'em?"

"Help them stop."

"Stop what? Crackin' up?"

"Yes."

Archie laughed. "Sheet. What the fuck you smokin', girl? You know what?"

"What?"

"Those skanks go in your place? Sleep. Use your bathrooms. Then they walk right back over here and buy shit from me. They crack it up, then go back and get what they can from you. You ain't stopping shit."

"We stopped you, didn't we?"

"Yeah, who's we? You and that fat-ass Bloom and his Muslim house niggers? That motherfucker be dead now, honey. I shot him. And the Muslim guy, too. I shot his ass full of holes. Cops couldn't stop me. That fuckin' cop you had around you? I'll kill him too before this is over. I'm might just fuckin' do it before I go. I got him where I want him. Got him standing out by the Hudson River right now. I can run his ass all over this town, sidle up next to him, and cap a round in his head anytime. Be gone before they know it.

"And nobody gonna stop me from burning your ass and this place to the ground. So what did you accomplish except getting everybody killed, you included? Nothing going to change. Crack ain't ever leavin' this neighborhood. Ain't me, it's just gonna be some other nigger selling dope. These people ain't got nothing else. Crackheads don't *want* nothing else."

Justine had enough sense not to answer him. As long as he talked, she didn't burn.

"Ain't a fuckin' thing you can give them they'll want more than crack, baby. Not one damn thing. What the hell gave you the notion they do?"

Justine forced herself to speak to Archie as if he deserved her response, knowing the longer he talked, the longer she would stay alive. Maybe someone would hear them. Maybe someone would see the flickering light. Maybe she believed somewhere inside her that Shaw would find her.

"They're human, aren't they? Do you really think they want to live like that? That the only thing left for them is crack?"

"What the fuck else is there for them? Jobs? Families? Place to live where someone ain't gonna take whatever they got, first chance they get? You gonna change that?"

"Maybe. Maybe for a few. For at least a few."

"Man, you don't know shit, girl. You got no idea what's goin' on here. This is the way the white man want it. His foot on the black man's neck. And they'll supply the crack and heroin and any other drugs they need to do it. They don't want these niggers living next to them. Goddamnit, Brownsville is a subway ride away from Manhattan. Might as well be on the other side of the world. None of these people gonna live there. You gonna need more than cops and Muslims and a place in this shithole to change that. You got fuckin' balls, girl, comin' in here like this. Causin' all this mess. But you ain't done nothing but get a lot of people killed and make the mess move to someplace else."

"I don't agree. I still think people should try."

"Yeah, right. What the fuck you know about it, anyhow? Ever try crackin' it up a little? Might do you some good."

"I don't have to try it to know how it ruins the lives of these women and children."

"Yeah, womens do love the rock, don't they?" Archie reached into his back pocket and pulled out a plastic bag filled with blue-topped vials and dropped it on the floor near Justine.

"That's the last of it. Used to have pounds of that shit stored up here. All the homeys used it up for themselves. Grabbin' what they can. You ought to try it before I burn your ass up. Be good going out high."

"Don't do this. What about the other people in this building? Why? Why do this? Just to kill me? Why hurt everybody else?"

Archie yelled, "So they'll remember not to mess with the Ar-Man next time!"

"You do this, and you'll die. They'll hunt you down wherever you go. Just leave. They don't know where you are. You can get away."

"You think they ain't gonna hunt me down anyhow? You think I'm going quietly? Put my nappy head down and shuffle off, hope the white man don't git me and make me pay? Fuck that. Come on, get your ass up, time to give your daddy a message. You want to talk to him?"

"Yes."

"Then get your ass up, girl, and don't be causing me any trouble or I'll just shoot you and get on wit' it."

Despite her injuries and hands bound behind her back, Justine managed to rise to her feet without Archie's help.

"Go over and stand facing that table."

CHAPTER 62

ALBERT J. DELUCA'S UNMARKED POLICE CAR HAD A POWERFUL engine, a full set of flashers in the window well and grill, plus flashing strobes next to the headlights. Shaw touched the brake only twice during the five minutes it took him to reach New Lots.

He drove the unmarked right up to the front gate, jumped out with his gun and badge out, striding toward the guardhouse before the two guards on duty even stood up.

"Police, open the gate."

They buzzed open the gate. Shaw burst through the opening and broke into a run, looking at the windows in Building E, trying to see a sign of where Archie might be but seeing nothing but a mean, dark, menacing building. The last stop in New Lots.

＊

Justine turned toward the table. Archie shoved her forward, pushing her off balance. She banged into the table's edge and doubled over onto it. She wanted to kick back at Archie, but he nimbly stepped to one side and pushed her down firmly against the tabletop into a puddle of napalm. She felt the noxious liquid soak through her blouse.

Still pressing her to the table, he picked up his cell phone with his free hand and dialed One Police. An operator answered, and Archie announced, "This is the Ar-Man, baby, get me the pohleece commissioner."

The call went through immediately. Commissioner Burton picked up the receiver. Speakers in the conference room broadcast the conversation to every man assembled.

"Commissioner Burton here."

"Yeah, Archie Reynolds here. Where's my fucking money?"

"In that plaza outside the Vista hotel."

Archie continued his call, still holding Justine's head down. "Yeah, but how come I see cops crawling all over the area?"

"The officer is alone. Where you said. You have my word—"

"Fuck your word."

✳

Shaw ran into the lobby of Building E. He pushed the elevator button. Nothing. No light, no sound. He ran for the stairwell, pulled open the door, and immediately caught the acrid, oily smell of doctored gasoline.

He ran up the stairs, pushed open the door to the first landing, saw nothing but darkness, turned back into the stairwell, aching to call out Justine's name, to warn people still in the building, but he didn't dare in fear he'd alert Archie. As he ran, the smell grew stronger. He continued up. Up toward the source of the evil.

✳

Archie yelled, "Fuck you and your money. How many cops you got running around down there, you chump? How many scanners you got tryin' to pick up this cell phone? Huh? Betcha got boats an' shit out there, too. You got that asshole standing out there with my money, huh? I hope someone mugs his ass."

In the crowded command office at One Police, William Burton realized Archie Reynolds intended to make him suffer. The men around him watched fear take hold of the commissioner. Something in Burton broke. He yelled, "Where's my daughter?"

As Archie moved behind Justine, even with her chest pinned against the sticky gasoline, she aimed a blind kick at his crotch. It was an awkward attempt. Archie twisted away from the kick, but Justine managed to hit the side of his leg. It seemed to amuse him.

"Uh-oh! Ain't this a bitch? Your girl just tried to kick me. She's right here, motherfucker, trying to assault me. Ought to have you arrest her ass."

The commissioner stood up at his desk, yelling at the tech crew, "Find him! Find him!"

Archie savagely kicked the inside of Justine's thigh, opening her legs so he could stand between them, behind her. He shoved his growing erection into her backside. Justine twisted and tried to push him away with her hip, screaming, "Get off me! Get away!"

Archie could not hold her down with one hand. He tossed the phone onto the floor so he could use both hands to restrain her. The sounds of Justine's screams filled her father's office.

Two flights down, Shaw heard a faint noise from above. He tried to run harder, faster. He stepped into the slick gasoline and went down, smashing his knee into the edge of a step.

His twisted ankle screamed again in pain.

He grabbed a handrail, feeling, stumbling, moving again, his lungs aching for air, his heart pounding. The stench of the gasoline burned his throat. He tried to suppress his gasps for air so he could hear better. It sounded like a woman's voice.

Justine twisted and writhed with such fury that Archie finally slammed a fist into her kidney, paralyzing her. As he pulled her skirt up, he yelled toward the phone, "Shit, man, she's a fighter. But I'm still gonna fuck her and cap a round into her head. And then burn her to a crisp."

He pushed Justine's skirt up over her hips and began to pull down his zipper.

"Man, she likes this. Bitch is wet, man! Wet an' wild, baby."

In the small office at One Police, Commissioner William Burton began raving, screaming threats and curses over the phone, but they emerged from Archie's cell phone lying on the floor as tiny, muffled noises buried by Justine's anguished snarls and shrieks.

✳

Walter Wang called police headquarters precisely twenty minutes after Shaw left. Twelve minutes after Whitey reported on the phone that he saw Shaw run into Building E. It took Walter three minutes to get through to the command center at One P P. The woman who took the call transferred it to the commissioner's conference room, but no one picked up the ringing phone. Everyone in the conference room was paralyzed by William Burton screaming death threats at Archie Reynolds.

✳

Archie heard nothing, except Justine Burton.

He pulled out his erect penis. He kicked at the inside of Justine's knees and thighs, forcing her legs to open wider, pushing her down harder against the table. In desperation, Justine grabbed blindly with her bound hands, hoping to grasp his genitals. Archie avoided her clutching hands, then gripped her tied-together wrists and pulled up sharply, nearly dislocating her shoulder sockets, pinning her to the table with unbearable leverage, forcing her face into the doctored gasoline. The liquid burned her open wounds and her eyes. She began to gag and choke.

✳

Shaw rounded the next flight of stairs. There was gasoline everywhere. He burst into the hallway. He heard Justine's choking sobs and screams. His Glock still in his hand, he stumbled and ran toward the sound. Unable to stop himself, he screamed her name.

"Justine!"

Archie stopped, turned, fumbled himself back into his pants, and pulled his Beretta from his waistband, keeping his other hand on Justine's back. He pressed the Beretta to the side of her turning head.

With one last desperate attempt, Justine twisted and turned halfway, maneuvering so she could kick Archie, knocking him back. The gun lifted from her head.

Shaw shouldered open the door and burst into the apartment. Archie turned, brought the gun around. In the flickering candlelight, Shaw launched himself toward the barely visible body near the center of the room. His shoulder hit Archie's stomach, knocking him away from Justine. Archie's Beretta fired. Justine heard both men hit the floor. She stood up off the table, shaking her head, blinking furiously to get the stinging gasoline out of her eyes.

Archie landed on his side with Shaw on top of him, his Beretta pinned underneath his hip.

Justine yelled, "Loyd!"

Shaw ignored her, rose up, and jammed his left forearm into Archie's neck, fighting to keep on top of Archie, who grabbed Shaw's wrist as he tried to point the Glock at Archie's face.

Justine wiped the stinging gasoline from her eyes with her sleeve.

Shaw yelled at her, "Justine, get out. Go! Now!"

Archie twisted violently, shoving Shaw off him, bringing the Beretta around. Shaw lost his grip on his Glock. He lunged for Archie's gun, grabbing for it. He felt the hammer moving back. He just managed to wedge his thumb between the hammer and the breech. He felt a fist smash into the side of his head. He tried to twist the gun out of Archie's hand and took another stinging blow to his head and ear.

Justine hesitated, looked at the burning candle, looked back at Shaw.

"Go!" he yelled.

She bolted for the doorway.

Shaw took another hit, this time a stinging blow to the temple. He felt himself losing consciousness. He couldn't take another blow. He let go of the Beretta to block the next punch. Archie pulled the trigger. The bullet flew past Shaw's head. Shaw banged his forehead into Archie's face.

Archie's nose splintered, but the intense pain only enraged him. He pulled the trigger again and again, but nothing happened. The gun was empty.

Shaw reared up to punch Archie, but Archie hammered the empty Beretta into the side of Shaw's head, knocking him away.

Both men got to their feet, backing off, gathering their strength.

Shaw looked around, blinking blood out of his eyes, making sure Justine had gotten out. He circled to his right, making sure to block the door. He heard Justine out in the hallway, kicking doors, screaming, "Get out. Get out."

Archie hunched over, panting, and smiled at Shaw.

"Fuckin' bitch still doin' her save the po' people act. Well, guess what, honkey, she ain't gonna save your ass."

Archie threw the empty Beretta at Shaw. When Shaw ducked, Archie pulled out his knife. Shaw heard the metallic flick and just managed to see the wing-knife blade flash open in Archie's right hand, down close to his right thigh.

Archie bent low, spitting blood and saliva at Shaw, holding the knife back near his right hip.

Shaw felt fear constricting his throat. He could tell from Archie's posture that the man knew how to use the knife. He would come in low, knife hand back, out of reach, almost invisible until he came within range, ready to punch the blade into Shaw's ribs, his liver, his kidney.

Shaw backed away. He knew blocking the knife would be nearly impossible. Archie moved forward slowly, patiently, waiting for Shaw to back into the wall where there would be no escape.

"Oh, this is going to hurt, motherfucker. You gonna wish you never messed with the Ar-Man. You gonna bleed now, asshole. Big fucking hero you are."

Shaw bumped into the wall. Archie smiled, ready for the kill.

And then, seeing Archie's malevolent, almost gleeful sneer, something inside Shaw snapped. He forgot about the knife. He stopped trying to see the knife. He stood erect, arms outstretched, and told Archie Reynolds, "Come on." Then he yelled, "Come on!"

Archie feinted once with his left hand and followed with his stabbing right hand, coming in fast. Shaw should have flinched at the feint, moved in the direction of the knife aimed at his side. But he never flinched because he had gone for Archie before the feint.

Archie's right hand came at him, but Shaw was close enough now to block Archie's right arm. Shaw felt a searing pain as the blade sliced across his lower back, but it meant nothing to him. He grabbed Archie's forearm with his left hand and Archie's throat with his right.

Archie tried to stab Shaw, but Shaw's rage and fear made him much too strong. Archie could not move his right arm. Shaw growled and slammed Archie against the wall, pinning Archie's right arm against the wall, jamming Archie's back and head against the wall, squeezing Archie's throat.

Shaw heard Archie choking, heard the knife drop, felt Archie trying to pull his hand from Archie's throat. Shaw tightened his grip and banged Archie's head against the wall again. Still, Archie struggled. Shaw thought about DeLuca and Mason and Impelliteri and Sperling. He remembered the faces of children he had seen in New Lots and their tired, defeated young mothers. He thought of Justine. He focused on Archie's eyes, watching the life go out of them. He thought of Justine. And the two of them together. And then Shaw felt his grip relaxing. Felt himself lift his hands from Archie's throat.

Archie crumpled onto the floor.

Shaw stood up straight, out of breath, dizzy now, steadying himself with one hand against the wall. He looked down at the murderous crack dealer. He watched Archie's head loll to the side, saw Archie's hand move toward his bruised throat. In a fresh rush of hate, Shaw kicked Archie behind the ear, turned him over, pulled handcuffs from his jacket, and snapped them on Archie's wrists.

He retrieved his Glock, doused the candle, grabbed Archie by the collar, and dragged him out of the darkened room.

Confused, frightened people had come out of the occupied apartments, hands to their noses and mouths, heading for the stairwell to get away from the gasoline-soaked fourth floor. There was no sign of Justine, but he thought he heard her on the floor below yelling for people to get out.

Shaw bulled his way through the tenants, dragging him through his own napalm, out into the stairwell.

As Shaw descended, he ran into more people. At first, the residents of New Lots let him pass, the men, women, and children, the old and the young, the people Archie had brutalized, preyed on, terrorized. But by the time Shaw reached the bottom flight of stairs, they knew who Shaw dragged behind him.

Someone yelled, "<u>Kill</u> that bastard."

Shaw pulled his Glock and pointed it in front of him to clear his way. When he dragged Archie out into the lobby, he heard the first kick land on Archie. He turned and pointed the gun. The gathering mob behind him backed off. Shaw felt exhausted. He was losing his grip on Archie's collar.

As Shaw dragged him into the light of The Pit, Archie regained consciousness. He struggled to get his feet under him, but Shaw kept dragging him, not letting him stand.

He backed out into the middle of The Pit and let go of Archie's collar. Archie rolled over and made it up to one knee, gasping in air through his bruised windpipe, coughing, choking on the blood still streaming from his broken nose. Hands cuffed behind him, he struggled to his feet. The crowd pressed closer. Someone threw a rock at him. It smacked into his shoulder. He turned and snarled at the crowd, "Get the fuck away from me."

Someone spit at him, a woman ran out of the crowd and scratched at his face. He kicked at her, almost falling, and she scrambled away. He turned to Shaw and yelled, "Shoot me, motherfucker. Come on, cop. Pull the fucking trigger!"

Shaw took one last look at Archie Reynolds, turned, and walked away. Something like a collective snarl erupted behind him. Police sirens sounded in the distance mixed with the sounds of fists and feet on flesh. Some in the crowd had knives. He heard the wet, slashing sounds. He heard Archie scream and curse. Shaw kept walking, feeling now as if he might not make it. Suddenly, everything began hurting. His head, hip, leg. And then he felt Justine at his side, holding him. Saying his name. He reached for her, clinging to her, and she to him, each helping the other walk toward the main gate.

Flashing red and blue lights filled The Pit.

The first patrol cars raced in through the main gate. A helicopter appeared in the sky, its blazing, white searchlight illuminated the flailing mass surrounding Archie.

As Shaw and Justine reached the main gate, someone set fire to Archie's gasoline-soaked clothes. By the time Shaw stepped out of New Lots, New Lots had turned Archie Reynolds into a torn, broken, bloody heap of flesh and fire.

EPILOGUE

OVER THE NEXT WEEK, LOYD SHAW PUT UP WITH THE DOCTORS telling him how lucky he was and with the police department putting him through five debriefings. His union lawyer had no problem with the interviews because Shaw told the truth, except for one detail. Shaw said he told Walter Wang to call police headquarters immediately. Wang had no problem with backing up Shaw's claim, particularly after the confusion and time wasted getting through to the commissioner's conference room.

On Wednesday of the second week, Shaw and his crew attended James Sperling's funeral service. Orestes Mason looked good, having lost about ten pounds during his recovery. Anthony Impelliteri looked quite dashing with his eye patch and cane. Even Walter had a bit of a swagger in his step. Impelliteri made sure to tell Walter he admired the way he had held his ground when the bullets were flying. When the service was over, Shaw told his partners that DeLuca had promised he would live up to his end of their bargain.

"Meaning what?" asked Impelliteri.

"Meaning our records are clean. But he made sure to say there'd be no more absolutions going forward."

"So, I guess we all gotta be good boys now."

"That's up to you," said Shaw.

The four of them shook hands and said they should have another dinner in a month or so, but they all knew it would never happen.

Shaw left for Massachusetts the next day. He retreated to his painting and Jack Daniel's. The whiskey felt good, but the color red had lost its appeal. He started thinking in shades of gray and brown and black.

Five days later, Shaw's phone rang. He let the answering machine take the call, but when he heard Justine's voice, he grabbed the receiver. She told him she'd be arriving at the Springfield bus station at 5:32 p.m.

Shaw was there when Justine stepped off the bus, a scarf covering her head and much of her face, dark glasses hiding her eyes. He made sure to be very gentle with their first embrace and kiss.

They hardly spoke during the drive back. When they arrived at Shaw's studio, they talked about everything but New Lots. They concentrated on being kind to each other.

Justine found solace in the outdoors, taking long walks with Mrs. McGovern's black Lab, Ellie. At times, the old lady hovered around Shaw and Justine, yet somehow managed to honor their privacy.

When night came on, Shaw would build a fire in his wood-burning stove, read, and slowly sip bourbon. Justine would spend time tidying up the kitchen, then drift into the bedroom to speak on the phone with friends and colleagues. After a while, she would come sit next to Shaw with a book or a day-old newspaper, read, and take an occasional sip from his glass. It made Shaw feel close to her.

Eventually, when they went to bed, they were able to fall into long, careful sessions of stroking and caressing. Because of Justine's injuries, Shaw had to be very gentle with her. In time, they were able to make love. Carefully. Which made the sex they shared somehow more intense and deeply satisfying.

They had survived. And they carefully embraced the opportunity to extract every bit of pleasure they could from each other.

The ugly bruises on Justine's beautiful skin broke Shaw's heart, even as his love for her soared beyond anything he had ever known.

Shaw had a great deal of difficulty handling what had happened to Justine. Especially at those times when he touched places on her body that still hurt. Bruises that he could not see. Justine would wince, and something inside Shaw would twist with searing psychological pain.

Knowing all that had happened to her, knowing that she would live with nightmares about Archie Reynolds, filled Shaw with familiar feelings of anger and regret. He couldn't seem to escape their grip on him, no matter how many times Justine reminded him that she was alive, that she was okay, that he had saved her. And Shaw reminded himself that Archie Reynolds had died the death he deserved.

Over the days that followed, Justine and Shaw met each other, in many ways for the first time. Shaw had never imagined how warm she could be. Even in their disarmed moments back in New York, the limited time and their differences naturally separated them. Now, for the first time in Shaw's life, a woman made him feel that he was her man. And she was his woman. Shaw had come through for Justine, and her stance toward him was absolute and entire.

Shaw knew that for the rest of her life, Justine Burton would care for him and about him, and he felt enormously gratified by that. He took her devotion to him and held it like a secret prize, not speaking about it for fear it would become less real.

Time passed slowly. The first two weeks seemed to provide them with the hours they needed for both themselves and each other.

By the middle of the third week, Shaw had begun to ease off the whiskey and accompany Justine on her afternoon walks.

One bright, sunny day, they whistled for Ellie and set out for a late afternoon walk. The April of their horrible time had evolved into a calm, mild May.

The first half of their walk took them a little over a mile along an overgrown pathway running through the scrub forest to their turnaround spot near a small pond set in a marshland clearing. They usually paused there to sit on a log facing the water. Justine turned her face to the waning sun and the twilight sky. Shaw watched the flickers of sunlight play on the surface of the water. He thought about trying to paint something so thin and ephemeral as that light sparkling on the liquid. The pond could have been bottomless, but for Shaw, all the action lived on the water's surface. He thought about how the weightless sunlight made everything visible and alive, yet never penetrated past even a molecule's depth.

Shaw seemed content with such thoughts, but on this day in May, Justine had had enough avoidance.

"I've been talking to my father."

Shaw nodded. He knew he didn't have to respond. He knew Justine would not force him. But he also knew it was time to talk.

"So what does he say?"

"Well, quite a bit. But mostly, he just wants to make sure I'm all right."

"And what do you tell him?"

"I tell him I am. Or I will be."

"Uh-huh."

"And I tell him about you."

"Oh."

"I tell him you're the reason I'm going to be all right."

Justine smiled at him. Shaw realized he could look at Justine's smile for a lifetime, and that it would dazzle him every time.

"How does Dad take that bit of information?"

"Well, he doesn't love you for it like I do, but he's grateful to you."

"You love me for *it?*"

"For it and for everything and for what's to come."

"Justine, I'm not sure the word love even begins to cover what I feel about you."

Shaw could see that what he'd said pleased her. Justine looked away, making believe she was trying to see where Mrs. McGovern's dog had wandered off.

Still looking away from Shaw, she asked, "So what's next, Loyd?"

"With us?"

"No. I'm not worried about us. With you."

"I haven't sorted it out yet. Have you?"

"Maybe halfway. First, I have to heal. And I'm making sure my community center gets set up. I'm just not sure how much I want to be a part of it."

Shaw said, "Okay."

Justine said, "What about you?"

"About the same."

"Why?"

He shrugged. "I don't know. Lately, I've gotten good at not thinking about that part of my life."

"You know, they're going to let you do just about whatever you want."

"Who's they?"

"My father. DeLuca. The department."

"Is your father sure about that?"

"I don't think there's anything about you he's sure about. He doesn't know you well enough. But he knows how much he owes you. And the department. He might not admit it to you, but he knows it."

Shaw watched the light sparkle on the lake for a few moments. Then he said, "Before I left New York, while I was in the hospital getting checked out, DeLuca visited me. He had his stooge Conklin guard the door, and then he gave me his speech."

"His speech?"

"Yeah, it started out with telling me I had done the right thing, although perhaps not in the right way. Of course, he couldn't complain about it much since he gave me his department car and unleashed me."

"Obviously."

"He told me the NYPD considered all past sins forgiven. I think he wanted to hear how grateful I was."

"Did he?"

"No. I told him I wasn't going to kiss his ring and thank him for keeping up his end of the bargain. And just in case he thought he could pull any shit on my guys, I told him I had tapes of Leon Bloom talking to his henchman, Conklin. And I let him know what I'd found out about Bloom and how he had used Archie Reynolds and his gang to ruin that housing project. And others."

"What did he say?"

"Nothing. Even after I made it clear to him that I had a line on who was getting what out of Arbor Realty if I decided to pursue it."

Justine nodded.

"I guess I ranted on about collusion and honesty and giving in to pressure from your father and Arbor Realty. I went on about sending men to die for their bullshit. I wanted him to know I knew the score."

Shaw stopped. Justine asked, "And?"

"He sat there and listened to me, then he told me I didn't know the half of it."

"Really?"

"Yep. Then it was my turn to sit and listen. DeLuca told me who was really behind Arbor Realty."

"Who?"

"A Korean investment group. That's where most of Arbor Realty's money comes from. They're putting a ton of money into distressed properties in Brooklyn. DeLuca told me Korean investors had not only pressured the NYPD, they'd also squeezed the mayor, threatened to drop financial support. It was a whole domino thing. There were also city council members complaining because their campaign coffers were threatened.

"There were way too many bodies dropping out there in Brownsville for a lot of people. Deluca told me just because your father was stupid enough to let you get involved out there, or just because Bloom was stupid enough to get involved with drug dealers, then come running to the department, didn't make him or your father complicit."

"Did you agree?"

"I suppose I did. But Deluca didn't care one way or the other. He stuck a finger at me and told me none of it meant anything."

"None of it meant anything?"

"He said whether I believed he was dirty or wasn't, or even if he was or wasn't, it all came down to the same thing."

"What?"

"After everybody makes their deals or their alliances or threats or contributions or bribes – after everybody does whatever the hell they can get away with, it's the cops who come in and clean up the mess and make it work. Guys like Impelliteri and Wang and Mason and Sperling…"

"And you."

"And me. We're the ones who stand with each other, with our guns and loyalty. The ones who make it safe for all the rest, good or bad. I have to admit it was a hell of a version of the

458 | JOHN CLARKSON

thin-blue-line speech. Without us, civilization ends. DeLuca really believes that."

"Do you?"

"In some ways, but that isn't really the issue, Justine."

"What is?"

"I know there have to be people like DeLuca. And like your father. The question is, do I want to be one of them? Do I want them to put me in a situation where I have to shove everything aside and push and push until I'm ready to pull the trigger? To kill a man with my bare hands?"

Justine looked at Shaw, and then out at the pond, thinking about what he had said.

Shaw felt he had to be perfectly clear about it, so he added, "Somebody had to make sure Archie Reynolds died. I just don't know if I want to be that somebody."

And then Justine nodded. She understood.

"Well," she said, "I believe you'll make the right decision, dear."

After a moment, Shaw said, "I believe you will, too."

They lapsed into silence. The sun edged down, touching the treetops, slowly turning the sky red. After a few minutes, Justine stood up and brushed off her bottom, turned to Shaw, and extended her hand.

"Shall we?"

Loyd Shaw took Justine's hand and said, "Yes."

A REQUEST TO MY READERS

IF YOU ENJOYED THIS NEW VERSION OF NEW LOTS, would you mind taking a moment to post a review and let other readers know you liked it? Books live or die by the number of Amazon reviews they receive. The Amazon algorithms only measure the number of reviews and star-ratings, so you can be as brief as you like.

It's easy to post a review:

- Go to the NEW LOTS product page
- Click where it says **"ratings"** next to the stars.
- Under "Review this product" click on **Write a customer review**

Thanks!

Also, for more information on my other books, publishing schedule, blog posts, and more visit www.johnclarkson.com